DAVID WILTSE

THE SERPENT

SOUVENIR PRESS

To my mother, Gretchen Wiltse Hawk,
with love and appreciation

PROLOGUE
TENNESSEE, 1948

The snakes were kept in a pit which was an old dry well, eight feet deep with vertical brick walls. The walls were uneven and pitted, offering many handholds to a human climber, and Thomas often worried that the snakes could climb out. None of them ever had, but every time he approached the pit the boy half feared to see their flat heads inching over the top, tongues flicking, waiting for him.

There were thirty of them, mostly diamondback rattlesnakes, but with a number of timber rattlers and a few copperheads and cottonmouths, too. The well was not really large enough for that many and they lay curled around and atop each other most of the time, forming a peaceful mound, like so many discarded and poorly coiled ropes; but when they were aroused, when they sensed food, they began to writhe and squirm and slither around and over each other, rattles shaking, tongues flitting, their heads lifted and looking at him.

Fifty yards away from the pit Sister Ludy Cater stood on the porch of the one-room Church of the Everlasting Redemption and swung the supper bell to summon the faithful to worship. The old bell atop the building was long since cracked, the clapper gone, the pull-rope rotted. The Sunday tolling of the bell to announce services was only ceremonial in any event. The parishioners of Everlasting Redemption came from miles around, traveling the hills and backwoods in their battered pickups, having left home hours earlier to get there on time. They needed no bell to remind them, and could not have heard it if they did.

Ludy was seven months pregnant and she swung the bell as

if it took all her remaining strength. Thomas could not remember when she hadn't been pregnant; the huge belly seemed always to bulge in front of her, leading her forward in her waddling gait. Even after she'd given birth, the belly seemed to diminish only slightly before it swelled to bursting again. The seams in her faded cotton dresses were permanently split, her feet always splayed out like a duck's, her head and shoulders always leaning backward to counterbalance her belly. And she was tired, always tired, wearier and wearier after each birth. Thomas was the third child in the Cater family, and four more had followed him. The oldest child was eight, the youngest barely a year, and Ludy was swollen to bursting again. Seven children in eight years had transformed Thomas's mother into a haggard, sallow woman whose brown hair, once full and rich, one of her beauties, now hung from her head in strings and knotted masses. As her body swelled again and again, her face began to shrink, the cheeks sunk in, the frail neck grew so thin that Thomas could count the vertebrae in her neck. The color fled from her flesh and blue veins appeared, tracing long, random lines across her cheeks and temples like ink under the skin. Only the eyes seemed to grow larger as the face receded around them, huge and faded brown with smoky smudges underneath that descended almost to the cheeks. Sister Ludy Cater was beginning to look like someone risen from the dead to warn the living.

It was an entirely misleading appearance, for Sister Ludy was as strong as most men, and her will—her will was invincible. Sister Ludy burned with the inner flame of a prophet. Each child she birthed was an offering for the Lord, each a new parishioner in Sister Ludy's own savage devotions. The ravages of her physical body were more than compensated for by the mental power that comes from knowing one is doing the Lord's work. And Sister Ludy was serving the Lord with a vengeance.

If she saw Thomas standing by the snake pit, she gave no sign. Ludy was so preoccupied with the next child—always the next child—that Thomas sometimes fantasized she was not his mother at all. She was a stranger who never noticed him unless he got in her way, never warmed him with her embrace nor lashed him with an angry tongue. In a way she was like the snakes, he thought. They had their young and slithered away, never giving them another thought.

As the last peal of the bell sounded over the mountaintop and faded into the valleys below, Ludy went back inside the church and Thomas went to work. In a large cage beside him three dozen mice squeaked and cowered, all of them trying to cram themselves into the safety of a corner. They had been frightened to begin with and the trip across the field from the barn, swinging back and forth at the end of Thomas's arm, had not helped. The mice were gifts from the parishioners—tithes, as it were, more vital to Everlasting Redemption than mere money. They brought the mice with them when they came to worship, the vermin of their own farms and backyards, trapped live; they had to be live, they had to be warm. When services ended today, there would be a fresh batch, donated by grateful worshipers, in the old barrel in front of the church. Occasionally they would bring frogs or toads if they couldn't find mice, but no rats were accepted. Sister Ludy had had a bad experience with a rat which had panicked and killed several mice. Dead mice were of no use.

It was Thomas's job to keep the mice alive from one Sunday to the next. Thomas was in charge of feeding the mice and the snakes. He fed the mice very little; he fed the snakes the mice.

Using his long pole, Thomas lifted the screen mesh off the top of the pit. He didn't want to touch the screen or any part of the pit with his hands if he could help it. The snakes were waiting for him. Their flattened heads lifted atop long necks, they rose as a chorus, swaying slightly like stalks in a breeze. A pulsating sound of hiss and rattle rose from the pit, urging the boy to get on with it. The snakes had not eaten since the last Sabbath, and they were hungry.

Thomas tossed the first mouse into the pit. It fell atop a mound of coils, feather-light, on its feet, ready to run. But of course there was no place to run. The mouse sensed its peril immediately and froze in terror. There was a pause which always mystified Thomas. The snakes were almost courteous, stately in their hesitation, waiting for the hostess before sitting down to dinner. The mouse stood, immobile but for its twitching nose, beneath a forest of swaying necks which towered two and three feet above him. Thomas counted to seven as the snakes watched their prey and determined that there was no danger there. The nearest snake suddenly struck downward, the fangs out and down. The fangs hit the mouse like twin knives, stabbing, not biting. Venom rushed down a canal inside the fangs from a gland in the head and into the wound. Immediately the snake withdrew, the head back into a strike position ready to attack again if necessary. It would not be necessary.

The mouse had squeaked when struck, but then froze again in shock. After a few seconds it began trembling all over as the venom started to work. Two toxic substances began to disturb the mouse's circulatory system. Haemolysin broke down the animal's red blood corpuscles and liberated the hemoglobin which carried oxygen to the mouse's cells. Hemorrhagin acted on the walls of the blood capillaries, changing their permeability and allowing blood to pass into the tissues. Blood seeped from the capillaries into the skin, lungs, intestines, and bladder, and the blood remaining in the veins and arteries ceased to carry oxygen. The mouse was dying simultaneously of internal hemorrhaging and asphyxiation. The mouse twitched, took two staggering steps, and fell. Only then did the snake lower its head and slide forward to take the mouse.

The reptile opened its jaws, the long lever bones connected to its cranium swinging free so that the snake could swallow prey larger than its own diameter. The two halves of the lower jaw were not fused in the center, so that they could act independently. The teeth bit into the mouse, still warm, still living. The right-hand side of the lower jaw moved slightly in advance of the left side, then the left side moved slightly ahead of the right. The teeth, which curved backward toward the snake's body, hooked into the mouse, making it virtually impossible for the prey to escape. The jaws continued to move forward, one side after the other, slowly pulling the mouse into the snake's body like the two-handed action of a man pulling on a rope.

One at a time Thomas dropped in the other mice, making sure that only one snake tried to eat each prey. Occasionally it happened that two snakes would start to swallow a mouse on either end. When they met at the middle, neither would release the half-swallowed prey, the recurved teeth making it difficult in any event, and so the larger snake would usually swallow the smaller one. When Sister Ludy lost a snake this way, she would be furious, and in his six years, Thomas had learned to avoid the Sister's fury whenever he could. If two snakes went for the same mouse, Thomas had to force one of them away with the long pole. The angry snake would lash out at the pole, striking it again and again, sometimes whipping its coils around the pole and starting to climb. When that happened Thomas would scream in terror and beat the pole against the bricks until the snake fell off. The last time it had happened, the snake came halfway up the pole before it finally dropped. When Thomas was able to stop screaming, he realized he had soiled himself. The Sister would beat him for that, too, but not as much as if he had lost a snake.

Thomas continued to drop mice into the pit until no more heads rose up on the stalky necks. Every body bulged with prey being slowly digested in gastric juices strong enough to dissolve bones, teeth, and claws. He dropped in just enough, and no more, remembering the time he had fed the snakes one mouse too many and the extra one had stood atop the motionless coils, squeaking for hours as the somnolent serpents ignored it, sated for several days.

Still using the pole, Thomas slid the screen back over the pit and walked back toward the barn with the six mice who would survive till next Sunday. In an hour the Sister would come to the pit and select the half dozen or so rattlers she would use for her devotions.

Sister Ludy stood before her congregation, the basket of snakes at her right hand, the Good Book at her left. The Word and the Act, two guides to lead the sinner to Everlasting Redemption.

"Sweet Jesus wants us to be saved," she said. Her voice was flat and hard, undertoned always by anger, and in her mouth the sweetness of Jesus turned bitter and sour. She did not cajole her flock with gentle words, she struck at them. It was a language they understood more readily than gentleness.

"He *wants* us to be saved," she repeated.

"Yes," said a chorus of voices.

"He *wants* it!"

"Yes!"

"He wants it!"

"Yes!"

"He truly *wants* us to be saved!"

The congregation was with her now, following the rhythm of her voice, caught in the tempo and the urgency that she had been building for the past ten minutes. It was a ritual that both sides understood, a necessary cooperation, yet the congregation slipped into it reluctantly every time. She had to work hard to get their hearts with her, to lift their energies, to bind their will to her own.

Sister Ludy was sweating as her voice strained and cracked with excitement and urgency, forcing her desires into these people who wanted to be saved, yet didn't want to give themselves up to her completely. She would take them there, take them to the peak with her strength, show them the abyss on the other side, then together they would leap in. When the chant was finished, they would all be in a state of ecstasy, a little bit mad. They needed to be a little mad for what they would do next.

"But do *you* want it?" she demanded.

The congregation was silent, the rhythm broken momentarily.

"I say, do you want it?"

They murmured slightly, not certain if they did want it. She would convince them.

"Do you *want* it?" She slapped her left hand down hard on the Book, building the rhythm again.

"Do you *want* it!" Slap.

"Do you *want* it!"

"Yes," but not convinced.

"Do you *want* it!"

"Yes."

"Do you *want* it!" She thrust her head toward them, lean and bony as a bird's skeleton, neck tendons straining.

"Yes!"

"Then tell me you want it!"

"YES!"

With a movement so quick and practiced that it looked like magic, the Sister flashed her right hand into the basket and pulled out a snake. She held the snake firmly at the base of the skull, her arm extended full length into the air. Thumb and forefinger squeezed tightly, forcing the serpent's mouth open and the fangs forward and out, into striking position.

The congregation gasped. The snake writhed and threw its coils around the Sister's arm, struggling, then instantly releasing and wrapping again in the other direction. As many times as they had seen the performance, the congregation was still awed. The Sister's arm had turned into a snake.

Even Daniel Cater, sitting in the front pew, even Daniel, who had seen his wife practice the act time and again until she had mastered it, even Daniel gasped in amazement. Daniel was perpetually in awe of his wife. Amazed at her inner strength, awed by her courage, afraid of her intensity. She was smarter than he, stronger, purer, better. He considered it a surprising, undeserved honor when her hands groped for him at night, pulling him toward her in the darkness. He knew he was but a sheep, she the shepherd. He did not resent it, he merely wondered dimly how he had deserved it.

The Sister felt the powerful muscles of the snake constricting around her arm. The scales of the dry, dry skin rasped against her flesh, seeking further purchase in its struggle to free its head. Close to seven feet of muscle and ribs did battle with the strength of the Sister, but ultimately Ludy was the stronger, in both muscle and will.

"I'm going to tell you that Christ can tame this serpent," she roared. "If'n he can tame this serpent in my hand, you know that Christ can tame the serpent inside of you. Do you want it?"

"Yes," they roared, eager now.

"Do you *want* it!"

"Yes! Oh, yes!"

"Then come forth!" she cried. "Come and let sweet Jesus tame you even as He tames this serpent of the Devil!"

Daniel came first, as always, stepping forward from the front pew without hesitation. Despite their readiness, they needed reassurance, needed to witness someone other than the Sister with her incredibly fast, magical hands. Daniel was the Judas goat who led them all to the altar.

Leaning down from the pulpit, the snake still high over her head, her left hand clutching Daniel's shoulder, the Sister stared at him intently for a moment.

"Do you love Jesus?" she asked sharply, her voice as much a threat as a question.

"I do," said Daniel.

"Do you love him truly, brother?"

"I do," he repeated meekly.

"Then Jesus' going to take care of you!" she roared, bringing the snake down with alarming speed and spreading the length of its body across his shoulders. The tail of the snake fell down the front of his shirt and onto his chest. The skin felt dry and cool, and Daniel was long since past caring, long since past the fear of the danger, past even awareness of the danger.

More carefully now the Sister transferred control of the snake's head to her husband's hand. When she was certain he had it, she let go. Daniel had been bitten three times, but he had survived. If his mind had grown dimmer each time, his soul had grown stronger. Ludy was not in the business of tending to her husband's mind. When she was pregnant for the fourth time, she had been bitten herself, causing her to miscarry the three-month-old fetus. It was a small price to pay for salvation, and she had become pregnant again in no time. Each bite was a test

by the Devil, and the Sister had passed the test, she was winning the struggle with the Enemy.

The next member of the congregation stood before her, Perlie Watts, a tired man of thirty-five who spent his days behind
the wheel of a truck, and his nights alone in his room. His eyes
were unfocused with ecstasy, but even so the Sister could sense
the fear that lay beneath. Again her hand flashed into the basket
and she pulled out another snake. This one was sloughing its
skin and the Sister had selected it for just that purpose. The
skin was halfway off, caught temporarily by the lump in its
stomach which had been a mouse only an hour before.

"If this creature of Satan can be reborn," she cried, holding
the sloughing snake aloft, "if this serpent can shed its skin and
start fresh, how can a servant of the Lord be denied rebirth?"
She lowered the snake's face to her own, staring into the serpent's unblinking eyes. Slowly, slowly she moved the snake toward her face, close enough so that the flicking tongue could
almost touch her nose. The snake had no way to hurt her without coiling and then lashing. It was powerless as long as Ludy
held its head and kept its body off any solid platform, but the
congregation didn't know that. They gasped at her strength, at
her courage, at the power Jesus gave this woman to command
the serpents.

Ludy transferred the snake to the parishioner.

"Hold his head firm, brother Watts, and look that devil in the
eyes. Look him in the eyes: they never blink. That's how God
looks down at you—He never blinks, He sees it all. Look this
devil in the eyes and think of Jesus!"

The truck driver held the snake and trembled, half with reli-
gion, half with fear.

The congregation was well into it now. All six snakes were
being held, the other members being led by the Sister in a
joyous, dynamic, hand-clapping spiritual. The noise did nothing

to bother the snakes; they were deaf. The sound of children laughing, squealing with delight, came from outside the church. The Sister turned to Daniel and frowned. Daniel had already passed his snake on to another parishioner, giving another man his moment of revulsion and flirtation with death in the house of the Lord. Mr. Cater silently left the church.

Sunday was one of the few times the Cater children had a chance to play. For the hour and a half or so while the Sister led the people to salvation, the children were supposed to be serving as lookouts for the despised authorities who raided the church occasionally, hoping to put a stop to the snake cult. In reality, since it was just about the only time during the week when the Sister's oppressive presence wasn't felt, the children acted like children. For the most part they were a sullen, defeated, listless bunch. Only Thomas had thus far retained the spark of vitality and mischief. He was a high-spirited boy, hyperactive by the standards of his family, curious and alert. Repeated beatings by the Sister had taught him to mask his rebellious nature, but they had not yet entirely quelled it.

Thomas and Kathy, his sister, were in their secret place under the corncrib, an eroded gully that formed a sort of cave with the floor of the crib as its roof. At seven, Kathy was the only one of the children Thomas really loved. She saved all her sweetness for him.

Kathy removed the last of her clothing.

"Now you show me, Tom-Tom," she said.

Thomas pulled off his pants and the two children stared at each other's sex. It was not the first time they had examined their bodies, but the mystery remained.

"Can I touch it?" she asked.

Thomas nodded. Kathy tapped his sex gingerly with a finger, as if it were a wound. She tapped it again, harder, and it bounced. Kathy laughed.

"Oh, Tom-Tom," she giggled, "it looks so silly."

"You're the one who looks silly," he said.

Kathy screamed. A hand snaked under the corncrib and grabbed her by the ankle, pulling her out. Seconds later Daniel pulled Thomas out, too.

"Oh, you children," he said. "Oh." He stared at their nakedness, then his eyes riveted on Thomas's tiny penis. A look of disgust came over him and without warning he slapped it with his hand.

"You devil," he cried. It was the only time Thomas could remember him showing such animation. He jerked away from the punishing hand and hurriedly pulled on his clothes.

"Don't tell her, Papa," Thomas cried. "Please don't tell her, please don't tell her!" Already Thomas had no name for his mother. She was never Mama, never Mother. The Sister was simply "her," a figure daunting and impersonal as God. And as terrifying.

"Oh, Tom-Tom, you *are* a devil," Daniel repeated, shaking his head sadly. Thomas reached for him, threw his arms around him, hugging his bony frame.

"You don't have to tell her, Papa," he pleaded. "Don't tell, please don't tell her!" He stared beseechingly at his father's face. Daniel's dull eyes looked back down at him, his head shaking slowly from side to side. For the first time in his life Thomas recognized the resignation of stupidity in his father's face.

"You don't *have* to tell her," he cried, knowing that he would. Thomas knew what his punishment would be and he didn't think he could stand it again. He pressed his head against the shiny serge suit Daniel wore to services, trying to will things to be different.

The Sister stood atop her hill and looked out over the peaks of the other rugged hills that were called the Appalachians. From where she stood one could see into parts of Virginia and Kentucky, but the Sister wasn't looking at geography, she was looking inward, seeking wisdom for dealing with the boy. She had beaten the boy, of course, and she had prayed with him, but it was not enough. The Devil was testing her again, probing for a weak spot. If Satan expected the Sister's vulnerability to be indulgence of her own flesh and blood, Satan would be disappointed.

The Devil had tested Ludy repeatedly, and Ludy was always too strong. He had tried her with the lust of the body, tempting her with the smiling faces and firm bodies of the men around her, but Ludy had resisted. He had tried her with her husband's dimness. He had tried her with poverty. He had tried her with her own sex, urging her to give in to the weakness of the spirit that tormented women. It was hard to be a servant of the Lord, harder still as a woman in a man's calling, but Ludy had withstood all temptations to give up. The Devil wanted her, but Ludy would not give in. It was all part of the same battle, the same unending battle directed at Sister Ludy. Now the Devil was coming after her own flesh and blood. The Sister had won before, and she would win this time.

Mother and son walked across the field toward the snake pit, the Sister holding Thomas by the neck.

They stopped beside the snake pit and Ludy pushed off the screen. Thomas could hear the snakes stirring at his approach, but he wouldn't look down. He squeezed his eyes shut, remembering when the Sister had brought him here before as punishment. Holding Thomas by the arms, she had lowered him halfway down the pit. Thomas had closed his eyes and screamed and screamed, but the Sister had refused to pull him up until she was convinced the boy sought true redemption. Thomas had become as terrified of his fear as he had been of the snakes. He had been afraid his heart would stop. He had been afraid his struggles would cause his mother to drop him. Finally he had calmed himself by imagining he was elsewhere, in another place, in another skin. He had willed it so hard that a peace had come and he had gone limp in his mother's hands. The Sister had pulled him out.

The boy had fooled Ludy that time; he had not changed. This time would be different.

The Sister took the long pole and pushed at the snakes until she had cleared a space in the center of the pit. She lowered a soapbox into the clearing. The top of the box was just about level with the heads of the snakes when they reared up on their necks.

"Take off your pants, boy," Ludy demanded.

Thomas stared at her stupidly, not comprehending. Ludy lifted the long pole threateningly.

"Take off your pants, I said."

Thomas took off his pants, still not understanding. Was he simply to be beaten again? Then why had they come to the snakes?

"You was showing your thing to your sister, boy," said the Sister, her voice in the flat, menacing tone she used in church. "You was showing your thing to your sister, and you have defied me, again and again, and you have defied the Lord, again and again, and our patience is at an end. Now you're going into the pit with the snakes, boy, and we are going to pray for the Devil in you to go into the Devil that is in them snakes. If you are truly repentant, boy, if you give yourself over to the sweet mercy of Jesus Christ, the Devil will leave you and go into them snakes. . . . And if you ain't, they will bite your thing off, they will bite it right off."

Before Thomas could run, the Sister grabbed him and swung him out over the pit. She lowered him until the boy's feet touched the box, then released him.

Thomas gasped and reached up, his fingers scrabbling for a hold in the brick. Ludy brought the long pole down on Thomas's hand.

"Hold still down there, boy," she said. "Don't you scare them."

Thomas refused to open his eyes, but he could hear the

movement of the snakes. They were confused. The pits between their nostrils and their eyes informed them that a warm-blooded animal was with them, but their other senses told them it was too large for prey, too still to be a threat. They waved back and forth slowly on their necks, waiting. The Sister was right; if the boy moved, he would scare them and they would strike. If he was still, absolutely still, they would accept his presence.

The stench of the pit was overwhelming, which meant that some of the snakes were mating. From atop the pit Ludy could see two of them, the female somewhat larger, entwined from tail to head, moving slowly in the copulatory dance that lasted for hours. The male had penetrated the female's cloaca with his twin penises after wooing her with his undulations and the fetid stench from his glands.

Thomas looked up from the pit. He could barely see his mother's face peering down over her pregnant belly. Her eyes seemed on fire. For a moment Tom-Tom thought he could see her belly pulse with excitement.

"You are my fault," said Ludy. "But I will save you. I will get the Devil out of you. Amen!" She stepped away from the pit, leaving Thomas alone with the snakes.

Despite himself, Thomas looked down at the dozens of staring serpents' eyes, the flickering tongues, the quivering rattles. One of the snakes, taller than the rest, began to cross Thomas's foot, attracted by the warmth. It rested its head atop the flesh of his bare foot, then slowly moved upward, entwining around his leg, climbing toward his groin. Thomas was in such terror he thought he would explode. In the far distance came the sound of his little sister, laughing. Thomas looked at the snake writhing toward his sex; he looked but he did not see. His body was rigid, but his mind, yearning to be safe, to be free, had broken out and was gone. Gone.

NEW YORK CITY, 1983
SUMMER

I

His name was Watts, or Waites, or something like that, but Alicia couldn't remember it exactly, although she had repeated it carefully when they met. She hadn't heard his first name at all. When they were making love she had called him Baby, as in "Oh, Baby, you do it so good!" a stock phrase of hers that she knew they responded to, but she wasn't going to call him Baby, now that the passion was spent. It hadn't even seemed terribly appropriate during sex—he was too big, too heavy, to be anybody's baby, and he smelled a bit, of sweat and liquor and a late dinner in the restaurant where she picked him up. Since she didn't know his name, she hadn't been calling him anything for the past ten minutes or so. For his part, he had started by calling her Miss Caro, as if the Miss were an honorary title she had earned by virtue of her stardom. When they arrived at her apartment he was calling her Alicia, during sex it was "Oh, Ali, honey," and now it was "You sweet thing," just a trace of a southern accent on "thing" so it sounded like "thang." And more than a bit of swagger to him, now, too. No longer awed by being with a Broadway star, he was now feeling inflated about having slept with one. As if it were a rare triumph. As if he had just bearded the lion in his own den. Oh, if only you knew how easy it is, Alicia thought.

She was tired of him now and wanted him to go, but she had to get his name first, for her book. She kept the names of all her lovers on file, and the dates when she had sex with them. She supposed many might consider it a fetish, but she wanted to retain *something* personal of the experience, and since it usually wasn't the sex that was different, and since their faces had all blended into one more or less homogeneous mass years ago, she kept the names. And the numbers. So far, not counting tonight, there had been 237. That was different men, not different times, since she had started counting, which was when the play opened to rave reviews and she knew she was going to be a star and ought to start paying attention to the details of her life. Someone would want to know someday, or maybe she would have to know herself, for her memoirs. Two hundred thirty-seven in a little over two years. She didn't know if it was a record, but it had kept her off the streets.

She pulled on her dressing gown and stepped into the bathroom.

"Oh. How do you spell your last name again, darling?" she asked.

He looked at her blankly for a moment. Not for the first time she thought he might be rather stupid.

"My name?"

"Your last name. How do you spell your last name?"

"W-a-t-t-s," he spelled.

She smiled gratefully. Sometimes they said, "Just the way it sounds," which wasn't much help if she didn't know what it was.

"I didn't take no precautions," he said, pulling on his shoe. "I figure I ought to tell you."

It was Alicia's turn to stare blankly. The phrase—even the sentiment—was so old fashioned that it took her a moment to understand.

"That's all right," she said finally. "None necessary. I'm already pregnant."

He looked up at her sharply.

"Didn't you know?" she said, merrily. "I thought everyone knew. It's been in the paper, I've been on the talk shows—darling, I've been dining out on it for weeks now. 'Star to be single mother.' How modern can you be?"

"I didn't know," he said dully. He looked at her body as if he could detect the signs through her dressing gown.

"You are an old-fashioned gent, aren't you?" she said. "You be sure to call me sometime, now, you heah?" She added the last with a touch of southern accent of her own. Hers was a Louisiana accent she had learned for a road production of Tennessee Williams and his had a harsher, more backwoods sound, but never mind. Since her phone number was unlisted and she had scrupulously removed it from all of her telephones in the apartment, it was not likely that he ever would call, but she'd let him figure that out later. It was a gentle way of easing them out. She pulled the bathroom door closed and turned on the shower. When she came out, he would be gone. Time had proven it to be a fairly effective way of getting rid of them. The bit about their calling sometime gave enough of a sop to their ego so that didn't become a problem. It amazed Alicia how vain some of them could be, and bruised feelings had led to bruised Alicia on more than one occasion. She was sure this one, Watts, the cornpone gent, was no troublemaker, however.

After her shower Alicia stood for a moment in front of the mirror in her bedroom. She was flattered that he hadn't noticed she was pregnant. She could tell, of course, but to the untrained eye she still looked—well, filled out, perhaps. Like a Rubens painting. In another month or so there'd be no hiding it at all, of course, and what that would do to her sex life she wasn't sure.

She wondered again about her decision to be an unwed mother. It had seemed a great idea when she learned she was pregnant; the publicity alone had been worth it. Now, however, it was getting close to the time when reality was going to set in. She was great in the part of a Liberated Woman, a natural. She was afraid she might be miscast as Madonna.

Alicia opened her notebook with the suede cover and turned to the last empty page. She made an entry: the date, then Watts, W (for white) 45 (his age). She wasn't sure at all about the age, he was a hard one to judge. His features weren't all that old, for he seemed weary, careworn. Or perhaps it was the courtliness of his manner that made him seem older. She thought for a moment of any distinguishing characteristic about this night or this man that would set it apart from any other. After a moment she added the word *southern* to the entry.

The first sound came as Alicia closed her notebook. It was faint, so faint she wasn't sure she had heard it at all. Then it came again, slightly louder, a grunt, very low. She did not know why, but it frightened her. The man had not gone yet, he was still in the living room. Well, it sometimes happened. She would have to get rid of him, but it was nothing to be afraid of.

As she started toward the living room door, she heard the sound again and froze with her hand on the knob. She realized that she was frightened because the person making the noise was frightened. She eased the door open and peeked into the living room.

Watts was standing in the middle of the room, his gaze transfixed on the *I, Claudius* poster that adorned one wall. He was trembling violently, his fist clenched in front of his chest, elbows pressed to his side. The sounds came from him, one after the other now, half grunt, half moan. Alicia realized they were the sounds of a man trying to keep from screaming.

She looked again at the poster. There was nothing to it, a simple mosaic used as the logo for a *Masterpiece Theatre* series she had much admired. A snake crawling across a stone floor. Nothing remarkable, not very realistically done, not great art, significant to Alicia only for the memories it evoked. But Watts stood trembling before it, transfixed with fear.

At first she thought of malaria. She had been in a television play once in which one of the characters had suffered from malaria and was shaken with fits of trembling like this. In the play Alicia had comforted the man with her body; it had been easy enough on television.

"Do you need a doctor?" she asked, stepping forward into the room.

The trembling stopped abruptly and Watts turned to look at her. Alicia knew immediately she had made a terrible mistake. It was the same man she had just slept with, but he had changed drastically. He carried himself differently, his smile was different, twisted and cruel, and his eyes blazed at her with hatred and madness. She realized almost at once that he was insane.

Run, she screamed in her mind. Run and cry for help. There was never any doubt he was going to kill her, none at all, and he still had not moved or said a word.

"I'll call one," she said, backing toward the bedroom.

He lashed out one arm and backhanded her across the mouth. She felt his knuckles smash her lip against her teeth and she rocked backward. It took a moment for her head to clear and when she looked at him again, he was holding his knuckles to his mouth, sucking her blood from them. He grinned at her, a terrible, demonic contortion of his mouth, her blood staining his teeth.

She ran past him, toward the hallway. She managed to turn the lock, but then his hand, coming from behind her, grabbed the knob. He yanked the door open, right in her face. The iron edge caught her on the forehead and she reeled back into the room. Her eyes were closed with pain. She opened them to see him swinging a fist at her, something metallic glinting from his hand.

It hit her with tremendous power in the stomach. She tried to gasp for breath that would not come, then hands closed around her windpipe. She lifted a hand, trying to claw at her attacker, but she was hit again in the stomach, then hurled against the wall. The baby, she thought. Her head smashed against the *I, Claudius* poster, shattering the glass and leaving a crimson stain.

She was kicked again, and hit, then slammed into the wall once, twice, three times. She was being battered by a cyclonic frenzy; she was being hurt, and hurt again, but she could never catch enough breath to scream.

She was hurled to the floor again. She tried not to move, hoping the attacker would think she was dead, but she was kicked again, and again. She was lifted and dropped, landing on her chin. A foot caught her in the spine, and then she really couldn't move.

The last thing she heard was her attacker's voice, a low, snarling guttural growl, raging in a language she could not understand. She knew she was being thrown against the wall again, but then she couldn't feel or hear anything anymore.

The killer awoke and for a moment did not know where he was. His head was resting on Alicia's abdomen and his ear was stuck to her skin with dried blood. He stood and saw her mutilated corpse, the apartment splattered with crimson, his own clothes as stained as a painter's coveralls. The murder came back to him and he laughed to himself. It had been marvelous. Such a release, so much better than sex at relaxing him. When he had finished and collapsed on her body, exhausted, for his brief nap, he had felt a sense of completeness and fulfillment he had never before known. It had been such a simple, natural act, he could not imagine why he had never done it before.

He picked his way out of the apartment, stepping around the puddles of blood. On the coatrack, just inside the door, he saw a man's trenchcoat. He put it on; it covered his bloody clothes nicely. Wearing the stranger's coat, he left, filled with a sense of well-being.

Whirling through the half-empty apartment, the light flashing in highlights off her long, soft brown hair, Sheila reminded Block of the sun. She brightened the world wherever she went. Her arms aloft, she gestured to the bare walls, the curtainless windows, making plans, decorating it all for his imagination, but Sandy Block was not paying attention to what she said. He was noticing the remarkable smoothness with which her arm flowed into her shoulder. He had never seen a lovelier shoulder. As she lifted her arm in the peasant blouse, the incredible perfection of that limb made itself clear to him. He had never seen a lovelier arm.

Sheila stopped and looked at him. "You're not listening, are you?" She put her hands on her hips in mild annoyance. "Don't you like my ideas for decorating?"

"I think they're terrific ideas," he said.

"What are they? You didn't hear any of it."

"I married a beautiful woman," he said. "How did it happen that I married such a beautiful woman? I'm forty-one years old." He did not add that she was only twenty-five and he felt that he had stolen her from a more deserving, younger man. He felt that way, but he did not regret it any more than he would regret stumbling across buried treasure and taking it for his own.

"Oh, cut it out," she said, but she gave him a smile that seemed to dance across her face, lighting it like summer lightning.

"I've been studying you," he said. "You are without flaw."

She laughed, a surprisingly robust sound coming from someone so feminine. Sandy knew it was the best laugh in the world.

"My forehead is too big, it bulges out."

"It does not."

"Of course it does, why do you think I wear my hair over it?" She pulled the hair off her brow, showing him her forehead, full face, then profile.

"See? It bulges."

"That's exactly the way a forehead is supposed to bulge," he said.

"My teeth stick out."

"They don't."

"They do so. I had to wear braces for years and they still stick out." It was true. From a dentist's point of view, her teeth did protrude. But they were perfect teeth, as white as porcelain, and they made her appear to be smiling slightly most of the time. Sandy had never seen lovelier teeth.

"I want your teeth," he said.

She laughed again and gently pushed him away as he tried to embrace her. He pursued her, and she ran from him, laughing, through the empty apartment. He followed, shuffling like a bear, arms out wide, snorting and growling. When he cornered her he pulled down the bodice of the loose scoop-neck blouse and kissed her breast. The breast was creamy white against the tan of her chest. He had never kissed a lovelier breast. He had been married three days.

They made love on the floor, then moved to the bed, one of the few articles of furniture in the apartment, and made love again.

After the second time they lay on their backs, studying the ceiling. Sheila was wondering whether to paint it off-white or cream, or maybe a pastel shade. Sandy was wondering if he had ever seen a lovelier nose. He decided he had not.

The doorbell rang insistently. Block opened the door to find Lou Florio there, leaning against the hallway wall, looking rather sheepish.

"I interrupt anything?" Florio asked.

"Like what?"

"A man's honeymoon . . ." Florio shrugged. "Couldn't get you by phone."

"We took it off the hook three days ago. Thought maybe you'd take the hint and stay away."

Florio nodded vaguely. "So, can I come in, or what?"

He sidled past Block and into the apartment with an easy familiarity. Florio was not only Block's partner but a good friend, perhaps his best, in the manner in which such men have friends. He was about Block's size, but something about him gave the impression of greater bulk. Sheila decided it was his darker coloring. He was the kind of man people gave plenty of room to, powerful and with an air of control that suggested great volatility underneath. She had tried, on their previous meetings, but Sheila had been unable to like the man. He had done nothing much to offend her, except, perhaps, to give her the feeling that she made him slightly uncomfortable. And yet Sandy seemed so relaxed with him. There was an air of complete comfort about the relationship between the two men that Sheila envied. Sandy was not that comfortable with her. He was loving and he was attentive, but always with a trace of effort, as if he had determined to be nice. She assumed that was only because their relationship was still new, still running the fever course of a love affair. Comfort could come later. Still, she envied Florio his ease with her husband.

"How are you, Mr. Florio?" she said, trying not to sound too cool.

He glanced at her as if noticing her for the first time and arched his head upward slightly. It was the sort of gesture one used upon greeting an acquaintance in a crowd, nothing personal, just an acknowledgment. Sheila resented it.

"We've been thinking about decorating, Mr. Florio," she said, waving an arm toward a window. "What would you think of balloon shades? Or maybe vertical blinds, what do you think?"

Florio nodded. "I'd like to consider that one."

"And as for light, there's a sconce, but I think the room needs recessed indirect overhead lights. What do you think?"

Florio turned to Block. "You got any aspirins?"

Block waved toward the bathroom. "Help yourself. Be sure to give us your opinion about the lights when you come back," said Block. He grinned. Block had a grin that seemed to work on only one side of his face. It lifted his left cheek, creasing it into a dimple, but left the right cheek virtually untouched.

"He drinks sometimes," Block offered when Florio had left the room.

"I suppose it's traumatic, having a partner get married," said Sheila.

"Why?"

"It interferes with all that male bonding, doesn't it?"

Block looked at her blankly.

"Isn't that what male partnerships are all about? Male bonding? Two buddies with their big guns, their car, guarding each other's backs. Suppressed homosexuality."

Block grinned at her again.

"I didn't think I'd given you any cause to suspect me of homosexuality."

She grabbed his arm and leaned her head against his shoulder. "Overcompensation," she said, a twinkle in her voice. "I read all about it in *New York* magazine."

Block laughed. She had steadfastly refused to be impressed by the fact that he was a homicide cop. That had been one of the first planks of their relationship, and the second had been that he would not try to change her mind. The less she knew about the realities of his work, the better, as far as Block was concerned. Her innocence was one of the things he loved about her. One of the many things.

"I wish you'd try to get along with Lou," he said. "He's really a good man."

"I am trying," she said. "What you're getting is the best I've got."

"Why don't you like him?"

"Because he doesn't like me."

"Sure he does."

"He ignores me. He never looks at me. All of his remarks are directed to you. He can't even bring himself to pronounce my name."

"He's shy," Block offered lamely. In fact, he had noticed all of it. Most of the time Florio acted as if Sheila did not exist.

"Well, I'm sensitive. But I'll try, I'll keep trying." She felt it was a pointless promise. She remembered their wedding, a peculiar affair that had been her introduction into the world of police. The men had kept to each other in one group, the women in another, like junior high school students at a dance. At any moment she had expected to see the frustrated women dancing with each other. Half of the policemen there were married, had their wives in attendance, but they still managed to clump together in their tight male group. It looked to Sheila as if they had all been dumped into a centrifuge and spun until they were divided according to their specific sexual density. Working-class Irish and Italians, joined in uneasy alliance against their common enemy—the woman. Misogynists to a man, she had thought. Even Block seemed restless locked away from the camaraderie of his fellows—temporarily—because he had the bride on his arm.

"They're no good with women, cops," Nell McKeon had said. She was the wife of another of Block's associates, a sharp-tongued skinny woman in a culture of women that tended to early puffiness.

"Sandy's good with me," Sheila had said quickly, defensively.

"He may be good with you, dear, but he ain't no good with women. They're asshole buddies, all of them." She indicated the men clustered around the bar, dismissing them with a jerk of her head.

Sheila had argued lamely for a moment, but in her heart she had recognized the truth of Nell's complaint immediately. They were a closed, male society. A woman might get close to one of them individually, but each of them shared a closeness, an intimacy born of common experience that no woman could share. A good man, her husband had called Florio. Why didn't "a good woman" mean the same thing?

She was jealous, Sheila realized, a bit shamefully. Florio had something with Sandy that she would never have, something that came from strapping on a gun, and had nothing to do with sex but everything to do with gender. Asshole buddies. Unpleasant phrase for an impenetrable reality.

Florio returned, one hand rubbing his temple.

"It's the alcohol," said Sheila.

"You do look a bit peaked, Lou," said Block. "Sort of like wilted lettuce." *He* could insult Florio, that was all right. Gentle insult and sarcasm was how they dealt with each other. Block just wished that Sheila could find another way.

"It's all that salt," Florio insisted. "I'm giving up Margaritas from now on."

"It was nice of you to stop by and tell us that, Lou," said Block. "We were concerned."

"I thought you'd want to know."

"We couldn't sleep last night for wondering about the salt in your Margaritas."

"I knew we were awake for some reason," said Sheila. To her amazement Florio seemed embarrassed and even Block appeared bothered. Not from a woman, she realized. They didn't want innuendo from one of their women. They could act like boys together, but women were only supposed to watch. To hell with that sort of working-class-cop prudishness, Sheila thought. She'd change Sandy soon enough.

"Captain wants you to come in," said Florio, the banter gone from his tone.

"I'm on my honeymoon."

"Yeah, well, you're coming back tomorrow anyway. What's a few hours?"

"You ever been on a honeymoon?"

"Captain's got a case for us."

"There's always a case," Block said. "This is murder month. New Yorkers love to kill each other in the summer."

"This case is different. Captain thought you should see it before they clean up."

"I did the Cap a favor by not taking a real honeymoon in the first place."

"Oh, go help them out, Sandy," Sheila said. "They obviously can't get along without you. I don't want to be blamed for a crime wave."

"We can get along without him, Miss," Florio said.

"No offense, Mr. Florio."

"I'm not offended."

"I see that you're not."

"It would help *him* if he was in on it from the beginning. You get a better feel of things that way. . . . And you could call me Lou."

"Fine. You could keep calling me Miss," she said. And laughed. But the laugh came a beat too late.

Florio looked at Sheila, then at Block.

"She's joking," said Block.

"I see that."

"Call her Sheila."

"So, you coming?"

"Go, go, go," said Sheila. "I can decorate better without interruptions anyway."

Block shrugged. "I guess I'm coming."

"You oughta be relieved I got you out of there," Florio said as they walked toward the car.

"Why?"

"I don't know about you—no offense now?"

"No offense."

"Well, I don't know about you, but the times I've been shacked up with a girl—no offense on the shacked up?"

"Get on with it."

"Married men get sensitive."

"Three days of marriage hasn't changed me all that drastically, Lou. Say what you want to say."

"Three days with a girl, I don't care how good it is, and I'd be dying to get away. This isn't anything against the girl, and of course not against your wife, but there's just so much domesticity I can take without my skin begins to crawl. They talk so much, the women. They want to know things—like how are you feeling, what are you thinking. How do I look? They're always asking, how do I look? I had this one girl was always trying on clothes in front of me. Tight stuff. She was a big girl, maybe twenty-five, thirty pounds overweight. She had this thing for tight clothes. She'd come out in these slacks, the shiny kind only a model can wear, and say, 'How do I look?' She's busting the seams, threads are flying, about six inches of flab is hanging over the waist, she can't do the top button, it's all held up by the zipper, which is holding only because it's jammed under the strain, and she asks me, 'How do I look?' I tell her she looks fine. 'Not too fat?' Not too fat for what? Not too fat for Orson Welles, not too fat for a circus act. 'You're sure I don't look a little heavy,' she asks. 'You look fine,' I say. 'You're sure?' 'Great, you look great.' 'Because I think I look a little heavy in these,' she says. 'Tell me the truth.' So I tell her the truth. 'They're a little tight,' I say. You couldn't believe the screaming! You'd think I stuck her with an ice pick. Standing there in these shiny tight pants, looking like a sausage that's gone bad, got that sheen on it, waving her arms, calling me names I never heard of. It was terrible. I'm not saying your marriage is like that."

Block laughed. "Thanks. It's not."

"I'm just saying, for me, about six hours with a woman is more than enough."

"Well, that's your problem, Lou. I'm happy to say I don't share it."

Block did not admit that Florio had come uncomfortably close to the truth. The honeymoon had been the most intense emotional experience he could recall, and too much ecstatic togetherness, like too much of anything, could be very wearing. He had been a bachelor for forty-one years and the prospect of marriage had made him so apprehensive that he had spent the night before his wedding walking the streets, hoping to stifle his anxiety with exhaustion. He knew he loved Sheila, but he wasn't sure that love alone could overcome a lifetime of solitary living. He had always been a very detached person, cruising on a tightly controlled emotional plateau that avoided both highs and lows. He had preferred it that way, felt it was safer. He was not entirely comfortable with happiness yet. Love was a danger to the equilibrium, and despite his denial earlier, Block felt that he was changing drastically already after only three days with Sheila. He was sure the change was for the better, but still he did not mind being back in a world where he was comfortable.

3

Block's new apartment was on Seventy-ninth Street, just off Amsterdam Avenue on the West Side. At the corner of Seventy-ninth and Columbus they drove through a small flood where the neighborhood children had tapped a fire hydrant in an effort to fight the heat. Fires became a greater danger in New York in the summer because the water pressure dropped, bled to a trickle by thousands of geysers from the hydrants. New York City did not adjust well to summer. There was nothing to absorb the heat, just brick and steel and asphalt. Every air conditioner installed to cool the indoors blasted heated air into the streets. The humidity which condensed in the air conditioners to make conditions livable inside dripped steadily onto the sidewalks outside, driving the humidity higher. The air conditioners worked harder to cool and dehumidify the outside air that came inside, thus depositing still hotter, more humid air outside. Et cetera, et cetera, et cetera, to the point of acute discomfort.

Those who could afford it fled New York City in the summer for the sea breezes or the cooler mountain air. Those who could not afford to flee stayed. They drank more, they fought more as tempers flared with the heat, they started more fires, they looted more shops, they killed more often.

The two detectives drove in silence for a time. Block broke it finally.

"How come you never call Sheila 'Sheila' ?" he asked.

"What do you mean?"

"You never use her name. She says you never look her in the eye. She thinks you don't like her."

"She doesn't like me," Florio said.

"Nonsense," Block lied. He felt as if he was having the same conversation with everyone. "She just doesn't know you very well."

"I like her fine," Florio said flatly.

"Just asking."

"We going to have trouble over this?"

"No trouble. You don't have to like her just because she's my wife. But it'd be nice. I'd like us to get along."

"You've changed, don't tell me you haven't. You used to be—what's the word—morose. That suited you better. Now you're all the time grinning and laughing."

Block laughed. "Sorry."

Florio swerved the car to avoid a pedestrian. The pedestrian glared at him balefully.

"I don't mind, marriage made you a little bit of a jerk—just don't expect everyone else to change, too. I'm only so sociable."

"Fair enough."

"But I'll try."

"Can't ask for more than that," Block said.

"You're so damned accommodating. It makes me nervous."

Florio nosed the car into a half-space between another car and a construction refuse bin, leaving the tail end of the pale-green Chevy to stick into the street. They walked the half block to Alicia Caro's apartment.

There were too many cops around. The building seemed to be swarming with them. There were uniformed cops in the street outside the apartment building, more of them in the lobby, standing around, making the passing residents of the building nervous by staring at them. Cops in groups made Block nervous, too. They made some people feel secure, but they reminded Block of maggots around dead meat.

A patrolman politely encouraged anyone who tried to step into the elevator either to take the stairs or wait until the forensic expert was finished dusting the buttons for prints.

"What do you hope to get off of there?" Block asked.

The forensic man didn't bother to look up. "Nothing," he said. "There's probably several thousand overlapping prints on each button. Whoever cleans an elevator button? There's probably a print going back to the day this was installed. Can't read any of them, of course."

"So?" asked Block.

The forensic man shrugged futilely. "That's what we do. We don't do it, somebody like you comes along and says, 'Hey, 'dja do the elevator?' "

There was another uniformed cop in the stairwell on the fifteenth floor. Block recognized him. He was an old-timer named Creavens who had been around to help on more than one of Block's cases. Creavens was sitting on the stairs, his head lowered between his knees. Block squatted beside him.

"What's the matter, Creavens? You sick?"

Creavens turned his face toward Block. The cop was very pale and Block guessed he had already been ill. But his eyes were angry.

"What kind of a job is this?" he demanded.

"You want a doctor?"

Creavens shook his head from side to side. Block wasn't sure whether he was saying no to the doctor, or shaking his head in disgust over the world.

"What's with him?" Florio asked as they approached the apartment door. Block didn't answer.

There were more cops inside the apartment. Another uniformed patrolman let them in the door, and inside a swarm of forensic experts knelt and crawled and stretched and craned and peered for evidence. One man was patiently scraping up samples of congealed blood. He had to be patient because there was blood everywhere in the room. It looked as if someone had slashed a major artery then pirouetted around and around and around, spraying a new batch with each pump of the heart. It was necessary to take a sample from each major splash and note the exact location within the room. If there was more than one person's blood spilled here, the lab would find out later.

"In here." Quayle motioned Block and Florio into the kitchen. Quayle had his pipe lit, which meant the examination was already well along. Despite his addiction to sweet-scented tobacco, Quayle had a very delicate sense of smell, and he always carefully sniffed for any unusual odors before he lit up. They had sophisticated instruments to check for the presence of gas or explosive or poisons, but normally the forensic unit didn't use them unless they already suspected they were necessary. Quayle, who was in charge of the forensic unit, made the initial determination with his nose.

"The corpus is in here," said Quayle, stepping back to let them into the cramped kitchen. Block nearly stumbled over the gray-green mound in the middle of the floor. The body had already been encased in a body bag, a larger, heavier, zippered version of a plastic garbage bag. The bags had two purposes. One was to cover the deceased. The other was to collect and hold any part or parts of the deceased that happened to fall or drain out en route to the medical examiner's office.

"Let's see it," said Block.

"Messy," said Quayle, hesitating.

"I gathered that from the other room."

Quayle bent with some difficulty. He affected suits with vests, which restricted his mobility but made him look unusually distinguished for a cop. But then Quayle didn't regard himself as a cop. He preferred to think of himself as a sleuth.

Quayle unzipped the bag. Alicia Caro lay on her back, her knees pulled up as if to protect her stomach. One hand lay in a normal fashion by her side; the other arm ended in a jaggedly cut stump, the blood congealed black at the end of the splintered bone. Her head was twisted at an impossibly sharp angle. Bruises and cuts covered her face and body. Her hair was clotted with blood; a dried crust of it spread from her nose to her chin.

A small soft brown pile was atop her stomach.

"What's that?" Florio asked.

Quayle looked at him for a moment. "You know what that is. Feces."

"Animal?" asked Block.

"We'll analyze it, of course, but I'm sure it's human."

Florio turned away and kicked at the refrigerator.

"One of many interesting features," Quayle said coolly. "I understand you had to leave your honeymoon. Sorry about that, but it's always best to see things in situ. Especially a case as unique as this one."

"That's a human being there!" Florio shouted.

Quayle tugged at his vest. "You're wrong again, Florio. That's a corpus, that has been a corpus for four days."

"How do you fix that?" Block asked.

"One of your henchmen, the Neanderthal, what's his name?"

"McKeon."

"Yes. He answered the first call and managed to rearrange things just enough to cause me minor problems before the Captain wisely sent for you. At any rate, McKeon spoke to the doorman, who says he last saw her four days ago. That seems perfectly consistent with what I can see, but of course we'll allow the illustrious M.E. to determine things for us." Quayle hated the medical examiner. Most of the department hated the medical examiner, but Quayle's hatred was a purer, finer instrument because Quayle had himself failed out of medical school. For some reason this gave him the reputation of a scholar and an intellectual among the detectives, a reputation which Quayle did everything to cultivate.

Quayle pointed to two long pink creases along Alicia's collarbone on either side of her head.

"Indentations caused by the edge of the sole of a man's shoe," Quayle said, pointing next at her ears and neck with the stem of his pipe.

Long, flat furrows, like the rake of blunt claws, spread from under her chin past her ears, where they disappeared into the hair. The ears were both partially torn away from the head.

"Fingernail marks," he explained. "Conjecture, of course, but it looks to me as if he sat here on the floor, put his feet on her shoulders, his hands under her chin, and tried to pull her head off."

Tapping the stem of his pipe against his lower teeth, Quayle studied the marks again.

"My guess is he did this in frustration after he failed with the hand. Might have been the other way around, of course."

"Where is the hand?"

"Not pretty," said Quayle.

"It's not exactly a beauty contest so far," said Florio.

"No," agreed Quayle. "As you say." Quayle pointed with his pipe toward a food processor on the kitchen counter. The beaker was half filled with a puree of flesh, bone, and blood.

"Christ!" Florio exclaimed. He tried to swallow twice, looking away from the beaker. "I'm going to find McKeon," he muttered.

"Don't be sick in the bathroom," Quayle called after him. "There's evidence in there." He turned back to Block, who was studiously looking at the floor. "Your friend's been boozing again, Lieutenant."

"He's all right," Block said. "Just get on with it."

"That's what I was doing." Quayle sniffed. "I don't enjoy this, you know."

"I didn't know."

"Well, I don't. I may appear detached, but I'm as appalled as you are."

"All right, you're a sensitive guy," Block said, realizing he would have to do better. The relationship between a detective and his forensic expert is complicated and often difficult. Although the detective is responsible for conducting the investigation of a case, the forensic man is technically in control at the actual scene of the crime until he completes his work. In reality, forensic squads are seldom given this kind of cooperation, and an annoyingly large part of their job is reconstructing evidence which overzealous uniformed cops or detectives have unwittingly rearranged.

Forensic experts determine the nature of the crime. The initial assessment of a death, whether it is murder, suicide, or natural causes, is made by the forensic expert. His judgment is later confirmed or denied by the office of the medical examiner, whose job it is to perform autopsies on the victim of every violent or suspicious death. Once murder is established, the work falls to the detectives. They deal with the living, trying to follow the trail first discovered by the forensic men through the tangles of human personalities. A proper assessment of the crime on the site is often an invaluable aid to the detective—but the detectives inevitably get the credit for the arrest. Not surprisingly, the forensic investigators resent this. They also resent the M.E.'s who disagree with them. Taken as a group, they are undervalued and testy. A wise detective knows this, and he also knows that a good forensic man can reconstruct a crime from clues the detective wouldn't even see.

"This is a grisly business and it has us all on edge," Block said soothingly. "I'm grateful you're able to maintain your detachment. I'd be lost if you couldn't."

Quayle tugged at his vest, mollified. "Well, again, just a guess, but I'd say he planned to make mince out of all of her, but gave that up when the blades jammed on the ulna—the forearm bone."

"Was he trying to destroy evidence? Fingerprints?"

"He didn't touch the other hand. Yanking someone's head off is not a very good way of destroying evidence, either. No, I think this was a crime of incredible rage, he wasn't thinking at all. There's a ring in there." He pointed toward the food processor beaker. "He didn't bother to remove it, but he must have known it would only gum up the works."

"Was she dead when he did this with the hand?"

"No, but probably unconscious, at least. She managed to pull her legs up before she died in a reflex to protect her stomach, which has been kicked pretty savagely. They wouldn't have stayed that way if he was dragging her to the counter, then throwing her down again."

Quayle led him back toward the living room. "Fury, that's the best word I can think of. He battered her to death, bounced her off the walls like a basketball. See all the larger splotches of blood? Each one of those is an impact mark. She's got glass in the back of her scalp."

Quayle pointed to the broken *I, Claudius* poster, shards of glass still in the frame. "That one happened first and until the business in the kitchen, it was the only time she was really cut. Everything else is an abrasion, very nasty ones, but not cuts. He slammed her around the way a child tries to kill a doll, by banging it against things."

Moving the uniformed cop aside, Quayle opened the door and showed Block the blood on its edge. "This is consistent with that gouge on her forehead. The first blow."

"Could I step outside, Lieutenant?" the uniformed cop asked. He looked queasy. "Get a little air?"

Block nodded. "Send Creavens in if he's feeling better." He returned to Quayle. "How do you figure it's the first blow?"

"The door had to be open." He released it and it swung shut by itself. "He didn't throw her around with it open. She comes to the door, opens it, suddenly he pushes against it, catches her in the head. The chain isn't forced. She opened the door for him."

"Someone she knew, then," said Block. Murderers almost always were someone known by the victim.

Quayle shrugged. "That's your department. All I know is it was someone strong, enraged—which could make him stronger—right-handed . . ."

"How so?"

"The majority of the impact wounds are on her right side. If a right-hander hits someone with his stronger hand, the blows are on the victim's left side. But if he pushes with his stronger side"—he nudged Block off balance; Block put up his right hand to keep from hitting the wall— "the victim lands on the right side."

"How big a man?" Block asked.

"There's a bloody footprint in the kitchen, just a partial, but it's a size ten shoe. That would put him between five ten and six one or so."

"Anything else on him? Hair sample or anything?"

Quayle laughed shortly. "Oh, we've got hair samples. Take your pick, the bedroom is crawling with them. Apparently she did a good deal of—entertaining. But there's nothing at all under her fingernails, no hair, no flesh, no blood. He must have hit her like a whirlwind and not given her any chance at all to defend herself."

Block moved toward the bedroom. Quayle hurried ahead of him to keep in control. "Now, the blood is a curious thing," he said. "She bled—well you can see how much—and he had to get some of that on him—a lot of it. He could have washed his face and hands—although there's no evidence of that, but what about his clothes? He had to walk out of here either nude or with his clothes splattered like a butcher's apron. How does he do that without anyone noticing?"

"Let's hope someone noticed," said Block. He stopped in the bedroom and stared at the wall next to the dressing table. About four feet from the floor, scrawled in lipstick, was the message:

TOM-TOM IS A ᗺAD BOY

Block studied the message for a long time. In a way, it was more troubling than the murder.

At length, he spoke to Quayle. "I'd like to hear what you make of this."

"A child wrote it," Quayle answered without hesitation.

"It didn't have to be a child," Block said heatedly.

"You mean you don't want it to be a child. Neither do I, but there it is. An adult could kneel and write at that level, but look at the printing, look how uncertain the characters are. Look at the way they're formed—the parts of the letters are produced almost at random, with no logical sequencing. They're drawn, not printed. You can tell by the pressure of the lipstick where each letter was started. Those *m*'s were each started three separate times, as if the child had to remember what stroke came next. Look at the reversal of *b* in *bad*. Someone with a learning disability might do that, but he'd do it consistently. The *b* is done the right way in *boy*. No, it was done by a child—a left-handed child, by the slant of the letters—and one who had just recently learned to print. That's what, six years old? Five? Seven at the most."

Block pressed the heels of his palms into his eyes and rubbed. Suddenly he felt very weary. "God damn," he said.

Quayle tapped his teeth with the pipe again. A trail of smoke curled out from the stem end. "You're looking for a raging maniac who takes a child with him. . . . Good luck."

"God damn," Block repeated softly. The honeymoon was over.

4

It had been weeks, but Tillie heard the sound of heavy footsteps overhead again. He was back, and pacing. She could picture him walking back and forth, hands moving slightly, lips twitching as he murmured softly to himself. With that southern accent his voice was so slow in cadence that Tillie equated it with slowness of mind; but his eyes were always a little anxious, never quite resting on the face of the person he was talking to. A conversation with him usually made Tillie want to look over her shoulder to see what he kept glancing at. Not that there were many conversations. You could talk at him, but he seldom responded beyond a polite smile and some formula southern courtesy. He volunteered nothing.

Tillie was more familiar with his accent from the times she had spent peering through his keyhole than from actual dialogues.

"He's back," Tillie said to the girl who was sitting listlessly in front of the television set. The girl, Shirley, turned a sullen eye toward her aunt.

"Who?" she asked in a tone of profound indifference. The girl had been bored since she arrived three days ago. First she had found fault with everything in the apartment from the sleeping arrangements to the fried fish for dinner, then, having exhausted her meager reserves of energy along with her even more meager supply of courtesy, she had fallen into the chair in front of the television set. During the few times that she had aroused herself since, she had complained about how boring New York was by contrast with Shaker Heights, which was the very pits to begin with. If she acted like this all the time, Tillie could well understand why her boyfriend had broken up with her. What she couldn't understand was how the girl had managed to get a boyfriend in the first place.

Tillie pointed upward to the sound of pacing. "Mr. Watts," she said. "He's a truck driver, he's almost never here. When he is, he walks a lot. Indoors and out. Sometimes he walks back and forth on the block, back and forth, back and forth, just the one block, for hours. I think he must miss the motion of the truck."

"A truck driver." Shirley snorted.

"Your grandfather was a taxi driver," Tillie reminded her sharply. "He managed to raise your mother and I pretty darn well." At least Tillie had always thought so until now. But judging by her sister's daughter, something had gone wrong with her sister somewhere. Marrying an orthodontist was one thing, a triumph no doubt, but you still had to instill your children with a proper sense of things.

"I didn't mean anything," Shirley said sullenly. "Is he going to stomp around up there like that all night?"

"Sometimes he does," said Tillie.

"How do you sleep?"

Tillie found the steady rhythm soothing, but didn't bother to say so.

"I don't know how you manage to sleep anyway, without an air conditioner," Shirley went on. "I haven't had a decent night's sleep since I've been here. It's so muggy."

Shirley pinched her blouse between thumb and forefinger and pulled it away from her body. Dark splotches of perspiration had turned the thin material translucent in spots, revealing both her navel and a sizable portion of one large breast. Tillie had never become comfortable with the fashion of going braless, particularly in one so chesty as her niece. She had tried to express her disapproval several times by pointedly staring but she hadn't said anything. Needless to say, it had had no effect on Shirley.

"He's quite the mystery man," Tillie said, forcing a note of animation into her tone. The girl was slowly driving her crazy. It would have been easier to sink down in a chair beside her and dissolve in the dancing light of the TV screen, too. But Tillie felt a responsibility to help the girl past her crisis, and if a little judicious fabricating would help, then there was nothing wrong with that.

"What's so mysterious?"

"He doesn't have a telephone. He never gets any mail except junk addressed to occupant. He never has anybody in his apartment."

"How do you know about his mail? Do you look?"

"I think he's hiding from a dark secret," Tillie said. She *had* looked at his mail, as a matter of fact, but it was her brownstone, she was the landlady, there was nothing wrong with checking things out once in a while.

"You mean he's a crook?" Shirley asked, intrigued for the first time. Tillie had meant something far more romantic, like recovering from a tragic love.

"Perhaps," she said.

"What kind of crook?"

"Well, I don't really know. . . ."

"An ax-murderer or something, I suppose?" Shirley snorted derisively. Still, the girl did seem interested. "What's he look like?"

"He's very attractive," Tillie said. "Quite handsome in a rugged sort of way." The older she got, the more Tillie was able to see the better aspects of every man. It was amazing how someone she would have considered as plain when she was young now could look so attractive and virile.

"How old is he?"

"It's hard to say," said Tillie. "Somewhere between thirty-five and fifty. He's a hard man to judge." She neglected to add that he looked considerably older when viewed through the keyhole than he did in the hallway.

"Sounds like a fruitcake to me," said Shirley, apparently dismissing the subject.

"At least he's a real person," Tillie said, waving a dismissive

hand at the television screen. "I'm going to have a glass of tea."
Tillie still preferred to drink tea from a glass the way her father
had done, although she let the sugar dissolve in the tea and
didn't clench it between her teeth the way the old people did.
"Would you like some?"

"How can you drink hot tea in this weather?" Shirley demanded, appalled.

"Hot drinks cool you off in hot weather," said Tillie with certainty. She had never understood it either, but some things you
just accepted.

Shirley's shoulders shook with contemptuous laughter as she
returned her attention to the television. As Tillie made her tea,
she wondered how she would keep from killing the girl. She
didn't notice when the pacing overhead stopped. When she returned to the living room, Tillie was surprised but relieved to
find Shirley gone.

Watts didn't hear the first knock on the door, he was so en-
grossed in what he had *seen*. It may have been a nightmare, he
told himself, it may have been a hallucination. God, he hoped
so. If it had been real, if it actually happened and he had really
seen it happen—his life was in danger, the very gravest danger.

At the second knock he stopped pacing and stared at the door.
For a moment he could only imagine it was a mistake of some
kind. No one came to his door. Ever. Warily, the fear of what
he had seen still with him, he approached the door and touched
the lock.

"Who's there?"

"I'm your neighbor," said the voice of a young woman. It was
safe. It wasn't *him*.

Watts opened the door. A young woman stood there, a
strange, provocative smile on her lips. His eyes saw the brown
mound of her nipple jutting against the wet fabric of her blouse.
He glanced at her face, into the corridor behind her, then back

at her face. He tried to keep from glancing at the nipple and the large breast again, but his eyes moved on their own.

The girl thrust her hand toward him and the breast jiggled. "Hi, my name's Shirley," she said brightly. "I was wondering if I could borrow some ice. Our refrigerator is broken."

Still smiling in that strange, seductive way, her eyes locked on his, she eased past him and into his room, her breasts grazing the front of his shirt.

Waving at a fly with a peculiarly girlish gesture that conveyed more annoyance than lethal intent, Captain Byrne lost his train of thought. He had a mild phobia about insects, and Block waited patiently as the Captain flapped away ineffectually. The swats were limp-wristed, and it was yet another gesture that Block wished Byrne would avoid. The Captain was one of the most effeminate men on the New York force; certainly among the nonclerical cops in Manhattan, the ones who did the actual police work, Byrne won hands down. A few years ago when he had taken over the precinct, most of the detectives thought he was gay.

New York City detectives may not be any more disturbed about serving under a homosexual than any randomly selected group of men—but they are certainly no less disturbed about it. For a month the detectives were so obsessed with finding out the truth about Byrne's sexual inclinations that they enlisted some fellow detectives, friends from a Bronx precinct, to trail Byrne in his off hours, hoping to catch him red-dicked, as it were, in the fundament of a young Forty-second Street hustler. After several weeks of following Byrne directly home to his wife and three sons every day after duty, the Bronx detectives wearied of the game and begged off.

Some of the more die-hard faggot hunters, like Detective McKeon, swore that Byrne's strict adherence to hearth, home, and heterosexuality was suspect in itself. A man truly comfortable with his maleness, they argued, could whore around a little bit, or, at the very least, trust himself to have a beer or two with the guys. That was the extreme view, however; most of the men came to accept Captain Byrne as a strange—but not truly queer—duck. Still, there were certain gestures that Block wished Byrne would eschew. Gay or not, there was no need to accentuate his girlishness.

The fly eventually tired of tormenting Byrne and flew toward Block, circling his head twice. On the third pass Block snatched it out of midair and held it in his clenched palm. Byrne looked on, mouth agape.

"Take it out of *here*," Byrne said at last after Block had sat for several seconds wondering what to do with the little body he could feel pulsing against his hand. Block had thought of slapping his hands together and squashing it just to watch Byrne's horrified reaction. The man might squeal, though, and that would make their future relationship difficult.

In a humane act that neither man would have felt compelled to perform if he were alone, Block tossed the fly out of the open window. By the time Block sat down again, Byrne was composed.

"I swallowed a fly once," Byrne said, as if that explained everything. "By accident." He gave a little shiver of disgust, then returned to business.

"So, anyway, where was I?"

"The shitstorm," Block reminded him.

"Right. You're a smart cop, I don't need to tell you that the last thing this city needs in the summer is a shitstorm. We got troubles enough. A psycho killer who kills Broadway stars is just the kind of thing that can cause a shitstorm. At least the psycho who was stabbing blacks on the street was getting his kicks in the winter. Can you imagine the kind of shitstorm that would have caused if he'd been sticking them in the summer? We would have had a race riot to make Watts look like a block party."

Block nodded. He could well imagine the trouble something like this could cause. The public had grown callous toward murder. As violence in general grew and each individual became defensively more insular, it was easy to shrug off events which did not affect them directly. Blacks killing blacks in record numbers, Puerto Ricans slicing each other in gang wars, old people mugged on subways, young people mugged in parks, rich people being slain by burglars—all of these could be discounted by the middle-class families in their individual fortresses. They didn't affect one because one could so easily avoid the problem. Stay away from blacks, stay away from Puerto Ricans, stay off the subways except in rush hours, stay out of the parks, don't be too old, don't be too young, don't be rich. But a psycho was different. By his nature he could strike anyone, anytime, any place. At least until the interior logic of his insanity was understood, he was a danger to all. And the worst kind of danger, tapping the deepest fear, because he was unknown. A monster. A maniac who did not have sense enough to avoid people who weren't black or Spanish or young or old or rich or in the wrong place. He just came and ate you up as you always feared he would when you used to hide under the covers at night.

The fact that the killer had chosen a famous actress for his victim assured that the city would know about things very soon. One killing did not make a shitstorm, of course, but it was certainly not too early to look for cover.

"What do you have so far?" Byrne asked, his short peptalk concluded.

Block blew out a small puff of air. "Not much yet, but we're working. The M.E. didn't have much to add to what we could see. She was battered to death sometime Thursday night, three and a half days before we found her."

"How was she discovered?"

"She missed two performances without calling in. Her agent tried to get in touch with her for two days, and finally got hold of the super and talked his way into the apartment. She was seen going up to her apartment that night with a man, not much of a description on him. Five feet ten or so, not too heavy, not too thin, age about forty, give or take, brownish hair. Apparently she goes up there with a different guy every night so no one pays much attention anymore. The doorman saw a guy leave about two in the morning, he thinks it was the same guy, but he isn't sure. He told McKeon all he remembered is the guy was wearing a raincoat—it was raining that night, we checked—and looked scared. The doorman said he'd looked like he'd seen a ghost, and the raincoat was buttoned up as soon as the man stepped out of the elevator. The doorman remembers that because he thought it was a little funny, it being so hot. The coat fits because we figure the killer would be covered with blood. . . . And that's about the extent of it; nobody else on the floor heard anything that night, but there wasn't anybody home in the adjoining apartment and the next closest one is a very old lady, very hard of hearing. She could barely hear me when I questioned her. I doubt she would have noticed anything lower than a gunshot. . . . Oh, there was something else. The M.E. confirmed that Miss Caro was pregnant."

"What do you mean *confirmed* she was pregnant?"

"We already knew she was because Florio told us."

"Florio's a gynecologist now, is he?"

"He says he read about it, it's been in the papers, apparently. Now, we do have one leg up, we think. She kept a list of names and dates. We showed it to her agent and members of the cast, and they could identify the first third or so. It seems they were her lovers. Apparently she ran out of people she knew and started dealing in strangers."

"You're telling me Alicia Caro was a nympho?" Byrne flapped his hand, palm up, elbow tucked close in to his body in one of the gestures Block wished he would avoid.

"She made friends easy," said Block.

"She was beautiful," Byrne exclaimed. "I wish someone had told *me* she was a nympho!" The suggestion of Byrne taking advantage of Alicia Caro seemed so unlikely to Block that for a moment he wondered if perhaps McKeon wasn't right after all.

Block brushed some imaginary dirt from his knee, looking away from Byrne, embarrassed by his attempts to appear virile.

"So, I've got McKeon out tracking down the first third of those names, the easy third, to see what kind of alibi they've got. Florio's got the last third, and I'm taking the middle. All she's got is last names, ages, and sometimes a comment or two, so it will take a while. Florio's after the guy we want to talk to most, the last name on the list, someone named Watts."

"How long is this going to take?"

"It's a long list, Captain," said Block. "Over two hundred names."

"Two hundred!" Byrne whistled and stood, putting his hands on his hips in a gesture of astonishment. As usual he did it slightly wrong, resting the wrist joints on his hips so his fingers hung loosely behind him. Block thought he looked like a disgruntled housewife with flour on her hands.

"Do you need more men?" Byrne asked, still looking as if he were in a huff.

"Let's see what happens when we find this Watts. If he's no help, I might need a few more to run down the list. . . . About McKeon—"

"I know, I know," said Byrne quickly. "He's dumb, but he's patient. Going down a list is his kind of work."

It was suspected among the detectives that McKeon had somehow managed to cheat on the exam for his detective's shield. The feeling was widespread that if McKeon could make detective, it made all the others look worse.

Block started for the door, but Byrne wasn't finished; he felt obliged to fulfill his duties as authority figure as well as cop.

"So, how's marriage?" he asked, stopping Block. "All it's cracked up to be?" He gave what Block could only consider a dirty little laugh.

"I've been home about three hours in the last forty-eight since this case got dumped on me, but before that it seemed promising."

To Block's amazement, Byrne offered to shake hands before he left. His clasp was weak and moist. "Marriage will do you a world of good," he said. "I know it did for me."

Block left the Captain's office wondering just what he might have meant. He knew what McKeon would make of the remark.

Block came to himself with a start. His mind had been off wandering on its own and it returned reluctantly.

He looked around, trying to find a familiar signpost to tell him where he was, and his eyes landed on the photograph of Sheila in its leather frame which dominated his meticulously tidy desk. She was smiling but looking beyond the camera, and her eyes were laughing as if she shared a wonderful secret with someone just out of the picture frame. It was the kind of look that could make most men wish she were sharing her secret with them—but she was sharing it with Block. Gently he reached out and ran his finger over the leather frame as if caressing her cheek. She's changed my life, he thought. She turned me upside down and shook me. She changed me from a frog to a prince. Her effect was a kind of magic and he was still looking for the trick behind the illusion. Or maybe he was the illusion to her, maybe she saw him as something he wasn't. Block dreaded that at any moment she might say "Oh, *that's* who you are! You aren't the man I wanted after all." This sense of insecurity, mild as it was, was part of the mix of gratitude, affection, and desire that he called love.

It was late; he should have been home by now, he realized. He thought of calling her to say he would be home soon, but realized she would probably be asleep by now anyway. Better to let her sleep.

He had gotten lost in his work again. A fierce and unremitting concentration was his greatest asset as a detective. He had been known to work for days on end without a break, concentrating so hard, burrowing so deeply into the intricate possibilities of motive and opportunity, alibi and lie, checking and rechecking every procedure in his mind, that he would suddenly come to himself with a start, and find himself in a strange place at a strange time, not entirely certain what had brought him there. His colleagues were used to his habits, knowing by the look on his face when he was with them and available for friendly banter—and when his mind was busy, scouring once again the chain of likelihoods that constituted the solution of a crime. Block was one of the few detectives in the precinct for whom absenteeism was no problem. If he was gone for days at a time, it was taken for granted that he was working in his own way. In a profession given to alcoholism and hypochondria, any detective not accounted for was considered a detective sloughing off. But not Block. Block's vice was work. Although none would say so, there was mild concern among his superiors that Block's marriage might weaken his monastic dedication to his job.

Block had been working his way through his share of the names in Alicia Caro's book. The first step was the phone book, checking all the entries under Sherman, to take one name from the list, in all five boroughs and calling each one until he had located and identified every male who fit the loose description of age given by Alicia. If she had given a clue, such as "banker," it greatly simplified matters; but for many there was nothing, only names and ages, for others, some personal reminder that was no help at all. Sherman, aged thirty-three, for instance, was listed as "sweet."

If the boroughs turned up nothing, he was prepared to go to all the surrounding areas of Connecticut, New Jersey, and Long Island. If this turned up nothing, he would canvass the hotels and motels, seeking anyone of that name registered on the date in Alicia's book. Once the possible suspects were found, the evidence had to be sifted again, every alibi checked carefully. It was an enormous task, and offered only an outside chance at best. But her friends and colleagues were already being scrutinized with little result. Successful detective work, Block knew, often consisted of sifting through mountains of manure with a teaspoon, then sifting the siftings to find the one bit of undigested information hidden there.

So far Block had made his way through about one tenth of

the names on his list, but it was a beginning. He had stood and was stretching his back, flipping through the pages of the suede-covered book, amazed at the woman's promiscuity, when suddenly a single word caught his eyes.

The entry was on the next to last page. The date was June sixth, four weeks ago. The name was Lowreo.(?) The age listed was thirty-eight. And the comment, written in Alicia's spidery handwriting, was "fuzz." Fuzz as in light downy hair? Or fuzz as in cop?

Block called central records and got a list of all the cops in the city with the name of Lowreo. The question mark after the name indicated she wasn't sure of the spelling, so he tried it spelled as many ways as he could think of. The list was a short one. He next checked out their ages, discarding those over fifty and those under thirty. Even allowing Alicia a ten-year margin of error in age assessment, he came up with only two names. One was Francis Loughery, a thirty-two-year-old patrolman who was hospitalized for the first two weeks of June following an emergency operation for a ruptured appendix. The other was Marian Loteo, a thirty-six-year-old meter maid in Queens. Block had seen nothing so far to indicate that Alicia favored meter maids.

When he let himself into the new apartment, it was six in the morning, and the heat outside was already getting oppressive. Sheila lay on her stomach, one slender arm reaching for the head of the bed, the other hand tucked under her cheek. She was naked, although whether because of the heat or in anticipation of Block's arrival, he couldn't say. Her lovely brown hair fell around her face and over her shoulders. He stood for a moment beside the bed, watching her sleep, wondering for the hundredth time how he had gotten such a prize. Just looking at her made him feel weak with love. She makes me think of roses, he thought. She makes me think of flowers. The truth was she made him think of metaphors, stirring the poet within him to come up with images which could contain the depth of his feelings.

She rolled onto her back, the arm above her bent over her head like a number seven. She lay completely exposed, even her palms open. Her lips were parted slightly, revealing those magnificent teeth. He had never seen her look so vulnerable. He loved her so much, he ached.

Her voice startled him. "Are you a voyeur?" Her eyes were still closed, her features completely relaxed, and for a moment it seemed as if she had spoken in her sleep. Then her lips curled up in a wanton smile. Eyes still closed, she reached out and touched his belt.

*

 The waitress looked familiar. She was dressed like all the others in the steak-and-salad restaurants—short-sleeved white shirt, black bow tie, black slacks a little shiny with wear, a black vest. On taking the drink order she had seemed to stare at Florio for a bit, but she hadn't said anything. If she remembered him, she wasn't going to bring it up. They seldom did. Florio frequently ran into people he thought he remembered, or thought he should remember but couldn't. Some of them were arrests he'd made at one time or another, or witnesses he'd grilled—not the types to want to renew the acquaintance. Or else they were former lovers. Occasionally they were both. Lovers, however, was a rather imprecise term. Florio and his partners didn't make love, they had sex. The difference, he knew, was monumental. Florio sometimes felt as if he led two lives; one during the working days when people and events were in sharp focus, and one during the night when alcohol lent events the fuzzy, disjointed quality of a dream. He awoke in beds not his own, not always certain how he'd got there, and, upon seeing the woman beside him, not always certain why.

The waitress could have fallen into either category of acquaintance. She had the hard, brassy look of a woman who was used to trouble. She was at the age when flesh seemed to compound itself without encouragement, and if she was fighting it, she was losing the battle.

"Do I know you?" Florio asked when the waitress brought the drinks.

She stared at him with a look of amused disdain.

"Obviously not," she said, walking away.

Sex, Florio decided. Arrests inspired fear. Sex inspired contempt.

He wished he could categorize and dismiss Sheila that easily. She didn't like him, he was certain of that, but not for the usual reasons. She was skittish around him, high-strung, as if just looking for a chance to bolt or start a fight. He couldn't imagine what he had done to inspire such a reaction. She didn't need to feel threatened by him; in truth, he was a bit afraid of her. She was so damned beautiful, for one thing. Not in the classical way, perhaps, but the more one looked at her, the more beautiful she became.

Florio considered himself an expert on beauty. There were more perfect faces than Sheila's to be seen in television commercials, in magazine ads, on the pages of newspapers where models pouted and jutted out their hips, bodies contorted to display the latest fashion and titillate the viewers. Florio studied these faces with secret passion. He had fallen in love with a face on a billboard more than once. Often he had spied a woman on the street whose face so captivated him that he had followed her until he had found something about her to break the spell— a nose not right when seen from another angle, a voice too shrill, the way she held her head in conversation. It was important to break the spell. Florio knew a fantasy for what it was, but defeating it was not always easy.

Sheila's beauty was not of that variety. The more imperfections he found, the more they seemed to compound her luster. None of her features was quite right alone, but in combination they worked a miracle. Not that it mattered, Florio thought. He didn't need to find a means of deflating this fantasy, it was built in. She was Block's wife.

It would never have occurred to Florio to compliment Sheila on her beauty. He wore shyness around women like a straitjacket. He could deal with men easily enough, and women were no problem as long as he encountered them in the line of duty. Business was business. But he found the delicate minuet of social intercourse impossibly difficult. His throat tightened, his mouth dried up, he could never think of anything to say. He retreated into a gruffness that protected him. Women thought of him as sullen, rude, indifferent, but that was his armor. Behind the armor he longed for them, yearned to hold their delicate hands, walk through meadows, serenade under their balconies. But instead he drank. Liquor allowed him to deal with women, after a fashion, but it was not a fashion that pleased either the women or Florio.

And now here he was, trying to entertain Sheila while waiting for Block to show up. It seemed such an ill-considered idea now that he was faced with the reality. A dinner together, get to know the wife, all three of them be buddies together. Block seemed to want it so much. Who could have known Block would come so late? Who could have known Sheila would be as awkward around him as he was around her? Florio would have preferred to be off somewhere alone, walking on hot coals. He hoped to hell that Block appreciated the gesture. Sheila certainly did not.

Sheila came out of the restroom and hesitated for a moment before crossing the room to her table. Florio did not see her, he was watching the waitress with something like a predatory stare. He's a strange one, she thought. He likes women, that much was obvious from the way he looked at them, but he seemed to like them the same way a wolf likes a rabbit. Just sitting and talking to them seemed to make him terribly uncomfortable. Well, that made him a typical cop, as far as she could see. Just then he tilted his chin up and stroked his neck, at the same time twisting to look in Sheila's direction. His large, moist brown eyes were unguarded, his features relaxed; the strong nose, the solid jaw, the dark, dark hair all seemed for just a second to have been subtly transformed to reveal the real person inside, and not the tough cop he presented for public consumption. In just that flash, Sheila saw a much younger man, a boy almost, sweet and shy. Then Florio's eyes focused on her and his mask dropped back into place. The boy was gone and the ill-at-ease cop had returned.

Florio leaped to his feet and helped her into her chair. It was an unwonted courtesy and for a moment she wasn't sure what Florio was doing. It seemed such an unlikely display of gallantry from the detective. But then so far the entire evening had seemed unlikely. Block had called from the office with the news that Florio had invited them both out to dinner. She suspected that Block had had a hand in it, part of his peacemaking campaign, but she had said only that she would be there. Block was to meet them, but so far he had not come and she and Florio had passed each leaden moment in awkward conversation.

"So, any luck?" he asked.

"He wasn't home, he wasn't at the office. Maybe he's on his way."

"He'll probably be here soon," said Florio. He finished his drink and waved for the waitress. Waved rather desperately, Sheila thought. All of his actions had the slightly exaggerated quality of a man trying to fill time.

"You don't suppose he forgot," said Sheila.

For a moment Florio looked stricken. He finds the idea of a dinner alone with me terrifying, Sheila thought. His panic was so obvious that Sheila had to fight an impulse to comfort him. I can't be as bad as all that, she thought. She remembered her thoughts at the wedding. "No good with women," Nell McKeon had proclaimed of cops. Misogynists to a man.

"He won't forget," said Florio. "Sandy's got a strange notion of time—I don't think he's got a clock in his head like everybody else—but he doesn't forget. It may take him a day or two to do it, but he doesn't forget."

He's thinking about waiting here with me for a day or two, Sheila thought. Poor man. What a fate. She found herself getting mad at him, even though she knew it was an irrational response. He doesn't *want* to be uncomfortable, she told herself. But it was insulting all the same.

Florio turned to wave at the waitress, and nearly bumped into her. She glared at Florio.

"Yes," said the waitress.

"We'll have another round here," said Florio. "That's a—Perrier—for the lady. And I'll have another Margarita."

"Without the salt," said Sheila.

"Oh, hey, that's right," said Florio, smiling for the first time with genuine humor. It wasn't a bad smile at all, Sheila thought. Too bad I had to surprise him into using it.

"And I think I'll switch to a glass of white wine," said Sheila, thinking she would probably need it.

Waiting for the drink, Florio played with his spoon, twisting it, turning it, standing it on end, then flicking it back and forth between his fingers like a baton twirler.

"So, Sheila," he said. He had been peppering his sentences with her name as if he were trying to commit it to memory. Sandy must have told him I'd complained, she thought. She wondered if he were deliberately coming late to force them to get to know each other. She hated being manipulated.

"So, Sheila, how'd you meet, you and Sandy?"

She fought an impulse to slap the spoon from his hand.

"We met in school. We were taking a course in modern cinema."

"Sandy was in school?"

"Night school. Adult education."

"He was taking a night course in 'cinema'? This is movies we're talking about? I never knew that about Sandy."

"There's probably a lot you don't know about him," Sheila said. "He's a very sensitive man." She could not keep the note of pride from her voice.

"You're a movie fan, too, are you?"

She laughed. "Sort of. I'm a film editor."

"Uh-huh. Which means what."

"Well, an editor is really the most important person when it comes to making a film. See, the director shoots thousands of feet of film, then somebody has to make sense out of it. The editor is responsible for the movie you finally see on the screen."

"That's an important job," said Florio.

"Oh, yes."

"That's a lot of responsibility for somebody your age, being a film editor."

"Well . . . I'm really sort of an assistant editor."

"What are some of the movies you made?"

"None, yet," she admitted, then threw her head back in the full-throated laugh. "I'm sort of a fraud," she said. "But I do have a job working on an industrial film. It's a beginning."

"You'll be running your own studio in no time," Florio said.

She smiled warmly, her lips parting over the full teeth. Florio realized why Block loved her. If she were mine, he thought, I'd show up on time and not leave her sitting and drinking with somebody like me.

"This is nice," he said, after finishing his second drink, and he halfway meant it. "We ought to do it again. Maybe I'll bring a date next time."

"Do you have a girl you're serious about?" she asked.

Florio thought of the waitress's glare of contempt. "I see a number of women socially," he said. "I'm not real serious—well, sort of semi-serious with a couple of them."

She was looking at him, her eyes wide with real interest for the first time that evening.

"Will you tell me something?" she asked.

Florio thought he would probably tell her anything at all.

"Does Sandy have another woman?"

"Sandy?"

"He keeps such strange hours. He works so late and he never likes to discuss it, I don't know what he's doing."

"If there's one thing he's not doing, it's fooling around. They don't come any straighter than Sandy Block. If he tells you he's working, he's working. You're the only woman I've ever seen him with, and I've known him for ten years."

"You're not just saying that to make me feel better—because you're his friend?"

"Well, I'm saying it because I *am* his friend. I know the guy. He loves you." The words sounded very strange on his lips, Florio thought. Awkward, embarrassing, and hard to say, but she seemed to like them. Sheila beamed at him.

"Thank you," she said, touching his hand gently.

Florio looked at her large slate-gray eyes and willed himself not to move his hand until she did.

"What was he like before he married me?"

"Sandy?" Florio thought for a moment. "Sad," he said at last. "He worked a lot, crazy hours, but I always figured that was to take his mind off his depression."

"He works like that because he wants to bring order to things. Order is important to Sandy."

"That's what he told you?"

"Yes."

Florio shrugged. "Order's got nothing to do with being a cop. It's the most disorderly job in the world. Especially a homicide cop. If he wanted order he should have been a gardener. Do you know what a honeywagon is?"

Sheila shook her head.

"In Korea they collect all the—uh—stuff from the out-houses."

"Shit?" she said helpfully.

"That's the word. They collect the human shit from the out-houses and spread it on the field for fertilizer. Very nice Oriental custom."

She was smiling at him, on the verge of breaking into laughter. Florio realized he wanted to make her laugh.

"So anyway they cart this shit around in a honeywagon. Being a homicide cop is like being the honeyman. You stand there under the crapper while people drop turds and you try to sort them out as they fall. If that's Sandy's idea of order, I'm not going to argue with it."

"You put that so well," she said.

"I got this way with words," he said, and she laughed at last. It was infectious; Florio laughed, too, covering his mouth with his hand.

Strange, she thought, how alike yet how different two friends could be. It had been Block's laugh she had first fallen in love with, a free, open, ready sound. He seemed to laugh easily, as if most of the world was amusing if only one looked at it the right way. She found it difficult to reconcile that with Florio's picture of the sad, obsessed man he knew. Unless it's me, she thought. Unless I bring the laughter out in him. She liked the idea. She wished she could do the same for Florio. He seemed so shy, laughing behind his hand. It was like wearing a mask, and he didn't need one, not really. He wasn't such a bad sort after all. At least not after two glasses of wine on an empty stomach.

When Block arrived at last, harried and apologetic, they no longer needed him. They were chatting like old friends and already seemed to have private jokes that Block did not understand. He had the feeling they were tolerating him, not welcoming him. A half-empty carafe of wine on the table accounted for some of it, Block thought.

"Looks like you two are getting along fine without me," he said.

"Isn't that what you wanted?" Sheila asked. She looked at him with a trace of belligerence, then reached for the carafe. Florio beat her to it and poured her some with exaggerated courtesy.

"Thank you, kind sir," said Sheila. Her words were slurred ever so slightly.

"My pleasure, madame," said Florio. He winked broadly at Block. Block felt a sudden twinge of jealousy, immediately repressed. He sensed he had upset some equilibrium they had established while waiting for him, and now they seemed to be exaggerating their parts to compensate for his presence. They spoke to him, but it seemed they did so reluctantly, as if waiting politely for him to leave.

Block took it stoically, trying to smile when they laughed together, trying to follow a conversation that did not include him. He gave no sign of the tension and growing anger he felt. By the time they had coffee, he had concluded that his wife should not drink so much in public, and that he liked his partner a lot more when he wasn't around his wife. He had forgotten that he ever wanted all three of them to be friends. It now seemed a very stupid idea.

•

Tom-Tom found himself in Grand Central Station, wandering across the crowded grand concourse. It was one of his favorite places in the city, throbbing with the possibility of action. He loved to watch the commuters passing by, their pudgy, well-washed faces staring straight ahead, avoiding eye contact with the other population—the derelicts, the perverts, the petty thieves, the homeless and the desperate who swirled and eddied in a constant motion through the vast building. Tom-Tom was amused by the commuters, their blindered stares, their assumption of superiority. But it was the others he came to see. The disenfranchised were so easily abused.

He did not know what to expect, but something would present itelf, it always did. He was a magnet for excitement. It was the Devil within him that called out to others, he knew. When the Devil spoke, there were always many who replied. Things were always provided for Tom-Tom, and he never questioned where they came from. One way or another, his needs were met.

Tom-Tom passed through the waiting room and its row on row of benches. Pews, they were, in a church for the lonely and afraid. Winos slept here on their backs, knees up, heads cushioned from the hard wood by newspapers, their bottles clutched in their hands even in slumber. Bag ladies came in from the heat of the streets and sorted through their treasured rubbish, counting again and again their precious bits of junk, muttering and cursing to themselves in a constant litany of abuse and invective. Kids were there, too, stoned, sitting like shell-shocked survivors of a chemical war. If any actual commuter ever stumbled into the waiting room by mistake, he did not wait for long before retreating to the crowded sanctuary of the concourse.

At one end of the waiting room, twin swinging doors opened to a long stairway which led down into the men's lavatory. Tom-Tom stood at a urinal, his head turned to the side, openly surveying the room. Next to him a man with hair as matted as a nest of ropes was bobbing over the groin of a commuter. The commuter faced the wall, eyes glued straight ahead, acting as if he were unaware of the man's head jerking up and down, his fingers stroking. His features were as composed as if the graffiti in front of him were an interoffice memo.

Tom-Tom grinned as a young man came down the steps and paused for a moment, looking over the scene. He caught Tom-Tom's eye and Tom-Tom's grin widened. As the young man approached, Tom-Tom could see he was sporting two tiny stones in one ear. A clear plastic case protected his shirt pocket from the clips of several ball-point pens. An office worker, Tom-Tom decided, a clerk of some kind, out for a quickie after work.

The young man led Tom-Tom to the toilet stall farthest away from the stairs. The doors of the stalls had been removed long ago, but it was possible to get a measure of privacy in the end stall unless someone stood directly in front. Shy, Tom-Tom concluded.

They stepped into the stall and the young man touched Tom-Tom's belt.

"Got a pencil?" Tom-Tom asked.

The young man paused, puzzled.

"A pencil?"

"Yeah, a pencil. You got a pencil?"

"Will a pen do?"

"A pen will do fine," Tom-Tom said. The young man pulled one from his pocket and handed it to Tom-Tom, who clicked it, making sure the point was out. He grasped the young man by the chin and pressed his head against the side of the stall, then drove the ball-point pen through the ear sporting the two small stones.

"Now you can have a diamond," Tom-Tom said. He dropped the pen into the toilet and walked away, leaving the young man gasping and clutching his ear.

Once on the street, Tom-Tom was annoyed with himself. He had just violated one of his rules. He knew himself well, knew what he had to avoid. He had to stay away from sharp objects, knives, broken glass—and now even ball-point pens. The temptation to thrust them into someone was too strong.

This time he had been lucky, he had exercised a measure of control. He might as easily have put the point into the young man's eye. And that might have caused trouble. He could get away with any number of minor transgressions as long as he picked his victims right. There were men and women throughout the city who bore his scars from cigarette burns, small cuts, blows. The right kind of person—the person who knew it would do no good—never reported it. The best kind—the person who knew he deserved it—even enjoyed it.

But the transgressions had to be small. The young man would not bother to cause any trouble. The police would not be sympathetic to anyone who already had two self-inflicted holes in his ear. But the loss of an eye would be different. They would look for Tom-Tom then. Not that they would find him. He knew them well, knew how to avoid them, but still there was no point in endangering himself.

There were other things he had to avoid. Other situations. Great heights. Open windows. He wanted to hurl people off the edges. Or if not others, then himself. The subway sang to him, the oncoming trains seemed to suck him toward the rails. He thought of it, the plunge, the suspension of time as he hung there, weightless, the crunch of the train against bones, the sizzle of the third rail. He dreamed of it. Once, he had pushed a young woman onto the rails. He had done it only to keep from leaping himself. His timing was off; she scampered out on the other side, raising a terrible hue and cry. Tom-Tom had been forced to disappear for a long time after that and had not come back until it was safe again. He remembered the incident only dimly now. All distant events were vague to him, like cries in the night. He had no real notion of his past, no sense of himself beyond the moment, and his needs, and his rules.

He had to avoid sharp objects, heights, the subway. Ropes posed no problem unless he had a woman with him. Then they were dangerous. Certain kinds of women had to be avoided, too.

And, of course, Christ. He had to avoid Christ.

Tom-Tom found himself staring at a store-window display of kitchen utensils. Cleavers, corkscrews, mallets, knives, more knives. Knives for paring and boning and slicing and hacking and mincing and coring. Each with its own special blade, each capable of inflicting its own special wound. It was wonderful, the violence we do to our food. In the center of the display, the latest masterpiece that could perform all forms of violence with speed and control, the automatic food processor.

Tom-Tom forced himself away from the display, but as he did so, he suddenly remembered the kitchen of the actress. Lying with his head stuck to her belly. He smiled to himself. The joy of it. The peace afterward. He had broken all the rules that time, but even then, even in the frenzy, the blood frenzy of the killing, he had been careful. He had left nothing behind for the police.

Recalling it made him excited. A girl came to his mind. He had known her sometime—he had no clear idea when—he had done a few things to her, and she seemed to like it. She was one of those who felt they deserved it. One of those who responded to the Devil's voice in Tom-Tom. He went off to find her.

With the sound of their tittering still ringing in her ears, Karen Holland walked into the hospital parking lot. She had just come off duty and was having a cup of coffee in a booth in the hospital coffee shop when the two men sauntered over. Mere boys, really, college age, probably, and not bad-looking, but she was a good ten years older than either of them. What did they expect? They flirted with her in their terribly obvious way, even after she prominently displayed her wedding ring.

All college boys seemed to have the notion that nurses were loose. She'd heard some of the stories that men told about nurses, and where they came from she had no idea. Did they seriously think she was going to trot on home with both of them just because they were kind of cute and obviously in some need? College boys were always in some need, at least they had been when she was in nursing school. They used to stand by the entrance to her dormitory and bay like wolves.

There was a time she might have accommodated them out of sympathy. Not because she was a nurse, though; because she had a good heart. She had supposed all of that was behind her now, but still it was rather flattering to have the pair of them jabbering away at her, trying to charm her. She pointedly tapped her wedding ring, but did it while smiling; there was no point in being mean about it. They paid no attention. She wondered to herself how she was going to get rid of them. But then, when she stood up, they both looked very sheepish and one of them muttered some sort of apology before they backed away. She had forgotten for a moment herself.

The parking lot was dark, some of the lights knocked out by vandals, as always. When Karen reached her car she heard a footstep behind her. She turned, expecting to find the boys had followed her.

"Oh, it's *you*," she said with a startled little laugh. She tried not to sound happy about it. "You're quite the stranger, aren't you? I haven't seen you for months."

"I've been away," he said. He had that mean but sexy look on his face, that smile that was half sneer. She didn't know why she liked it so much.

"Well, too bad for you," she said. "I'm married now." She turned around and faced him squarely, holding her ring out. But he didn't look at her ring, he looked at her swollen belly.

She giggled. "That's why," she said. He looked crestfallen, absolutely stricken. She had never seen anything wipe that self-satisfied look off his face before. Karen realized that he must have cared for her very much, after all. He must have loved her to be so upset.

"I can't see you anymore, of course," she said, feeling sorry for him. "But we never did get a chance to say good-bye. I guess one last time won't hurt." She touched his cheek. He finally looked her in the face again. His eyes were blazing.

"We can't go to my place," she said. "My husband might be there. We'll have to go to your place."

"I don't have a place," he said.

"But where do you live?" she asked. "You must live somewhere."

After a pause Tom-Tom said, "I live with a creep. We can't go there."

Karen smiled sweetly at him. He really was so upset; it was touching.

"Never mind," she said. "We'll think of something."

He took her arm roughly and shoved her into the car.

"It's your own fault, you know, Bill," she was saying. Tom-Tom never told them his right name. They knew nothing about him he didn't want them to know. "I could just never count on you. You show up—and you know I'm glad to see you—and then you disappear for months at a time. A girl has to think of her future, you know."

"That's right," said Tom-Tom. He had started just with the idea of a quick screw and a bed for the night, but now as he watched her driving, the steering wheel almost touching her obscene belly, a much better thought occurred to him. Using his sleeve he carefully wiped his prints off the door handle and tried to think what else he had touched. Only the outer door handle. Easy enough to clean when he stepped out, and he would be careful not to touch anything else from here on. Except her. Oh, he would touch her, all right.

"I don't mind being with you this time—for old times' sake," she said. "But this will have to be the very last time. If we can think of a place."

"I know a place," he said huskily, tearing his eyes off her belly with difficulty. He had to control himself until he had her where he wanted her. He directed her toward the river.

He was seething with anticipation, the temples in his head were pounding with excitement, but there were too many people around; he had to be careful. He managed to keep his hands off her while she undressed, folding her clothes so nurselike and prattling on in her silly way about her husband.

When she turned to him and he saw her nude swollen stomach, he nearly swooned. A giggle of nervous anticipation burst involuntarily from his throat.

"My, you really are excited, aren't you?" said the nurse. "Look at you, you're quivering."

Tom-Tom had tucked his hands into his armpits and clamped them there in an effort to keep them from attacking her. He was trembling all over and the giggle of excitement continued to burble out.

"Why, you're shivering! How long has it been?"

The noises from the people next door rose into a communal

roar of laughter. The music was loud, but Tom-Tom was not sure it was loud enough. He had to do it quietly. He wanted to tear at her right now, to rip her head from her shoulders, but he knew he mustn't. The frustration was making him buck spasmodically.

Karen Holland removed her panties, added them to her tidy pile of clothing, then lay back on the bed. He was staring at her belly, his head shaking, piping that high-pitched giggle. Karen did not remember ever having seen a man so excited.

"Take off your clothes, too, silly," she said.

The noise from next door had fallen. Tom-Tom knew he had to wait for it to peak again—if he could wait. He wanted at her so badly. He bit his lip until a drop of blood appeared. Barely able to control his hands, he began to undress. It would be best to do it naked, anyway, he knew. Fibers could be traced sometimes; it would not do to leave any under her fingernails.

"Oh, come here," she said. "Let me do that." She brushed his hands aside from his belt where they were fumbling with the buckle. He gripped the railing of the top bunk while she undid his trousers and dropped them to the floor. They landed with a metallic clunk and burnished nickel glinted from the folds of cloth.

"Why on earth do you carry those?" she asked.

The noise next door was getting louder again. Tom-Tom's knuckles were white as they gripped the railing. He suddenly realized what he was doing and used the sheet to rub off his fingerprints. He must be careful not to touch anything else. Except her.

"Well, come on," she urged. She tugged his loins toward her. He touched her belly and jerked back.

"Oh, don't worry about that," she said. "You won't hurt it. It looks like it will be in the way, but it really won't." She pulled him down on her.

"You must be freezing, you're shivering so hard." She put her arms on his back and rubbed. Tom-Tom's jaw was locked with the effort to keep from screaming. The excited whimpers seemed to burble from his nose.

The noise next door swelled to a peak again.

"Come on," said the nurse. "Don't be shy. You won't hurt me."

So Tom-Tom put his hands under her chin and pushed her head back until the neck snapped. He felt so good that the joy burst from his throat.

The sun had barely lighted the Manhattan sky when a man named Tarshis took his dog, a lean, sleek Doberman pinscher, for his morning stroll along Riverside Park. As they passed the boat basin, the dog started to act up. Tarshis could see there had been one hell of a party aboard one of the yachts. Streamers and funny hats floated in the oily water. A sneaker bobbed upside down against the hull of a neighboring boat, empty cartons of bottles were in evidence on the deck. But the dog was reacting to another boat closer to the pier, a thirty-foot Chris-Craft named *Lisalore*. Someone had attacked it with a crayon, smearing the gleaming white side with black letters. Growling low in its throat, the dog tried to push its way through the fence that surrounded the basin.

Tarshis saw the maintenance man who pumped gas on the dock for the boats coming to work. He took one glance at Tarshis and the dog and hurriedly slipped through the gate.

The dog leaped forward with a bound and the chain snapped as Tarshis had feared it might. In three jumps the dog was at the gate, then through it. The maintenance man threw up his arms to protect himself but the dog raced past him and onto the Chris-Craft *Lisalore* with the black writing on it.

For a second Tarshis considered running the other way and never coming back. That dog was going to kill something sure as hell, and Tarshis would be blamed. But he had already been seen by the maintenance man, and too many people knew his bald skull for running to do him any good.

Tarshis leaped aboard the Chris-Craft and nearly tripped over a tube of mascara that lay on the deck. Although he never actually thought it, he realized that was what had made the letters on the hull. He could hear the dog snarling belowdeck, and wondered how in hell he was ever going to pull it off some-one—the dog would hang on until it killed. Tarshis had paid a good deal extra for it to be trained that way. But when he found the dog, he knew he was safe on that count, at least. The nurse had been dead long before the dog got her by the throat.

Block let himself into the apartment quietly, not to wake Sheila, but the phone rang as soon as he opened the door. When he got to the bedroom, she was already sitting up, the receiver pressed to her ear, her eyes half open as if she were hoping to take the message without truly waking up.

Block wondered whether it was her age or her natural beauty that allowed her to look so lovely even now. He knew what he would look like, being jarred awake like that; sheet imprints on a face that seemed to sag lopsidedly toward one shoulder, eyes so small he could barely find them in the mirror, hair contorted into spikes and tufts. The older he got, the more it seemed to him he awoke wearing a mask of some sad monster from his dreams.

"Just a minute," Sheila said to the phone, her voice still thick with sleep. Instead of handing the phone to Block, she pressed it against her stomach to cover the speaker.

"Are you just getting in? Did you work all night?"

Block shrugged sheepishly.

"Stay," she said. "Don't go out right away again. I haven't seen you for twenty-four hours."

"All right," he said. "You look terrific waking up."

"Too bad you weren't here to see me go to bed," she said.

Block touched her cheek, then let his hand trail down inside her nightgown.

"What's your name again?" she said. She handed him the phone. He left his hand inside her nightgown as he spoke his name into the telephone.

Sheila dreamily put her hand atop his, but when his demeanor changed and his attention shifted completely to the telephone, she rolled impatiently away from him.

"I have to go," he said, as he hung up the phone.

"How'd I guess?"

"I'm sorry. It's important."

"Yeah, okay," she said coldly.

"Don't be mad."

"Why not?" She sat up completely, drawing her bare legs underneath her.

"It's important," he repeated.

"Oh, well, that's okay, then. As long as it's important. Crucial to the public safety, is it?"

He rose from the bed. He couldn't blame her for her anger, but he didn't like to be on the receiving end of it.

"Go ahead and be mad, then," he said. "But try to get over it by tonight. I'll be home, I promise."

She gave him an icy smile. "As long as it suits you," she said.

It wasn't much of an argument, Block reflected, but it was their first, and he hated to leave it on that note. When he reached the lobby of his building he turned back with the intention of taking her in his arms and kissing her into forgiveness. But when he reached his door, he hesitated. What was the point? He would still have to leave her, and knowing that he had to go, he would not be able to give his full attention to her. It was a half measure and would please no one. He left again, vowing to make it up to her that evening. By the time he reached the street he knew he had made a mistake, but by then it was too late. He kept going.

Quayle was standing on the deck of the *Lisalore*, puffing his pipe and gazing out toward the water like a sea captain, when Block arrived. He was resting one hand on the railing, so Block knew the fingerprinting was over, which was a relief. Block hated to be present when the forensic experts went through their

search for prints, inside open food containers where the perpe-
trator might have stuck a finger for a taste of something, under
toilet seats, in every conceivable nook and cranny a person puts
his hands. It was too intensely private for Block's taste; like
watching a doctor give a complete physical exam to someone
else. And usually it was all of no great help to Block, anyway.
The chances of finding a really clean print are fairly remote.
Prints are usually smudged, or overlaid by other prints, or only
a portion of the print, called a partial, is readable. The New
York City police keep a print file on criminals and suspects booked
in New York City. They have difficult but technically possible
access to the files in the other major cities in the country. Again,
for known criminals. But if the prints belong to someone who is
not a criminal at all, then things get tricky. The FBI maintains
a massive file of fingerprints on former servicemen, civil ser-
vants, anyone who has ever had a security check, et cetera; but
the operative word here is FBI. The prints are in their files,
and they stay in the FBI files unless a federal crime has been
committed. Murder is not a federal crime. The FBI will not run
a random check of prints for every requesting police force in
the country. The amount of computer time that would involve
is enormous, not to mention cost and manpower. The notion
that leaving a fingerprint at the scene of the crime is tantamount
to walking away with paint on your feet is simply not true unless
you're a known New York criminal, in which case you're already
high on the list of suspects. But if you're caught anyway, you'd
better hope you didn't leave a print on the murder weapon.

Block stopped when he saw the letters on the side of the
boat. They were upside down from Block's point of view on the
dock. Someone had leaned over the edge and scrawled them.
They had the same childlike quality of uncertainty, the same
left-handed slant. The message was TOM-TOM.

"Done with the victim's mascara," Quayle said.

Block stepped aboard. "Tom-Tom shows us new dimensions,"
said Quayle, leading the detective belowdeck.

Karen Holland had been murdered with her clothes off. Her
uniform and underwear were placed in a neat pile on the top

bunk, the uniform carefully folded. The shoes were placed together, side by side, under the bunk. She lay on the bottom
bunk, her head over the edge. Most of her throat was missing
and there was a large pool of blood on the polished mahogany
floor directly under her head, but very little elsewhere.

"This was done by a dog that found the body," Quayle explained, gesturing at the woman's throat with his pipestem. A
small body bag lay a few feet away from the bed. "The patrolman had to shoot the dog to get it off."

"You're sure the dog didn't kill her?"

"The M.E. will have to verify this," he said with resentment,
"but I'm sure of it. You can still see the bruises under her jaw.
Fingers did that—thumbs, to be precise. The finger marks are
on the side of the neck. Give me your hand."

Quayle took Block's fingers and placed them under the back
of Karen Holland's neck. "Feel those vertebrae? Feel how far
out of place they are? Someone stuck her head over the edge
of the bed, used the edge as a fulcrum, and broke her neck."

"A man in a fury, again?" Block asked.

"It takes a lot of force to kill somebody like that, but there's
no other sign of rage like last time. Of course, he may have
simply been careful. There was a party going on in the next
boat."

"Is a man in a rage capable of being careful?"

"I think Tom-Tom is capable of quite a bit," said Quayle.

The Captain stepped down from the deck, sniffing the air in
the boat as if it were heavily and offensively perfumed.

"You the only one here?" he asked.

"So far," said Block. "McKeon's on his way."

"Where's Florio?"

"He's not due in yet."

"You're here."

"We worked late last night. I just got home myself when I
got the call. It's Tom-Tom again," said Block.

The Captain nodded. "I saw the side of the boat. Anything
good from you, Quayle?"

"I'll have a full report in a few days. . . ."

"Come on, come on, come on." Captain Byrne wiggled his fingers prissily.

"I doubt we'll have much to help you," Quayle said.

Byrne sniffed again. "This whole river stinks. What is that smell?"

"Diesel fuel, probably," said Block.

"Don't you hate that? It goes right up into my sinuses. What about witnesses?"

"We may have some," said Block. "There was a party in the next boat."

"Thank God," said the Captain. "Let's pray we've got some witnesses."

Block let McKeon and Florio run through the list of the party guests. The party had been very loud, very drunken, and when everyone fell asleep they slept in a stupor.

"It's like getting witnesses out of a graveyard," Florio complained. "If they weren't passed out, they were so high they didn't know what they were hearing anyway."

"Where did we get this list?" Block asked.

"From the 'host,' " said Florio. "A very nasty guy, lots of money, lots of unpleasant friends. Just the age when he likes things a little perverted."

Block held the list in his hand, as if by weight alone he could determine its veracity. "I want you and McKeon to go back and talk to all the party guests again, but this time don't talk to the same people. You might get something different. And I want every one of those people to give you their own list of everyone they can remember at the party. What's a party without gate crashers?"

When Block compiled the new lists, he found three new names. Two of them were caterers who had left early. The third was a young woman named Maeve Kline. Block interviewed her himself.

She was a pretty young woman who wore her hair in the current style that made it look both stringy and frizzy at the same time, as if she had just stepped out of a steambath. He could not imagine who thought it was attractive.

"I understand you left the party early. Well, relatively early for that party."

"It was between one thirty and two," she said nervously.

Block smiled at her. "No one holds you responsible for the party, or what went on there," he said.

She relaxed visibly. "I don't approve of a lot of those things they do," she said. "I don't want to seem like a prude, but all those drugs and some of those people . . . I mean, really."

"How did you happen to go?"

"My boyfriend asked . . . well, he's not really a friend at all, that's pretty obvious, isn't it?"

"Why is that?"

"I thought you knew why I left."

"No."

"He kept insisting I should sleep with the old guy who was giving the party. I mean, what am I, a hostess gift? I got tired of it, so I left."

"When you left, how did you get to the dock?"

"I took the shortest way, across the deck of the next boat. That isn't illegal, is it?"

"No. Miss Kline, I want you to try very hard to remember when you walked across the deck of that boat, anything you heard or saw, anything at all."

Maeve Kline thought for a moment while Block held his breath. It was a long shot, he knew, but it was the only shot he had.

"Yes, I did hear something," she said at last. "But I don't know what exactly. I mean it was a man's voice coming from belowdeck on that boat. It was a very excited voice, but strange, kind of garbled. I couldn't make out what it was saying. For a second I thought it was coming from the party but when I got off the boat I heard it very clearly."

"What was it saying?"

"I haven't any idea. It was a foreign language, but I don't know which one."

Block took Maeve Kline to the Columbia University Department of Languages and introduced her to Professor Harvey Aaron. To his colleagues at Columbia, Aaron was something of a legend. Some people have a gift for music, other prodigies excel at mathematics. Aaron had a perfect ear for language. Raised in Europe by a father who made his living in import-export, Harvey could speak eight languages by the time he was six years old. By the time he entered Oxford he was fluent in sixteen languages and could read seven others. By the time he acquired his Ph.D. in linguistics, Aaron himself no longer bothered to keep track of how many he could speak, but his usual estimate was around twenty-five. Although he was an intelligent man, Aaron's intellect had nothing to do with his ability; in fact, if he had used his reasoning powers, they would only have gotten in his way. His one true talent was for keeping his mind blank and simply absorbing the language through the ear, the way a child does. The associations, the similarities and differences between one tongue and another all came later; in the beginning he didn't think about those things, he simply listened.

It was boasted of Aaron that he could be plopped down in any country on the planet, and within a week he would speak like a native. It was no idle boast. In a celebrated case of twin girls who spoke in a language all their own, Aaron spent three days with the girls and was able to translate everything they said.

Block explained the problem to Aaron, then let the diminutive professor take over. Aaron took Maeve to the language lab, fitted her with earphones, and began to play tapes. Twenty-four hours later he called Block back.

"I started with the most likely European languages," Aaron

said. "French, German, Italian, Spanish. I played tapes of Spanish dialects—Cuban, Mexican, Puerto Rican, and so on. Then I went through the more obscure Europeans—Hungarian, Russian, Serbo-Croat, Romansh. She hesitated over one European language, Flemish; but she didn't think that was it. I then ran through the major Oriental groups, and she had the same response to Fukienese as she'd had to Flemish. Close but not it. After the subgroups of the major Orientals didn't turn anything up, I went to Africa. She picked one out there, the !Kung."

"The what?"

"!Kung," Aaron said, his tongue making a sound like a stick hitting a hollow block of wood at the beginning of the word. "It's a tribe of Bushmen who live on the edge of the Kalahari Desert. There aren't more than a few hundred of them living. It's highly unlikely that's what she heard, and she wasn't certain that was it anyway."

"What was she certain of?"

"Nothing, which is to be expected. She heard a few words under difficult circumstances; you're asking her a day later to pick out the language from a tape, spoken by somebody else, saying different words. It's no wonder she can't be precise, but she has limited possibilities for you. Flemish, Japanese, and !Kung wouldn't appear to have anything in common linguistically, grammatically, or structurally, but they do have a similarity. They all make a pronounced use of the glottal stop."

"You want me to ask?"

Aaron made a sound deep in his throat that sounded like a small explosion. "A pronounced glottal stop," he said.

"It sounded like you had something caught in your throat," said Block.

"Exactly," said Aaron. "It is not a sound that comes naturally to English speakers, and I think that's the point. She was responding to those three languages because they sounded extremely foreign, she'd never heard anything quite like them before. Miss Klein is a fairly sophisticated woman, linguistically speaking. She's traveled in Europe, she's listened to Russian opera, she's been exposed to the sound of Arabic, Vietnamese, and so forth on television. Whoever she heard on that boat was speaking a language totally foreign."

"You know, it sounds a little bit like the grunts that karate people give when they hit something."

Aaron, whose ear was too refined for so coarse a comparison, murmured politely. "It could be she simply heard the sound of a man in exertion."

"She was sure it was a language, though."

"Yes," said Aaron, "she seemed quite certain."

"That's all, then? I'm looking for somebody who speaks a very foreign language?"

"Without more to go on, there's not much I can add. . . . Oh, she did say one thing that was rather interesting."

"What was that?" Block asked.

"She said he sounded very happy."

Block haunted the pier like a wraith borne on the night air. The evidence had been gathered, sifted, tagged, and stored. The forensic men had combed the area within a radius of several hundred meters, rummaging through the garbage bins, searching the rocks on the shore, scrutinizing the sidewalks again and again for any telltale sign Tom-Tom might have left behind. Divers had even searched the waters around the yacht on the chance that something had been thrown overboard. Block did not expect to find anything new; he was trying to jog his memory into giving up something that was nagging at him.

From the moment he had arrived on the murder scene he realized there was something familiar about the *Lisalore*. He had never been there before the murder, never seen it, never met the owner or any of his family or friends. Still, the idea that he knew something about the *Lisalore* troubled his mind like a mote on the eye. He could see it until he looked directly at it, then it swam away with the motion of the eyeball.

After the normal working day he came to the pier and paced,

hoping that the proximity of the yacht would draw out the answer. His presence made the yacht owners uneasy until they learned he was a cop; and even then they were uncomfortable with the lonely figure stalking back and forth in the darkness, vanishing for minutes, hours, then resuming his restless pacing. There was something in his intensity that made them think of a giant cat, a tiger hunting at night. But whether the cat was stalking its prey or pacing within a cage, they could not have said.

As it frequently did, the breakthrough came when Block had finally relaxed and was about to give up. He rushed back to the station and headed for the files. Some months ago a painter had killed a friend in a bar, stabbing him with a screwdriver in the chest. The painter was even more surprised than the victim when the result was death. Block had not investigated the crime but he had given the case report a cursory glance. He reread it now with careful attention. The murder had occurred in a bar on Broadway and Ninety-seventh Street, but the arrest had taken place on a yacht where the painter had a temporary job refinishing the deck. The yacht was the *Lisalore*. The arresting officer and author of the report was Detective Lou Florio.

 He was back, and more agitated than ever. He had
been pacing so much Tillie thought he would wear a
hole in the floor and crash down on her head. His trip
must have been a very short one; Tillie could not remember when he had returned so quickly. She had always assumed that he drove cross-country, a moving van perhaps,
because his visits were so infrequent and unpredictable. It would
have been much cheaper for him to stay in a hotel room, he
was home that seldom, but she supposed a man liked to have a
place he could call his own. And she certainly couldn't complain. When he was gone, he was the perfect tenant.

"If he doesn't stop, I'm going to scream!" said Shirley.

"It's the truck," Tillie said, trying to soothe her. "He misses
the motion."

"Oh, that is so dumb, I can't believe you keep saying it!"

Tillie turned away and clenched her teeth. Shirley had started
making savage remarks in the last few days, and Tillie was determined not to let her know how much they hurt. She realized
that if Shirley knew her barbed tongue was drawing blood, she'd
never stop. The girl was vicious—mean, sullen, and vicious, even
if she was her niece. She hated to say it, but her sister's child
was a spoiled brat, and Tillie had almost decided to send her
home, boyfriend crisis or not, broken heart or not. She certainly
didn't seem to be mending in New York.

"Stop it!" Shirley yelled, her face to the ceiling.

"That does a lot of good, I'm sure," said Tillie. "I thought you
were such a good friend of his."

"Boy, when you get hold of something, you never let it go,

do you? I told you fifty times, I went up there and we had a little chat, all right? A little talk. I asked for some ice . . . and do you want to know what really happened? He gave me some ice. And he did it with his clothes on, too. A perfect gentleman."

"I never suggested anything about his clothes."

"You thought it, don't pretend you didn't. Well, I don't think you need to worry about it, your Mr. Watts isn't straight."

Tillie stared at her. "What do you mean?"

"I mean he's gay, of course."

Tillie walked to the kitchen to get away from the girl. She wanted to poison everything with her malice. There was no possibility that Mr. Watts was gay; Tillie had spoken to him herself. She was sure she would have known.

"He shares that room with another guy," Shirley said, following her.

"That is not true," said Tillie.

"You should have heard him talk about him. It must be some kind of S-and-M thing, because Watts is afraid of this guy."

"You are only saying that to get me upset."

"I told you, we had a nice long chat, and all he could talk about was his friend Frou-Frou or whatever."

"And what did you talk about?" Tillie sniffed.

Shirley smirked. "Myself. I told him my life story. With particular emphasis on that dirty little shit Richie Skolnick."

"You didn't tell him!" Tillie exclaimed, too upset to even reprimand her for dirty language.

"What, about being knocked up? Listen, Aunt Tillie, it's a new day, nobody cares anymore."

"But did you tell him?"

"Oh, don't worry, I didn't tell him. But I might. I'm not ashamed."

Around two in the morning Shirley gave up trying to sleep and walked upstairs. She started to knock on Watts's door, then on impulse bent to look through the keyhole. She could see him clearly as he passed back and forth through her line of vision, pacing as he had been nonstop for hours. He held a Bible in his hands and he read from it as he paced, muttering to himself, his words too low for Shirley to hear. But after a moment she realized he wasn't reading to himself, his words and his gestures all seemed directed toward the closet. The door was ajar and a light shone from within. Was someone in that closet? Shirley grinned knowingly. Probably the butch partner with his whips and chains, putting on his leather. No wonder Watts looked so worried, no wonder he was sermonizing.

When it appeared that Watts would pace forever and the lover would not come out of the closet, Shirley grew impatient and knocked. For just a second before he composed himself, Shirley thought Watts's face showed sheer terror.

"You've got to stop the pacing," she said, trying to sound and look as if she'd just awakened.

He stared at her as if she were a ghost. His look was so strange that Shirley buttoned the top button of her shortie pajamas.

"I'm sorry," he said finally, as if he had at last understood where he was.

Shirley eased past him, into his room.

"That's all right, I understand," she said. "I get awfully nervous just sitting around the house, myself. You need to get out, meet some new people. I think your friends are getting you down." She stopped by the closet and winked, letting him know that she knew what was going on, and didn't disapprove. He hurried forward to stop her as Shirley reached for the closet door. He caught her wrist and held it with a strength that surprised her.

"Okay," she said. "Don't get excited." She tried to pull her hand away but his grip was too strong.

"I'm not trying to pry," she said. "You're entitled to your privacy—but I'm entitled to my sleep. I'm going to have a baby." As she said it, she realized that she enjoyed the feeling of superiority it gave her. For once in her life she could pull rank. Being pregnant entitled her to consideration.

Watts squeezed her wrist harder for just a second, then let go. "I'm so glad," he said, but Shirley wasn't certain if he was congratulating her, or glad that she was leaving the room.

Shirley watched through the keyhole for a few minutes after she had left the room, hoping to catch a glimpse of whoever was in the closet. But Watts wasn't going to oblige her. He stopped pacing and stood by the closet door, still murmuring. Shirley couldn't hear what he was saying or if anyone answered. Finally she tired of it all and went back to bed. Watts was the first person outside of her family—and of course the little shit Richie Skolnick—she had told about being pregnant. She liked hearing it; maybe this ordeal wasn't going to be so bad after all.

Shirley awoke, sick to her stomach. As she was returning to bed, she heard a whimper. She lay in bed for several minutes, trying to figure it out. An insistent crying came from overhead where Watts had been pacing earlier. It sounded like a child crying herself to sleep. But what would a child be doing in Watts's room?

He was hardly the paternal type, hardly one to be bringing children into the house. Shirley remembered the look on his face when she told him she was knocked up. A look of blank incomprehension at first, then, briefly, disgust. And finally nothing at all, as if he hadn't even heard. Shirley had expected a little understanding, a little sympathy, so that he would realize he couldn't be making noise all night long.

Shirley walked up to Watts's room and the crying grew louder. There was definitely a child in Watts's room. A light shone dimly under the door. She glanced through the keyhole again, but could not see Watts. There was no response to her knock, and the whimpering continued. Shirley knocked again, angry at Watts's lack of consideration. Looking again through the keyhole, she saw only the light coming from under the closed closet door. The whimpering was coming from the closet, too. Had he shut a child in that closet? Furious, Shirley knocked again, then tried the door. It opened and she stepped into Watts's room.

There was no sign of Watts, and no place to hide in the room. The Bible lay on the floor outside the closet. Shirley went to the closet and listened for a second. The whimpering continued. She heard a girl's voice say, "Mama." The door was locked.

"Hello," Shirley said.

The whimpering stopped for a moment.

"Hello," replied a mournful voice. Shirley guessed the girl was five or six years old.

"Are you locked in?" Shirley asked.

"I can't find my mama," the girl said.

"Where did your mama go?"

"I don't know," the girl said, and started to cry again.

Shirley looked around for a key to the closet. She couldn't find one and she wondered at the extreme bareness of Watts's room. She had never seen anyone live with so few possessions. It was almost as if the man did nothing in the room but pace and read Scriptures. If he left at any time there would be scarcely a trace left behind.

"How did you get in the closet?" Shirley asked. She bent to look in the keyhole. A blue suit hung on a hanger and something was on the floor; it looked like a man's trench coat with large black buttons. She could not see the girl, who must be in the very corner.

"I'm hiding," said the girl.

"Who are you hiding from?"

"Tom-Tom."

"Why are you hiding from Tom-Tom?" Shirley asked.

"Tom-Tom is bad," said the girl.

"My aunt must have a key," said Shirley. "I'll be right back and get you out of there." Shirley hurried downstairs and found Tillie's ring of keys where her aunt kept them beside her bed. Tillie stirred and rolled over. Shirley waited until her aunt was settled, then softly left the room. She wanted to do this alone. She was proud of herself, she was doing something good and even a little brave, and she didn't feel like sharing the credit with anyone.

As she reached Watts's room, she paused just inside the door. She had sensed a movement within the closet, and then utter, unnatural stillness. For just a moment she had the feeling that something was waiting for her, coiled to pounce. Ridiculous, she told herself, ignoring the sudden brief chill. The moment passed, and she returned to the closet. There was a child there who needed help.

"Did Mr. Watts put you in the closet?" Shirley asked, going through the ring of keys, trying to find the right fit.

"No," said the girl.

"Where is Mr. Watts?"

"He ran away," said the girl. "He's afraid of Tom-Tom, too."

Shirley found the key and opened the door.

"Who is Tom-Tom—" Shirley froze. Watts sat in the corner of the closet. The end of the trench coat was balled in his fist and pressed against his cheek, in the manner of a child with a blanket. Tears ran down his face, his lips were in a pout, his eyes had the mournful look of an abandoned child.

"I'm Kathy," said Watts. His voice was that of a six-year-old girl. "I don't know where my mama is."

For a moment Shirley was so stunned she couldn't move. A cold tremor shook her as she realized she was looking into the eyes of insanity. Something had been scrawled in a child's hand on the closet wall. Shirley saw the word *Tom* and the word *bad*, misspelled.

Shirley gave an almost soundless cry. She felt as if she were in a nightmare and Watts's gaze had somehow welded her to the spot. When he moved she could see a wad of clothing, covered with dried blood, thrust up into the corner of the closet.

She turned to run but his hand gripped her ankle. He was still on the floor, his face still pleading for comfort, his voice still a child's—but his grip was like iron.

"Please," he said. "Stay with me." His other hand took her arm and pulled her down. Shirley slid down the wall till she was seated on the closet floor, one leg turned uncomfortably under her, the other out straight, Watts's grip still on the ankle. He put his head into her lap.

"Mama," he whimpered. "Mama."

Shirley sensed that the worst thing she could do was to scream. This was no child in her lap, no matter how he acted the part. His grip on her ankle reminded her of the power of the man. She put out a hand and carefully stroked his head.

"It's all right," she said. "It's all right."

His body seemed to relax under stroking and he lifted his head, like a cat whose back is being scratched. His face nuzzled against her breasts.

"It's all right," she repeated. "It's all right."

He continued to rub against her breasts, a low moan of contentment coming from his throat. His eyes were closed, his mouth open slightly. His face looked peaceful.

I'm going to make it, Shirley thought. I'm going to get out of this somehow. She stroked his head, murmuring softly to him, over and over. It's all right, it's all right, it's all right. She began to believe it.

He crawled right into her lap, pulling his knees up into the fetal position. He was very heavy and the leg turned under her body began to hurt, but she didn't dare to move yet. He put his right arm around her waist, holding himself against her, but his left hand released her ankle. He resumed his nuzzling against her breasts, dragging the material of her shortie pajamas back and forth across her nipples. Shirley felt her nipples respond and harden as if they had a mind of their own. He's going to nurse! she thought, with disgust. And she was going to let him. She couldn't get away if she tried.

He began to move his head back and forth more rapidly, his mouth open wider, making little cries of distress. The fabric was in his way, but he didn't seem capable of moving it. His hand was now by his cheek, fingers loose and uncoordinated. A tiny bit of drool escaped his open lips. He really is a baby now, she thought. She didn't know how or why, but he had regressed completely. He was a baby, she the mother. Moving very carefully, Shirley lifted one hand and freed her breast. He stopped his mewling and began to suck. As she felt his wet lips on her skin, Shirley shuddered. She closed her eyes and tried to think of something else, anything else.

Watts slept. His breath came in the short, shallow gasps of a child. His fist was pressed against his cheek, and under his eyelids his eyeballs moved rapidly in dreams.

Shirley watched him for a moment, scarcely daring to breathe herself. She put her hands under his head, supporting it while she slowly, so slowly, eased her leg from under his weight. If she could get her second leg free she might be able to make it out of the closet before he came fully awake. He would be disoriented, surely, sluggish, slow to respond. She moved another inch. He stirred and she froze, forcing herself to count to fifty before she moved again. There, almost there, almost.

His hand came up and touched her neck. His thumb pressed into the cavity of her collarbone. She felt pressure, but no pain. She looked into his face. His eyes were open and blazing. He was grinning. He was no longer a child, no longer Watts. She had never seen him before. His thumb continued to press her carotid artery. Shirley thought of lunging, making a run even though he was awake, but her mind had grown confused. She blinked twice and passed out.

She woke thinking she was going to gag. Something was pressing against her tongue, forcing it back toward her throat. There was a pain in the back of her head and in her cheeks. After a moment she realized she had been gagged; he had thrust something into her mouth and tied it across her face with a towel. The knot pressed painfully against the base of her skull. She twisted her head to either side and saw that her hands had been secured by belts, stretched out at shoulder level and tied to the coatrack. Her feet just barely touched the floor and they were tied together at the ankles by a necktie. She had been trussed up in the closet as if tied to a cross.

An incessant muttering came from the outer room but she

could catch only glimpses of Watts as he paced back and forth in front of the half-opened closet door. He had his Bible in one hand again and was reading from it as before—only this time Shirley was in the closet, not in the safety of the hallway, peering through the keyhole.

He paused for a moment in front of the door. There was a snake on his shoulder, around his neck, moving, writhing. Somehow the snake was more horrible than being tied and gagged, than having nursed a madman. The snake was worse than anything the man might do to her, she thought.

Watts opened the door and stood in front of her. The thing on his shoulder writhed again. It lashed its tail, she could hear the rattle clearly.

"I have been praying," he said to her. He was Watts again, she could tell that. He was the meek, shy man she had known before the night began.

Shirley tried to scream, but it came past the gag as a muffled groan.

Watts nodded as if he understood. "I know. I am frightened, too, but I can't let you go. If I did, he would kill me. He would kill me."

He stepped closer to her. The snake's head was pinched by his fingers, just behind the gaping jaws. Shirley turned her head and squeezed her eyes closed.

"I'm sorry," he said, contritely. "It's nothing to be afraid of. I've been praying. Very very hard. It may stop him. He may not kill us."

Shirley watched as he stepped away from her and dropped the snake into a shopping bag. He placed the first bag into a second bag with the name *Gristede's* emblazoned on it and pulled the drawstring tight, then wound it around the top and tied it.

Shirley screamed again and Watts turned back to her.

"I want to help you, truly I do," he said. "But I can't."

He followed her gaze, which went past him to the table. There on the table were a hammer and three nails. Only three nails. Long, heavy, almost spikes. Only three. Shirley knew why she was tied in this position. She knew what he planned to do with them. To her.

Watts looked at the hammer and nails and seemed surprised to see them.

"I'll hide them," he said, sweeping them into the table drawer. "Maybe he'll forget. Maybe he'll forget."

Shirley began to cry and shake her head furiously from side to side. For a moment Watts was at a loss. He looked at her, disturbed by her distress, as helpless as an old woman.

"I'll get help," he said finally. He ran from the room, taking the shopping bag with him.

At 3:07 A.M. the same night the police emergency number, 911, received the following call:

POLICE: Police emergency.
VOICE: He's going to kill me. I saw him do it and he's going to kill me for it.
POLICE: What is your name, sir?
VOICE: Help me, you have to help me, he knows I saw him.
POLICE: What is your name, sir?
VOICE: What?
POLICE: Your name, sir.
VOICE: Watts. Help me.
POLICE: What is your phone number?
VOICE: Phone number?
POLICE: I need your phone number, sir.
VOICE: I don't have a phone.
POLICE: What is your address, Mr. Watts?
VOICE: Help me. He has to kill me. He'll kill her first, then he'll kill me.

POLICE: Mr. Watts, we will help you, but we have to know your address.

VOICE: No one can help me. I can't stop him.

POLICE: Mr. Watts, please tell me where you are now. . . . Call terminated at 3:08 A.M.

The tape of the call was routinely stored for ninety-six hours in accordance with police procedure, then erased.

Shirley had almost managed to free her right hand. By lifting her feet and putting all her weight on her arms, she had been able to loosen the hook that held one of the belts. It hurt incredibly, the leather bit into her skin as if it had teeth, and she feared her shoulder blades were being wrenched from the sockets—but it was better than staying here and waiting for insanity to return. And she knew he would return.

It was impossible for her to gauge the time. It had to be night still, she supposed, although it had seemed ages. For a time she had tried to waken Tillie by pounding on the wall with her feet, but she had no leverage and couldn't swing enough to take a real kick. If she counted on Tillie to save her, she would probably deserve to die. She had to rely on herself. She was bracing herself for another agonizing effort to free her right hand when she heard a key in the door. She held her breath.

The man walked in and she knew it was all over. He was wearing that grin, the blazing look of insanity. He wore white gloves, simple cloth work gloves. Pausing before Shirley for a moment, he grinned even more broadly. He looked to Shirley like a wolf baring its fangs. A tremor shook him and he shivered from head to foot. A high-pitched giggle escaped him; then he seemed to bring himself under control.

Methodically he went through the little apartment wiping every surface with the white gloves. He touched everywhere he could reach, tops, bottoms, sides; and all the while he kept his eyes on Shirley, drinking her in, his eyes wide and fierce, filled with some kind of savage joy. Every now and again he would stop suddenly and tremble again, then return to his work with difficulty. Finally Shirley realized it was a shiver of anticipation.

When he had finished dusting the room, he returned to the table. For a moment he seemed puzzled. He searched the table, the chair beside it, underneath it.

"Where did he put it!" he roared suddenly. It was the first time Shirley had heard him speak.

He yanked open the drawer and stood, satisfied, as he pulled out the hammer and the nails. He laid the nails, one at a time, side by side on the tabletop. He studied them for a moment, seemingly pleased with them.

"He tried to pray me to death," he said to her suddenly. He sneered and repeated it, as if he hadn't said it right the first time. "Tried to pray me to death."

He came to the closet, the hammer in one hand, but he passed Shirley and took the clothing. Ignoring Shirley now, he laid out the spare suit on the floor. He straightened the legs, put socks where the feet would be, folded the arms of the jacket over the chest. The suit looked as if it had been laid out for a funeral, then the corpse removed. Tom-Tom put the Bible where the head should have been.

As Shirley watched, dumbfounded, he began to tear at the clothing, holding it in his teeth and ripping it. After each segment was torn, he laid it carefully back in place and proceeded to the next part.

Finally, the clothes in tatters but neatly arranged, Tom-Tom stood and looked at Shirley once more. He was rocked by a series of spasms so severe that they seemed to shake the noises out of him. It was a joyous noise, half giggle, half unintelligible words, his voice quivering as violently as his body.

Picking up one of the nails, he approached Shirley. Maybe the pounding will wake Tillie, she thought, clinging to the hope as he raised the hammer. It was her last thought that wasn't a scream.

Tillie's body was found first. She had been smothered by her own pillow as she lay in bed. There was no other sign of violence. Searching for witnesses, the detectives found Shirley's body in the empty closet of the apartment overhead. They also found a pile of men's clothing in the center of the room. The clothes had been torn violently to shreds, smeared with blood, then laid out to form the shape of a man, a corpse, with arms folded across the chest.

Block sat with Quayle and Florio in Captain Byrne's office. Byrne had been beside himself at first, fulminating about the shitstorm that was sure to come now. For journalists, two murders are a trend and three are a killing spree. They now had three, one of them a crucifixion. Because it was New York, the news of the murderous "Tom-Tom" was destined to be a national story before the day was out. Publicity could help, of course, in finding a suspect. It could also clog the police switchboards and inundate every desk sergeant in town with helpful citizens turning in their brothers-in-law. Volunteers would crawl out of the woodwork, confessing to every murder since Lizzie Borden's hatchet job in order to get some attention. All the cases would have to be checked out; the chances of any of them being helpful were pitifully small. Manpower would be strained and the already tight budget stretched even further. The mayor would be irate that anything might disturb the tourist business in peak season. Heat from the mayor was exaggerated in the public mind. There was really very little he could do to most career officers, still the heat would be felt and even filtered by several bureaucratic lawyers it could singe a bit. Probably the worst part of a "crime wave" for the average policeman, however, was all the negative publicity. Policemen are people, too, with friends and neighbors, and they don't like public suggestions that they are doing an incompetent job any more than anyone else does.

After his tirade, which Block could not help thinking of as a huff, Byrne calmed down and asked for the facts. There weren't many and they weren't encouraging.

"His name is Watts," said Block. "We have that much from the landlady's records. Aside from that, it's like he wasn't there. One of the other tenants was surprised to hear there was such a man. Another knew the room was occupied but never saw Watts. He paid in cash, we have no signatures. No description. No one who ever saw him."

"Any prints?" Byrne asked.

Quayle shifted uncomfortably. "No," he said. "No prints at all. None. He cleaned the place."

Byrne stared at his forensic expert.

"I know how it sounds," Quayle said. "I figured somebody screwed up when I read the report so I went over there myself. I couldn't have cleaned this guy Watts's room better myself. He may be crazy, but he knows what he's doing."

"I'm not sure he's just a psycho," Block said. "Look how he handled the nurse. They got aboard that boat like mice even though there was a party going on next door. No one saw them, no one heard them. She had to be cooperating. My guess is she took her clothes off and folded them neatly herself. I think they were going to make love, which means he wasn't a monster all the time."

"So he's a madman one minute and some kind of genius the next?"

"He's clearly able to cover himself. He must have killed the landlady because she could identify him. He certainly didn't kill her in a passion the way he did the others. That was cold blooded, just as wiping the fingerprints was cold blooded."

"So we've got a killer who kills in an uncontrollable rage, then immediately calms down and wipes up the fingerprints?"

Block sighed. "I'm not so sure he kills in an uncontrollable rage. Rage, maybe, but let's look what he did. With the Caro woman, he killed her right there in her apartment, probably after he slept with her. All right, that might have been a spontaneous act. But with the nurse he obviously lured her to the yacht first, then killed her quietly. That took some planning. For this last one, he did it in his own room. He set a trap for the girl, baited it somehow, and pulled her in. He took a long time killing her, and he had to plan it. He's getting more deliberate each time. He's enjoying it."

Byrne groaned. "He's getting to like it and we don't have a fingerprint, we don't have a witness, we don't have a description, we don't even have a motive."

"I think we have a motive of sorts," said Block. He glanced at Florio.

"Not a motive, maybe," said Florio. "But part of the pattern."

"What?"

"The M.E.'s report just came in on Shirley Halper. She was pregnant," said Block.

Byrne stared at Block for a long, silent moment.

"The Holland woman was pregnant," said Block.

"Alicia Caro was pregnant," said Florio.

"The landlady?"

"The landlady just happened to be in the way, we figure," said Florio.

Byrne looked to Quayle. "What are the odds?"

"Of what? Coincidence? No odds at all. It's got to be deliberate."

Byrne closed his eyes and rubbed his temples with his fingertips. "You're telling me Tom-Tom is murdering pregnant women?" he said at last.

"That's it," said Block.

"Christ! My father was a fireman," Byrne said. "I always thought that was a crazy job. . . . I'm no longer sure. I don't suppose there's any chance you're wrong?"

He looked at each in turn. The three men looked back at him impassively. Byrne felt in some subtle way as if all the weight had suddenly been dumped on him.

"Better see the Kanter," he said.

The Kanter was Charles Kanter, M.D., the police psychiatrist. The job of police psychiatrist is not one that qualified men clamor for. Not many aspiring analysts set their sights on tending to the psyches of the city cops at a civil servant's pay. The Kanter, however, had needed pull to get it.

He had started his career well enough, establishing himself with the aid of his wealthy father—a prominent owner of discount record stores—on Park Avenue. The Kanter set himself up as a specialist on anorexia nervosa, and soon found himself with a number of clients from the Society pages, fashionable young women who were fashionably starving themselves to death. Some of them were actually anorexics; others were merely thin but knew a chic ailment when they heard of one.

Dr. Charles Kanter (who had waged a lifelong but futile campaign to be called Chuck) knew what was wrong with his patients. They were blocked emotionally. They did not need food, they needed sex. Sex would stimulate their appetites, so to speak. More specifically, they needed sex with Dr. Charles Kanter. It was convenient, since they were lying down anyway, and it was scientific, since the doctor himself was there to observe. And, at sixty dollars for a fifty-minute session, it wasn't all that expensive, either.

As it turned out, it was a bit dangerous for the Kanter's health. An enterprising reporter found out about the Kanter "cure" and gave it wide and unwanted publicity. Because Kanter's clients were who they were and wanted to stay that way, none of them was willing to testify against him in court. The case was dropped, Chuck kept his license, and the AMA looked the other way after a few stern words in private.

Charles Kanter, suddenly known as "the sexy shrink," looked for a refuge in the storm of criticism and abuse that came his way. When he applied for the job as police psychiatrist, the cops wanted nothing to do with him, but his father, the discount-record king, was a sizable contributor to the Democratic political coffers in Manhattan. The mayor of the city, who was a sizable recipient from the political coffers in Manhattan, believed that every man deserves a second chance in life. Some deserve it behind bars and some deserve it within the city administration. He also attended the same temple as Kanter's father. In the manner of democracy, a deal was worked out. The discount-record king sold a few more pirated tapes and records and donated the proceeds to his second favorite cause—the party. His first favorite cause, the sexy psychiatrist, got the job as head shrink to the cops. As is often the nature in a case of political compromise, nobody was happy, but they were all stuck with it.

Block filled Kanter in on the case, then showed him the picture of the pile of men's clothing left in Watt's room, ripped to shreds, soaked in blood, and laid out like a corpse.

"Tell me about the clothes," he said.

"The clothes?" Kanter asked.

"Am I right, or is that some sort of ritual slaying?"

"It does look that way," Kanter agreed.

"So why would a man kill his clothes? He's just murdered two women, wiped his apartment clean of fingerprints, then he takes the trouble to put the clothes down in the shape of a man and rip them up. Why?"

"Maybe he was killing someone in absentia," said Kanter. "The clothes represent someone else he wants dead."

"They're his clothes," said Block.

"So he wants himself dead," said Kanter. "Maybe he even thinks he is dead now."

"Symbolically, you mean?"

"He may feel that he's literally done away with one side of himself. Maybe these killings have expunged it."

Block struggled to keep his tone polite.

"Doc, the man has killed four women. I doubt that this last batch has expunged anything."

"You may be right, of course," Kanter agreed hastily. "It's very difficult to tell without talking with the man himself."

"We're trying to arrange that," Block said.

"Of course."

"In the meantime, what's your best guess about this?" Block had found it was always wise to word things vaguely, putting things off the record, as it were. Experts—however inexact their sciences—tended to be conservative to the point of muteness unless it was understood that they were simply speculating.

"Well," said Kanter, "just off the top of my head, you understand . . ."

"Sure," said Block.

". . . I'd say the man is disassociating himself from another aspect of his personality. He's saying, 'I wash my hands of you, you're dead as far as I'm concerned.' This on the assumption we're dealing with a psychotic here."

"I'm assuming he's a little psychotic, yeah."

"Yes. So he's saying to his murderous impulse—'I'm through with you; it's over'—and whether or not it will last, of course, who knows?"

"You're saying Tom-Tom has two sides? A good side and a bad side."

"I'm not saying that. This is just speculation."

"Let's make sure I understand this," said Block. "You're saying—you're speculating—that Tom-Tom is a split personality?"

"That's your phrase, not mine, but it conveys the meaning."

"Come on, Doctor. Dr. Jekyll and Mr. Hyde? Come on."

Kanter shrugged. "You asked for speculation. Do you want my official position? I don't know. How's that?"

"So you're telling me—hypothetically—that someone could be

so split in two mentally that one half of him would try to kill the other half?"

"There've been a lot stranger things than that, Lieutenant. The psychopathic mind is a mare's nest; you might find anything in there."

"Does one half know what the other half is doing?"

"It might, but it wouldn't be able to control it at all. His awareness would probably be like watching another person's dream. . . . I'm trying to avoid clinical terminology, I assume that's what you want."

"I appreciate it. And now you think that symbolic corpse means Tom-Tom's good side has killed the bad side?"

Kanter paused. "If any killing was done, I'd think the bad side did it. Maybe that corpse is the good side and what's left of Tom-Tom is the murderer."

Block got home by eight o'clock and found the apartment empty. By ten o'clock he began to worry. He called the film lab where Sheila was working and learned that she had left more than an hour before. He called her friends, trying to keep his tone casual, not wishing to alarm them. Not wishing to alarm himself.

He considered calling the police, but realized he was overreacting. Instead he tried to watch television, ate more than he was hungry for, and worried.

A sense of deep anxiety swept over Block. It was an emotion he had no experience with, was unprepared for. He felt as if Sheila were going to be taken from him. In a way he had expected it, he had never felt he deserved her, and now fate was proving him right. A dreadful sense of loss and sorrow filled him. It had happened to him before, the only other time he had dared to come out of himself and love a woman.

Block had been in love only once before in his life, in college. Alone even then, both parents dead so long he could scarcely remember them, Block was working his way through Baruch Community College, clerking at night in a delicatessen. In the evening hours he would keep a school book beside the cash register and study when business was slow, which was a good portion of the time. Although his job was dealing with people, he had little to do with them, and the work made him lonelier than if he had been alone. He would close and shutter the deli at eleven and walk home to his one-room kitchenette with the bathroom in the hall. He had been supporting himself since he had wandered into Manhattan in his late teens and neither knew or expected much better than a bathroom in the hall shared with strangers. At least it was a bathroom. He had known worse.

He had met Rachel Tempkin in a sociology class and been overwhelmed by her attentions. A plain girl with thick glasses and a nose of such dimensions that not even surgery had been able to tame it completely, she was as lonely as Block. But where Block collapsed in upon himself, Rachel exploded with gregariousness. She latched onto Block with the grip of a drowning man and seemed to follow him everywhere, weak eyes gleaming, smiling, chattering happily to him about a universe of concerns that Block knew only from reading. At first she annoyed him, then she amused him. And finally, because she insisted it was so, he loved her.

After six months of Rachel, Block was becoming a different man, more outgoing, more garrulous, happier. And then she disappeared, vanished entirely for three weeks without a word to Block or her family. Finally she surfaced, literally, her bloated body rising from the depths of the Hudson. The coroner said her neck had been broken in several places before she was tossed into the river. The police investigation proved barren and futile, filling Block with a rage at the incompetence of the authorities.

Block dropped out of college and became a cop. He continued to study, getting his degree after five years of night school, attending classes with other students as solitary but dedicated as he. But by the time he was finally eligible to seek employment as an accountant, Block was being pushed for the detective list. For good or ill, he was a cop, and lonelier than ever.

Until Sheila, he had preferred to stay that way. The memory of Rachel had seemed to demand it. Now, as he paced his apartment, he felt the pattern of the past repeating itself, dooming him to solitude.

When Sheila came home just before midnight, he shook her angrily. "Where have you been?" he demanded. "I was worried silly!"

"Louise and I went out for some coffee after work," she said, startled.

"Why didn't you call?"

"You haven't been home before morning for a week," she said. "How was I to know you weren't working tonight, too?"

He shook her again. Her slate-gray eyes went wide. "Sandy!" she said.

He stopped abruptly and pulled her to him, hugging her. "I'm sorry," he murmured against her ear. "I'm sorry. I was so worried."

Sheila slid her arms up his back. "I didn't know you were home," she said softly.

"I love you too much," he said, surprised at the strength of his reaction.

Later, in the dark, he promised to try to be home more often.

It was one of those nightmares in which Florio knew he was dreaming, but still couldn't wake up. He dreamed that he was sleeping, trying to waken because he was in danger, but coming awake was like rising to the surface of the ocean from a great depth, and as he struggled toward the edge of waking, consciousness seemed to recede before him. He knew, at least in the dream he knew, that someone was standing in the room at the end of the bed, looking down at him. His gun was somewhere he couldn't remember, somewhere careless where he had left it when he fell into bed the night before. If he didn't wake immediately, the person in the room would find the gun. But he couldn't wake up, couldn't quite lift his head from the pillow and sit up. Gravity was stronger than his sense of danger.

The person moved, said something, edged closer to the gun. Florio wanted to open his eyes, but he was afraid of what he would see. The person was right next to the gun now. Feeling it was the hardest thing he had ever done in his life, Florio opened his eyes. His mother stood at the end of the bed, her face twisted into a look of hatred. She was drawing his gun and pointing it at him, squeezing the trigger.

This time Florio woke for real and sat up with a start.

" 'Bout time," said the woman.

Florio shook his head, rubbed his eyes, and felt the sweat that had broken out on his forehead. He tried to remember who the woman was and where he was. She was black, as black as anyone he had ever seen. Her skin was so dark it seemed almost blue. In the inner thighs where it was particularly smooth, it seemed to glisten, even in the dull light of the lamp on the night table. Florio had once seen a black horse which appeared to change colors in the sunlight. When he stroked the horse's neck, the black surface hairs moved and revealed a russet layer of hairs beneath. This woman was like that; as she turned, her skin seemed to change from black to blue to black again.

Florio fell back on the bed and covered his eyes with his forearm. He wished she'd put some clothes on. Christ, she was ugly. Her face was dominated by an enormous nose, long and bony, that seemed to begin somewhere in her forehead and descend to her chin. The flesh on her body, for all its intriguing color, was fat and loose, growing fatter the farther it was from the pervading influence of the nose, so that her bottom half swelled out like the base of a pear. Florio thought that if he pushed her over, she would bob right back up again, like a weighted punching bag.

"What time is it?" he asked.

"Look at your watch," she said. "You didn't take it off. You didn't bother to take off much of anything."

Florio realized he was fully dressed except for his shoes. He must have tucked the gun in the shoes. Sitting up again, he groped under the bed until he found them.

"You got any coffee?"

"There's a coffee shop three, four blocks down," she said. "If you hurry, you can just get there."

"How late are they open?"

"Twenty-four hours."

He risked another glance at her. Judging by her hostility, he had turned in another sterling performance last night. He had to stop living this way.

She had undone her hair and it fell halfway down her back, incredibly full, black, and wavy. A bright red dot had appeared between her eyebrows, just above that plow of a nose.

He began to remember. She was from India. No, something stranger than that. Sri Lanka, wherever that was, but a long time ago, if command of the idiom was any indication. Christ, where did he find them? And how drunk must he have been? A Sri Lankan. New York was supposed to be a melting pot; why did Florio always manage to end up with the undissolved clotted bits that clung to the side of the pot?

He stood up, clutching the edge of the bed until his dizziness passed.

"I'll call you," he said.

She laughed, a mean, mean laugh.

"Don't catch your ass on the doorknob," she said.

Florio stepped into the street, squinting against the light. The streets felt like a steambath. His rumpled clothes clung to him with his own sweat before he'd gone a block.

Passing a shop window he caught a look at his reflection and for a second didn't recognize himself. If he was still on a beat and saw somebody who looked like that, he'd run him in on a drunk and disorderly, he thought.

As he gazed at his reflection, he suddenly had a gut-wrenching desire to see Sheila. He remembered her wide smile, her laugh, her eyes sparkling with interest. He remembered she had touched his hand when she talked and he had felt it was on

fire. Not only her beauty and her charm, but her wholesome-
ness assailed him. Her decency seemed as strong an attraction
as her body. For the moment, before he caught himself, he
resented Block deeply.

Kathy was frightened. She had seen Tom-Tom when he was
hurting the ladies, she had been there every time, and she had
seen him hurt them again and again. She had tried to stop him
but he was much too strong for her. Kathy was only a little girl,
she couldn't stop Tom-Tom. She didn't think anyone could stop
Tom-Tom. She had warned everyone, though. She had left her
messages every time he made her go with him to one of those
places.

He was getting meaner each time. He had hurt that last lady
for a very long time before she stopped hurting, a very long
time, and Kathy had been forced to watch. She was a good girl,
she didn't know why she had to be with Tom-Tom and watch
him do those things. He was the meanest person in the world
and she hated him.

Kathy had liked the last lady. She had looked like Kathy's
mother, she had felt sorry for Kathy and had tried to comfort
her. Kathy remembered cuddling in the lady's lap. She remembered nuzzling the lady's breast, just like she used to do with
her mommy's. The lady had smelled so good and stroked
Kathy's head. She had been so nice. It wasn't fair that Tom-Tom
had come then. He ruined everything, he always ruined everything. She hated him, even if he was her brother.

And then he had done that to Mr. Watts. He didn't have to
do that. Kathy had liked Mr. Watts. He was a lonely man, but
always very nice. He would read the Bible out loud and Kathy
liked to listen to the words, even though she didn't always understand them. She didn't know why Tom-Tom had made Mr.
Watts go away forever, except that Tom-Tom was mean. Mama
had always said Tom-Tom was the very Devil, and she was right.

With Mr. Watts gone, Kathy had to take care of his pet. She

didn't like to, she thought snakes were disgusting and no kind
of a pet, but she couldn't let it die. That wouldn't be right.
Someone had to take care of it, and she was the only one. Tom-
Tom would never do it. Tom-Tom only liked to torture animals.
He liked to tie things to them and stick things in them and
make them swallow stuff that would make them sick. When they
lived in the country it was awful, Tom-Tom was always hurting
the animals. Since they had moved to the city, he had started
hurting people, instead. And recently he had been hurting them
until they were dead. He had never done that before. Well,
once. But that was a long time ago.

Kathy walked through the great big station where so many
people came to catch the train. It was a big, scary place with a
funny, hollow sound, and a lot of people who a good little girl
shouldn't talk to. She kept her head down, careful not to stare
at strangers, and walked all the way to the lockers. She took
Mr. Watts's key and opened the locker where he kept his pet.
The locker was empty except for a Gristede's plastic shopping
bag carefully tied at the top. Kathy carried a paper food container, the kind used in Chinese restaurants. Kathy thought that
was funny. She wondered if the pet store man who gave her the
mouse in the container had known it was the take-out dinner
for Mr. Watts's snake.

The mouse was such a cute little thing. His eyes and ears and
the tip of his nose were all pink and his fur was so white. He
let her stroke his fur and didn't even try to run away. She liked
the mouse much better than the disgusting snake and for a moment she thought she would save it, but then she remembered
Mr. Watts, poor Mr. Watts, reading his Bible aloud, and she
felt even sorrier for him, being killed like that, than she did for
the mouse. She put the mouse in the bag and tied the top again
and closed the locker. She didn't want to have to listen to the
mouse squeal.

After a moment she opened the locker again. There was neither sound nor motion coming from the bag. She took the bag
from the locker and walked away. She would have to move the
snake to some place more convenient. The station was all right

for Mr. Watts, but Kathy didn't like it, she thought it was scary with so many people around and she didn't like to have to come here.

Some men watched her walk away. Dirty men, she thought. The kind little girls had to stay away from. She kept her head down and walked quickly away from them and out of the station.

Kathy walked a long way. It was far, so far, and she was so little and her legs hurt, but she had to do it. She owed it to Mr. Watts to take care of the snake. He had tried to help her. It wasn't his fault he wasn't as strong as Tom-Tom. Kathy didn't think anyone was as strong as Tom-Tom.

Finally she entered a private garage in the basement of an apartment building. The attendant nodded at her, but Kathy turned her head away. She found the car she wanted, a tan Citation. She opened the trunk and put the Gristede's bag beside the spare tire. The snake wriggled once, then settled into its new home. It was warm and well fed. It could wait for as long as necessary to come out again.

Excerpts from taped session between P. Riordan and client Thomas Cater, August eighth:

RIORDAN:	Good morning.
CATER:	Good morning, Doctor.
RIORDAN:	Won't you sit down, Mr. . . . do you pronounce your name to rhyme with later?
CATER:	Cater, that's right.
RIORDAN:	Mr. Cater, I'm going to tape our conversation. I find it very helpful. Is that all right?
CATER:	Okay.
RIORDAN:	Your full name is Thomas Cater? How old are you?
CATER:	Forty-one.
RIORDAN:	And your address?

CATER:	I don't have one.
RIORDAN:	You're in transit?
CATER:	That's right.
RIORDAN:	Is there any place you can be reached?
CATER:	(Pause) I never know where I'll be.
RIORDAN:	I see. What is your profession, Mr. Cater?
CATER:	I want to talk about my family, Doctor.
RIORDAN:	I'm not a doctor. I'm a psychiatric social worker. You don't need to call me doctor.
CATER:	You can help me, can't you?
RIORDAN:	I think that working together we can help you, yes. We've been able to help many families with problems. How did you happen to come to me, who recommended me?
CATER:	The police.
RIORDAN:	The police sent you?
CATER:	My family . . .
RIORDAN:	Yes?
CATER:	I don't know what to do with them.
RIORDAN:	All right, we'll get your statistics later. Tell me about your family. In what way don't you know what to do with them?
CATER:	They're fighting.
RIORDAN:	(Pause) They're fighting each other?
CATER:	Kathy is afraid.
RIORDAN:	What is she afraid of?
CATER:	She's afraid of *him*. He has the Devil in him. He already got rid of Perlie Watts. He was a nice man, a lonely man, he never hurt anyone, he gave me a sucker once.
RIORDAN:	Who . . . who gave you a sucker?
CATER:	Perlie Watts. He drives a truck but he got rid of him. Kathy's afraid he'll get rid of her, too.
RIORDAN:	Mr. Cater, I'm having a little trouble following you. I'm not sure who the members of your family are. How many children do you have?
CATER:	I don't have any children!

RIORDAN: I thought . . . Who are these members of your family?

CATER: I used to be able to control him, but I can't anymore. He hates the other one. He's going to get rid of him, too. He wants to be the only one.

RIORDAN: Watts?

CATER: Watts is gone. He got rid of him because he saw him and was going to tell. I used to be able to control him.

RIORDAN: Mr. Cater . . . Mr. Cater, I don't know what you're talking about. If you could just back up and identify the members of your family for me, then I could follow you. Are all these people members of your immediate family? . . . Where do they live?

CATER: They live with me.

RIORDAN: Can you tell me their names, one at a time? (Pause) Mr. Cater? Can you tell me their names? (Pause) Are you all right, Mr. Cater? . . . Uh, for the record, the client just walked out.

New York City began to twitch with a nervous tic.

In mid-August, when the media furor over the "Tom-Tom killings" was at a peak, a pregnant woman killed a man who she claimed was attacking her. The woman, Mrs. Christine Samose, said she had met a man at a bar where she worked as a waitress. He had introduced himself as Tom and paid what she considered unusual and unwarranted attentions to her for several hours. The primary focus of his comments was her pregnancy, which, in her sixth month, was quite evident, and he repeatedly voiced his disapproval that she had chosen to keep working. At one point he pulled off her apron and tried to propel her out the door, saying he was sending her home for the sake of the unborn child. The man was then ejected from the bar.

Mrs. Samose returned to her apartment after work. As she searched for her key—her husband was asleep and she didn't want to wake him by ringing the doorbell—she heard heavy footsteps in the hallway behind her. She ran into her apartment, got her husband's .22 caliber pistol, and aimed it at the door, vowing loudly that she would shoot if anyone entered. The door opened, a man entered, and Mrs. Samose shot him four times, killing him.

The fact that the murdered man was the innocent superintendent of the building, summoned by the husband to deal with a broken air conditioner, did not dampen the Tom-Tom fever. The damage had been done. A pregnant woman had defended herself against Tom-Tom—that was the message that reached the public, and with it a precedent was set.

Nervous women began to "defend" themselves all over the city. Three more men were wounded, one seriously; and half a dozen were arrested following complaints of threatening behavior. Two of the men were former husbands, one was a teen-age boy, one was a tourist from Senegal asking for directions to Radio City—none of them was Tom-Tom.

Block was not surprised. Captain Byrne had predicted a shitstorm, and it had come. The city was always on the verge of panic anyway, Block thought. Like the Sword of Damocles, the threatening clouds were always hanging above the city—they needed but a seed, some single incident around which all the fear could coalesce and start to precipitate. As rainmakers sprinkle the clouds to draw down the rain, not to make the moisture, so Tom-Tom had just given the fear an excuse to come forth; he had not created it.

"This city lives on fear," Block said. "Fear is the engine that keeps it going. It's like one of those giant planets, Saturn or Jupiter, they tell us it's got a heat engine, the tides are constantly pulling it apart and gravity's pulling it back together and all that pulling and pushing are making it hot. The plates are sliding back and forth across each other and the oceans are boiling, and it's doing it all to itself."

"What are you talking about?" Florio asked.

They were investigating yet another false lead. Because they knew it was false and because they knew they had to investigate it anyway, they were ill tempered.

"New York provides its own friction, is what I'm saying. Too many parts grinding against each other, too much friction, too much heat."

"It's August," said Florio. "It's supposed to be hot. How's Sheila?"

"Sheila's fine, what do you mean?"

"I was just asking. Being polite."

"Well, she's fine," Block said, wondering when he had ever heard Florio being polite before. He decided he never had.

"She worried?"

"What about?"

"What all the rest of the women in the city are worried about—Tom-Tom."

"She's not," Block said. "But I am. I'm about half frantic with worry, to be honest with you."

Florio looked closely at his partner. Half frantic with worry. It was a phrase he couldn't connect with the Block he had known. It was a sentiment he would never have suspected, a suggestion of the sensitivity Sheila had mentioned. Florio could easily picture himself half frantic with worry, but the admission of such vulnerability in Block made him uneasy. Cops did not discuss such things with one another.

"She's not in any danger. He's only after the pregnant ones."

"So far," said Block. "Who knows how long that's going to last? Maybe it's just coincidence so far. Neither Caro nor this last one *looked* pregnant."

"He's not going to pick Sheila out of all the women in the city."

"That's easy for you to say."

"You know it's true."

"As a cop I know it's true. As a husband, I worry. And what happens if Sheila gets pregnant?"

"Are you trying?" Florio asked, then wished he hadn't. He didn't want to know, didn't want to think of Block and Sheila making love.

"We're trying."

Florio started to make a perfunctory joke about how the trying must be worth it in itself, but the words died on his lips. He was sorry to hear Block's news. Somehow, to this point, he had managed to see Sheila in a state of purity, virginal, no matter what the physical reality. It might be an image difficult to sustain if she were pregnant.

"Good luck," he said, after such a pause that Block turned to him, puzzled, not certain what he was referring to.

"Did you stop drinking?" Block asked after a time. He had not seen Florio with a hangover for at least two weeks. His color in the morning seemed more nearly normal, the pale tone of a city person, not the deathly white of the sick.

"I cut back a little," said Florio, twisting uncomfortably. Block thought he seemed suddenly shy.

As their car eased its way through a small lake formed by yet another unauthorized open hydrant, Florio popped a small mint in his mouth. Block could not remember when his partner had ever expressed concern over his breath, either.

"Anything up?" Block asked.

"What do you mean?"

Block shrugged. "In your social life."

"I don't have a social life."

"You're out with someone every night," said Block.

"That ain't social," said Florio flatly. "I do that like a spasm. Like a reflex. There's nothing sociable about it." His voice was sour with bitterness.

Sheila worked late because she had learned that her husband was probably working late, too. As much as possible, she had been warned about his hours before they married. Block had told her what his life was like, that many of the stoolies, the informants, the witnesses who made up an indispensable part of a cop's life, were available only at night. Like nocturnal creatures fearing the exposure of the sun, they came out only after dark, and Block sought them out then after a full day of work. If midnight was the only time he could get a vital piece of information, then he went out at midnight. Or, more likely, simply stayed on the case until then, never coming home until he was finished.

Warnings were one thing, but the lonely reality of this kind of life was quite another. If she had married the man, she felt, then she had married his hours as well. She might not like it, but she had a responsibility now. It would not be fair to ask him to change. At least it would not be fair yet—she had been married only a month. And Block was so attentive, so loving, so totally hers when he was with her that it almost made up for his being gone so much. Almost.

Sheila had come to her marriage expecting happiness. Not from naiveté but from solid example. Her parents were so clearly, exultantly happy in their marriage that she had come to think of that as the normal state of affairs and all of the obvious marital failures as exceptions to the rule. The key to her parents' marriage, she had always thought, was the patient, enduring quality of her father's devotion to both mother and daughter. A commercial artist, he worked at home and took as much part in the running of the household as her mother. He never missed an anniversary because of a business trip, never failed to show for Sheila's dance recitals, school plays, gymnastics meets. He was there for all the scraped knees, all the schoolgirl squabbles, all the wounds to her ego. He was the rock on which the family was founded.

And Sheila had needed him. She had come into beauty late and unexpectedly. A gangly, bony child, with a face that seemed tyrannized by her mouth and her forehead, she had affected bangs to cover the brow and had gone for protracted periods in her adolescence trying not to smile, forcing her lips closed over her teeth as if she had a shattering secret to preserve.

She had thought of herself as ugly, and it was only her father's steady, patient, understanding reassurance that she was not that gave her some small share of confidence. When she finally staggered out of adolescence and her features shifted just that last tiny fraction to change imperfection into stunning originality, Sheila was amazed. She was still not used to it. She thought of it at times as a magical gift bestowed upon her by her father's belief in her.

When she met Block, she saw many of the same virtues of her father in him, although, of course, she didn't think of it that way. He was steady, patient, understanding. He laughed easily and loved hard. She would never have suspected that he would be there so seldom when she wanted him.

As had been happening with increasing frequency, Sheila was once again the last person in the office. When she rose to go, the rest of the divided loft was in darkness. The only light shining was over her work area. Sheila made an effort to tidy up before she left, but as always she managed to reshuffle things more than straighten them up. Midway through a chore she would be distracted by another and then another, often starting three projects and deserting them all rather than finishing one. She counted her untidiness among her failings and vowed to correct it one day, knowing full well she probably never would.

The light switch for her work area lay at the end of her subdivision of the loft. Normally she would turn off her light then walk in darkness down the aisle that led between the racks of film canisters to the next light switch just outside the elevator. As she was about to turn off the lights, she thought she heard a sound coming from the darkness ahead of her. She paused, listening. She heard nothing, and somehow it was the silence that frightened her. Sheila felt as if something was there, hiding in the darkness, holding its breath.

She waited, staring into the darkness, until her eyes adjusted and she could make out shapes in the shadows. The film canisters were in their familiar racks, each the rounded silhouette of a human head.

Sheila gasped and realized she had been holding her breath. Nothing moved in the darkness, nothing made a sound; but she knew someone was there. Knew it with the nerve endings on her skin that had reacted with goose bumps as certainly as if she had been hit with an icy wind. Her scalp tingled with the awareness and her intestines protested with fear. Someone was waiting for her in the dark.

She backed away from the darkness. She didn't want to see him, didn't want eye contact to provoke him to action. As she backed away, her footsteps sounded horribly loud and hollow in the loft. They obscured another noise coming from the darkness. When she stopped to listen the other sound stopped, too. It had been a high, nervous, excited sound, something halfway between a giggle and a whimper. She wasn't sure the sound was human, although she knew that whatever had made it was.

Keeping her eyes fixed on the darkness, she felt behind her

for the telephone. She didn't know if he would come at her with a rush or slowly, grotesquely, dragging himself across the open floor; nor could she imagine which would be worse. Her groping fingers knocked the telephone receiver from the base and she clutched at it, bringing it to her ear as if brandishing a club. Her other hand found, on her desk, the scissors she used to cut film. They felt pathetically small and harmless. They would harm no one, not even slow him down, but she gripped them tightly.

She thought she heard the sound again just before she spoke into the telephone. It sounded very much like a suppressed giggle now.

"I am at the Film Center at Fifty-seventh and Tenth Avenue," she said, speaking clearly and precisely, as Sandy had taught her. "Man with a gun." That would bring every cop within range to her immediately, she knew. That was the ultimate distress signal, Block had said, the one which took precedence over all others, and should bring cops on the fly.

She thought she heard the scrape of metal against metal, but it was farther away, receding. The air pressure seemed to change as if a door had been opened, then closed. She knew he was gone with the same certainty that she had known he was there.

The recording of the querulous operator sounded in her ear, urging her to hang up and dial again. Sheila had never dialed in the first place. She had been afraid to turn her back to the darkness long enough to face the phone, and she knew anyway that the police would never have arrived in time to save her if he had come at her then.

She sat down, realizing how weak her limbs felt. For a moment she wondered how she had known so much, or thought she had known so much, with so little evidence to go on. One sound from the darkness, an unnatural stillness, another noise that may or may not have been heard—may in fact have been her own excitement. If she thought about it rationally she would soon convince herself it hadn't happened, but Sheila knew it had. She had had a brush with someone in the dark and it had terrified her.

She could no longer bear to be alone in the loft and she ran for the elevator, her body cringing as she passed through the racks of film. She half expected him to be waiting for her in the elevator, and she considered pushing the button then waiting a few steps away in the stairwell till the elevator doors opened. But then she realized he might be waiting in the stairwell for her, too. He was not in the elevator and she rushed into it, waiting an eternity for the doors to close. The elevator, at least, was well lighted and it took her safely to the ground floor of the building.

She ran into the street, her senses grabbing at the sights and sounds of the city at night as if they were lifelines thrown into the ocean. It was just past nine and the city was finally relinquishing the long summer day.

The block between Tenth and Ninth Avenues was industrial, given over on both sides of the street to film labs, video centers, an automobile body shop. A sculptor quietly violated the zoning code by using the top floor over the body shop as a home-cum-studio, but he was the only resident on the long expanse of the city block until one encountered two crumbling brownstones on the corner of Ninth Avenue. There being no one living on the street, cabs never needed to venture toward the Tenth Avenue end of the block after business hours. Sheila walked gratefully toward the oasis of human activity. Latin music could be heard from the corner; people went in and out of a bodega on the corner, their voices rising above the steady hum of the traffic.

Sheila had gone only a few yards when she realized she was not alone on the street. Footsteps echoed between the squat brick buildings and for a moment she wasn't sure if she was hearing her own footsteps twice, or if there was really someone back there, his steps slightly out of synchronization with her own. She glanced over her shoulder, instinctively hugging her purse tighter against her body. She saw the form of a man, keeping close to the shadows of the building, moving quickly toward her. He was coming faster than she was, and would overtake her easily long before she reached Ninth Avenue. The safety of the human activity now seemed hopelessly far away, the voices totally indifferent.

If she ran now, she just might make it to the corner before he caught her. Surely he would be deterred from hurting her if she made it to the safety of those lights and voices. But she feared that running might force him to act. Thus far, despite her imagination, he had been content to watch her. A panicked move on her part might signal weakness, might trigger his aggression as the erratic motions of a fish in trouble bring on the rush of the shark. She walked faster but forced herself not to run.

The footsteps came closer, then slowed, falling into rhythm with her own. He was following her. Sheila felt her whole back shiver. She could almost feel the knife slashing through her clothing, into her flesh. Now he was closer still, right behind her, close enough to reach out and touch her. She wanted to scream; instead she whirled around to face him, one arm already flying up to defend her face and chest from the blow.

"Hi," said Florio, his manner one of great surprise and innocence. "I thought it was you but I wasn't sure."

"Oh, my God," said Sheila, clapping one hand to her heart. She tried to overdo her relief, to make a joke of it to let him know she hadn't really been scared. But her lips were quivering and her voice was shaking.

"What's the matter?" asked Florio. "I didn't scare you, did I? I didn't want to scare you."

Sheila sagged against him in relief, allowing herself that second of complete collapse. She would be brave again in a moment.

Her hair brushed against his face, one hand touched his chest. She leaned her head on his shoulder.

"I thought you were Tom-Tom," she said, laughing, and surprised that she could laugh so soon. But even before she spoke she could feel Florio's body go rigid. He stood, taking her weight like a board. No hand came up to pat her shoulder as another man's might have. Sheila thought she might have embarrassed him by throwing herself on him, and she quickly pulled away.

She did not realize Florio was afraid to touch her because he wouldn't want to stop. Maybe wouldn't even be able to stop.

"So, what are you up to?" he asked, forcing his voice to sound casual.

"I'm on my way home from work," she said.

"Is that right? I didn't know you work around here."

Sheila pointed out her building.

"What are you doing around here?" she asked.

"Just bar-hopping," he said. But she knew there were no bars on that block, and his breath smelled like a minty oral spray.

"Whyn't I take you home?" he said. "The streets aren't what you'd call safe these days. Maybe you heard."

"Distant rumors," she said. "But I never let mass panic or waves of terror affect me." She shook her hands and rolled her eyes and wobbled her tongue in a parody of fright. They laughed, and Florio put his hand on her elbow, steering her toward Ninth Avenue.

"I'll just take you home," he said.

He held her elbow with the greatest of care as if fearful it might come unhinged.

"I usually catch a cab on the corner there," said Sheila.

"Well, I'll take one with you," he said. "I'm not doing anything exciting anyway."

"It's not necessary," she said.

Florio kept his eyes straight ahead, as if afraid of looking at her too directly. "No problem," he said. Then, as an afterthought, he added, "Who's to say Tom-Tom isn't a cabdriver?"

Sheila invited him into her apartment, hoping that Block would be there. She was not afraid of Florio in any way, merely confused by him. There was something so proper in his attitude, not in anything he said, but in the way he said it, the way he held her elbow like an escort at a formal ball, the way he opened the cab door and insisted on following her into and out of the elevator, something so restrained and out of character that it puzzled her. Sheila could not recall being treated with such deference since her first date when she was thirteen years old. It seemed that all the progress they had made at their dinner had been lost completely.

She brought coffee cake to the table along with the coffee,

setting it down on the plates then returning to the kitchen. When she came back with napkins and forks, Florio took a small bite of the cake. He put the fork down and delicately dabbed at his mouth with the napkin.

Eating was torture for Florio. He was certain that at any moment his throat would seal itself shut entirely. As it was, it seemed that the smallest crumb was too large to force its way down his esophagus. When he drank the noise sounded like an ocean washing against his ears. He was reminded of a plastic transparent mockup of a body used for anatomical demonstrations. He thought she could see everything he ate, watch it pass through his cotton-dry mouth, force its way down his throat, and fall noisily into the churning acids of his stomach. He was so gross, so obvious in his disgusting alimentary processes, that she would be revolted, he thought.

When he spoke to her, he looked all around her, his vision flicking over her mouth, her nose, her hair, carefully avoiding direct contact with her eyes. If he let her see into his eyes, she would see everything he was trying to hide. If he let himself look into those large slate-gray eyes of hers, he would fall in and be lost completely.

He had never been so uncomfortable in his life.

The conversation had grown exceedingly cryptic, Sheila thought. Somehow they had wandered into the area of love and lasting relationships and why Florio wasn't married. Sheila was certain she hadn't taken matters in that direction, but then she couldn't specifically remember Florio doing it, either. The conversation just seemed to drift there by itself, as if pulled by its own gravity.

When they'd hit upon love, Florio had became very vague. If he had not been such a large hulking man, Sheila might have used the word "coy" to describe his avoidance of any direct statements. But if it was coy or cryptic, it was not unfamiliar. Sheila thought she recognized what Florio was doing with all his veiled statements about what he wanted to do if only he could, about fate taking nasty turns, about loyalty weighing more than selfish happiness. She had seen it before. In his bashful bumbling way, Florio was paying court.

While helping her return their dishes to the kitchen, Florio bumped shoulders lightly with Sheila. The contact sent a shiver through him and made him jerk away so dramatically that Sheila turned to see what was wrong.

"I got to go," he said gruffly. "You don't want me hanging around."

He paused, giving her a chance to say, yes, she did want him around.

"It was nice of you to see me home," she said, striving for the right note of polite formality. She walked him toward the door.

"Tell Sandy I'll see him in the morning," said Florio. He lurched forward suddenly and for an instant Sheila thought he was going to try to kiss her. She turned her head and flinched backward involuntarily before she realized he was only offering to shake her hand. She took his hand with a nervous little laugh.

"I wasn't going to hurt you," he said gently. Sheila realized for the second time that evening that the idea of Florio's hurting her was not very surprising.

"No, of course not," she blurted. "You just . . . I was startled."

The gentle smile stayed on his face, but his eyes were filled with pain. As he left, Sheila knew there was a great deal more to Lou Florio than she had realized.

When Block finally came home, Sheila was asleep. In the morning they made love, and afterward she mentioned Florio's visit of the night before. She told the events plainly, omitting the emotional subtext she had sensed. It was not fair to Florio to impute her own imaginings to him. And there was just enough of a thrill of innocent excitement about the incident that she wanted to keep it to herself. Mentioning it would only exaggerate it and transmute it into something it was not.

"He just appeared out of nowhere?" Block asked when she had finished.

"He said he was bar-hopping," she said.

"Was he drunk?"

"No . . . maybe he was about to start bar-hopping when he saw me. I don't think he'd had anything to drink yet."

"It doesn't sound like Florio to spend the evening sipping coffee and nibbling cake."

"It wasn't the whole evening," she said, wondering why she felt defensive.

"And he just ran into you by accident?" asked Block.

"That's what he said," said Sheila. "I thought he was a mugger for a minute when he came up behind me in the dark. Or Tom-Tom." She laughed, able at a distance to ignore the real fear she had felt.

"Why Tom-Tom?" said Block.

Sheila paused. "I had a strange experience in the loft just before I came home," she said at last. She told him of the incident haltingly, trying to make light of it now. She did not expect him to take it seriously; she found it hard to do so herself at this distance.

"It was probably my imagination," she said. "An animal, maybe. Pigeons get trapped in there sometimes. Or a rat, maybe."

She shivered. She knew it was no rat, disgusting as that thought was to her, that had filled her with terror. It may have been her imagination, but it was no rat.

"Why did you think it was Tom-Tom?" Block asked.

"He's on everybody's mind, isn't he?"

"I suppose so. Tell me about it again."

Sheila repeated her story. Then Block took her through it step by step, questioning her to bring out every detail she could remember.

"Why are you so interested?" Sheila asked.

"My wife tells me she thinks Tom-Tom is in her office at night. Shouldn't I be interested?"

"But he wasn't. Not really. It was in my mind."

"Sheila, you don't really believe that, I can tell. Why do you want me to think it's your imagination?"

"I don't want to look silly. Not to you."

"You don't look silly."

"I am silly, Sandy. I'm a very superficial person—but I don't want you to see that. You're never silly."

"I can be silly, too," he said, surprised.

"Not you. You're so stern."

Confused and hurt, he hugged her to him. Why did she think him stern? He had tried so hard to be fun for her. He would give her anything, prance around naked to make her laugh.

"And I want to think it's my imagination because . . . I don't want to think it's true. You don't think it's true, do you?"

"No," said Block quickly. "It's not true. Statistically it's practically impossible. You may have heard something, but it wasn't Tom-Tom." He said it as convincingly, as sincerely, as he could manage. He hoped that she did not see through his apparent sincerity—or she would be as frightened as he was.

"Now, tell me about Florio," he said, trying for a lightness in his tone that he did not feel. "You thought he was Tom-Tom?"

"I connected him—not Florio, but the footsteps I heard, the sense that someone was following me—I connected that to whatever happened in the loft. I was wrong."

"He just popped up? Was he coming from the direction of your office?"

"Yes, but—"

"Did he do anything that reminded you specifically of what happened in the loft?"

"Like what? There wasn't anything in the loft. There wasn't any real connection. It was just a coincidence that Florio was behind me at that time. I just connected the two by coincidence."

"Of course it was coincidence," said Block. "I'm just trying to put myself into the picture. Would you have thought any man at all on the street at that time was Tom-Tom?"

"Or a mugger," said Sheila. "I thought he might have been just a mugger."

"All right. That's always a possibility. Did he do anything to make you think that, or was it just his presence?"

"He seemed to be following me. No, but he really wasn't. See, I'm being silly. I didn't want to be, but you're making me. He just *seemed* to be following me because he was going in the same direction."

"No, he probably was following you," said Block.

"What?"

"Well, he recognized you. It was dark, maybe it took him a minute or two to be sure it was you, so he followed for a little bit, then he hurried to catch up. He probably was following you, you weren't being silly at all."

"He hurried, that's right, that's what really scared me," said Sheila. "He hurried after me. If a man hurries after you on a dark street, it scares you."

"And that made you think of Tom-Tom?"

"Until you catch him, I guess it will. . . . Are you making any progress?"

Block shook his head. "It's funny. I feel that I am, but I don't know why. I've got nothing concrete, but something about this case seems awfully . . . close, I guess. The answer is just a membrane away, but I can't see it. It's like trying to step on my shadow, every time I move it moves. But I'll get it, I'll get it. Meantime . . . if men are going to bring you home at night, I guess I'm glad it's Florio."

"Why?"

"Well, he's a cop. Not a bad idea to have a cop with you when there's a madman loose in the city."

She snuggled against him. "I'd rather have you," she said, but without recrimination.

Sheila's story had left Block very uneasy. Despite her protestations, he knew his wife was not a silly person, not given to flights of imagination just because she was alone in the dark. It was unlikely to the point of impossible that it had been Tom-Tom, of course, he knew that. And yet . . . Block sat at his desk and methodically thought through the possibilities. Most probably, it had been nothing, a random sound, a rat, a bird, amplified by the Tom-Tom hysteria. That was most likely. But Sheila clearly didn't believe it, and neither did Block.

The second possibility was that someone had been there, but not Tom-Tom. The city was filled with weirdos, peeping Toms, perverts of all descriptions. Most of them were harmless, a few were dangerous. At its worst, it could have been someone who intended to rob her, rape her, kill her. Block shuddered as he thought of it. It was not likely but possible; but that didn't mean it was Tom-Tom.

The third possibility was that it had been Tom-Tom. Not only was it extremely unlikely that Tom-Tom was stalking any given woman in the city—there must be close to a million of them in Manhattan alone—but it was astronomically unlikely that he would be randomly stalking the wife of the detective who was hunting him. The key word was random. If Tom-Tom were aware of Block, however, the odds came tumbling down. If Tom-Tom knew the identity of the man who was after him, if he had selected Sheila on purpose . . .

Block hurried out of his office, trying to control his sense of panic. He could not have said exactly why, but the idea felt right and it made his skin crawl.

Block squatted on the roof of the building, training his binoculars on the office across the street. The day's blistering sun had made the asphalt soft and sticky and Block didn't dare to put a supporting hand down anywhere for fear of drawing it away stained with tar. Every surface was hot, even after the sun went down, and Block's thighs ached with the strain of squatting. He did not think of rising to stretch them, however, nor of moving to a more comfortable position on the roof. It was imperative that he not be seen, and this was the best vantage point for both Sheila's office and the entire street below, comfort or no.

He adjusted the focus on the Zeiss-Ikon's and his wife's image seemed to leap across the street. She was reaching to clip up a strip of film, and her long, bare arm stretched upward, traced in gentle contours, soft yet firm. Her breasts strained against the material of her blouse as she arched her back. She had risen on her toes to reach the clip, and her calves stood out in high relief beneath the soft summer skirt.

Block had been watching her every evening for three days, seeing her come out of the building after work, following her with his glasses until she was safely in a cab on Tenth Avenue. At first he had felt like a voyeur, watching her from hiding, seeing her vulnerably exposed, innocent of his presence. But after a time he had come to understand the pleasures of that lonely activity. He was seeing her for the first time every day, seeing her as a stranger would see her. Since she thought she was alone, in a way he was seeing her at her most natural. It was erotic and fascinating. Block found he could study her in a way he never could when they were face to face. The nape of her neck had a contour he had never noticed before, for instance. Working with such excellent binoculars, he could study her as if standing only feet away, but cloaked in invisibility, and both of them were spared the embarrassment of staring.

The more he studied her, the more beautiful she became to him, and the more he came to appreciate her innate sweetness. She looked like a nice person, not only when she was acting nice for the sake of politeness, but all the time, alone or in a crowd. He found that he liked her even better than he had before—perhaps because from this distance he was not overwhelmed entirely by his love. He also found that he desired her even more, and in its way his lonely vigil on the rooftop took on something of the air of self-denial of the monk in his cell.

Sheila came out of the office, leaving with the last employee, as Block had requested of her. He would be of no use to her if Tom-Tom was in the office alone with her, but from his eyrie he could pick up anyone who followed her. Not that Sheila knew Block was watching her. That would only have made her more frightened, and he felt she had been scared enough.

As soon as his wife was on the street Block stopped watching her and scanned the sidewalks, the parked cars, the other windows that had a long-range view of the street below. This was the fourth day and Block had yet to pick up any consistent pattern among the random pedestrians. No one had seemed to take anything more than a casual interest in her.

A shape moved in the shadows of a warehouse door. It was on Block's side of the street and he could not see it clearly without leaning out over the edge of the building. He could not risk being seen and scaring it—him—away, so Block waited, tensed, for the shadow to move again. His thigh muscles screamed out with the strain.

The shadow stirred and started across the street, dashing quickly in front of a passing truck. The truck obscured Block's view for a second, and when it was passed, the man had stepped into another darkened doorway. Sheila was halfway up the block, chatting obliviously to her colleague. The man started to walk after her. His pace was slow, no faster than her own, but everything about his carriage spoke of tension. He reminded Block of a panther stalking its prey. The man glanced around occasionally, again like a predator, checking its environment at all times, gauging distances, perspectives.

Sheila and her colleague stopped, Sheila gesturing broadly as she concluded a story. Block could hear their laughter floating upward on the rising heat, but his eyes never left the man, who turned away like a professional spy. He had his back to Sheila and was looking back and forth confusedly, trying to give the impression, should she look his way, that he was just a lost stranger. But Block knew he wasn't lost and he wasn't a stranger.

When Sheila started walking again, the man fell in behind her once more, matching her step for step, keeping a steady twenty yards between them and hugging the greater darkness at the side of the buildings. So far Block had only had a vague profile of the man's face, which he kept turned away and in the dark. Block had to see it clearly once, had to make very sure.

At the end of the block, emerging into the frenetic energy of Latin music and neon lights, Sheila said good-bye to her friend and hailed a cab. The man following her hung back until Sheila got into the car and drove off. Block stood erect, risking discovery. He had to get closer, get a better angle. With the asphalt sucking softly at every step, he hurried to the edge of the building and jumped over the narrow airshaft onto the next rooftop. Sprinting to the edge of the next building, Block thought for a moment he had lost the man. He searched among the faces of the chattering Puerto Ricans, looking for the body that was bigger, heavier, the face that was familiarly tight and clenched like a fist. The man stood in the bright light of the tungsten streetlamp, watching Sheila's cab disappear; then he sighed enormously, and all the tension seemed to drain from him at once. Relaxing like that, so completely, he almost seemed to change personality. As he did so, he glanced all around him, as if deciding which way to go. For a second he looked back in Block's direction, his face turned squarely up toward Block's position on the rooftop. Block ducked down, quite certain that he had not been seen. But Block had seen what he wanted to see. In the last instant, the focus clear, Block had seen Florio's face in his lenses.

Block worked late again that night, returning to Alicia Caro's notebook list of lovers. Feeling both depressed and expectant as he did so, Block checked the entry under the name "Lowreo (?)." This time he followed it up the way he knew he should have done the first time. Pulling the work sheet on Lou Florio, he discovered that Florio had been off duty on the evening of June sixth, the date of the Lowreo entry.

Hoping to clear his desk so he could sneak in a long weekend with his family at the Jersey shore, Quayle was working late. He was not surprised when Block walked into his office; the detective was notorious for popping up at the strangest times in the strangest places.

"Glad I caught you," said Block with such sincerity that Quayle knew he might have a great deal of extra work.

"I was just on my way out," said Quayle, slipping the folder on which he had been working back into the file. Block worked bizarre hours, but that was no reason for him to expect others to do so.

"Just one question," said Block, crossing to the file cabinets which lined the walls. "It won't take a minute."

"A minute you can have," said Quayle. It annoyed him that Block went to the files as if they were his own. In fact they were Quayle's preserve and he had worked particularly hard to keep them as precise and professional as they were. He was tempted to take over and find whatever Block was looking for, just to assert his authority, but he realized that to do so would be to commit himself to helping further.

"The Alicia Caro thing," said Block, searching through the cabinets. "There were a couple of details. . . ."

Overcome by a sense of property, Quayle found the folder and laid it on his desk.

Block clucked in approval. "You've got that set up great," he said, knowing Quayle was as susceptible to flattery as most men.

Quayle shrugged. "Organization," he said, uttering the secret to good living.

"I wish some of the others around here would learn from you," said Block. "The fingerprints you found at Caro's apartment. Some of them were police, right?"

Quayle snorted contemptuously. "Half of them were police. They usually are. McKeon's, yours, Florio's . . . I mean, I've asked you guys a thousand times, just keep your hands in your pockets till we're done."

"I know," Block agreed. "It's sloppy. Did you find any other cops' prints?"

Quayle cleared his throat and studied his pipe. "A couple of my guys," he said. "I talked to them about it."

"It's understandable," Block said sympathetically. "Do you know where you found McKeon's prints?"

"Where in the apartment, you mean?" Quayle looked at the folder. "On the telephone receiver, on the base of the telephone, on the lamp by the telephone."

"How about Florio's?"

Quayle paused. "On the iron frame of the bed behind the headboard. On the doorknob—"

"Which doorknob?"

"The bedroom and the hallway door, actually. Also on the toilet bowl."

Block nodded. "That was probably when he was sick."

"I warned him away, I told him to go outside."

"Not your fault," said Block. "I'm going to have a talk with those guys. This is happening entirely too much. Thanks for your help.

"Is that it?" asked Quayle.

"Just one other thing," said Block. "I seem to remember something about hair. You found a lot of hair?"

Quayle sighed and opened the folder again. "In the bedroom, in the bed, on the floor, some in her brushes. She had a lot of visitors."

"You can't identify anyone by a hair," said Block.

"No."

"But if I brought you a hair and it matched with one of the ones you found at the scene . . ."

"I can't match it exactly, I can only match it as to type. It won't do you much good in court, you know that."

"I know that," said Block. "But it might narrow things down a bit. You don't mind waiting while I go get a hair, do you?"

"Now?"

"Won't take long, and I want you here to do it. I want to make sure the work's done right."

Block left quickly, not waiting for an answer. Quayle cursed to himself and went back to work. The one good thing, he decided, was that this really justified the long weekend.

As he stood outside the door of Florio's apartment, Block felt a sense of guilt. He was not certain of his motives, but he did know they were not as pure as he would like, else why the feeling that he was belittling himself?

Using a credit card, Block slipped the lock on the door with practiced ease. Florio was not the type of man to work hard to keep people out; there was no reason for them to want to get in.

A comb in the bathroom supplied the hair Block was after; then he hesitated for a moment before Florio's closet. Block was not sure what he was seeking, or even whether he wanted to find it or not, but finally he opened the closet and went through Florio's clothes.

There were two suits, one brown, one blue, both cheap and long since stretched out of shape by Florio's habit of stuffing heavy objects into his pockets. There were a few shirts, fewer ties, none of which matched the suits, a heavy winter coat, a lightweight raincoat. A pair of black wingtip shoes and a pair of ancient basketball sneakers with ankle-high black laces. Block held the wingtips sole to sole against the sneakers. The wingtip was a size ten and a half; the sneaker an eleven.

Once he'd started, Block could not stop. Feeling slightly guilty all the while, yet strangely excited, as if he was onto something, he went through the drawers of the night table, the shelves of the medicine cabinet. He searched the kitchen cabinets, which held a motley collection of flatware that looked as if it had been purchased at the Salvation Army.

With the smell of dust in his nostrils, he got down on the floor and peered under the bed. In the living room he held himself just off the floor with his arms and toes, his hands pressed into the carpet, while he looked under the couch.

Then he turned to the drawers of the dresser, rifling quickly through frayed socks and tattered shorts, two shirts carefully folded and pinned by a laundry, a comb with missing teeth, long forgotten. In the top drawer amid a scattering of mismatched cuff links and tie clips he found a photograph. Block took the photo out and held it in the light. He studied it for a long time, turned it over and glanced at the blank back, then studied the woman's face again. The photo had been photocopied from an original and the picture was dark and grainy, but there was no mistaking the face. It was a picture of Sheila, a copy of the one on Block's desk.

Block felt as stunned as if he had found Sheila herself curled up in Florio's bed. She had not given Florio the picture, Block was certain of that. He had slipped it out of the frame on Block's desk and made the replica on the office copier. The quality of the reproduction testified to Florio's haste. He had wanted to get it back quickly, fearing he might be caught. The whole scene suggested recklessness. Why had Florio wanted a picture of Sheila so desperately that he would risk being caught and settle for such a poor reproduction?

There were many possible explanations, Block supposed, but

he could think of only one. Florio wanted the photo because
Florio wanted Block's wife.

Block was surprised by his own reactions. In a way, finding a
picture of his wife was so much less than he had feared to find.
And yet so much worse. What *had* he expected, a dragon in the
closet, crouched over a pile of bones? Instead he was confronted
with the possibility of something so much more common. Block
was not the first man to be cuckolded and live to tell about it.
If indeed he had been cuckolded, and that was far from certain.
Why, then, did it hurt so very much? Why would he have preferred to find the dragon to his wife's picture?

As he left Florio's apartment, Block had a sense of walking on
shifting sands. The very earth was moving under his feet. Nothing any longer seemed quite as it should, nothing could be
trusted.

Quayle opened the buff-colored envelope and extracted the
hairs which Block presented him with a tweezer. He fiddled
with the microscope for a moment, humming to himself, then
urged Block to look at the image projected by the electron microscope onto a screen.

Something huge and sinuous seemed to be afloat on an island
of clarity in a surrounding sea of shimmering air. Block knew he
was looking at the hair from Florio's comb, but only because he
had seen Quayle place it under the microscope. This thing before him was enormous, with all the grains and texture of a
garden hose. Like a hose on a hot day, it seemed to be sweating
blobs of moisture, and tiny hairs upon the hair poked upward.
It was more like a cable than a hose, Block decided. A cable
that was coming unraveled.

As Quayle continued humming to himself, Block kept his eye
on the screen long enough to show he had really tried, then
began to cluck in consternation. Quayle staged these little demonstrations periodically to show the detectives how difficult fo-
rensics was. He knew Block would not understand what he was

seeing, and Block knew it, too, but part of the ritual was to go through the charade before expressing amazement and respect.

"I can't make any sense of it," Block admitted. It was easy enough to be impressed by Quayle's exotic arts, since they happened to supply the truth.

Quayle smiled benignly and waited. If he was going to have to work late and do favors for Block, he was at least going to have his tribute in full.

"I don't know how you do it," Block offered. "It's amazing."

"Well, it takes practice," said Quayle, still smiling. "Lots of practice. And talent. You need a gift for science just like you do for art."

"I can see that," said Block. "Did you learn how to work one of these in med school?" Block found it odd that Quayle took pride in his greatest failure. At any mention of his stay in medical college, Quayle preened himself like a body builder on display.

"Not this one specifically," said Quayle. "This is an electron microscope. They were not so common then, but yes, you would have to say that my medical training has been very helpful."

Mollified at last, Quayle turned to the business at hand. "It's a Caucasian hair," he said, turning the focus on the microscope. "Of the variety we classify as rhomboid because of the shape of the cross section. It's not rhomboid, of course, but it's not as nearly circular as some others. It's not young—you can see it's frangible, that is, it breaks easily."

"How old?"

"Oh, well, I can't be precise, but over twenty-five, certainly. Under sixty. Now if you brought me a follicle, I could tell you things."

"I don't have a follicle," said Block.

"You seldom do," said Quayle, as if faulting Block for improper techniques. "I'd have to do a chromosome test to get the sex, and that takes a while, but my guess would be male. The guy has fairly oily hair, but he doesn't use hair oil or anything artificial. Probably has a moderate case of dandruff."

"That's it?"

"What do you want? He's six feet tall, weighs a hundred eighty pounds, has a scar on his left cheek, and comes from Jersey? You gave me a single hair and three minutes to look. Let me do a chromosome test and I can maybe tell you if he's criminally insane or has diabetes, but that's it at best."

"Does it match any of the hairs you found at Alicia Caro's apartment?"

Quayle flipped another slide under the microscope. Block dutifully took a glance.

"It looks the same to me," said Block.

"It is the same. At least it's the same as to type, general age, and so forth. This one is definitely male."

"So's the one I brought," said Block.

"Okay," shrugged Quayle. "You prove that your guy was in her apartment and I'll have a little corroboration for you. Not much, since there are a few million other guys who have the same type of hair, but it won't hurt."

"Where did you find that one?"

Quayle glanced at the file notes. Every piece of evidence was carefully, painstakingly described and located within a grid which could be placed over a photo of the Caro apartment. This particular hair had come from grid Cf7-3—the lower right-hand quadrant of section seven of room C, the bedroom.

"We vacuumed it up from the floor beside the bed. The maid service came once a week and had been there six days earlier. Assuming the maid did a thorough job, your white Caucasian of middle age had been to see Miss Caro no longer than a week earlier."

"Assuming the maid did a thorough job," said Block.

"Yes," agreed Quayle. "We can't date it for you. The only one we can date approximately is the one we took from the grill on the shower drain."

Quayle put another slide under the microscope, checked his notes, then focused the machine. "There are too many possibilities for this to stand as evidence," he said, "but if I were looking for somebody, I'd look for this guy. Either the hair got stuck on her body and came off when she took a shower that night, or he took a shower there himself. It wasn't stuck, it wasn't caught, it was hanging on the grill ready to be washed down next time she took a shower."

The forensic expert motioned Block to look again. "Notice the stuff around the hair, that stuff with the jagged edges—that's the residue of soap. Soap suds might feel smooth, but at this level they're not. One more good rinse and that residue would have been washed off. I'm not saying that's your killer, but my guess is he was in her apartment that day or the day before at the earliest."

Block stared at the hair magnified thousands of times, trying to make any sense of the gigantic scene, as if blown up far enough the killer's face would magically appear.

"Is this rhomboid, too?"

Quayle shook his head. "Close, but not the same. This one is what we call semi-rhomboid. If it was Oriental, it would be nearly round. If it was black, it would be almost flat. This is Caucasian, too, but not the same. Also male, also over twenty-five. This particular specimen is a pelvic hair."

"It's the same color as the one I gave you," said Block.

"Means nothing. Color is no use to us at all. You've got several different colors on your head, everyone does, and pelvic hair is generally darker, which gives you another shade. If you doubt it, grow a beard, you'll find you've got red and blond as well as brown."

"So what good does all this do us?" Block asked, knowing the answer, but feeling obliged to ask.

Quayle checked off on his fingers. "One, the hair you brought me is similar to one we found in Alicia Caro's apartment. Which means your man might have been in her apartment, maybe within a few days of her death. Might and maybe. Two, your man is not the man who got his pubic hair mixed with hers or washed it off in the shower on the night she was killed. Three, it's all speculation and don't quote me on any of it."

"One more thing," said Block. "You had a partial footprint in blood from the kitchen. What was the shoe size?"

Quayle flipped a page in the file folder.

"Ten and a half," he said.

"Did you ever hear of anybody wearing two different size shoes?"

"Sure. That's not uncommon. A shoe made in Italy or Taiwan or someplace is going to be narrower in relation to length than an American shoe, so if you're going to be wearing an Italian number, you'll take a half size or so larger to keep it from pinching your toes."

"You're saying they've got different size feet in different countries?"

"That's what I'm saying. Either that or a higher tolerance for pain. . . . You don't look too pleased, Block. Did I screw up a theory?"

Block shrugged. "I don't know what my theory was anyway."

Quayle saw him to the door like a host bidding good-bye to a guest who has stayed too long.

"You work too hard, Block," he said. "It's my job to examine hairs, I enjoy doing it, but let's not kid ourselves. You're not going to find Tom-Tom from his hair or his shoe size."

"How am I going to find him?" Block asked.

Quayle looked surprised. "Who said you are? He may just quit. He may move away. He may get reformed. Or you might get lucky. It happens."

"It happens," Block agreed.

When he left Quayle, the image of Sheila's photograph in Florio's apartment returned to his mind, and Block nearly staggered under a wave of apprehension and sorrow. He had felt the same way in the early days when Rachel Tempkin had disappeared. Frightened, puzzled, and certain that in some way it was his fault. Had he loved her too little? Loved her too much? Driven her from him with excess or neglect? He tried to tell himself that this was different, Sheila was not Rachel, nothing like her. And Rachel had not left him as he had feared at first.

She had been taken from him, wrenched out of his life. . . . Was Sheila being taken, too? There was more than one way for him to lose his love. He vowed it would not happen again.

Sheila felt she could see through her eyelids to the time on the glowing face of the digital clock beside the bed, but she was determined not to open them, her dream was too good. The woman she had been talking to, a pert young thing in an antique bathing costume with long skirt, cap, and stockings, had just changed into a man and was slipping into bed with her. She felt his hand upon her thigh, steaming hot, moving slowly up the leg. She was walking toward the ocean where the tide was coming in and somehow his hand was still on her leg.

She knew that she was not dreaming, that a man had just gotten into bed with her and if she opened her eyes the clock would read 4:07 in the morning—she knew that with a certainty although she had been asleep for hours—but the feeling of a dream persisted. The sea, surprisingly warm, as warm as blood, was lapping at her body, engulfing her legs, splashing higher as she moved deeper into it.

Sand moved beneath her toes, shifting under her weight, and she sank slowly lower into the sea. Its creatures came to her, welcoming her. A crab moved across her leg, its legs soft and gently kneading, not at all frightening or unpleasant. Another crab moved across her stomach, inching lower, seeking union with its brother. The muscles of her abdomen rippled in small convulsions, forcing the crab lower. A wave came, a tiny one, no more than a murmur, and brushed strands of seaweed between her legs. She arched her pelvis forward to meet it.

If she opened her eyes the clock would read 4:08, but she didn't need to open them, she could see anyway, and this was all really happening to her, she knew it. She was in her bed and there was a man with her but so was the sea.

A fish came toward her, huge, larger than she was. She felt its great bulk brush against her body. It was enormous, large as a whale and was surely going to swallow her, but Sheila was not afraid, she welcomed it. Instead the whale put its mouth to her breast. Its lips were incredibly soft and dry, but there was something within the whale, another fish, bumping urgently against her breast, wet and persistent, trying to get out.

One of the crabs had nestled into the seaweed and she heard a low sigh and knew it to be the murmur of the deep. The creatures of the sea were making love to her, she realized. But how had they known that she could breathe underwater? It was all very mysterious and she would have to report it to her husband who was a policeman.

The whale left her breast and one of the crabs replaced it, tugging gently at her nipple, trying to take it. She pushed toward it, wanted the crab to have it. The whale moved beside her, nudged her onto her side, crowded against her back. It was even larger than she'd realized, but so warm. A shiver ran through her and she wriggled backward toward the warmth.

The crab between her legs was exploring insistently now and she moved and writhed to open herself more to accommodate it. The whale's organ was pressed against her buttocks and she alternately pushed back against it and forward toward the fingers.

She was really awake now and knew exactly what was happening, but still Sheila did not open her eyes. For just a moment as she came fully awake, she did not know who the man was. And when she recognized it was her husband—of course, she realized that—for this brief moment at least she didn't care if it was or not. It could have been any man just as she had been contented to have it be a whale and other sea creatures. She did not open her eyes, hoping to prolong the sense of being made love to by a stranger. No, not a stranger, something more impersonal even than that. She was being made love to by a male, that was all she needed—all she wanted—to know. As he penetrated her she thought she had never felt less self-conscious, never so completely open to sex just as sex. Taken by surprise, in mid-dream, she could have this lover be anyone she wanted. For just a moment Florio flashed in her mind.

Immediately she felt disloyal, but the feeling didn't last, any more than the image of Florio lasted. She was becoming too caught up in her orgasm to think anything coherently. Her body was straining, the nerve endings tingling as if she were being rubbed under the skin by thousands of pine boughs, and her mind became a chaos of random, flashing images.

She screamed when she reached her climax, startling herself. It was something she had never done before. He withdrew and left the bed and still Sheila kept her eyes closed. She knew why people had used to believe in an incubus who visited women in the night, ravished them, and vanished like a dream.

The man was Sandy, of course, it had to be, and Sheila didn't really want it to be anyone else. But still she did not call out to him, was content to hold the notion of a phantom lover just a few minutes longer.

She couldn't hear him anymore, couldn't sense him in the room. When the silence stretched out, she became alarmed. She finally opened her eyes. A man stood at the end of the bed, looking down at her, not moving, still as the shadows that surrounded him. It was too dark in the room to see his face.

"Sandy?"

The figure watched her in silence a moment longer before speaking.

"Yes?" His voice sounded puzzled, as if he were surprised to be called upon. Sheila felt for a moment as if the phantom had needed that extra moment to return to the body of her husband.

From the corner of her eye she could see the clock. She had been right about the time, and wasn't even surprised. He had just come home from work. There were advantages to having a husband who worked this late, she thought contentedly.

"Good night," she said, curling up and closing her eyes again.

"Good night," he said, his voice still strangely unfamiliar with his body.

Sheila was relieved that it had been her husband—but just slightly disappointed, too.

Notes on meeting between P. Riordan and Thomas Cater, August twenty-eighth:

The following transcript is taken verbatim from the taped meeting with client Cater, but due to the unusual nature of the meeting, I felt it was useful to add my own annotations in parentheses in the body of the transcript.

(Client burst into the office while my secretary was out to lunch. He had no appointment. He seemed extremely agitated.)

CATER:	I have to see you.
RIORDAN:	Hello, Mr. . . . uh . . .
CATER:	Cater. Don't you remember?
RIORDAN:	Yes, of course. Do you have an appointment?
CATER:	I have to talk to you.
RIORDAN:	I'm having my lunch, Mr. Cater. Why don't you arrange a time with my secretary.
CATER:	I don't know when I'll be here again. You have to take me now.
RIORDAN:	As I recall, you left before our first session was finished, and now you come in without an appointment. It's very important that we establish a regular time and a regular system for helping you. . . .
CATER:	He's going to do it again, he's going to do it again, I can't stop him.
RIORDAN:	Now you see, this is what I was talking about. Because I didn't know you were coming I

haven't looked at your file and refreshed my memory. . . . Please sit down, Mr. Cater.

(Client was pacing back and forth in a state of extreme agitation, and speaking under his breath. His comments were not recorded and I could not understand them clearly myself.)

RIORDAN: Please sit down, it's much easier for both of us if you sit down.

CATER: You have to help.

RIORDAN: I'll try, of course.

CATER: He's coming again. I want to keep him back, but I can't. He was under control for so long, for years, for years, but now he doesn't like the way things are going. It's the woman, she's giving him strength, she's making him do it. I could control him until the woman, now he's stronger than I am.

RIORDAN: Who is he?

CATER: He's stronger than anyone. He has the strength of the Devil, the Devil is in him.

RIORDAN: Is he a member of your family? Are you afraid this person will harm you in some way?

CATER: He might do to me what he did to Perlie Watts.

RIORDAN: What was that?

CATER: He got rid of him.

RIORDAN: What do you mean, got rid of him?

CATER: He wants to get rid of all of us. He wants to be the only one—but needs us to hide him.

RIORDAN: You said a woman was responsible. Who is the woman?

CATER: She knows who she is, she knows what she's doing. She wants him to act that way.

RIORDAN: You said you hide him. Why do you hide him if he harms you?

CATER: Kathy is very frightened.

RIORDAN: Who is Kathy?

CATER: She saw him, she saw him every time, Watts
            wasn't the only one who saw him. She saw him
            with the actress and she saw him with the nurse
            and she saw him with the girl downstairs. They'll
            blame Watts for that but he didn't do it.

RIORDAN: Mr. Cater. Let's try to take this one step at a
            time. Who is Kathy?

(The client was seated at this time. His entire physical attitude began to change as he hunched in upon himself as if to
make himself smaller. He pulled his legs under himself on the
chair, clasped one arm with the other, and pressed his hand,
which was closed into a fist, to his mouth. His entire facial
expression took on the appearance of what I can only describe
as childish petulance. When he spoke, the client's voice was no
longer that of a grown man, but a child's voice. Listening now
to the tapes and trying to ignore the extraordinary scene that
accompanied it, I would guess the voice to belong to a girl of
five or six.)

CATER: I'm scared.
RIORDAN: What?
CATER: Scared.
RIORDAN: Mr. Cater, what—
CATER: Cater's gone.
RIORDAN: Cater's gone? Is that what you said?
CATER: I . . . wa . . . I . . . wa . . . wan . . .

(The client was breathing in the heaving sighs of a child who
has been crying and is trying to stop in order to speak, but
cannot quite control his breathing. Much of what she—he—said
is indecipherable.)

RIORDAN: Mr. Cater, what is it?
CATER: I'm Kathy. Cater . . . Cater's . . . Cater's gone.

(There follows a rather lengthy pause. I admit to being ini-
tially dumbfounded by the complete psychological transforma-

tion of the client. Had I not known better, I would have sworn that somehow this unhappy child, Kathy, had been trapped within the body of the client, Thomas Cater. In a manner of speaking, of course, that is precisely what happened. Which is only to explain, at least to myself, why it took me so long to realize what was happening and to respond to it. As I sat stunned, "Kathy" stayed curled up in the chair and whimpered—the only word for it.)

RIORDAN:	Kathy. Kathy can you hear me?
CATER:	Yes.
RIORDAN:	Kathy, do you know where you are?
CATER:	Yes.
RIORDAN:	Where are you?
CATER:	In a doctor's office.
RIORDAN:	I'm not a doctor, Kathy. But I'm going to try to make you feel better. Do you want that?
CATER:	I want my mama.
RIORDAN:	Do you know how you got here, Kathy?
CATER:	I came with him.
RIORDAN:	With Mr. Cater?

(No response.)

RIORDAN:	Do you go everywhere Mr. Cater goes?
CATER:	No, I don't go everywhere with *him*.
RIORDAN:	You say that as if you go everywhere with someone else. Do you always go with someone else?
CATER:	Yes.
RIORDAN:	Who?

(No response.)

| RIORDAN: | Who do you go with, Kathy? . . . Does someone take care of you? |

CATER: I go with him but he doesn't take care of me.
            He's bad.
RIORDAN: Who's bad, Kathy? Mr. Cater?
CATER: Mr. Cater isn't bad.
RIORDAN: Who is bad, Kathy?
CATER: Tom-Tom is bad.

(A series of dramatic murders have been committed in the city in the last month and the police refer to the killer as "Tom-Tom." I assumed this to be a reference to the same "Tom-Tom.")

RIORDAN: Yes, Tom-Tom is bad. He's a very bad man,
            isn't he?
CATER: He scares me.
RIORDAN: Yes, he frightens all of us. Did Mr. Cater tell
            you about Tom-Tom, Kathy?

(She began weeping.)
(Response muffled.)

RIORDAN: Well, I don't think we need to worry about him
            anymore, Kathy. The police will take care of
            him. Where is Mr. Cater, now, Kathy? Do you
            know where he went?
CATER: Away . . . he went away.
RIORDAN: Will he come back?
CATER: I want my mama.
RIORDAN: Who is your mama?
CATER: Mama.
RIORDAN: Where is she?
CATER: I don't know. I lost her.
RIORDAN: Is she with Mr. Cater?
CATER: No.
RIORDAN: Is Mr. Cater your father?
CATER: Nooo . . . I don't like my father.
RIORDAN: But you do like Mr. Cater?

(No response.)

RIORDAN: Why don't you like your father, Kathy?
CATER: He's mean. He's bad.
RIORDAN: Why do you say your father's mean?
CATER: He's mean to Tom-Tom.
RIORDAN: Let's just forget Tom-Tom, Kathy. I want to talk
             about you. Why did you come to see me?
CATER: To find my mama.
RIORDAN: You came to see me to find your mama? . . .
             Did you come to me because I'm a mama, too?

(No response.)

MRS. SIMMS: I'm back, Mrs. Riordan.

(My secretary, returning from lunch, looked in, as she usually
does, not realizing I had a client.

Without a further word or sign of any kind, the client hurried
from the office. I tried to follow him to get him to return, but
to no avail.

This was my first experience of a so-called "multiple personality." I must do some reading in the literature of the subject to
prepare myself in the event the client returns. The torment of
both "Cater" and "Kathy" is so obvious that I suspect he will
return.)

Block drove to Queens, parking his car in front of one of a
row of semidetached houses, each with a small square of cement
serving as a porch, surrounded by a wrought iron rail, with three
concrete steps leading down to a sloping lawn. Each house was
sided with asphalt shingles, the outer surfaces covered with bits
of colored grit. The colors ran from red to green to blue, then
back to red to start the cycle over. Block selected a house with

green shingles and was met on the little porch by a burly man a few years older than himself.

"Block," he said in greeting. He wore a scoop-neck sleeveless T-shirt, revealing a small red-and-green tattoo of a dragon that breathed fire continuously on his left shoulder. A much larger tattoo of a heart and piercing arrow with the name of Roz written underneath, a memento to a long-gone love during his stint in the Navy, had been removed at the insistence of his first wife, now also long gone. The only remnant of the valentine to Roz was a light-blue tint that rode his bicep, like a perpetual bruise.

"How are you, Keiner?" Block asked as they shook hands.

"Keeping," said Malcolm Keiner. He led Block into his house.

It was like stepping into a florist's, Block thought. Flowers were everywhere, crowding the windows, jamming the shelves and counters, neatly lined like soldiers on parade underneath fluorescent bulbs, hanging from the ceiling in plastic pots, the blossoms trailing over the edges and dangling down like vines.

Keiner watched Block's reaction carefully, closely.

"Pretty, huh?"

"Like plants, do you?"

"Not plants. Flowers. Most people grow rubber plants indoors. Avocado trees. Bromeliads." He named each plant contemptuously, as if reciting a list of public offenders. "Aloes. Ivy. Saber plants. Any asshole can grow a cactus. I grow flowers."

"I see that."

"Impatiens," said Keiner, jerking a finger in the direction of a large decorated clay pot, a riot of pink and red blossoms forming a halo around it. "Also known as 'Busy Lizzy.' Hell of a producer, blooms all year round. You make new ones by taking a cutting and sticking it in water. Want a cutting?" Without waiting for an answer, Keiner snipped off a length of the impatiens, removed the bottom leaves, and stuck it in a jelly glass of water.

"Your wife wants a cutting," he said. "Tell her to pinch it back when it gets new growth, that'll make it spread out. Want me to write that down?"

"Pinch it back," said Block.

"Don't even know what that means, do you? You wife will know." He continued his tour around the room, jabbing a finger at each plant in turn as he named it. "Browallia. Blue flowers. Blue is rare in nature. Geranium. You know a geranium when you see one, Block? Easy to grow outside, not so easy to get to bloom inside. Petunias. Underrated as a houseplant, very prolific."

"It's summer," said Block. "Why don't you have any of these outside?"

Keiner snorted in disgust. "Jesus!" He shook his head, exasperated over a student who just would not learn. "You think like everybody else. Do I grow these plants for the assholes on the street, or dc I grow them for myself?"

Block was pleased to see that a chromium steel plate in his head and enforced early retirement had not stifled his old partner's pugnaciousness.

"You grow them for yourself," said Block dutifully.

"Correct. And do I live outside or inside?"

"You live inside."

"Violets," said Keiner, never one to belabor the point once he had made it. "Pissy little plants, pissy little flowers. I'm not sure they're worth the window space. I'll give you a cutting. Take a leaf, stick it in moist sand. Your wife will know how."

"Thank you," said Block as Keiner snipped off a violet leaf, wrapped it in aluminum foil, and thrust it at him.

"Pissy little plant," said Keiner. "So, what kind of job do you have for me?"

"Who says I have a job? Maybe I came to say hello."

"We said hello at your wedding. That was only a couple months ago and you're not that friendly. What have you got?"

Block searched for a place to sit down. There was lots of furniture to accommodate the plants, very little for humans. He finally settled on a small bench, one end of which was stacked with empty plastic pots, and perched there uncomfortably, brushing a trailing strand of petunias away from his head. Keiner made no attempt to sit. He stood in the middle of the room, hands on his hips like a gardener surveying a pile of compost that had to be turned and mixed. Block glanced around and saw that there was no other place for Keiner to sit.

"Have I taken your seat?" he asked.

"Go ahead, you're tired," said Keiner.

"I'm not tired."

"You look it."

"What do you do if you have a guest?" Block asked.

"If it's an asshole like you, I let him sit on the bench. If it's a woman, I let her sit on my face."

"My guess is you don't get too many visitors."

"That's what makes you an asshole, Block. Bad guesses."

Block struggled with some difficulty to remember that Keiner's unique method of expressing affection was the insult.

"What you got?" Keiner demanded again.

"You know my wife," Block started. He inched a bit farther to one side to get away from the dangling plant and felt the bench begin to teeter beneath him.

"We met at the wedding. She was the one in white. Of course I know your wife. She leave you already?"

"Of course not!" said Block angrily. "What makes you say a thing like that?"

"Touchy, aren't you?"

"I don't see any humor in that kind of remark."

"So, how is your married life?"

"Great."

"That's what I thought of it, too," said Keiner. "Both times. For about a month."

"We don't all have your peculiar problems, Mal."

"You were too old to marry," said Keiner. "And too much of a hermit. If anybody'd asked me, I could have warned you. No wonder you got problems."

"I don't have problems!" said Block, knowing as he did it that he was showing too much heat. "Besides, I've changed since you knew me."

"Uh-huh," said Keiner. "They say a good woman will do that for you."

"Sheila's done it for me," said Block. "She's a very special girl."

"No one's blaming her, pal," said Keiner. "No one's blaming her."

"Could we get to it?" Block asked.

"That's what I've been telling you," said Keiner.

"I'd like you to watch Sheila for a while, specifically in the evenings, from the time she leaves work until she gets home. I've been doing it for a few days, but I can't always be gone from work, the evening's some of my most productive hours."

"Yeah, things start crawling out from under the rocks around then. What am I watching her for?"

"I think she might be in some—" He stopped. He did not want to say "danger," didn't want to formulate it that concretely, as if putting a name to it would make it happen.

"She had an incident of some kind," he said. Block told Keiner of Sheila's experience in the loft and of his own instinct that it was possible, just possible, that somehow Tom-Tom knew he was after him and had doubled back. Keiner wandered through the room checking his plants as Block talked, pressing a finger into the soil here, pinching back a shoot there.

"You don't have much to go on," Keiner said when Block had finished.

"Nothing at all, really," said Block. "That's why I can't request official police protection. It's just a feeling. I love her, Mal. I'm worried about her."

Keiner dropped his eyes to the floor at the sight of sentiment on Block's face. Like Block, he had spent most of his adult life avoiding displays of sentiment, and it embarrassed him. He suspected it embarrassed Block as well.

"So, you want a bodyguard for her."

"No. I don't want her to know about it. It would scare her out of her wits if she thought she needed a bodyguard. I just want you to tail her, see she gets home safely. I'll make sure she doesn't spend any time alone in the loft. . . . See if anyone's following her."

Block did not mention Florio. If he really was following Sheila,

Keiner would discover it. And if he wasn't, Block did not want to give any fuel to Keiner's cynicism. The innuendos were bad enough in Block's own mind, where he could control them. To hear them voiced by an outsider might be more than he could take without exploding. He didn't know how to explain Florio's relationship with Sheila to Keiner; he didn't know how to explain it to himself.

"I can pay your expenses, Mal," he said. "That's about all."

"Don't insult me," said Keiner. "When do you want me to start?"

"Tonight."

"Why not?"

As Block left, Keiner hurried out of the house after him.

"Don't forget your cuttings," said Keiner. "Your wife will want them."

Block took the cuttings in their aluminum wrappings and put them on the car seat. He left them there for days until they dried, then threw them away.

The audience was a tough one and Rosemary was
working hard. No harder than usual, maybe, but then
it was always tough gouging a laugh out of the late-
night audience. The early show was usually a much
better crowd, a married crowd, Mom and Pop out for a drink
and dinner and some entertainment, glad for it, happy to laugh.
She had worked the *Merv Griffin* show once and had been delighted and surprised at how easy it was. That audience came
wanting to be entertained. Not defying you to entertain them,
like the late-show people.

Rosemary knew she was in trouble as soon as she hit the stage
and saw the solitary guy sitting alone at the table right down
front. People didn't laugh much when they were alone. They
might think it was funny, but they wouldn't laugh unless someone was with them. And this guy didn't look as if he'd laughed
for the past decade or so anyway. He wasn't drunk, either. Just
sullen and mean looking, sitting there, glaring at her. What did
he think she was doing, *Hamlet?*

"Rosemary Schwarz, is that a name?" she demanded, heaving
her bulk from one side of the stage to the other.

"That's not a name, that's a contradiction in terms. Rosemary
Schwarz? Rosemary's a Catholic name, right?"

She stood in front of the solitary guy. "Do I look Catholic to
you? Tell the truth." She tipped the hand mike toward him.
As she had hoped, he kept glaring and said not a word.

"Sorry to disturb you," she said. "It takes time to get over
those lobotomies, doesn't it?" If you can't amuse them, use them.

The audience tittered, craning to see if she had provoked the customer to a response. He continued to stare at her as if he didn't realize she was making fun of him. He was beginning to unnerve her a bit.

"I hope you remembered to leave a wake-up call," she said. Again no response from the man. Rosemary turned away to work the other side of the stage.

After a few minutes she swung around again. The guy was still staring at her as if she were a pork chop slapped down on a Moslem's plate.

"Hey, are you still staring?" she said. "Somebody ask him what he sees in me, will you? I'd like to tell my husband . . . I'd like to *find* my husband. No, but listen, you think I got this way by my husband?" She patted the front of her maternity dress. "That's what he thinks, too. You're both wrong. . . . No, seriously, this was a miracle. If you saw my husband, you'd say, 'She let *him* do that? That's a miracle!' . . . No, I feel like I've been pregnant forever—you know the feeling, don't you, ladies?—I've been like this so long, whoever's in there's never coming out. She's set up housekeeping, you know what I mean? . . . Hey, you got to get out of there, the place is going co-op! . . . Get out, what are you, crazy, I just put in new kitchen cabinets!"

The guy was staring at her with even darker intensity. Rosemary sashayed her huge bulk toward him again, rolling her hips.

"I love to see the customers having such a good time," she said. "Look at this guy," she urged the audience. "I'm killing him. You'd never know it but he's dying from internal bleeding."

When she glanced back at him he was grinning at her with a vicious sneer. It was more like a snarl than a smile, and Rosemary wished she hadn't seen it. It looked like a death's head sneer.

Backstage, in the overgrown closet the management called a dressing room, Rosemary scrubbed away at her face with cold cream while her manager, Marvin Green, spoke to her in his soft, breathy voice.

"Did you see him, did you see that guy?" Rosemary growled.

"No, I missed him, Rosemary," said Green.

"He sat there like a stone, like a boulder, like Mount Rushmore," she said.

"Like Mount Rushmore." Green chuckled softly. "That's funny, Rosemary."

"No, it ain't funny, Marvin." She glowered at her reflection in the mirror as she rubbed the cold cream into her chin. Nature had given her an oily, hairy complexion which she loathed. Nature had also given her the ability to make people laugh. The obesity she had developed all on her own.

"Then all of a sudden he was snarling at me like a dog. Like Mount Rushmore with an orthodontia problem."

Green smiled uncertainly.

"That's funny, Marvin."

Green chuckled appreciatively. "It was a good show, Rosemary," he said.

"Uh," she grunted. "They're a dead crowd, Marvin. I've done better shows in a cemetery. When are you going to get me a decent booking? I'm not some *unknown*, you know. I killed them on the Griffin show."

Green shifted uncomfortably. "You were terrific on the Griffin show," he said, wondering how long she could expect him to continue to parlay a one-time visit three years ago into bookings. "You know, Rosemary, watching you tonight I had an idea. Just an idea, you understand, you might not like it, it's just off the top of my head."

"Off the top of your head, what's it, dandruff? You keep it, Marvin, I got enough problems."

"No, no," he protested, chuckling. "It's a thought, Rosemary. Probably not a good one."

"All right, what is it?"

"Maybe you could drop the pregnancy jokes? I mean, they're very funny, they're really dynamite material . . . but you've been doing that pregnancy routine for four years. I mean, I don't think anyone really thinks you're pregnant anymore."

"What am I supposed to do, fat jokes? I hate fat jokes! Fat isn't funny, Marvin."

"Totie Fields did some really funny stuff. . . ."

"Don't give me Totie Fields! Get me a decent booking, that's your job, Marvin. I'll do the comedy, you do the booking! All right with you, Marvin?"

"Sure, Rosemary," he said meekly.

"You want a fat joke? I'm going to change clothes, you stick around, you'll see a fat joke."

Green edged toward the door.

"Come on, Marvin, stick around. You think fat is so funny, I'll give you hilarious."

"I'll talk to you tomorrow, Rosemary," he said, closing the door quickly behind him as she began to pull the maternity dress over her head.

Fairly early in their relationship, Green had made love to Rosemary. They were on the road, somewhere outside of Pittsburgh, and both were lonely and a little drunk. Marvin had made a manly attempt, but when it came right down to it her mountainous bulk had been too repellent to him and he had failed. He had been gallant, blaming the booze, but it had never happened again, and Rosemary did not blame him. She found her body as unattractive as Marvin did, as most men did. There were those who were drawn to her, of course, men who liked obesity, but with the contrariness of the human spirit, Rosemary would have nothing to do with them. Any man who was attracted to her was, by her definition, a pervert. The only men she wanted were those who were right-minded enough not to want her. She had arranged things in her cosmology so that her self-loathing was constantly reinforced. When people looked away in embarrassment from her bulk, she ate more to assuage the pain. When they laughed at her on stage, she felt as if it were only a continuation of the endless laughter she heard behind her back in real life. Rosemary loved to hate herself, but she was not happy about it. She made others laugh and had the saddest life she knew.

As usual, you couldn't get a cab when you wanted one. Rosemary walked the four blocks to the subway, unworried about the late hour or the dark streets. She felt shielded by her bulk against muggers, as if no one would want to harm her since she was so intent on harming herself. As for rape, the specter that haunted countless women in the city, Rosemary thought it was more likely that her weight would snap an elevator cable and she would fall to her death than that anyone would think of forcing himself on her. Rapists have *some* taste, she thought. Whether there was any justification for this sense of invulnerability was hard to say, but Rosemary tested it every chance she got, walking wherever and whenever she wanted in the city. Walking soon made her fatigued and breathless, however, so she never went far.

About a block away from the club she thought she noticed the guy who had stared at her through her act walking behind her. He was on the other side of the street and she couldn't be sure, but he seemed to glance her way more than once. People did that sometimes. They would recognize, or half recognize her, from her appearance on the Griffin show, and follow her for a distance until they could put name and face (or body) and circumstances together. Rosemary didn't really mind, it was one of the prices for semi-celebrity. Sometimes they would come up with a name and confront her with it. "Aren't you so-and-so?" they would demand, as if she had been trying to fool them and they were triumphant in their small victory. The fact that they usually had the wrong name wasn't really important. Sometimes she would say yes, she was so-and-so, and let them go off happy. A star had a responsibility to her public, after all. To anyone's public, for that matter.

When the guy followed her into the subway station, she put him in a different category. He wasn't curious, he wasn't starstruck. He was what he had appeared to be in the club, a creep. He stayed at the other end of the platform from her but she could feel his eyes on her all the time. She hated to be stared at except by a fan, and whatever else this guy was, he wasn't a fan. She considered confronting him, demanding what he wanted, threatening him if he didn't leave her alone. Creep or not, she wasn't afraid of him; her size gave her certain advantages, and one was the power to intimidate. If she chose to lean all her weight on him, only the strongest of men could withstand it.

The subway arrived and Rosemary entered; the creep got into a car at the other end. She surveyed the people in the car—the usual motley assortment of blacks, Hispanics, drunks, and hopheads. No one else took the subway at this hour of the night unless they traveled in pairs. One of the Hispanics looked at her and made some sneering comment in Spanish to his companion, but Rosemary fixed him with such a hostile glare that he soon looked away in confusion.

Just before the train squealed to a halt at her stop, Rosemary saw a face peering through the door that led to the next car. The creep was standing in the little vestibule between cars, balancing in the roaring darkness and watching her. For the first time Rosemary felt a little bit frightened.

Her apartment was less than a block from the subway station and she covered it as quickly as she could without running. He was still behind her, but not trying to catch up with her. She told herself she was being silly, no one would care enough about her to want to hurt her, but still she felt a surge of relief when she closed the lobby door behind her. She made sure the lock clicked into place before walking up a flight to her apartment.

As she always did, Rosemary had a late-night snack before going to bed. Remembering her manager's hesitant advice, she took out her tape recorder and worked on her new routine as she ate. She knew she needed new material and had been working on it for weeks, trying to keep things within the old format, but shifting the ingredients, taking the emphasis off the pregnant bit.

She listened to the material she had recorded earlier in the day, then started to record and recited it all again, working on the timing, the pauses, the delivery that turned an ordinary line into an irresistible joke.

"They say living in New York City is tough," she said to the machine as she sliced herself a slab of chicken breast. "Hey, tough? What's tough? . . ."

Then she knew he was in the apartment with her. He had been here all along, waiting for her, had slipped in ahead of her. She didn't know how she knew he was there, she hadn't seen him or heard him, but her body knew and a chilling shudder shook her whole body and the hairs on the back of her neck prickled as if jerked by static electricity.

The telephone was in her bedroom, impossibly far away. To get to the door she would have to pass the darkened mouth of the bedroom, stand with her back to it while she turned the lock, released the chain, opened the door. Her back would be exposed every step of the way. She had never known this kind of fear before, never felt it on the street where others hurried looking over their shoulders, hearts jumping at the sound of footsteps behind them. She had never felt it in the deserted subways where others sat and trembled in expectation of swift and certain harm.

But now, cowering in her kitchen with the man with the death-head's grin somewhere in the other room, Rosemary Schwarz, who had often wished she were dead, decided she wanted to live. Looking down at the carving knife she held in her hand, she decided it was not big enough. Still watching the door that led into the kitchen, she found a cleaver, a short, heavy thick-bladed utensil with obscure Oriental markings on the handle. The very weight of it in her hand was reassuring.

Rosemary stood in the door of the kitchen and listened. She

could hear nothing. From this vantage she could see most of the living room she had to cross to get to the hallway door. There was no place to hide. If he was here—and she was already beginning to doubt that he was—he would have to be in the coat closet next to the door, or in the bedroom. If it was the closet, she could lean against the door and keep him in there and still reach the locks on the door. If he was in the closet, she could make it. If he was in the closet.

She inched into the living room, reluctant to leave the kitchen behind her, as if it were home base and she would always be safe there. She took another step, her eyes glued to the bedroom, the cleaver up, ready to strike. She had a weapon, which made her feel a little better, and her bulk was a weapon, too. Unless the guy was a sumo wrestler, she should be able to flatten him with her weight. If her fright didn't paralyze her first. She took another step toward the hallway door. There had still been neither sight nor sound of anyone and the humor of the situation—if there was no one else in the apartment—started to force itself on her. Well, she could put it in the act, she thought, once she got safely out that door. Rosemary the elephant tiptoeing through her apartment, brandishing an ax—she would make it an ax, that sounded sillier. . . .

She heard the sound of a child crying, a brief, muffled sob, more of a hiccough of sorrow. What the hell was this? Rosemary wondered. Someone was in her apartment, all right, but it wasn't the creep, it was a kid. She heard the sob again, still muffled, so it was hard to locate exactly. She moved toward the bedroom, baffled but relieved.

"Hey, kid," she said. "What are you doing in here?"

Behind her the coat closet door opened and Tom-Tom stepped out quietly. He saw the cleaver in her hand and flicked off the light switch by the hallway door, plunging the room into darkness.

Rosemary wheeled around, swinging the cleaver violently through the darkness in front of her. Her eyes had been used to the light and now in the sudden darkness she was effectively blinded. She could not see the guy in front of her, but she sensed that he was there. She swung the cleaver again, then back, then across, then back, grunting each time with the effort.

"Come on, Tom-Tom," she said, defiantly, realizing for the first time that it was he. She had seen the phantom killer who dominated the news, she could identify him—if only she could survive him.

There was a whizzing noise and something hit her on the side of the head. It did not hurt her, but it stunned her and she took too long to react. When she swung the cleaver, it was only flailing at air. The thing hit her on the other side. It was soft, but had concussive power, like being hit hard by a pillow. She lashed out to her left, too late. The cleaver struck the wall and jarred in her hand. She yanked it out of the wall with both hands and waited for Tom-Tom to move again.

The third time she was ready. As she heard the sound of the thing coming at her she stepped forward, unafraid of the impact. The thing caught her on the raised forearm and pushed her off balance. Her other hand grasped at the blackness and touched cloth. With her grip squeezing his shoulder, she lunged forward and slammed into him with all three hundred pounds.

Tom-Tom was pinned against the wall with all of Rosemary's weight against him. She raised the cleaver and brought it down, felt it rip into something soft. She swung it again and felt it strike its target once more, wondering why he didn't cry out.

As she tried to swing again, he caught her wrist. She was heavy but not strong, and he forced her arm backward, the cleaver dangling helplessly. With his other hand he grabbed her hair and yanked downward. His entire fist was wrapped in her hair, pulling back and down until she thought her neck would break. She tried to scream then, but because her neck was bowed so severely, only a strangled gasp escaped her lips. The cleaver clattered to the floor and Tom-Tom hit her exposed throat with something metallic. She couldn't believe the pain. After that she couldn't cry out at all.

Still pulling on her hair, he kneed her once in the belly and she toppled backward. Once on the floor, her bulk worked against her. On her back she was like a turtle tipped onto its shell and all she could do was try to cover up with her hands as his kicks and blows hammered at her.

Toward the end she could hear him talking, yelling almost, but she didn't know what he was saying. She only knew he was killing her.

13

Marvin Green stuck close to Block, glancing nervously at Florio, who had finally released him after a grilling that left Green feeling weak and guilty.

"He acts like I did it," Green whined. "I reported it, I came here and I found poor Rosemary, and I reported it."

"I know," said Block, giving Green only enough attention to avoid an appearance of rudeness. The little man had just had more than enough rudeness from Florio during the examination, which Block had listened to from a distance. Florio was not a subtle questioner, his entire manner bristled with suspicion as if everyone were lying to him, but the implicit threat of his presence and demeanor usually got the truth. Or at least the truth as perceived by the witness, which was as close as one could hope for.

"If I'd killed her, would I have reported it?" Green demanded.

"It happens," said Block. He was examining a velvet bolster from the couch. It was as long as a man's arm and thicker than a man's thigh, and it had been slashed deeply twice by the meat cleaver that lay on the floor beside it.

Rosemary's body had been removed but white chalk marks traced the outline of where she had lain. The outline seemed large enough for two people.

"How big a person was she?" asked Block.

"Rosemary? You never saw Rosemary Schwarz?"

"How big was she, Mr. Green?" Block asked patiently. "Was she a big person?"

"She was *famous* for being big," said Green, insulted for his client, still struggling for recognition even in death.

Block tapped the chalk outline with his toe. "Does this look right?" he asked. The size was difficult to associate with a woman.

Green looked down at the silhouette of a body lying supine on the floor and remembered the motel outside Pittsburgh, Rosemary lying naked on the bed, beckoning him, arms outstretched, like a whale waiting to eat him up.

"I would have thought a little bigger," said Green finally.

Block nodded. She must have been huge, that would explain why she hadn't been hurled around like the others. Judging by the pattern of bloodstains, she died where she had fallen, trapped by gravity. At least she had made a fight of it, he thought, looking at the slashed bolster.

"This man she saw at the club, the one she was concerned about, what'd he look like?"

"I told the other officer," said Green. "I never saw him. I was in the back of the club, watching the act and having a drink. To tell you the truth, I wasn't paying a whole lot of attention to the act, I've heard it an awful lot of times. There was a guy, she was working him over pretty good. She told me about him later. I suppose he was the one, but all I ever saw was the back of his head."

"All right," said Block. "Tell me about the back of his head."

"What are you, kidding? What can I say about the back of a man's head?"

"Was he a white man?"

"Yeah."

"Did he have hair, or was he bald?"

"He had hair. A full head."

"What color?"

"It was dark in there."

"Red? White? Gray? Blond?"

"Brown," said Green. "Brown or black."

"Curly, wavy, straight?"

"It wasn't curly, that's all I remember. What are you going to learn from the guy's hair?"

"I'm going to learn all I can," said Block.

Green inched closer to Block as Florio came in from the bedroom carrying a dress.

"You said she wasn't pregnant!" said Florio, waving the dress in Green's face. "This is a maternity dress. They're all maternity dresses!"

"It was for the act, she pretended to be pregnant," said Green, edging away from Florio's anger.

"What was she, doing the act all the time? This is the only kind of dress she's got!"

"It was the only thing that would fit," said Green, and for the first time since he discovered her body he was overcome with a real sense of sorrow for Rosemary. At first he'd been too stunned for it to sink in, then too bewildered by the police activity. Now the pathos of Rosemary's life, condemned to clothe herself in tents designed for women bursting with life while she was stuffed by an urge for self-destruction, welled up and threatened to drown him. Tears were in his eyes as Florio turned disgustedly away from him.

"I think I saw her once," Block said suddenly. "A fat woman who joked about being pregnant? I think it was on television. The Carson show?"

"Merv Griffin," said Green. "She killed them on the Griffin show, they loved her."

"She was very funny," Block said. Actually he remembered her as being rather distasteful, but the case had taken a sudden turn, wheeling back upon itself, and in some oblique way Block felt that Tom-Tom had touched his pursuer. Other than Rachel, Rosemary Schwarz was the first person Block had ever known in any way who was the victim of murder. He had heard of Alicia Caro, but never seen her, and all the other victims over his long career had been faceless entities who had never touched upon his life before their deaths. Here, represented by chalk marks, was a person whom Block had seen alive. He had chuckled or grimaced at her, she had worked on a stage to amuse him, and he felt that his life had been diminished a small amount by her death. He sensed that Tom-Tom had passed close by him in the dark and he had caught a whiff of his foul odor.

Preceded by a puff of smoke from his pipe, Quayle emerged from the kitchen, holding a tape recorder in his hand.

"You'll want to hear this," he said to Block.

"We'll need you for more questions later," said Block to Green as he gestured to a uniformed officer to remove the manager. Block went into the kitchen with Quayle and they listened to the tape once.

Back in the laboratory, technicians made two copies of the tape and gave one to Block. He listened to it in his office, playing it over and over. After the first time he had given up any hope of understanding the words; what he wanted now was to recognize the voice. Recognition skirted around the edges of his consciousness. There was something familiar about the voice at the same time that it was utterly alien. It was like trying to think of the name of someone from the past—suggested answers kept presenting themselves, and while he knew they were wrong, he also knew they had some underlying connection with the truth. The harder he tried to remember, the more it eluded him. Finally, Block took the tape to Harvey Aaron at Columbia.

"First is just her monologue, rehearsing for her show," explained Block. He and Aaron sat in the professor's office where the walls were decorated with Dürer prints of hands and rabbits and plants.

Block started the tape on a protracted silence. Faint noises were audible in the background, sounds of Rosemary moving about the kitchen, dropping the carving knife, scraping the cleaver across the table.

"Her machine was a good one," said Block. "We're analyzing those background noises at the lab. They'll amplify them and maybe learn something about what was going on, but I doubt it. This is what I want you to hear."

There was the sound of a muffled scream and Aaron winced. After another pause, he heard the voice.

"Right there," said Block, reversing the tape to a point just after the scream. "This is Tom-Tom. I want to know what language he's speaking and what he's saying." He started the tape again and a man's voice leaped out at them. Harsh and explosive, totally foreign and yet somehow familiar. Words were punctuated by the eruptive sounds which Aaron had told Block were glottal stops. The voice continued for about three minutes, speaking its foreign tongue in an increasingly higher pitch until it finally stopped abruptly. There was a moment of silence, then the sound of a child whimpering. The tape ran out with an audible click.

"There was a child there?" Aaron asked, aghast.

Block studied the print of the rabbit. It looked alive enough to twitch its nose.

"We're trying to find that out," he said.

"God, I hope not," said Aaron. "I mean, Tom-Tom killed somebody during this, didn't he? Can you imagine a child's witnessing that? Can you imagine what it would do to the child's psyche?"

"I've been imagining it for a month," said Block.

"You mean—there was a child at the other killings?"

Block nodded.

"The same child?"

The detective exhaled suddenly as if he had just climbed a great height. "It looks that way," he said.

"My God," said Aaron.

"Help us find the son of a bitch," said Block. As he said it, he realized that he truly hated Tom-Tom, and the thing he hated about him most was not the appalling fact that he had a child with him when he killed—Block had become as used to that idea as one could—but something new that had come out on the tape. The witness Maeve Kline had suggested it, but Block had not fully appreciated it until he heard it himself.

"The bastard sounds like he's enjoying it . . . no, it's more than that. He sounds—joyous."

"Ecstatic," said Aaron. "I would have said ecstatic."

Block was summoned to the medical examiner's office by Dr. Bobby Ching, an assistant coroner. Ching was an expert at his craft, as good at dissecting cadavers and discovering what had made them that way as anyone in the trade. Like virtually everyone else, Ching hated the M.E., but unlike most everyone else, he also loved his job. There was a quiet beauty to the human body stripped and laid bare to the bone that Ching could never convey to anyone else. The genius and symmetry of nature was revealed to Ching every day on the dissecting table, giving him a deep and secret look at the mystery of life even as it lay cloaked in death. He also thought he had a good shot at the M.E.'s job if he could hang on for another couple of years.

Rosemary Schwarz's huge bulk lay on the table, stitched down the middle by a heavy black thread that closed the incision running from sternum to navel from which her internal organs had been removed. Block was moved by the serenity on her face, as if death had been a gentle acceptance of ultimate peace instead of a brutal, insane battering.

"A curiosity here," said Ching, pointing at Rosemary's neck with a marking pencil. "Thought you might like to look at this." With a pencil he drew a sketchy circle around a red mark.

There was a clear imprint, three quarters of an inch across and nearly four inches long. Her body was covered with contusions, but none of them had the clarity of this mark.

"What did he hit her with?" Block asked.

"I have no idea," said Ching, "but it was enough of a blow to crush her windpipe. You'll notice it's the only mark that's really clear. All the rest of them have the diffuse appearance. The reason, I suspect, is that this is one of the few times he hit her where she didn't have any clothing. It takes a very sharp instrument to leave a specific mark through clothing, even hitting her as hard as he did. He's been very careful up to now, the only marks on the face have been kicks. You notice these?"

He drew three smaller circles, leading away from the large one. In each circle was a smaller welt, distinct from the next one.

"What do you make of those?" Block asked.

"Don't know," said Ching. "Just thought you might want to see them."

"Did any of the other victims have marks like this?"

"I went back and checked the photos—nothing. As I said, he's been very careful about hitting them where nothing incriminating would show up."

"She must have given him quite a struggle," said Block. Looking at the grotesque size of the corpse, he could imagine it. "He must have been a little desperate."

"Funny," said Ching. "I know you don't mean it, but when you say that about his being desperate, it almost sounds as if you feel sorry for him."

"Not him," said Block. "I feel sorry for his mind. How could anyone live with all that hatred?" He turned away from the corpse abruptly. "I'd like a close-up of those marks, actual size. Can you do it?"

"Sure," said Ching, although it had not really been a question.

Block paused outside, his hand arrested on the door of his car. His remark to Ching had left him puzzled. Since when had he felt any sympathy for Tom-Tom? He was closer to this case than to any he had ever had. Everything about it seemed vaguely familiar, as if he had seen it all before. Even the marks on Rosemary Schwarz's neck seemed recognizable if only he could clear the film from his eyes. He wondered if he was giving the case his best effort. Maybe the hours he was putting into it were only a mask for the one obvious leap of intuition he refused to make.

"My wife thinks we haven't found him yet because we're men," McKeon was saying. "She says it's like the birth control business. If Tom-Tom was killing men, she thinks we would of caught him by now."

Florio laughed aloud and the others smiled. They all knew McKeon's wife, Nell, and pitied their colleague—when they weren't thinking that he deserved her.

"It's not funny," McKeon continued. "She's making my life hell."

"That's her job, isn't it?" Florio asked.

"You think it's a joke, Florio?"

"I don't think Tom-Tom's a joke. You and your wife might be. Depends on your sense of humor."

"It's easy for you. You don't have any women to worry about. You don't have a wife who thinks this lunatic might decide someday that she looks pregnant."

"I have women to worry about," Florio said quietly.

Block stared at him.

"I don't mean hookers," said McKeon.

"I'm going to excuse you, McKeon, because you're stupid and can't be held accountable."

McKeon jumped up angrily, thrusting his chest out. A dark stain spread across his shirt front.

"I ain't stupid!"

"How would you know?"

"Cut it out, Lou," Block said sharply. "Sit down, McKeon."

"I don't have to take that crap from him," said McKeon. But he sat down, grateful that Block had interceded. He wanted no part of Florio in a fight.

Captain Byrne studied the tiny desk fan which provided him with the only small comfort in the room. Originally he had debated whether his own comfort was sufficient to negate the anger his detectives would feel when they realized the fan worked only in his direction—and decided it was. Now he kept his eyes on the fan, ignoring the Florio-McKeon exchange. Behavior he did not notice he would not be compelled to act upon, and the tight collar of discipline was the last thing his men needed now. They were all hot and uncomfortable, nerves were frayed, tempers short. The pressure of the Tom-Tom case had gotten to all of them.

Pressure is something a cop lives with. The greatest sense of urgency comes from the policemen's friends, neighbors, family. Where was he when they needed a cop? What was he doing to make the streets safe? Why doesn't he see to it that fewer traffic tickets are issued and more thugs put behind bars? This is normal, everyday pressure that comes with the job.

The Tom-Tom case provided an extra pressure to every cop on the force. There wasn't one of them who didn't know a niece, a sister, a cousin, a friend's friend's wife who was a potential victim. And in the case of the homicide cops, the situation was unusual. Agatha Christie notwithstanding, murder is normally the easiest crime to solve. Many people have reason to steal. Very few have reason to murder. Homicide cops know that most of the time the murderer is a member of the family or a friend, someone who can work up enough passion to pull a trigger or thrust a knife. Sometimes, though rarely, the killer is motivated by greed, and again the chain of circumstance and profit is easy to establish. It is only the unmotivated murder, the seemingly random killing that is difficult. A series of such killings is proportionately very rare—and always takes a long time to solve. Homicide cops fear such a killer as doctors fear an unknown virus. In both cases, the sleuthing is long, arduous, and frustrating. A pathologist, however, does not usually have his neighbors accusing him of dragging his feet.

Although McKeon's case was exaggerated by the shrewishness of his wife, they all understood what he was going through. They laughed, but without amusement.

Byrne had spent the last twenty minutes adding his own weight to the pressure. He had gone over the facts in the case, dragging the pathetically thin skein of data into the open so they could all examine it. The overriding fact was that they still knew alarmingly little about Tom-Tom. Routine policework had turned up next to nothing. Which left science.

Byrne adjusted the fan a millimeter and turned to Quayle. He did not bother to speak, merely waited for stillness, then raised an eyebrow at the forensic expert.

Quayle was waiting.

"Don't look to me for miracles," he said. "I can examine what you give me, I can't create evidence."

Quayle was sweating profusely. The beads of perspiration stood out on his forehead and on his left cheek several of them had formed a rivulet that ran down under his collar. Block could not understand why the man didn't take off his suit coat. Quayle was the only one in the room not in shirt-sleeves. Even Captain Byrne had long since shed his jacket and ripped off his tie.

"I have absolutely nothing new to tell you. I know what you want. You want me to find a thread that proves he's wearing a suit made of rhinoceros, the only one sold in New York in the last five years. Well, he's not. He buys his clothes off the rack just like all the rest of us. He wears shoes like everybody else, too. His heel isn't built up, he isn't a clubfoot. He doesn't kill with a garrotte used only by hill tribes in India. He uses nails and the women's own kitchen implements. I can only tell you what he isn't. He isn't black, he isn't female, he isn't weak. That leaves us with one or two million candidates in the city. Give me more evidence and I can tell you more, but don't expect miracles from me."

Byrne let the silence hang for a moment after Quayle had finished, trying to control his annoyance at the man's manner. Quayle had not been alone. Virtually everyone to speak had been defensive. They had all done the best with what they had, they argued. And Byrne believed them. They had. The problem was that what they had amounted to so very little.

Byrne surveyed the assembled men, looking for some positive note on which to end the meeting. His gaze came to rest at last on Block. Block started to speak, then stopped.

Byrne raised his eyebrow again, but Block shook his head. After Byrne had dismissed the men, he detained Block.

"You were going to say something," Byrne said.

"Nothing I want to defend in front of everyone," said Block.

"Just to me, then."

Block paused. "I think we're getting closer to him," he said.

"How?"

Block shrugged. "I said I wouldn't want to defend it. I just have a feeling. He's making a few mistakes. . . . Let's just leave it that I have a feeling."

How does a spider know when a fly has hit his web, Block wanted to say. I can feel the tremors of the creature thrashing. But he did not say it.

14

Sheila felt as good as a woman with morning sickness could. The first morning the nausea overcame her she ascribed it to something she had eaten. The second time she began to suspect and after the third time she hurried to the doctor. It was easy enough to keep it a secret from her husband. Block was so immersed in his pursuit of Tom-Tom he paid little attention to anything happening at home. Which was just as well, because she wanted to be absolutely sure when she told him. She was aware of his ambivalence about having children, but she knew he would be overjoyed when she revealed the surprise at last.

He did not disappoint her. She came from her morning bout with nausea and saw him looking at her oddly. The doctor's report had come the day before, but he had not been there to share it.

"Sandy, we're going to have a baby."

The film of concern on his face cracked and he burst into a laugh. He grabbed her and whirled her around the room with joy. Stopping at last because he feared she would get dizzy, he put her carefully on the sofa. Kneeling beside her, he stroked her face adoringly, then kissed her softly on the lips, the cheeks, the eyes. Then, laughing, he pressed his ear to her stomach in a wildly premature effort to listen to the baby. As Sheila stroked his head, she thought how much alike milestone moments of joy are for everyone. We must look like a cliché from a greeting card, she thought. The thought did not diminish her happiness at all.

When she came home from work that evening she found a gift-wrapped box with a single red rose laid across the top. Block had come to the apartment during the day and scrawled a note on a sheet torn from the telephone scratch pad:

Rose is for you, the rest for our baby. Love and Love, S.

Holding it to the sunlight still coming through the kitchen window, Sheila regarded a tiny quilt, elaborately filigreed with delicate lace. A wave of love for her husband swept over her. Theirs would be a special child, she thought. Bathed in love from both parents, endowed with his mother's vitality, his father's decency and dedication. Sheila and Sandy would love each other all the more for having the child, and they would love the child all the more for loving each other. They would live happily ever after. At that moment it seemed a certainty. It was easy to forget there was a madman preying on pregnant women who all had had much the same dream.

It was a short walk from her apartment to the obstetrician's office on Seventy-second Street between Amsterdam and Columbus, and Sheila made the journey in the morning before work. She loved sitting in the waiting room with all the other pregnant women. It was as if she had joined a large but exclusive club and they all shared a wonderful secret that the rest of the world didn't know and couldn't understand. She felt adult in a way she had never felt before. Being a mother forced one into maturity, ready or not, she thought, and she welcomed it. Much as she loved Sandy, she had always felt that being childless had kept her at one remove from the real world of grownups. Being childless seemed to her like two single people living together, playing at house. She was no longer playing, and was enraptured by the realization. At the same time she felt very youthful. But not in a callow way. Young as springtime is young: greening and fertile.

She walked briskly, happily away from the office, a pretty
young woman, her long soft brown hair swaying behind her.
She was smiling, pleased with herself, revealing her large, perfect, gleaming teeth, slightly protruding from her lips. As she
walked she unconsciously cradled her stomach—still perfectly
flat—with both her arms.

Sheila did not glance at the coffee shop on the corner. She
did not see the man who sat in the booth by the window, watching her. He had watched her go into the obstetrician's office
and had waited until she came out. When she passed by, almost
close enough to touch him, the man began to laugh silently, his
shoulders shaking, His face was twisted into a sneer. Occasionally a sound burst forth, harsh and startling. The waitress looked
at the man staring so raptly at the pretty young woman, but she
did not rush to fill his coffee cup. She knew he was no tipper.

Tom-Tom left the coffee shop and watched Sheila until she
turned the corner and left his sight. He did not need to follow
her now. He knew where to find her. And he had seen her
come from the obstetrician's office. He knew all he needed to
know about her.

Florio took Sheila's photo from his drawer and propped it on
the night table. As it always did, the picture evoked an immediate response from him, a tingling that spread from his scrotum
and stomach into his chest. It was a strange mix of excitement
and anxiety, as if just looking at her made some demands on him
which he was not sure he could fulfill. Melancholy warred with
stimulation.

With the picture still in view, Florio lay on the floor, his feet
on the bed, and did sit-ups until his stomach muscles quivered
with fatigue and burned with pain. Love was making him a better person. He would slim down, tone up, and spread the
warmth of his newly discovered joy on others. Already he was
nicer with other people, he thought. The few tarts he had slept
with since their dinner when he realized he loved Sheila had

been the recipients of his new generosity of spirit. He had neither abused nor belittled any of them, and on one occasion he had struggled to see that the woman was fulfilled as well as himself, a courtesy so unexpected she had pushed him roughly away, accusing him of not knowing when he was finished.

Afterward he had come home and slept in his own bed, awaking sober and feeling chaste. Florio burned with a flame that did not consume. He expected nothing of Sheila but to be. His was the same purity of love that the knights of chivalry had espoused, love that needed and expected no requiting. It was sufficient to bear the lady's banner, to do good in her name.

Sheila left work earlier than had become her custom, planning on a long stroll through the streets at twilight. The heat was bearable by then and the humidity had started to lift. The sun dipped below the skyscrapers nearly an hour before it fell beneath the earth's horizon, casting the city into a prolonged dusk that would allow her to walk as long as she liked and still be home before it was truly dark.

On Broadway a man was playing the bagpipes, the shrill notes of Scotland skirling through the warm, alien air of New York, as out of place as kilts and a tam o'shanter. The bagpiper was dressed in jeans and a work shirt, however, and his long hair was pulled back in a ponytail secured by a rubber band. Funny, he doesn't look Scottish, Sheila thought wryly. A black cloth lay on the sidewalk at his feet and a few coins had been dropped into a cigar box. Sheila loved the idea of street musicians, preferring to think of them as troubadors, bringing song and mirth to the scattered castles of a feudal landscape—not as street beggars, playing on sympathy as much as mediocre talents. She stood at the edge of the cloth, rummaging for coins, becoming as much a part of the spectacle to the other passersby as the bagpiper himself. Sheila felt herself being watched, by the piper and the spectators, to see how much she would give. Self-consciously she scooped all of her change and knelt, dropping it carefully into the cigar box so it wouldn't bounce onto the pavement. She glanced at the man to see if he had noticed, but his eyes remained fixed on the middle distance. Once the money had been given, the donation made, it seemed superfluous to stay and actually listen to the music. Much as she wouldn't take a pencil from a blind man after dropping a coin in his cup, Sheila didn't feel she should take the sounds of the bagpipes now that she'd paid for them. She hurried off, chased by her charity.

New York City was attempting to contort itself into a medieval street fair, twisting itself backward in time as if trying to deny the towering buildings, the technology, the frantic pace of modern urban life. Samples of the worst of the cuisines of many nations, all simplified and Americanized for easy vending from a pushcart, vied for the passing dollar with entertainers of all kinds. A hapless juggler continued a nonstop comedy patter even though few stayed long enough to get the point of any of the jokes. An escape artist encouraged strangers to wrap him in ropes and chains. Sleight-of-hand artists cheated foolhardy customers at three-card monte played on upturned cardboard boxes placed atop trash baskets.

All that was missing was a dancing bear and multicolored costumes topped by jesters' caps with tinkling bells. If New York was not medieval London in the summertime, it was not for lack of trying. On the Avenue of the Americas where the recessed buildings and mini-courtyards allowed crowds to assemble, the artists had gathered in clusters. A wild-eyed violinist sawed away at a curious composition of discordances that seemed to be improvised from a nightmare. Sheila thought the sound so terrible she could not imagine how the man expected to make any money, but his violin case was nearly overflowing with crumpled bills, conscience money from those who had no appreciation of classical music, but thought they should.

Less than fifty yards away a weary but earnest-looking young couple were playing a flute duet. Unamplified, the music wafted away, rising upward with the heat, inaudible beyond a few feet. The music was as unassertive and self-effacing as the couple who were playing it. They were reading the score set on a wobbly music stand and the man kept reaching out with his foot to steady it. The young woman, barely more than a girl, was wearing a sleeveless T-shirt, within which her breasts drooped noticeably; her hair was twisted into braids. Her face was pale and washed out; all the features, like the music, were evident only upon very close scrutiny.

Wishing she hadn't given all of her change to the bagpiper, Sheila put a dollar bill in the open flute case. As she stood up she realized she was being followed.

She turned and looked back the way she had come. The crowd on the sidewalk was jammed with office workers on their way home and it was difficult to see past the bodies for more than a few yards. Sheila couldn't see him now, but she was certain she had caught him in the corner of her eye a moment before, just as she had glimpsed him ten minutes earlier when she turned to get one final look at the escape artist.

Walking quickly, she hurried away from him, more confused than frightened. Why would he be following her? What did he hope to gain? Had her husband sent him for some reason? The dream of seduction in the sea came back to her again, and she remembered that Florio had flashed in her mind at one point while her husband was making love to her. Florio had no more business in her sex life than he did following her on the street, and her reaction to both was bewilderment.

As she walked she was careful not to look directly behind her again. She wanted to know if he was really there, she wanted a convincing glimpse of him, but she did not want to look directly at him and possibly drive him off. Sheila told herself she should be offended at this invasion of her privacy, but she was flattered.

She glanced in shopwindows, pretending an interest in shoes and skirts and trips to scenic Erin, hoping to catch his reflection in the glass. She saw herself instead, the high rose-and-cream complexion that had labeled her as a "typical English beauty" since her teens, the high brow, the prominent teeth, the slate-gray eyes wide and searching. I look excited, she thought. I look as if I'm enjoying this. She wondered if she were so vain that she responded to any kind of attention, however strange, from whatever source. She had never thought of herself that way, but heaven knew it could not have been Florio causing this excitement. Not Florio.

If he was still behind her, she never saw him. Had she really expected to? But didn't he want her to? Weren't police detectives skilled enough to follow people without being detected, particularly by someone who had no reason to be suspicious? If she had seen him, hadn't he intended her to see him?

A quartet of brass players was torturing Vivaldi at the steps leading to a fountain outside the Plaza Hotel. A semicircle of listeners had formed around them, and Sheila walked to the farthest reach of the audience so that she could look back the way she had come while still seeming to watch the musicians.

Keeping her head facing the center of the musicians, she let her eyes roam over the people on the sidewalk. He wasn't there. She freed her head and searched openly, standing on a higher step so she could see clearly over the little crowd in front of her. He wasn't there. Sheila was surprised at the depth of her disappointment.

Then he stepped out of a doorway and walked away. He had been perfectly hidden, his back to her; she would never have found him. Was he letting her see him? If he wanted to be seen, why was he walking away from her? As she watched he turned a corner and disappeared, going back downtown, the way they both had come. He never glanced in her direction.

Sheila wondered if she had misjudged the entire situation. Perhaps he had not been following her at all, perhaps he was out on business of his own that had just happened to coincide with the path she was taking. That had happened once before—they had run into each other by accident. Or so he had said.

For a second she toyed with the idea of following him. It had seemed almost as if he had wanted her to do that, getting her attention when she had lost him, then ambling slowly off, hard to miss, easy to follow.

She turned instead for home. But when she reached the first corner, she swung on impulse and stepped into the nearest doorway. To her amazement she noted that her breath was coming in short gasps. The act of stepping into the doorway, of laying the trap, made her feel like a spy. Her breathing was quick and irregular and she realized she was excited by the game.

People passed, some of them glancing at the woman standing in the doorway. But Florio did not come. Sheila forced herself to be patient and counted slowly to thirty under her breath. She counted another fifteen, then gave up. Why had she expected him to follow when she had seen him go the other way? She was letting her imagination run away with her good sense.

Wondering what on earth she would have done if he had come after her, Sheila stepped onto the sidewalk and came within a foot of bumping into Florio.

He stepped away from her as if she might explode on contact, holding his hands in front of him to fend her off.

Sheila found herself blushing unaccountably.

"Imagine meeting you here," she said, and the inanity of the statement made her blush even more. Her face felt as if it had been set on fire.

Florio muttered something unintelligible, still looking at her as if she had suddenly materialized out of the sidewalk. Sheila wondered again if she had been wrong about his following her.

"It's a lovely time for a walk, isn't it?" she said.

Florio took a minute to come to himself, as if pondering her statement at length.

"A nice day," he managed at last.

He had bought some new clothes, his white shirt was crisp and clean, the tie looked brand-new. His hair had been neatly trimmed. He's really quite good-looking, Sheila thought. Handsome, if he'd give himself a chance. Not as handsome as Sandy, she added quickly, guiltily. But very nice-looking when he made the effort. She couldn't help but think he had made the effort for her.

"I'm on my way home now," she said. "Are you going in that direction?"

Florio nodded. She noted his Adam's apple dancing in his throat as if he were having difficulty swallowing.

"Would you like to walk with me?" she asked. She almost added "instead of behind me," but she thought better of it. Let him cling to whatever pretense he needed to save face.

"Sure," he said. "Why not?"

They walked in silence. Sheila could sense his discomfort; it seemed to surround him like an aureole. When the jostling of other pedestrians caused her to bump into him, he jerked quickly away.

She felt that she was walking with a bear, exercising control of something large and wild with the strength of her will and mind. She had to be aware of every step she took lest she startle it and it swiped at her in reflexive power.

When Florio spoke, she did not at first understand. She looked at him questioningly, smiling automatically.

"You all right?" he asked again.

"I'm fine," she said. "I just didn't hear you."

"If you're ever not all right, you let me know," said Florio.

The offer of assistance, if that's what it was, seemed so strange and uncalled for that Sheila laughed nervously.

"That's very kind of you," she said.

"I mean it," he said, and his tone was so grave, his look so intense, that Sheila now believed him. "If you ever need any help, let me know."

As if to seal a bargain, he offered his hand and shook hers with a curious formality. His grip was too strong and Sheila realized he was not used to shaking hands with women. For a moment as he unwittingly compressed her fingers, she was aware of how easily this bear of a man could squeeze her, break her in two, rip her apart. Then he released her hand and shuffled back a step, his eyes focusing unthreateningly on a spot just below her chin. He was not a grizzly, Sheila thought, but a large, intense teddy bear.

"Wait," she said, grabbing at his arm as he started away. "What's this all about?"

He held his arm rigidly away from his body, not moving it a fraction with her grasp, as if her touch had paralyzed it.

"What's what about?"

"You know," she said, smiling. "Following me. Why does Sandy want you to follow me?"

He glanced at her face, then away. She was still clutching his arm, and he was still stiffly holding it out as if it were in a cast. Anyone else would have dropped his arm by now, Sheila thought, or let her draw him closer.

"Oh, come on," she said, teasingly, in a tone that usually got men to do things for her. "You can tell me. I'm not blaming you, you're just doing your job. I just want to know why Sandy's doing it."

"You don't understand."

"Then tell me," she said. "Come on. . . . Come onnnn."

"Stop it," he said quietly.

Sheila gripped his arm tighter, shaking it, exhorting him to join her team.

"Come on, Florio! Tell me! Tell me!" She laughed. He looked so much like a recalcitrant schoolboy, refusing to rat on his buddies by telling the teacher who threw the rock through the window. She laughed again, throwing her head back, releasing the tension and anger that had been building with her full throaty laugh.

"Stop it," he said again. She could barely hear him over her laughter.

He looked so malleable, standing there, arm rigid, eyes studying the sidewalk, that Sheila put her other hand on his arm and tugged.

"Come on, you big ape!" she said. "Tell me or I'll beat you up." She pulled at his arm, then pounded it lightly with her fists, feeling as she did it how pathetic was her strength compared to his.

He stepped back from her and she came after him, laughing, thinking he was playing, too. She started to pound his chest, hammering his clean white shirt.

"I'll beat it out of you," she said manically.

Florio grabbed her wrists and held them.

"You don't know what you're doing," he said, staring at her in amazement. "You don't know, do you?"

Instinctively she tried to pull her wrists free, but he held them tightly.

"That hurts," she said. He held her immobile so easily.

"You just don't have any idea," he repeated. He looked at her with a mixture of bewilderment and sympathy.

"I was only joking," she said. "Let go."

Instead he pulled her closer to him, drawing her wrists up to her collarbone. She stumbled forward. Her thighs rested against his. She was forced forward till her breasts brushed his chest. Although she tried to pull back, he held her.

His face was just inches above hers. She could see that his lips were trembling, and his jaw muscles were clenching and unclenching repeatedly, as if he were trying to control the chattering of his teeth. He stared down at her for what seemed a very long time, his eyes boring into her, his nostrils flaring as he breathed. He seemed like a man on the verge of exploding, but Sheila detected only tension, not anger. She was uncomfortable, but not afraid. The teddy bear had decided to hold on to her for a moment, but it would let go. That was the nature of teddy bears.

Eventually Florio did let go, with a sigh that seemed to ripple throughout his body. He eased the grip on her wrists, but his thighs were still pressed against hers, his chest still touching her breasts.

"You must be very careful," he said slowly. "Since you don't know what you're doing, you must be very careful." He stepped back half a step. Suddenly off balance, Sheila fell against him. She felt the rock-hard shape below his belt before she could pull away and right herself. She realized that her nipples were erect, too.

Without another word Florio walked away. She watched him for half a block to see if he would turn and look back. When he did not, Sheila entered her apartment building.

Shaken by her encounter with Florio, Sheila telephoned her husband. As usual, he was not in his office, and Sheila hung up with a rising sense of resentment. If Block could assign Florio to do his bidding, if he could have other detectives waste their time shadowing her, why could he not just as easily delegate some of his other work to them so that he could spend some time with his wife?

Restless and disturbed by Florio's strange behavior—and by her reaction to it—she paced the apartment. There was no point in denying it to herself, she had been aroused. Was that what she liked, she wondered, the heavy-handed, brutish approach? Did the feeling of vulnerability which Florio had evoked really stimulate her? She had chosen Block, had loved Block, for precisely opposite reasons; for his gentleness, his tenderness, his patience. There was something of the animal in Florio, an untamed, undomesticated bestiality that threatened her at the same time that it excited her. He was everything that her civilized husband was not, and she should have despised him for it. Because she didn't despise him, she disliked herself.

Sheila was not accustomed to disliking herself. Her greatest asset in life, her greatest appeal to others, had always been an air of confidence that was rooted in a contentment with herself.

Drawn by the same impulse that had made her turn the corner and hide in the doorway, Sheila went to the window and looked out. The attenuated twilight had finally collapsed into night. Cones of light spread out from the streetlights, not quite intersecting and leaving thin strips of blackness in between.

A man stood in one of the strips of darkness, just beyond the nearest cone. With the light on behind her in the room, it was hard for Sheila to make him out. She turned off the light and returned to the window, standing in darkness more complete than that on the street below. The man was still standing there, his face turned up toward Sheila's apartment.

He was staring up, his eyes looking for her in the darkness of her apartment. Sheila knew he couldn't see her with the light out, but he stared straight at her and she felt a shiver race through her. Sheila had the sense of being spied on by a lone, hungry wolf.

She drew the curtains and went into the kitchen. She sat there, her back to the wall, until Block came home. But when he asked her about her day, she did not mention Florio.

Professor Harvey Aaron haunted his language lab the way he imagined Block was haunting the trail of Tom-Tom. He had worked for the police before and had never been impressed by the intelligence involved. There was little abstract thinking necessary in police work, little theoretical castle-building of the type Aaron and his university colleagues pursued. It was not, after all, a calling that brought forth genius. Doggedness was called for in a good detective; a willingness to work hard was of much greater use than the ability to deal in hypothetical speculation.

Of the policemen he had known, Block had impressed Aaron most because of the special intensity of his devotion. The man seemed to care more about catching his quarry than any of the others, as if something personal were involved. Aaron had the suspicion that if Block were not able to impose a sort of order on his chaotic world, something within Block himself would be threatened. Like a snapping turtle that will cling to its prey even after its head is severed from the body, Block would keep working on a case long after reason or expediency had said to let it go.

Aaron found an inspiration in knowing that Block was working that hard, because now he was working that hard himself. The tape recording of Tom-Tom defied Aaron's efforts to decipher it. He had tried the easy way first, playing the tape for the assembled members of the language department without explaining that what they were hearing was a murderer in the act.

There had been theories in abundance, but no one recognized the language.

Next Aaron settled down to the labor. Counting regional dialects, many of which are different enough to be nearly indecipherable to other speakers of the parent language—Cockney and Louisiana Cajun, for example—there are more than three thousand different known tongues in the world. That number includes only the living languages. Addition of the known dead languages would make the total much larger.

All of the living tongues are recorded somewhere on tape or record if one knows where to look. Aaron knew where to look. After he had exhausted the sizable files of Columbia University, he turned to the Library of Congress. Using a two-reel tape player, he first played the known language, listening to it long enough to get a feel for the sonorities and rhythms; then he replayed the tape of Tom-Tom, comparing the two, listening not for exact matches, but similarities in tone, pitch, consonant and vowel repetition and combination, unique sounds (such as the click of !Kung).

To Aaron's gifted ear, the unintelligible grunts and glottal stops and frictives and sibilances of a foreign language made a diagram he could follow. Not a precise picture, but a contour map, showing him the general shape of the terrain. Tom-Tom's language fit the shape of none of them.

He turned to the computer, breaking each syllable of Tom-Tom's speech into vowels and consonants. Each sound was quantified and given a numerical value. The numbers were converted to binomial code and fed into the computer.

Using the logic of its own special language, the computer analyzed Tom-Tom's speech, looking for the patterns which Aaron sought with his ear. It was the same basic technique used to break codes, seeking the repetitions that make up the essence of any language invented by the human mind.

In the end, the computer did no better than Aaron had done. It told him what he had known for some time—Tom-Tom was not speaking Chinese or Russian or Fiji or Farsi. He was not speaking any of the encoded or recorded languages known.

That it was a language, Aaron still had no doubt. He could hear it clearly on the tape. Tom-Tom was speaking; Aaron could hear the words, he just couldn't make sense of them. There was no sense to it, no sense at all. And when the professor finally admitted that to himself, he found his answer.

Responding to Aaron's summons, Block and Florio drove through the streets of Harlem. Block felt, as he always felt in a black neighborhood, like an interloper, a stranger passing through a strange land without a safe-conduct visa. The badge and shield offered some comfort, but they did nothing to protect him from the hostility of all the glowering eyes. Block was not a man to ponder ironies, but the presence of Columbia University, one of the great pillars of wisdom and learning in the white Western world, in the middle of one of the white Western world's most famous black ghettos, was a juxtaposition he could hardly have missed.

Columbia squatted atop its rise on Morningside Heights like the castle of a king perched on the high ground, surrounded at its base by the squalid hamlets of the vassals. The university was not of the black community—despite years of public relations efforts—any more than the monarch was of the peasantry because of occasional condescending largesse.

No philosopher, Block did not consider the situation, he merely recognized and accepted it. If Florio recognized it, too, he did not say. He sat in a self-involved silence beside his partner.

Aaron was waiting in his office with a pale, thin, ascetic-looking boy whom he introduced as Professor Whit Cummings. Block had assumed the boy was a student. He was, in fact, closer to thirty than seventeen, and, like Aaron, something of a genius in his field.

"I think I've found out what you want to know about Tom-Tom," said Aaron after the introductions. "At least I think I've found out all there is to find out."

"What language was it?"

"Well, that's just going to be an educated guess," said Aaron, "so let me tell you how I came to this conclusion."

"You don't know the language?" Florio asked.

"Language is not the right term," said Aaron. "Let me bore you for a second with a few facts from my field. Every language has a basic grammar. Now, I don't mean diagraming sentences or not ending with a preposition, I mean something *fundamental*. Each language puts words together in a special way in order to make sense out of them. Some do it by word order in the sentences. Germans, for instance. The verb is always in the first or second position. Always. In the first position it's a command or a question, in the second position it's a declarative. Very straightforward. In other languages the grammar is indicated by the tone of voice. It's very difficult to read various Chinese languages out of context, for instance, because without the tone of voice you don't know whether it's a question or a statement, and consequently you don't know how to interpret the several possible meanings of most of the words. All right, that's more difficult, but once you know how it works, you can make sense of it. If languages did not have some sort of grammar, we could be restricted to using one word at a time, most of them nouns. Are you with me?"

"I guess so," said Block.

"All I'm really saying is that all languages are built, in their different ways, to enable us to communicate with each other. Well, to get to the heart of it, I used every means I know and some I just made up, but I can't find any sign of underlying grammar in Tom-Tom's speech. It *is* speech, I'm sure of that, every instinct tells me it is. We have more than three minutes of him on tape, and there's no question in my mind that he's speaking—but he is not trying to communicate. What I'm saying is, Tom-Tom is not speaking to another human."

Block paused, waiting to be sure he understood.

"What is he speaking to?" he asked, finally.

Aaron glanced at Whit Cummings.

"God," said Cummings. "He's speaking directly to God."

"We think," qualified Aaron.

"He is," said Cummings with certainty. "What you've got on those tapes is glossolalia."

Block stared at the young man who was speaking to him with such assurance about murderers who spoke to God. He reminded Block of someone fresh out of school, so full of himself, so arrogant in his newly acquired knowledge, that older, wiser men could only shake their heads and say, "He'll learn."

"Glossolalia," Aaron volunteered, although Block had not asked. "Whit is more convinced of it than I am, but it's really the only explanation I've got."

"So far it's no explanation at all," said Florio angrily. "What the hell is glossolalia?"

Block lifted a hand slightly, palm up, silently urging patience.

"Speaking in tongues," said Cummings quickly, eager to take the floor from his colleague. "It's a manifestation of intense religious excitement. To a believer, it's a sign of possession by the Holy Spirit. To a psychiatrist it's a phenomenon of self-hypnosis resulting from extreme religious agitation."

"And which are you?" Block asked.

"Pardon?"

"A true believer or a psychiatrist?"

"I'm into contemporary theology," said Cummings.

"That means a little of each with no belief in either one," said Aaron, smiling.

Cummings gave him a pained expression.

"Tell us about it," said Block.

"Speaking in tongues is first mentioned in the New Testament," said Cummings. "The Apostle Paul claimed to have exceptional ability in the spiritual gift of translating glossolalia. Not translating. Interpreting is a better word. He felt that speaking in tongues without a proper interpretation for the congregation was just an indulgence. He was quite strict about it, he gave instructions that no more than two 'speakers' per service should be allowed, and then only when someone was present to draw the proper theological inferences in order to edify the congregation. The practice continued throughout the centuries. It was used by mendicant friars in the thirteenth century, Montanus was excommunicated for practicing in defiance of Paul's strictures, the early Quakers and Shakers were said to have used it, et cetera, and I realize that's not relevant to your needs. Here's what is. In the early twentieth century a man named A. J. Tomlinson founded the Church of God and the Pentecostal movement, which believed in a literal interpretation of apocalyptic passages. They practiced divine healing, glossolalia, and other rather bizarre manifestations of the Holy Spirit. This movement was called the 'Latter Rain.' After Tomlinson died, there were a number of schisms as numerous groups broke off—not so much over their rather minor differences in belief as on account of major political disagreements—and when his two surviving sons quarreled over control of the parent church in Tennessee, there were even more splits.

"Some of the better-known splinters are the Assemblies of God, the United Pentecostal Church, Pentecostal Holiness Church, the Calvary Pentecostal Church, the Pentecostal Fire-Baptized Holiness Church."

"And they all babble like Tom-Tom?" Florio asked impatiently.

"It's not babble," said Aaron.

"It most certainly is not babble," said Cummings. "These people are swept up in a feeling of great exultation which bursts forth in speech, speech of a nature that no one else can understand—except the angels. I don't think there's any question—no matter what your religious belief, or lack of it—that it is an involuntary act. On a conscious level, these people are not aware of what they are doing. They may be doing it because the Holy Spirit has possessed them, or they may be doing it to please their minister or the congregation, that's entirely possible, but they are not doing it consciously."

"These are southern churches?"

"Not exclusively; they began there, but by now they've spread all over the world. I just mentioned the more official ones. There are dozens of storefront churches right here in New York with no affiliation with any other group. The congregation is the entire church."

"Blacks?"

"Blacks, whites. The revival even flourished in Italian communities in New York and Chicago for a time. There are literally millions of worshipers of the Pentecostal movement in this country. Not all of them practice glossolalia, of course."

"But Tom-Tom does."

"Oh, yes," said Cummings. "Tom-Tom definitely does."

Block was surrounded by black bodies, swaying and clapping in time to their own music. They had no instrument to lead them or give them the right key. They did not need one. This was percussive music, as close to drumbeats as the human voice could get. Jungle music, thought Block, imagining a steady, insistent beat being hit on a hollow log somewhere in a clearing and another drum answering in the distance, the two rhythmic beats meeting somewhere in the air over the rain forest. Now and then a solo voice would rise up and a woman, heavyset, little eyes squeezed shut from the effort, would sing a melody in tones more bold than beautiful. The congregation would continue their steady, pulsing beat, clapping their hands, stamping their feet, thrusting their heads forward with the effort.

But the melody was insignificant, an excuse for the background beat, the chorus of fifty human drums. The heat in the storefront church was stifling and everyone was sweating, black skins glistening in the light, each body a furnace contributing to the rising temperature.

Block and Florio had come late, after the service had started, hoping to slip in unnoticed in the back. They had not been unnoticed—their white skin stood out as if they had set off a flare the moment they entered, but they had been ignored. Another white worshiper—or curiosity seeker—was nothing new to the congregation of the First United Church of the Cleansing Light of New York. Whites had come to the Cleansing Light before, some to be healed, some to gawk. All were welcomed and most made a healthy contribution once they had seen Brother Eastus work.

There were other white folks in the storefront church tonight, scattered throughout the congregation like chips of granite on an asphalt road, and these were the people Block was interested in. Tom-Tom, from all the available evidence, was white. Just what he would be doing in a storefront church of Holy Rollers in Harlem, most of them Haitians, newly arrived or a generation removed from the homeland, Block could not say. But Block and his team were checking out all Pentecostal churches, whether the search seemed promising or not.

Block watched an elderly white man come in, slipping behind Florio, who had taken a position across the room from Block, and making his way to one side of the congregation. He moved with a total lack of self-consciousness which Block envied, as if he didn't know he was white in a room full of blacks. As if he didn't fear blacks; not because he was armed or powerful, but because he was used to them.

The music was getting louder, faster. Block could feel the floor shaking beneath his feet. The music ceased to be music and was becoming just a pulse, a steady throb that Block felt as much as heard. It's like sitting inside a drum, he thought, but at the same time he could not resist it. His head began to bob with all the others, thrusting forward sharply with the effort of the clap, the stomp, on each downbeat.

The beat had reached its most frantic, the air reverberated with fifty people expelling their breath in a grunted "Huh!" at every clapping, stamping beat.

With a cry a man hurled himself into the tiny clearing at the front of the room. He was dressed in a white robe that fell loosely, secured only at the neck. A large white feather thrust itself into the air above his head, held in place by a thin leather cord that crossed his forehead. In his right ear a platinum ring glinted in the light. Something white and blurry was in his hand. He held it over his head, shaking it once, and Block could see a flash of red and yellow above the white.

The congregation exhaled a sigh of excitement, but never lost a beat. If anything, the music got louder, more insistent, as the man in the robe, Brother Eastus, whirled around in a circle, his robe flying out around him like the tent of a carousel.

Eastus said something else that Block could not understand, pumping the white thing in his hand up and down over his head. The congregation responded with a word and Eastus spun faster.

Despite himself, Block began to go along with the congregation. He did it tentatively at first, clapping halfheartedly, as if Eastus were an entertainer who had urged everyone in the room to sing along, but as the throbbing beat continued, Block could no more resist it than he could the beat of his own heart. Stomping, lurching forward, grunting, he found a release in the group action. No one cared what he did and it was so much easier to go along than to resist. Block glanced across the room. He was relieved to see that Florio had given himself over to the music, too.

Eastus stopped his spinning, both hands raised over his head now. The congregation stopped abruptly, collectively holding its breath. Block found the pause even more compelling than the music. He yearned for the rhythm to start again as he ached for the next breath, the next heartbeat.

The white thing moved in Eastus's hand, shifted of its own accord, and Block could make out some details amid the blur of white. A yellow beak curved under a scarlet comb, an eye, black and moist, perfectly round, glazed now and dull. Eastus was holding a chicken, brandishing it above him like a savage with a spear. The fowl was alive, but stunned, in shock.

Eastus called out again in the foreign tongue, a sharp, brisk command. In answer a young woman stepped forth, propelled by the hands of the women around her. It was clear to see the woman was not well. Though she was lush, full-bodied, and young, and her ample breasts strained against the fabric of her simple shift, her dark skin had an ashen undertone. She carried her head tilted to one side, as if her fading strength were insufficient to keep it upright, and her arms were crossed over her stomach, protecting it.

As soon as the woman stepped into the clearing, Eastus gave a triumphant cry and the congregation began again to sing their curious, grunting chant, clapping and stamping their feet. The rhythm resumed immediately, as if it had never really stopped but continued during the pause, inaudibly, in the head and hands of everyone there. Block welcomed it back and this time joined in with familiarity, as if he had called and stomped like this many times before.

Eastus moved around the woman, calling to her in strange, alien noises, dancing in a curious two-dimensional dance, heaving up and down from the hips and shoulders, his head bobbing, his feet nearly leaving the ground with each upward thrust. As he bounced, he punctuated his movements with a guttural "Hu! Hu!," each sound torn from him by his efforts. The chicken was still in his hand, where it dangled by his side, temporarily forgotten.

The rhythm of the congregation changed subtly, fell into synchrony with Eastus until the entire building rocked to the same sound, pulsed to the same heartbeat. It was mesmerizing, nearly impossible to resist.

The young woman began to move with Eastus, up, down, up, down, shoulders and hips, grunts bursting forth every time the shoulders fell. Eastus moved closer, his body almost touching hers, then reached out with the chicken, stroking the woman's body with it. The inert body of the chicken rubbed against the woman's hips, her stomach, her thighs, her arms, her head; downward, slowly, across her breasts, the white feathers trailing over her stomach where the shift was slick and translucent with perspiration.

The woman was totally lost, her head thrown back, her body jerking with uncontrollable movements that superimposed themselves over the constant up-down thrust.

Eastus put the chicken between her legs, holding it there for a moment as she thrust her pelvis against it. Her entire frame twitched as if she were in convulsions. Her eyes were wide open, staring at the ceiling as if she saw the Lord God Himself coming out of the plaster.

Totally out of control when Eastus removed the chicken from between her legs and stepped away, the young woman bucked her way across the floor, spasm after spasm propelling her as if she were having electric shocks administered to her. Head shaking violently up and down, she began to utter little cries of ecstasy and pain that sounded very like the cries of a woman in orgasm. The entire scene had turned wildly sexual: the excitement in the eyes of the congregation, the jerking movements of Eastus, the frantic bucking of the woman's buxom body within her sweat-soaked shift. Block expected a miracle or a climax. There seemed no other possible resolution.

Suddenly throwing her arms toward the ceiling, the woman planted herself in the middle of the clearing, quivering all over, her hands trembling like leaves, her legs shaking so the muscles in her calves threatened to burst from her skin, her breasts trying to rip through the shift. She was waiting now for Eastus to come to her again, and the entire congregation waited for him, too.

He took his time, moving at her like a snake, holding the chicken in front of him, shaking it, testing the air like a serpent's tongue. The woman stood planted, quivering, like a bird, as Eastus insinuated himself toward her, still in rhythm to the chant, but different now, making her wait for it, making her want it.

In front of her once more, he shook the chicken all around her face like a tambourine. The woman stayed in place, quivering, but straining forward, needing it, needing it.

When it seemed that to wait one more instant would be a kind of death, Eastus jerked the chicken's head from its body. The young woman screamed and fell to her knees, the blood of the bird spurting onto her upturned face.

The entire congregation called out in release, and the chanting stopped. From his position against the wall Block turned to look at Florio.

Florio's eyes rolled back in his head. He fell backward into the packed bodies of those around him. As arms grabbed him, holding him up, a white froth dribbled from the corner of his mouth.

Byrne fiddled with a pencil, twirling it back and forth between his fingers. The action made him look impatient, but actually he was embarrassed.

"You had a what?" Byrne asked, afraid he had understood the first time.

"I had a religious experience," said Florio. "I don't know what else to call it." Florio *did* know what else to call it. He feared that he had had an epileptic seizure in the Church of the Cleansing Light, but to admit as much was tantamount to asking for early retirement.

Byrne glanced at Block, who stood behind Florio, looking at his partner curiously. Block had been acting a bit strange himself lately, Byrne thought. For a man with a beautiful new wife, he spent an incredible amount of time away from home. With an old wife, he could have understood it, thought Byrne, his mind considering his own spouse for the moment, but not with someone like Sheila. It was the Tom-Tom case, of course. It was getting to all of them.

"I whited out," said Florio. "There was this flash of light and I heard a sound, not a voice exactly, but like a voice."

"Like Saul on the road to Damascus," said Byrne.

"Who?"

"Has this ever happened before? Do you have this reaction in church all the time?"

"Come on, Captain. I'm a Catholic."

"Does this mean you're born again?"

"No," said Florio, indignantly. "It doesn't mean anything. I'm just telling you what happened so you'll understand when I say I'm not going back to any of those churches. I'm sorry, you can put me on anything else you want, but I don't intend to go through that again."

He had come to his senses lying on the floor of the Church of the Cleansing Light, Block's face the only white one among dozens of black faces staring down at him. He could not have been out for more than a few seconds when he struggled to his feet again. Using his sleeve to wipe the spittle that had run down his chin, he had looked around him. Everyone had been smiling, as if happy for him. As if passing out were an accomplishment to be proud of. Only Block was different; his face was enigmatic, unrevealing as stone.

The young woman had been standing at the edge of the throng, glaring at him angrily. I stole her show, Florio realized. They had gone through all that to cure her and a white cop wanders in and faints and ends up the star of the evening. No wonder she looked mad. But she also looked cured, Florio noted. Apart from the chicken blood drying on her clothes and hair, she looked much better than when she'd first stepped forth to meet Eastus in the middle of the clearing. In fact, everyone in the church had looked better, more radiant, revitalized. Except, of course, for the chicken.

"Do you want some time off?" Byrne asked. It was a routine question. There was more annoyance than solicitude in his tone.

"No, I'm fine," said Florio. "I just ain't going back there."

Byrne looked again at Block and shrugged.

"You can manage without him?"

"Sure," said Block. "I'm just wondering if he ought to go back to work right away."

"I'm fine!" Florio insisted. "Christ, I knew I shouldn't have told you."

"See the Kanter," Byrne said, then looked to Block. "That satisfy you, if the Kanter says okay?"

"Screw the Kanter, I don't need him," said Florio.

Block addressed Byrne. "I suppose it will have to," he said.

"I don't know what else to tell you," said Byrne. They spoke as if Florio were no longer in the room. "I can't remove a man from duty because he's found Jesus."

"I didn't find anybody!" Florio cried. "It was just an experience."

"I don't want him removed from duty," said Block. "I just want him secure in his own mind."

"I'm secure, goddamn it!"

Byrne turned to Florio. "See the Kanter," he said.

After Florio had had his session with the Kanter, Block went to see the "sexy shrink."

"I can't tell you what we talked about," said Kanter. "That's privileged information."

"Did I ask?"

"Weren't you going to?"

"No, as it happens," said Block. "I wasn't going to ask anything that you couldn't tell me with a clear conscience."

The Kanter removed his glasses and rubbed the bridge of his nose. The glasses had silver rims. A very heavy gold chain necklace hung around his neck, nestled like a gleaming serpent in the thick high hair of his chest. Kanter seemed to gather himself and when he lifted his head he flashed a bright smile, the best display of porcelain the discount king could buy.

"How come you guys are so hard-ass?" he said, chuckling, charming his way into Block's heart. "I mean, your friend Florio, I thought he was going to punch me out. And now you come in here, you're bristling—did you know this? You're absolutely bristling with hostility. What do you guys have against me?"

"It's nothing personal," Block lied. "Most of us spend our time judging other people's mental makeup, trying to decide if they're lying or not, if they're capable of killing or not. We analyze all day long, we know how inexact it is. We don't like to have it done to us."

"I'm here to help, not to judge."

"Did Florio tell you about his—'religious experience'?" Block asked. "Let me rephrase that. I know he told you about it, that's why he came. Is it going to incapacitate him?"

"No."

"He's fit to work?"

"Yes, certainly. But I wouldn't send him back to one of those places right away."

"It could happen again?"

Kanter shrugged. "I'd say it's quite possible. Don't tell your priest I said this, but that kind of extreme religious response is a form of hysteria."

"What does that mean, exactly?"

"It means he got too excited. There was too much stimulation in that scene for him to handle—so he blacked out. It's like a built-in circuit breaker, too much current, the brain says, 'Enough!' and clicks off."

"It's a safety device," said Block.

"That's it."

"And what would happen if he didn't pass out? What is he trying to protect himself from?"

"Well, that's very hard to say," said Kanter. "I talked to the man for less than an hour, I don't know his history, I don't really know anything about him. There's no way to answer your question without spending quite a bit of time with him."

"This kind of reaction, this blackout he had—is it possible that a man could do something he wasn't aware of during a blackout like that?"

"Offhand, without knowing more about it, I'd have to say no."

"Could this unconscious period extend for a length of time?"

"I doubt it," said Kanter.

"Could it trigger some change in a person, lead him to do something he wouldn't ordinarily do?"

"Lieutenant Block, you're trying to lead me somewhere, but I don't know why. From what little I know of Detective Florio and his case—and it is very little—the answer to all of your questions is no. . . . Why do I feel you don't accept my answer?"

"Do you know about glossolalia?" Block asked.

"Yes, I've heard of it."

"Would you call that a form of hysteria, too?"

"Actually, hysteria is out of fashion as a psychiatric term. I used it simply because it's an easy concept to grasp."

"Does glossolalia have anything to do with overloaded brain circuits, too?"

"I haven't read the literature on glossolalia," said Kanter.

"An educated guess," said Block. "Would a man who had fainting spells at a religious meeting be the type to speak in tongues, too? Off the record."

"That's very difficult to say. I mean, both are manifestations of a high susceptibility to the so-called 'religious experience,' but I don't know that that means the two are that closely related."

"But it's possible."

"Is that a question?"

"Is it possible?"

"It's possible. I don't know if it's likely, but it's possible. What are you getting at? If I knew the general thrust here, I might be able to help you more."

"If I told you that a hypothetical man who got so carried away at a religious service that he passed out, blacked out, also got so carried away at—certain times—times of intense excitement—times that probably had some sort of religious connection for him—if this same guy who passed out when he got too excited also spoke in tongues when he got excited, would that seem reasonably consistent to you?"

"It doesn't sound *in*consistent," Kanter admitted.

"It wouldn't surprise you if the same man did both things?"

"Are we talking about Florio?"

"A hypothetical man."

"It wouldn't surprise me about a hypothetical man. It would surprise me about Florio. It would shock hell out of me."

"Why?"

"Because I know Florio, at least a little bit."

"All right, Doctor, let's change the subject for a second. Let's talk about Tom-Tom. You told me that that pile of clothes laid out like a corpse meant that one side of his character had symbolically killed the other side."

"That was just speculation."

"I appreciate that. Now, would you speculate that if a person had two sides of his personality so distinct that one could kill the other, he could have a third side, too?"

"What are you getting at, Lieutenant?"

"The child with Tom-Tom. I can't find a trace of her. There's not a single piece of physical evidence that she exists except for her writing on the walls. Not a trace at four different murder sites. Now, a single man—an experienced and knowledgeable man—might be able to slip around in this city and cover his tracks the way Tom-Tom is doing. But with a child in tow? No one has seen her. You might not pay too much attention to a single man at two in the morning, but a six-year-old child? Someone would notice her, someone would wonder why she wasn't in bed. And when Tom-Tom is killing these women, why doesn't this child ever touch anything? We've never found a child's fingerprint. We've never found a child's footprint in rooms spattered with blood. She's never dropped anything. She's left no trace of her clothing, not so much as a thread. That doesn't sound like any child I've ever heard of. I don't think there is a child. I think Tom-Tom might be the child, too. Is that possible?"

"You're asking for one hell of a lot of speculation, Lieutenant."

"We're not getting anywhere the other way."

"All right. Theoretically, yes, it's possible. If Tom-Tom is a multiple personality. He might be a child, part of the time. He might be anything."

"Could he duplicate a child's writing well enough to fool an expert?"

"Yes, but he wouldn't really be *fooling* anyone. If he thought he was a child, he would be a child."

"How's that work?"

"Well, I'm not that familiar with the literature. . . ."

"I understand."

"You don't understand! I know how it sounds, but there's a lot of literature in my field, new studies come out all the time. I do keep abreast, you know. But glossolalia. Multiple personalities. How often do you think I run into this kind of thing?"

"I do understand," said Block, placatingly. "No one expects you to know everything. I'm sure that now that I've told you what I need you'll do a study and give me a fuller answer in time."

"That's right."

"But right now I don't think we have a whole lot of time. Which is why we're speculating, and it's extremely helpful, believe me. Now, Doctor, tell me what you mean if he thinks he's a child, he is a child."

Kanter toyed with the chain around his neck for a moment, calming himself. Not for the first time he thought wistfully of his patients in private practice. They never made him feel inadequate. They didn't second-guess him, assuming their knowledge of human nature was as profound as his own.

"Well," he said finally, "as I recall it, a multiple personality develops a number of personalities that are each complete in themselves. For instance, if from the age of ten you think you're not only Block, but also John Doe, during the time when you think you're John Doe you will act like him, think like him, feel like him—be him. You're not pretending you're him, you *are* John Doe. By the time you're twenty, you've got ten years of memories separate and distinct from your memories as Block. If at the age of six you spend part of your time thinking, believing, hell, *knowing* you're a little girl, then you're going to know how to write like a child. Not because you remember it and are trying to reproduce it, but because that part of your mind is still that child."

"And could that child be left-handed and the man right-handed?"

"The mind is capable of just about anything. The child could be a Zulu if she'd had any exposure to that, and Tom-Tom could be a Swedish statesman. If you start early enough, there's no limit. You take a child of four or five or six and put it in any culture in the world and within six months it will be perfectly at home there, it will speak that language, observe the customs, relate to the people, and think of itself as a member of that society. At that age we have almost infinite mental flexibility."

"So Tom-Tom could be Watts and the girl, too?"

"I don't know about Tom-Tom. A person is capable of living many distinct personalities, that's all I'm saying."

"And he could have a fourth personality, too, couldn't he? One that allowed him to walk around as a member of society? He could be a psychiatrist, for instance."

"Or a cop," countered Kanter. "Theoretically he could be anything."

"And would he know?"

"Who is 'he'?"

"Would the psychiatrist know about the little girl or Tom-Tom?"

"I really do have to read up on this."

"He wouldn't know, though, would he?"

"You're a persistent man, Lieutenant."

"He's killing people."

"No, I don't think the psychiatrist would know about the killer. . . . You had this all worked out before you asked the questions, didn't you?"

"I wouldn't want to form any definite conclusions without consulting expert opinion," said Block.

"Yeah."

"If he's had these personalities since childhood, he's had the bad side, the Tom-Tom side under control. He only started killing very recently. Why?"

"I don't know why, Lieutenant. Something happened."

"What?"

"I don't know. Something traumatic. It's impossible to say."

"How about a woman. What if he fell in love with a woman? Could that be traumatic?"

Kanter sighed. "You're off on your own, you know. I don't know this person, I don't know where you get these hypotheticals, I . . . Yes. All right, why not. If falling in love with this woman threatened the stability of his life in some way, I suppose it could be traumatic enough to do it. He's killing women, after all. Actually, I would think falling in love would be a fairly plausible cause."

"Why is that?"

"Most of the personality changes would be as a result of pressure. If life is getting too difficult as one personality"—he snapped his fingers—"right into another one where there's no pressure. When pressure builds up on that one, pop into another. The pressure might be internal—fear of thinking certain thoughts that aren't consistent with that character. If one of them is clean and pure and thoughts of sex come up, it would be easier to deal with them with the personality that is more liberated with sexual thoughts. Or the pressure could be external. Say someone is making demands of him that he can't deal with in that personality; job pressure, let's say. Commitment to a career change. Easier to change the personality than the situation."

"So in that sense falling in love—with another man's wife, for instance—could provide the necessary pressure."

"Well, falling in love would have to have very serious consequences for him to bring forth the personality of Tom-Tom, which has been suppressed—or at least has not been murderous—until now. There would have to be some very very strong threat, some connection with women in his past—well, of course, that's rather obvious. . . . My turn for a question. If all you've got is the handwriting, why do you assume this child is a girl?"

Block looked at Kanter for a moment, puzzled.

"We've heard her," he said finally. "We have her voice on tape."

"Then you can tell if it's the same person, can't you?"

"Shit!" Block exploded. He really was too close to the case, he wasn't thinking clearly. "Thank you, Doctor. I think I'd better do some reading of my own literature."

As Block left, Kanter sat at his plain metal desk on his un-

comfortable chair and wondered how much longer he had to do
his penance among these hard-ass men.

Block called Quayle.

"I want you to analyze the voice on the Tom-Tom tape," he
said without preamble. "I want you to compare it with the voice
of the child, the crying."

"Compare it how?"

"There are certain elements of the human voice that are as
unique and individual as fingerprints, isn't that right?"

"That's right," said Quayle. "They use voice ID in some very
high security government installations."

"Even a trained mimic can't hide his voice if you analyze it
with a computer, isn't that right?"

"True."

"Good," said Block. "I want you to find out if Tom-Tom's
voice is the same as that child's."

There was a pause on Quayle's end of the line. "We don't
have that capability," he said finally. "That calls for very sophisticated technology."

"So go where it is," said Block.

"And I'm not sure they can do it anyway. The child is crying
and Tom-Tom is shouting gibberish. I think they have to speak
the same words so a comparison can be made."

"Try," said Block. He hung up and turned to the photo which
Ching had provided of the marks on Rosemary Schwarz's neck.
It lay on his desk, the gooseneck lamp shining on the color shot,
encircling it with light. In closeup, with the distractions of
Rosemary's face and body removed from the picture, it was like
studying an aerial photograph. Somewhere within the light and
shadow lay the truth, an illegal missile silo, a camouflaged tank,
a murder weapon.

Block had had the photo in and out of his desk for more than
a week, studying it whenever he had the chance, burning the

pattern of marks into his mind so that they would make the necessary connection on their own, within his unconscious. This time he didn't hesitate. He placed his knuckles across the large mark. The bruise extended a fraction of an inch farther on either side.

He rummaged for a moment in a desk drawer and took out a dark blue rubbery substance used to clean the typewriter keys. The type cleaner still had the imprint of individual letters where it had been pressed against the keys and lifted away the ink. Block stretched and kneaded the rubber putty until the ink was absorbed into the general color. He flattened the stuff into a block shape on his desk, then he removed the handcuffs from his belt where they hung over his hip pocket, beneath his suit coat. Sticking his hand through the loop in the cuffs so they covered his hand like brass knuckles, Block slammed his fist into the putty. Next to the larger mark of the cuffs was a series of smaller indentations where the chain had whiplashed into the putty.

Block held the putty next to the photograph. The putty mark was much clearer, but the shape was the same. Rosemary Schwarz had been hit with a pair of handcuffs.

A security check is run on every man who enters the police academy. When he applies for Detective Grade, a much more thorough examination is made of his past. The resources of the New York City Police are limited, however, and for those candidates who spent their early years out of the state, not too much is known. A police record shows up, of course, but not much else.

According to the questionnaire he had filled out fifteen years before, Florio was born in Detroit and spent most of his formative years in Cincinnati before coming to New York as a young man. The file had virtually nothing to offer beyond that, and after an hour of checking sources and trying to read between the lines, Block tossed the file aside in frustration.

17

 From where he sat in his car, Keiner could see Florio by keeping his head back against the seat. That it was the most restful position possible was fortunate, for Keiner had been seated for a long time. Keiner realized he had forgotten how tedious most police work is. He was often bored in his retirement, but that was for lack of entertainment, a condition he could rectify whenever he gathered enough initiative to read a book or take a walk or repot a plant. If he got bored on his own, it was only because he was too lazy to think of something to do. But the enforced tedium of policework was a different matter. There was no cure for it; anything that distracted him from the dullness of surveillance also took his mind off the job.

As he had in the past, Keiner found some relief in hating his quarry. Since he was supposed to be concentrating on him anyway, Keiner concentrated intensely, letting the pain in his lower back, the stiffness in his legs, the burning in his bladder, be converted to anger at the man who was causing them. Some detectives thought of the men they tailed as game, deer or bighorn sheep, which they kept in their sights, waiting for the right moment to squeeze the trigger. Keiner had known some cops who actually pretended to shoot their prey, practicing assassination the way boys will simulate firing at a low-flying squadron of geese.

Keiner's spirit was not that playful. He thought of them as insects, and he regarded them as he might study the activity in an ant hill. Their movements took on the senseless, random patterns of bugs, scurrying here and there, resting for unpredictable periods, then bursting forth with equally inexplicable vigor, their motives unknown and unknowable. Unlike insects, which Keiner found interesting, particularly when they were pollinating his flowers, Keiner did not view the men he tailed—or used to tail—with detachment. Men had personalities, even in the way they moved and stood and slouched, and almost without exception, Keiner disliked them.

Florio, for instance, he had disliked almost immediately. From his vantage point, half a block away, Keiner thought Florio looked like nothing so much as a lovesick bear, standing on its hind legs and staring moodily at the lighted window across the street where Sheila Block could occasionally be seen.

For three nights running now Florio had taken up his position across the street from Sheila's office, mooned about for an hour or so, then silently followed her home, not even attempting to speak to her, just trailing her from a distance even as Keiner was shadowing him. Keiner was fairly certain that the woman knew Florio was back there, too. She walked very quickly, very deliberately, never looking behind her, as if she were trying to outdistance him and afraid to find out she hadn't.

Sheila stepped into the street and Florio felt his heart quicken. It seemed to him that she glanced quickly in his direction before turning her back and walking rapidly toward the corner of Ninth Avenue. As always happened when Florio was near her, his breathing became shallow and difficult.

He stayed well behind her, not wanting to frighten her as he sensed that his presence often did; but at the same time he knew that she had to take comfort in knowing someone was there for her if she needed him. He watched her walk, her long legs swiftly clipping off the distance, her hips and buttocks rolling beautifully with each stride. Like the gentle swell of the ocean, he thought, watching her hips. Like a ship gently lapped by the waves.

He was completely obsessed by her. She filled his thoughts, night and day, causing him to smile suddenly, inexplicably, his face creasing with a curious serenity when her image came to mind. Being with her—and he thought of these nightly vigils as being with her—was a time for observing her with a fanatical devotion so that when she was gone he could remember it all, going over and over each motion, each nuance of her expression, interpreting the tilt of her head for signs of displeasure, reading hope into a glance. In many ways he loved her even more when she was away from him, for his fantasies had freer rein without her presence to inhibit him. He was capable of falling into breathless, heart-fluttering episodes whether she was with him or not.

Florio dogged her steps to her apartment door, feeling a satisfaction at having seen her safely home. To his surprise she turned in the doorway and looked back at him. He stood half a block away, trapped by her forthright gaze. This was breaking the rules. After confronting him that first time on the street, she had been scrupulous about ignoring him, saving them both from further embarrassment.

She waved at him, beckoning him to come to her. As Florio approached her, Keiner lifted the camera from the passenger's seat. It was a Konica FS-1 fitted out with a zoom lens. Keiner was no photographer, but he knew how to point it and the machines they made these days took care of most of the work themselves. He focused the lens as Sheila took Florio by the arm, smiling at him. Keiner clicked.

Florio moved stiffly, reluctantly, it seemed to Keiner, as she tugged him by the wrist across the lobby of the building. Keiner snapped the shot, then hurried out of the car to get directly opposite the lobby. He arrived in time to see them getting into the elevator. Sheila was beaming up at Florio, who turned and stared in Keiner's direction just as the shutter clicked. The elevator door slid closed and they were gone.

Poor Block, thought Keiner. Poor son of a bitch thinks he's protecting his wife and what he's really got is a divorce case. He was too old to get married. Keiner could have warned him. Keiner was an expert on failed marriages.

Sheila led Florio into her apartment and across to the sofa. Placing her hands on his shoulders, she forced him to sit, then stood before him, legs spread, arms akimbo, in what she hoped was a stern schoolmistress pose.

"This has to stop," she said. "I know you mean no harm by it, but it's going on much too long and I don't think it's good for either one of us."

When Florio spoke his voice was husky, as if he hadn't used it in a long time.

"I haven't done anything," he said.

"You've been following me. Do you think I haven't seen you? You've been out there every night, waiting for me to get off work, then following me home, then sometimes hanging around outside for an hour or more. Why do you do it? You don't have to do it, you know. I've made an effort, haven't I, to be friendly? If you want to walk with me, then come and walk with me, I'm happy to have your company."

"I haven't been hanging around," he said. "I make sure you get home safe, that's all."

"Sometimes you do," she said. "I've seen you in the doorway across the street."

"No," he said, puzzled.

"All right, I don't want to argue about it. Anyway, I know you're doing it because you want to protect me, but I don't need it, really I don't. I know you feel you owe it to Sandy for all he's done for you. . . ."

A shadow of incomprehension passed over Florio's face and Sheila knew she was wrong. Good God, she thought, that isn't it. He's doing it because he loves me. All that tongue-tied shyness when they were together, the recoil at her touch, the strange intensity whenever he was near her—she knew now with instinctive certainty that she was right.

"I am so stupid," she said. "Please forgive me." She sat on the sofa beside him, not yet certain enough of her reaction to look at him.

Florio waited, studying her face. Even troubled and perplexed, she was the most beautiful creature he had ever seen. Being this close to her made him feel weak, as if the love that filled him was not sturdy enough to support the weight of his body.

She looked in his face again at last. Her lips smiled weakly, but her eyes appeared ready to weep.

"Florio . . . I'm happily married. I love my husband. If I've ever led you to believe otherwise, I'm so sorry. But I love my husband."

He nodded slowly, politely.

"Yes."

"Yes," she repeated.

Florio slid off the couch onto his knees. He felt as if he were melting. He put his head in her lap and closed his eyes.

"Oh, Jesus," he said.

"Please don't," she said softly, putting her hands on his shoulders and pushing gently. He was impossible to move with such a feeble effort.

Florio said something into the fabric of her skirt, his lips moving against her thigh. Sheila didn't understand him, but she could feel his warm breath going through the cloth, heating her skin.

"Please get up," she said.

"Love you," he said hoarsely, his lips still pressed against her skirt. He sounded so torn, so sorrowful, that Sheila instinctively put her hand on his head. Who could turn love roughly aside?

"Oh, Florio," she said. "You mustn't be unhappy. I didn't know, I really didn't know." She stroked his hair but stifled the impulse to cradle him.

"Come on, now," she said brightly, trying to jolly them both out of the mood. "Sit up and we'll have a cup of coffee and talk about it. I'm really not worth it, you'll see."

But he put his hands under her skirt, gripping her thighs. She gasped with the suddenness of it.

"No!" she said, sharply. Sheila pushed him again, harder, but he was too heavy, his body weight kept her immobilized from the waist down, pinned against the sofa.

His head moved so that it was pressing firmly against her abdomen, his chin digging between her legs. His hands slid higher up her thighs, the thumbs caressing the soft inner flesh, the fingers insinuating themselves under the elastic of her panties. The thumbs joined and rubbed her where her legs met.

"Stop!" she cried, and even then she thought he would. She felt as if she could still control him if only she could remain calm.

His thumbs rubbed her again and she realized she was responding despite herself. Dismayed as much by her reaction as by his activity, she struck him on the back with her tiny balled fist. She hit him again and again with both hands. Her blows seemed so pathetically weak against his broad back.

With one heave he gripped her buttocks and jerked her flat on the sofa. His head lay on her chest, his lips atop her breast. His warm breath cut through the thin muslin blouse as if it weren't there. She could feel her nipples stiffen in response. His hands were still active under her skirt. The thumbs stopped stroking for a moment while they burrowed their way under the edge of her panties. They met again, under the cloth, ruffling her pubic hair.

Florio gave a long, shuddering sigh as his thumbs touched the moisture between her legs.

"I'll scream!" said Sheila, but she didn't. She tried to get a knee up but his weight was too much. She couldn't move except to hit his back. He controlled her completely; at least part of her liked it. She detested herself for it.

He was firm and he was forceful, but he was not hurting her. She willed herself to struggle more, but she knew that she was fighting now only enough to be able to tell herself she had resisted. His mouth closed on her breast, pulling gently at the nipple. One of his thumbs entered her, the other moved up higher and caressed her.

"Don't," she pleaded. "Don't do this. I'm pregnant."

Florio stopped immediately, pulling his hands away from her as if they were burned. Slowly he sat up, turning away from her. He sat on the edge of the sofa as she righted herself and straightened her clothes.

"Pregnant," he said dully.

"Yes, pregnant," she said. She was amazed that her voice was calm.

"Congratulations," he said, after a pause. She listened for a note of irony or sarcasm, but there was none. His voice was flat, toneless.

"Thank you," she said. For a moment they sat on the opposite ends of the sofa. The cushion between them still held the impression of their bodies. Sheila massaged it back into shape. I can't believe this, she thought. We're both acting as if nothing happened, and a minute ago I was nearly raped. Or seduced.

"How pregnant?" he asked.

Sheila laughed. "Completely," she said, thinking of the old line that there was no such thing as being only a little bit pregnant.

"Two months," she added. She knew to the day. It had happened the night of that odd dream, she was certain of it. She believed that a woman could always tell.

Florio stood and turned to her. His face was impassive, his eyes full and expressionless. The longing that had animated them only moments before was gone, and now there was nothing there at all.

"I'm sorry," he said.

For a moment Sheila didn't know how to take it. Sorry that he had attacked her? Sorry that she was pregnant? She had a sense that he was referring to something different, some past or future transgression of which she had no knowledge.

"Well," she said finally, groping for the right phrase. "I understand. I'm willing to forget all about it if you are."

She expected him to answer, to agree to forget it, maybe even ask her not to mention it to Sandy, but he seemed not to have heard her. He continued to stare at her blankly. The real Florio had withdrawn very far within the shell.

He started to go, then stopped and reached out for her hand. She pulled it away instinctively, now suddenly afraid of him. He insisted, caught her forearm. Then, with a slow grace she had never seen in him before, he lifted her hand to his lips and kissed it, bending slightly like a cavalier. His lips moved on the back of her hand with infinite tenderness, then he pressed her hand against his cheek for a second, his eyes closed.

"Good-bye," he said, dropping her hand. There was life in his voice again, although whether it was self-mockery or contempt Sheila could not say.

When he had gone, Sheila stood in front of a mirror and re-garded herself. Her blouse still held a dark ring above her breast where his mouth had touched, but the moisture was already fading. Aside from that, there was no sign at all of what had just happened. Except for her flushed cheeks. Excitement or out-rage? She admitted it was both.

"You are a slut," she told her reflection.

Glancing out the window, she surveyed the street to see if Florio was still out there, huddled in the night, watching for a sign of her. He was gone. Sheila looked for a long time, think-ing he might appear again.

When her husband came home and took her in his arms, she told him she did not feel well.

Tom-Tom had been aware of the man watching for some time. A burly, balding man with a tattoo on one shoulder and a blue bruise on his bicep, his short-sleeve shirt too tight for him, as if he had been smaller once and had never adjusted in his mind— he was either a cop or a longshoreman, and dockworkers did not sit in stakeouts. Tom-Tom had caught the glint of light on the long, unwieldy camera lens. Circling around behind him had been easy enough, and then it had been just a matter of time, waiting for nature to take its course.

When Keiner left his car to find a bathroom, Tom-Tom slipped into the back seat. A heavy tarp covered the back seat and it in turn was covered with a half-empty twenty-pound bag of top-soil, half a dozen clay pots, a bag of peat moss with a leak in one corner, a seed catalogue, a pair of work gloves covered with dirt, an old trowel with the wooden handle broken off. The car smelled of earth and humidity. Tom-Tom put on the work gloves and lay on the floor, pulling the tarp over himself. Under the tarp he worked the handcuffs loose on his belt and slipped them over his knuckles, but then he had a better idea. The steel rod of the trowel handle was still securely attached to the blade, even though the wooden haft was gone. The rod was slightly thinner than Tom-Tom's forefinger and longer.

Skewer the son of a bitch with his own toy, Tom-Tom thought. He laughed soundlessly. Shame on you, he thought, you're even going to enjoy killing this one, and he's just a nuisance, not a pleasure. You're beginning to like it too much, you naughty boy. He giggled. Naughty-naughty Tom-Tom. He lay under the tarp, very pleased with himself, until Keiner came back to the car.

Keiner heard the sound behind him and started to turn just as he caught a glimpse of Tom-Tom's face in the rearview mir-ror. Tom-Tom's eyes were glinting with excitement even though his mouth was twisted and his teeth bared.

"What the fuck—" Keiner said, just before Tom-Tom drove the spike of the trowel handle straight down toward the chrome plate buried under Keiner's scalp. Tom-Tom felt it was a little like puncturing a tin can with a nail. The spike broke off of the blade and Tom-Tom could not pull it out for a second blow, but it didn't matter by then. Keiner was dead and Tom-Tom was laughing out loud.

18

 Feely, the photo technician, gently agitated the print in the developing solution and silently cursed the photographer. The first of the shots was coming out very blurry and underexposed, the work of an amateur. The man with the camera had used the wrong film and the wrong shutter speed and as a result Feely was going to have to attack it with a variety of techniques before he had a blowup that could be identified. He didn't mind the work—in fact he enjoyed the challenge—but it meant he would have Detective Lieutenant Block breathing, literally, down his neck that much longer.

Block had brought the camera in and had not left the technician's side since. He was with him now, peering over his shoulder, his features taking on an eerie glow in the red working light. Block took the wet print from Feely's hand.

A man, or the shape of a man, loomed in a darkened doorway. There were no identifying features to the doorway, it could have been anywhere. The man, the shape of the man, appeared to have his head tilted, looking up.

"I can't make this out," said Block, but he thought he could. Vaguely, fleetingly, the image tugged at his memory. Something about the tilt of the head, the turn of the shoulder, looked familiar.

"No, sir," the technician agreed.

"It could be anybody."

The technician doubted it. A camera enthusiast might take a picture of a random face, an interesting shape, a darkened doorway. But this guy wasn't an enthusiast, he barely knew which end to point. This wasn't experimentation, it was rank amateurism. Whoever it was, the photographer wanted his picture.

The second shot was as bad as the first, maybe worse. The subject had shifted his face away from the camera slightly, revealing what the technician assumed was the back of his head. Feely was forced to assume, because as the subject turned he also stepped deeper into the darkness. Black on black, shadow merging into man and man into shadow.

He heard Block grunt as he clipped the second shot onto the wire.

"Not very good," said the technician. "Not much of a photographer." Feely wanted Block to realize it wasn't *his* fault.

But Block was struck by something other than the quality of the film. He was seeing not the pose but the arrested motion. It seemed so familiar, it nearly shrieked its name. Nearly—not quite. He had to be careful, he had to be sure.

As a younger man Block had played handball on the outdoor courts of the city playgrounds. He had not been a good player, but he had been a very observant one. Without making a conscious effort he found that he had absorbed the subtle nuances of movement of a vast number of players. Frequently he found he could identify by his walk alone a man he had seen only once or twice in his life. And almost as frequently, to his amazement, he could be wrong. He would note the slightly pigeon-toed walk of certain athletes, the way of carrying the arm away from the body, the tilt of the head, all of it declaring that this person was a man Block knew—or at least a brother. But when he pursued the connection, it would vanish. Close, Block had learned, was not good enough. His eyes and memory were flawed.

They might be wrong now. He had to remind himself he was looking at very blurry photos of a man without features. They were photographs, they were not cloaked in flesh and blood and moving in familiar action, no matter how much his instincts said that they were.

"Blow this one up," Block said. "Blow both of them up."

"I will certainly blow them up, sir," said Feely, "but they'll be blurrier."

Block was not listening to him. He had taken the next photo out of Feely's grasp, jerking it abruptly away, and was studying it now with faintly quivering hand. Feely thought he looked as though he were seeing a pornographic picture of his mother.

Sheila was holding Florio's arm, smiling at him. He was looking down at her, his face frozen, solemn. They were standing outside Block's apartment building. Keiner had had no trouble with this shot. It was Sheila. It was Florio.

The next shot was worse. Sheila was holding Florio by the wrist, tugging him across the lobby of the building. The expression on her face as she walked backward, pulling him, was playful. Florio had his back to the camera, but Block could imagine his expression, and the thought sickened him.

A third shot showed them in the elevator just before the door closed. Sheila was still smiling and Block thought she looked achingly beautiful. Florio had just turned his head away from her and was staring, surprised, across the lobby. He was looking straight at the camera. He was looking, Block realized, at Keiner.

"The rest of the roll is blank," said Feely. "I guess that was the last shot he took."

"Yes," said Block dully. It was the last shot Keiner took. A full face of Tom-Tom with Sheila. Sheila smiling and unsuspecting. Keiner marked for death by the photo that had captured his murderer.

Block steadied himself for a moment, leaning against the vat of solution. He felt as if he was going to be sick. He had hidden from it, tried to rationalize it, tried to ignore it. He had waited too long for Keiner and Rosemary Schwarz and maybe even those two women in the brownstone. Yes, he had suspected even then. He could add two more lives, deaths, to his conscience. He prayed he had not waited too long for Sheila, too.

First Block called Sheila. He told her she was to go straight home with the patrolman who was coming to pick her up. She was to lock the door, throw the chain, and stay in her apartment, opening the door for no one until Block returned home. When she started to demand why, alarm making her voice rise, he simply repeated his instructions. By the time he had gone through it all a third time, her voice had calmed and he knew she would obey. There would be time enough to explain it all to her later.

It was not true, as Sheila had at first protested, that not knowing was worse than the facts. Whatever dangers she imagined for herself would not exceed the danger she was already in. Also, Block knew, if he told her that Florio was Tom-Tom, she would not believe him. How do you convince a woman that her lover is planning to kill her? How, as a husband, do you convince your wife that there is no measure of personal enmity in this judgment? Indeed, Block wondered, how do you convince yourself? How much was he convinced that Florio was Tom-Tom because of what had happened to Keiner, because of what Keiner's camera told him, and how much because he wanted to be rid of the man who was cuckolding him?

There was no point in going to Byrne. Block could order a simple thing like a ride for his wife in a squad car, but he could not give her police protection beyond that without telling Byrne what he knew. And what he knew would look like a cuckold's revenge—Block was aware of that. There was no evidence, none at all, to *prove* Florio was Tom-Tom. A name, misspelled, in Alicia Caro's diary, a voice on tape that sounded familiar in its ecstatic ramblings, a blurry photo of a man hiding in the shadows, a startled face in an elevator glaring at Keiner. Even Block did not know it, but he sensed it, feeling the truth of it on a much deeper level of conviction than the mere rational. Block had been in the lair of the beast, he had its scent in his nostrils, he had felt the beast stirring in the dark. His skin crawled with the certainty that the beast was here now, crouched in the night, waiting to pounce on the one person Block valued above all others. He did not need *proof* any more than a man in a graveyard who feels the frigid grip of skeletal fingers on his ankle needs to be told to be afraid. He *knew.*

When Sheila called to say that she was safely home, the door locked, Block went to find Florio.

Setting the bait was simple. He told Florio that he would be away from home all night, pursuing a lead on Long Island. And then he told him Sheila was pregnant.

"Congratulations," Florio said. He did not seem the least bit surprised. When he offered to shake Block's hand Block thought he saw a shift behind his eyes, as if different shapes were moving past each other.

"I couldn't be happier for you," Florio said.

Block kept smiling until he thought his face would break from the effort. Only when Florio had walked away and left the office did Block allow himself to react. He rubbed his right hand against the cloth of his trouser leg. He had felt the monster's scales scrape against his skin. Tom-Tom would come tonight, Block was sure of it. And this time Block would be ready.

Block settled himself in the stairwell outside his apartment. He sat on a folding chair and peered through the crack of the door, the door wedged open an inch by a matchbook. He could see the entrance to his apartment clearly, he could be at the door at the first sign of trouble within a few seconds. He could not see the elevator, but he could hear it when the doors opened or closed. If Tom-Tom chose to come up the stairs, Block would be able to hear and see him a full two flights ahead of time. The door to his apartment he had checked out himself. Even an expert—and most detectives had to be considered expert—could not get through that door without taking a lot of time and making a lot of noise. The only quick way in would be for Sheila to open the door from the inside.

Confident in the security of his stakeout, Block leaned back in the chair and prepared himself for what he would have to do when Tom-Tom showed up. He forced himself to think of him as Tom-Tom now, not Florio. It was Tom-Tom who must be dealt with, not his friend. If there had been any evidence on which to arrest Florio, to protect him, get him treatment, Block would have done so. But there was no way to help him except to stop him. Block's one fear was that he would hesitate, that at the crucial moment he would see his friend, not the madman, and fail to fire.

He settled back and waited for Tom-Tom to come. He knew he would come with the night. He felt it with every fiber of his being. Block would encounter the beast one final time, and already he could sense the rush of its madness, hear the slither of its tail on the stairs. The stairwell seemed heavy with Tom-Tom's presence. Block removed the automatic from its holster and placed it on his lap.

As darkness fell, Sheila tried to busy herself in the apartment, but it did not take long enough to cook a meal for one, or do the dishes for one, or to tidy up after just one. She wondered where Sandy was now. Had he eaten? Was he safe?

In the middle of a television show Sheila found herself looking out the window, staring blankly at the darkness. She rose and stood by the glass, looking down at the street, down at the spot where night after night she had seen Florio keeping his lonely vigil. Had it been Florio? She had assumed so, but he had denied it.

With the light on behind her she could not tell if anyone was out there tonight, and she did not really want to know. She was frightened enough, she realized, without making it worse.

She returned to her chair, this time with a book, but her eyes continued to drift toward the window.

•

Florio had haunted the streets during the day, walking every-where, using the motion to alleviate the pain and disgust he felt with himself. Fumbling at Sheila, his hands up her skirt. Telling her he loved her! Pawing at her like a rapist.

Florio walked to the tip of Manhattan, to the shadows of the Twin Towers, then turned and walked back uptown again. He paused only long enough to take sips from the bottle of bour-bon in his pocket, using it as fuel for the exercise and the tor-ment. When the bottle was empty he bought another and kept walking. By nightfall he still did not feel drunk.

He had to apologize, that much was clear. He had to tell Sheila he was sorry. He had to see her one last time and tell her he was sorry, then he could do whatever he had to do.

He waited for her as usual outside her office, but when all the lights were off and she didn't appear, he went to her apart-ment building. He stood in the dark, watching the light in her window. She appeared suddenly, silhouetted in the window, looking out, and Florio's gasp of pleasure was irrepressible. He knew he had to go up.

Sheila was a little girl again and someone was hurting her and she was crying, but it wasn't she who was crying, it was her daughter, her unborn child. She struggled awake, surprised that she had managed to sleep at all. The child was still crying and she realized she had not dreamed it but merely incorporated it into her dream.

She had fallen asleep in the chair and her neck was stiff. Mas-saging it, she stood and stretched, arching her back like a cat. The child in the hallway cried again and she started for the door, only then remembering her promise not to open it.

She crossed to the window. If anyone was out there now, she could not make him out.

TS - P

"Mama," cried the child. "I want my mama."

There was the sound of a grunt and a body hit the floor in the hallway. A man's voice cried out in pain, then there were more sounds, less clear, sounds of violence and sudden movement. Sheila looked through the spyhole and saw two men struggling with each other. At first she could see only their bodies, two large, strong men, straining against each other. Then she could make out Block's face, distorted with effort and anger. Block was lashing out with his handcuffs, striking at the man whose hands were closing around Block's throat. It was Florio.

Sheila screamed and opened the door. The two men crashed against the wall and fell. Florio was on top, still choking Block. Block's blows were growing feebler. Sheila ran to the kitchen and grabbed the first weapon she saw, the carving knife. In the hall she hesitated for just a second, knife raised overhead. Block's eyes fluttered up toward hers but he gave no sign of recognition. He's dying, Sheila thought. She brought the knife down with all her strength, plunging it deep into Florio's back.

Florio jerked backward, then turned so Sheila saw his face.

His expression was one of dismay, as if she had hurt his feelings more than anything else.

"I saw him. . . ." Florio said. His tone was quite reasonable, but one hand was twitching behind him, trying to find the knife. He stood, reeling badly.

"I saw him. . . ." he started again. He took a step toward Sheila, the one hand still clawing at his back, the other reaching for her. His fingers brushed her cheek. Sheila screamed and jumped aside as Florio fell forward. His face hit the wall and slid down it. His eyes were open but already unseeing.

Sheila screamed for quite some time before it occurred to her to call an ambulance and the police. When she returned to the hallway, Block's eyes were closed but he was breathing evenly, and Florio had stopped twitching. She wasn't sure if he was breathing at all.

SEPTEMBER

Sheila sat on the screened porch of the beach house, looking at the sea. The summer season was over and they had the beach to themselves most of the day. The other clapboard house they could see stood empty, deserted by the summer occupants. The year-rounders in the next house on the other side had returned, but their house was out of sight around a curve in the shore and on the other side of some ponderous dunes.

Block and Sheila were quite alone, which had seemed a good idea at first, but developed into a bad situation. They were the worst company for each other. Away from the distractions of his job, Block was hit with remorse, plagued with guilt. He had set a trap for his friend when—with hindsight—it seemed there might have been a better way, a route to safety that didn't endanger all three of them. It had seemed an uncharacteristically risky move on Block's part, and she could only guess at the emotional turmoil that had forced him into it.

On the sand, Block jogged by, head down, arms pumping. He was a joyless runner. His legs moved heavily across the beach, his feet barely clearing the sand. Sheila realized he did it not for exercise or pleasure, but to exhaust himself, and he ran until he slowed to a lurching walk. He would return to their beach house and collapse on the sofa, too drained to speak. More important, Sheila knew, he was too tired to think. Later in the day he would rise wearily and do it all again.

Sheila had gone with him at first, taking long walks along the shore, but the silence had been too much. Each was suffering with memories and they only served to remind each other. After a few days she let him go alone and he turned to running to burn out the pain.

After the incident with Florio they had tried at first to stay in the city. Block had had the easier part of it then. He was kept busy by the reporters, the official inquiry, all the little details of cleaning up. Sheila was left to her thoughts and Florio was never out of her mind. The look on his face when she stabbed him was burned onto the back of her retina. She saw that look as a final plea for understanding. "I saw him," he had said. "I saw him." And Sheila had seen him, too. She had seen Tom-Tom and Florio merged into one, cop and killer and lovelorn man all the same, all just wanting understanding.

And she continued to see him. His image seemed to have multiplied and bled throughout the city. In the evenings when she left her office she could not stop herself from looking everywhere, searching the crowds for his face. When she reached home she found herself drawn to the window to see if anyone was standing in the shadows across the street. Because she sought him, she found him, in the shadows, in the crowds, in the fleeting glimpse of a stranger, head turned just so, shoulders set just so, a flash of Florio, then gone. Sometimes he wore the pleading expression. Sometimes, in the night, the shadow across the street still had the knife sticking from his back.

She had tried to tell Block about it at first. Without mentioning the rape-seduction and her subsequent silence about it, she told him of the few times she and Florio had been together, of the odd, ritualistic courtship air of Florio's presence.

"I was . . . I liked him," she said, lamely, knowing she was not doing justice to the situation. Her relationship with Florio was more ambiguous than that, more emotionally charged, but exactly how, she couldn't define to herself, much less describe to her husband.

He looked at her curiously, his head tipped to one side. She felt that he was trying to suppress something, but whether mirth or anger she didn't know.

"I know you liked him," he said, his voice deliberately flat. "I liked him, too."

"He meant more to you than that," she said, feeling the need to defend Florio's memory. "He was a very special friend."

"Was he to you, too?"

Sheila looked away. "There was something special about him. I didn't know him that well."

"We've discovered what was special about him," said Block.

"I don't mean that. There was something special about him as Florio, not just as Tom-Tom. We can't deny that man now just because of what happened. If we do, it will be like the good side didn't exist at all. And it did . . . didn't it?"

"Yes, it did," said Block slowly.

"Oh, God," she cried, bursting suddenly into tears. "It was so awful. So awful!"

Block tried to comfort her, but it was the same as it had been since that night. The guilt of each evoked guilt in the other. Silence became a less painful course.

But as her days became somehow more manageable, her dreams became worse. She woke time and again, screaming with horror or begging forgiveness. Block would hold her sweat-drenched body and murmur, "It's over, it's all over," again and again.

But of course it wasn't over.

The nurse was late and Florio was worried. He had come to depend on the regularity of the hospital routine. In a world gone mad, it was a constant he could cling to. Breakfast at such a time. Pill. Visit by doctor and nurse to check the status of his wounds. Loosening of his restraints so he could sit up, examination. Healing nicely. Doctor leaning over, checking heart, pulse, lungs. The doctor would be easy enough to take right then, but Florio would never get to the nurse before she spread the alarm. Not with thirty-nine stitches in his back. After the visit, replace the restraints. Boredom until lunch. Another pill. A visit in the afternoon, sometimes police, sometimes Kanter— the one variable. Another pill midafternoon. Dinner. Restraint loosened for mealtimes, of course, but there was an orderly with every meal, a burly, suspicious man who stood at a distance from Florio and never looked away. What did he think, Florio was going to disembowel someone with a plastic spoon? That was the main problem, everyone was so damned wary. Except the doctor. He didn't seem to be afraid, but then maybe he didn't read the newspapers.

Florio had read the newspapers. He was well aware of what he was supposed to have done, he had read Block's account, seen the picture of Sheila, eyes still wide with panic, looking startled by the flash of the photographer's camera. He had tried to chew the picture off the page, using his teeth as scissors since he couldn't use his hands. He wanted to save it, but they thought he was having a fit, trying to eat his enemies or some such.

The nurse arrived, only a minute or two late, after all. Florio tucked the pill between his cheek and gum and drank from the straw. He let some water dribble out of his mouth as if his lips weren't working quite right. It was a nice touch. It made him look like the zombie the pills were designed to create. He would dispose of the sedative when the orderly took him to the bathroom. Even the orderly wasn't so suspicious as to check his stool.

When the time came, he shuffled along to the bathroom, pausing every so often as if exhausted. The orderly stayed well away. While appearing to move haltingly because of chemical exhaustion, Florio was actually using the time to test his back. Moving it, flexing the muscles. It still hurt badly, but not too much anymore. He could contain the pain now.

The doctor had explained it all patiently enough. Sheila's knife had penetrated the heavy trapezius muscle on the upper portion of his right back, sliced through the rhomboideus major and the underlying splenius. The blade had missed the scapula and slipped neatly between the third and fourth ribs. The doctor had sounded almost respectful as he described the surgical neatness of the incision. The point of the blade had nicked the right lung before coming to a stop. If the blade had been a bit longer, it might have reached his heart and Florio's problems would be over. If it had been a bit more to the right, it would have struck bone and Florio would not have passed out. What then? According to the police, Florio, that is, Tom-Tom, would have killed Sheila and Block. They were wrong, of course, but Florio couldn't convince them of it. It was a neat type of madness they had assigned to him. He would be the last to recognize it, because he was the very one his personality had split in order to protect. The saner he seemed, the crazier they thought he was inside.

Kanter, of course, had been doing mental gyrations like a hooker, trying to entice Florio's other personalities out into the open. As if he expected Florio to dissolve into a puddle and rise up again as a monster, or a girl, or a saint. Oh, he understood the theory by now, he'd heard it often enough. The thing was they had the wrong man. The whole thing would be ridiculous if it weren't so dangerously mistaken. Sheila's life was in peril. Florio faced a lifetime in a mental hospital. It was all a disastrous mistake which only Florio could correct. If he got out. No, when he got out. He had to . . . so he would.

Returning from the bathroom, he stood in the middle of the hall, swaying slightly as if dizzy. At the end of the hall was the door he needed to get through. Locked, of course, with thick wire mesh on the window. But only one door and he was out of the forensic section and into the regular hospital. From there he would take his chances.

In bed once more, he made his final plans. If the afternoon visitors were the police, he would simply have to wait. He would ask once more to see Block. Tell them again he was innocent. Inquire about Sheila. As usual they would tell him nothing about Block, but they wouldn't have to. The district attorney's man was a young one and he had let slip early in the game that Block was on vacation. Florio knew what that meant. He knew Block's habits well. He would be on Long Island now. On the beach. The same beach house he rented year after year. Florio even remembered the address from a visit in years past. It was amazing the things you could remember if you had all day to think.

If the afternoon's visitor was Kanter, then it was time to go. The psychiatrist required that they be alone during the examination. Florio might not be ready to tackle the orderly yet, or even the nurse. But he knew he could handle Kanter.

He began to chew the inside of his cheeks. Whoever was coming would be here soon, and if it was Kanter, he would need plenty of blood to look authentic.

The door opened. It was Kanter.

"How are you feeling today?" Kanter asked, settling himself in the chair by Florio's bed. He had his notepad on his lap. The tape recorder in his inside pocket had been turned on before he entered the room. He didn't want Florio to freeze up at the sight of the recorder, as many patients did, but he wasn't going to risk losing a chance to record one of the personalities if it emerged. Kanter had been trying everything he knew to elicit one of Florio's other selves. It was an opportunity few psychiatrists would have in a lifetime. A case study of the multiple personality who had rocked New York City would lift Kanter out of his current mire in police work, not to mention a movie sale . . . and of course it would help Florio, too. That was the main thing.

"Are you on the mend?" Kanter asked, smiling brightly. It was important to become the one person Florio trusted, the one he would talk to.

Florio shook his head slowly from side to side, his eyes half closed. He coughed discreetly a couple of times, his mouth closed. Kanter thought he did not look well, worse than yesterday. His cheeks looked sunken.

Florio coughed again, a disquieting noise, even though his mouth still remained closed. A tiny trickle of blood came from between Florio's lips.

Kanter stood up, startled. There had been some fear about the damage done to his lung where the knife blade had nicked it. It seemed to be healing well, but one could never be sure of injuries in that area.

Florio's mouth and jaw were working, the sides of his cheeks now alarmingly sunken, almost as if they were being sucked inward. He coughed, a distressingly rich, liquid sound, and this time spat a gout of blood onto his shirt.

He's coughing up blood, Kanter thought with alarm. He moved to the bed to press the button for the nurse. Florio's leg whipped out from under the covers and around Kanter's chest. Kanter was yanked back against the bed, his neck scissored between Florio's calves.

"Reach up with your right hand and undo the restraint," said Florio.

Kanter tried to pull the leg from his neck. Florio tightened the grip. Kanter was amazed at the strength. He could feel the knot of Florio's calf muscle constricting his throat. He reached up one hand blindly and clawed at the restraint that held Florio's arm.

It all happened so bewilderingly fast that Kanter was not quite sure how he had wound up in the bed himself, tied down tightly by the restraining straps. I should have struggled more, he thought. Maybe I should have cried for help before he stuck the pajama top in my mouth and covered my head with a pillow. He could still hear Florio, even though the pillow cut off vision, as Florio tried to fit himself into Kanter's clothes. Kanter lay very still, careful not to draw any more attention to himself. All he wanted now was for Florio to get dressed and leave. Kanter would be content to lie here until the nurse came. To hell with struggling, to hell with yelling. He was no hero. He was no cop. He waited to hear Florio leave and the door close before he even took a deep breath. He could always tell them later that he had fought like a tiger.

Captain Byrne shuffled the photos back and forth across his desk, trying them in varying positions, trying to make sense of them. They were the first two shots on the roll of film that had been in Keiner's camera when he died. Feeny, the technician, had blown them up, processed them through a series of filters, then subjected them to some sort of computer enhancement which Byrne did not pretend to understand. Block had requested the treatment, according to Feeny, and the result was good—if confusing. The shape in the darkened doorway, black on black, had been transformed into a recognizable image.

Byrne sighed. If there was anything about the Tom-Tom business that *wasn't* puzzling, he had yet to hear it. One of his men half killed and now locked up in the bin with his arms strapped to his bed, another, his *best* man, out of commission from guilt and sorrow. The newspapers were having a wonderful time and the past few days had been the first time in two weeks that Byrne had been able to stick his nose outside without getting a microphone thrust under it. Byrne had already had two offers from publishers who wanted to do a quickie paperback on the Tom-Tom case. Who knew what Florio's memoirs would be worth—if he were sane enough to write them.

McKeon entered cautiously, as always, hanging back after knocking, leaning just his head into the room first, as if sniffing for danger. He reminded Byrne of a dim-witted dog.

"Captain?"

"I already said come in, McKeon."

"You're going to hate this, Captain."

"It's not a joyous job, McKeon. What have you got?"

"Florio's gone."

"He died?"

"Escaped."

"Escaped! You'd better be joking."

"Not really."

"How in hell did he do it?"

"The Kanter was in with him, trying to determine if he was sane enough for a trial and all that, when Florio starts coughing up blood. Well, Kanter figures maybe the lung is bleeding again. He's concerned, he's a doctor, he goes to take a look. Florio got ahold of him."

"How in hell can a healthy man be overpowered by a sedated man who's coughing up blood!"

"Kanter doesn't think he was sedated. He doesn't think he was really coughing up the blood, either."

"He's doing a hell of a lot of thinking after the fact."

"He had lots of time to think, I guess. They found Kanter in Florio's bed, tied down and with a pillow in his mouth. Florio's got his clothes, his money, his cards, his car keys—"

"I got the idea. How much of a lead does Florio have?"

"About an hour, I guess."

"Shit. He's out of the city by now, you can bet on that. Christ, the man's got holes in his back. How far can he get?"

"He didn't have any trouble with Kanter."

"You wouldn't have any trouble with Kanter."

"What's that mean?"

"What do the doctors say? Can he travel in his condition?"

"They think he'll be in a lot of pain. They say it all depends on how bad he wants to get wherever he wants to go."

"We better assume he wants it bad. All right, notify the state cops and send out an APB to our guys."

"Yes, sir."

"McKeon . . . Block's wife. She's pregnant, isn't she?"

"Yes, sir, I think so. The Kanter thinks Florio might go after her. He says Florio—or Tom-Tom, whoever in hell he is—had been kind of fixated on Block and his wife, asking a lot of questions and all."

"That had occurred to me, McKeon. Notify Block."

"That's kind of a problem. We don't know where he is."

"He's on vacation."

"Yes, sir, but we don't know where, exactly. He didn't leave an address or phone number the way he's supposed to—I figure to duck the reporters. We assume he's on Long Island, that's where he usually goes, but nobody ever visited him out there as far as I know, except . . ."

"Except who?"

"Florio."

Byrne pursed his lips and pressed his fingertips together in front of his chest, a mannerism of his when thinking. McKeon thought he looked like a praying mantis.

"Alert every police force on the Island, and then get hold of a list of rental agents out there. If he went through one of them we can get his phone number. Go. Do."

McKeon vanished, bobbing his head in agreement. Byrne felt as if he had sent him to fetch a stick.

Florio drove Kanter's car directly to a midtown indoor parking lot where patrons parked the cars themselves. After less than a minute of looking, he found a Volkswagen Beetle with the door unlocked. He hot-wired the VW and drove out of the lot, paying off the ticket issued to Kanter's car. Let them think he was still in Kanter's car, it would give him time.

He passed through the Midtown Tunnel, and half an hour after coughing blood for Kanter's benefit, he was on the Long Island Expressway heading east. Traffic was light at this time of day—the rush home wouldn't begin for another hour—but Florio kept his speed down to fifty-five. The last thing he wanted was a run-in with some zealous traffic cop. He passed through Queens and without transition into the series of Long Island towns that bordered the expressway but never touched it.

Passing signs to Jericho, his back began to hurt badly. He had wrenched it when he threw his arm around Kanter's throat, and some of the stitches had torn. His back was moist and sticking to his shirt and Florio realized he was bleeding. Kanter was not a small man, but he favored form-fitting European style clothes, and Florio had left the shirt unbuttoned to the navel in order to get it on. The jacket was tight across the shoulders— all part of Kanter's sexy image—and Florio felt as if he would rip a seam with every move.

He turned north on Sunken Meadow Parkway, then east again on 25A. He was off the expressways now, traveling much slower, letting the flow of traffic carry him. At one point he passed a slow truck, pulling rapidly into the other lane, then swiftly back to avoid oncoming traffic. The effort caused a shooting pain from his back all the way down his right arm, and after that his wounds seemed to ache even more. He cursed himself for not having stolen a car with power steering.

At East Setauket Florio pulled off the highway and cruised slowly through town until he found a pharmacy. He bought a bottle of extra-strength aspirins and swallowed six, then asked directions to the nearest sporting goods store.

Florio asked the clerk in the sporting goods store for a riot gun.

The clerk was a big man with a full brown beard peppered with gray, the kind of man who could sit for hours in a duck blind, thinking the few seconds of firing, of killing birds, were worth the wait. He handled the weapons with something more than respect, a kind of lambent sensuality. He stroked the black barrel of the riot gun as if soothing a nervous animal.

"The Remington 11-48. Twelve gauge, semiautomatic," he said proudly. He jerked the chamber open, let it fly shut, yanked the gun up to his shoulder with a practiced move. "Holds five cartridges. Just keep pumping the trigger and you can down a whole flock. If you're close enough."

"How close?" Florio asked.

"Well, that depends what you're after," the man said. "This is an eighteen-and-a-half-inch barrel. There's very little choke on a barrel that short, the pattern spreads pretty fast. It depends what you're shooting at and what kind of ammunition you're using. For woodcock, for instance, I'd use number-nine shot. You'd have an effective pattern at—oh, maybe thirty-five yards."

"I'm not after birds," said Florio.

"Oh, yes," said the man, nodding, as if he understood everything completely and at once. It was not hard to look at Florio and realize he was not a man for hunting birds.

"Something larger," suggested the man.

"Yeah."

"As big as—"

"A bear," said Florio.

"As big as a bear. You want protection against a bear."

"Yeah."

"I see," said the man, still unflinching. He did not bother to point out that no one would go hunting a bear with a riot gun. It was clear enough that Florio was not interested in the nuances of hunting. He was not the first to buy a shotgun to protect himself from bears. Black bears, usually. Black bears were much on the minds of many in the city. And this customer was clearly from the city.

The clerk placed a box of shotgun shells on the counter. "Double-ought buck," he said. "Nine pellets per cartridge. Hit a bear at ten, fifteen yards and you'll put a hole through him big as a basketball. At thirty yards you might miss him altogether."

Florio had seen the results of a riot gun at close range. He and Block had drawn a case of a man who had turned the weapon on his wife's family. Father-in-law, mother-in-law, brother-in-law, wife; he had arranged them on the living room sofa as if for a group portrait. Instead of using a camera, however, he had focused the riot gun on them—from ten feet. The first four shots were for his in-laws—relations had not been good—and the fifth for himself. Parts of the in-laws had been blown through the back of the sofa and through the wall into the adjoining apartment. When it came his own turn, however, the man had apparently changed his mind, and decided to fire on the first policeman responding to the scene. He fired at him through the apartment window at a range of half a block. Six bystanders were sprayed with pellets and not one of them was injured. They described the experience later as like being hit by a heavy rainfall. The riot gun was extremely variable in its effects.

"I'll take it," said Florio, and only then asked the price. He produced four one-hundred-dollar bills from Kanter's wallet and laid them out on the counter, tapping each one with a finger after putting it down. Since the price of the gun was $275, it was not difficult for the clerk to understand that the extra was for his trouble.

"You'll have to sign some forms and give proof of New York

State residency," the clerk said, a new note of diffidence entering his tone.

"Of course," said Florio. He placed Kanter's driver's license on the counter.

The clerk glanced at the picture on the license, then smiled at Florio. "Thank you, sir," he said. "Should I call you Doctor?"

"No," said Florio. As the clerk completed the forms, Florio wondered why anyone would carry as much cash as Kanter did. Thank God for fools.

As he left, Florio asked directions to Jericho. The clerk patiently spelled out the way, and Florio asked several questions to make sure the man remembered his destination in case his conscience should overcome his greed and he notified the police that someone with the wrong driver's license had purchased a very murderous weapon. The police might not believe he was going to Jericho, but they would be forced to check it out, and that would take time.

When his customer left, the clerk noticed the spreading spot of damp on the back of his lightweight suit coat. Well, it was hot. A man's back would sweat if he had to drive very long. Particularly if the man's clothes were as tight as the customer's. It was strange to see a man in such expensive clothes that fit so poorly. That was but one of several irregularities to ponder about the customer, but he would ponder them with himself alone. A man who sold guns for a living learned to keep his mouth shut almost as soon as he learned how to take a bribe with aplomb and grace.

Back on 25A until it turned into a secondary highway and changed its name to Sound Avenue, Florio continued to head east, hugging the north shore now through a succession of small towns. Sound Avenue became North Road and grew even smaller. He was nearing the end of the island. At a town called Stirling, he left the highway and traveled the back roads. He passed a golf course, then came upon the beach, only a few hundred yards north and sloping downward from the road. The houses were very sparse now, people even scarcer. He cruised slowly past several hundred yards of empty beach, a house, browned and cracking in the sun, then more deserted beach. He read the mailboxes now, inching along whenever he neared a house.

Sheila was in the kitchen, pounding chicken breasts with a rolling pin, when the phone rang, startling her. It was the first call they had received since coming to the beach house.

"Yes?"

"Mrs. Block?"

"Yes . . ." she said, warily, fearing a reporter. She would hang up, she decided, if it was.

"Mrs. Block, this is Detective McKeon. You've given us a heck of a time finding you. I had to call about thirty-five numbers so far. Are you all right?"

"If it's police business, I won't call him to the phone," she said. "He needs to be away from it awhile."

"Mrs. Block, listen carefully a minute. This is important. Lou Florio has gotten out of the hospital . . . Mrs. Block?"

"I'm still here," she said weakly.

"Did you hear what I said?"

"Lou Florio has gotten out of the hospital, you said. How?"

"It's complicated. Is Sandy there?"

Sheila looked around vaguely as if she expected to see Sandy next to her, his hand out, waiting for the phone. The shock of the news had temporarily disoriented her. She felt as if she'd been kicked in the stomach.

"He's out jogging."

"Shit. Pardon me. Mrs. Block, I don't want you to be alarmed, but I do want you to take this seriously. Florio might be coming your way. He might not, we don't know for sure, but just to be on the safe side we'd better assume he is. Now I'm going to call the local police there—you're in Stirling, is that right? . . . Mrs. Block?"

"I'm sorry. This isn't all registering. What did you say?"

"What town are you in? Are you in Stirling?"

"Yes, Stirling, that's right."

"What's your address? Do you know your address?"

"We don't have an address."

"Mrs. Block . . . I think you have an address. What's the name of your road?"

"I don't know. You make a left just after the golf course and then go straight on the beach road. Maybe it's called Beach Road, I don't know. I know I sound stupid." Calm down, she said to herself. Calm down. Tell him where you are. Florio coming after her?

"Is there a name on the mailbox?"

"Yes." She tried to visualize it, tried to see the mailbox in her mind. It was black, with the name in white letters. She knew it, why couldn't she remember it! All she had to do was walk out to the road and look, but the thought of leaving the telephone right now terrified her.

"What is the name on the mailbox, Mrs. Block?"

"I know what it is, I know what it is, just a minute." She could see Florio, rising up by the mailbox, waiting for her, the knife in his back, and then in his hand. She opened her eyes.

"Peck. The name on the box is B. Peck, and there's a decal of flying ducks under the name. Mallards. And cattails in the background."

"All right, good, very good. Now I'm going to call the police in Stirling and tell them to get out to you right away. Now, what I want you to do right now is find your husband and tell him what has happened. Can you do that?"

"Of course I can do that." Which way had he gone? Why didn't she pay more attention?

"Find him and tell him what has happened. He'll know what to do. And, Mrs. Block?"

"Yes?"

"I think you might want to get away from the house for a while."

"When will he be here?" she asked.

"The police?"

"No. When will Florio get here?"

"We don't know that he's coming, Mrs. Block. He may not come at all. This is just a precaution."

"When will he get here?"

She could hear him pause, sense him looking at his watch, calculating.

"I'd find your husband right away, Mrs. Block." When McKeon hung up, Sheila gasped. It was as if her back was suddenly exposed now that she was alone. She hung up and hugged her arms around herself. Which way had Sandy gone? Where in hell was he? The thought of being alone on the beach was even more frightening than staying in the house.

She caught her breath. She had heard something. Somewhere in the distance a car's engine had stopped. She ran to the front window, then recoiled, afraid to look. Don't stand there, she screamed in her mind. He can see you! She ran to the kitchen, then the back porch, looking up and down the beach. Which way had Sandy gone?

Florio stopped the car, pulling it onto the sand on the road's shoulder. A hundred yards away a man in a track suit jogged by on the water's edge. Florio caught only a glimpse of him from the corner of his eye, and then he was gone and Florio was alone as far as he could see in any direction. He swallowed four more aspirin. One of them caught in his throat and he nearly gagged before he got it down. Slowly, mindful of his back, he got out of the car and stretched. When he felt as if the knife was still in his back, he stopped and leaned against the car. After a moment he brought out the shotgun and loaded it. If his calculations were correct, Sheila was just over the rise in the dunes.

McKeon reappeared in Byrne's doorway, leaning around.

"I got hold of Mrs. Block, Captain. That's under control. Local police will be out there soon."

"Okay, good. Keep me posted."

"And, Captain, there's a woman out here with a kind of weird story."

"So, take it down."

"I did, but I think you'll want to hear this story," said Mc-Keon.

"I can't think why. You deal with her."

"Well, sir, I think you ought to see her. She's telling some very weird shit about Tom-Tom."

"If you can't handle her, I guess I'll have to," said Byrne, wearily. "What the hell, McKeon, I wasn't doing anything anyway."

McKeon vanished, bobbing his head in agreement. A moment later a woman entered.

"My name is Phyllis Riordan," she said. "I won't take up much of your time, but there's something I thought you ought to know."

"Yes, ma'am."

"I'm a psychiatric social worker."

Byrne cringed inwardly. Another psychiatric theory about multiple personalities. The last thing he needed.

"I had a patient recently who was suffering from multiple personalities, one of whom was a young girl, one of whom was a man named Watts, another was a man named Cater, and a fourth one, who was never named specifically, was apparently very violent and was terrorizing the others."

Byrne nodded politely. So far she was telling him exactly what she could have read in the newspapers.

She opened her purse and removed a creased photograph clipped from the afternoon tabloid. Byrne knew it well. It was actually three shots in one, showing Block at the press conference, sad and weary, Sheila, wide-eyed and frightened, and Florio, staring straight at the camera in his official ID picture.

"I do not normally read this newspaper," she was saying. "I happened to see it by accident when putting out my garbage, which is why I'm late reporting this." Byrne was always amazed at the number of people who never read that newspaper but happened to know what was in it.

She pointed at the trio of pictures on the tabloid. "This is the man who came to me," she said.

Byrne nodded. "Yes, ma'am."

"You don't seem surprised," she said.

"I'm grateful that you have come forward," said Byrne. "You may be called to testify at the trial."

"But . . . is that all?"

"For now," said Byrne. "We do have the man in custody, as I'm sure you realize."

"Not that man, Captain," said Mrs. Riordan. "*This* one." She jabbed her finger at the paper again.

Byrne blinked. "That man was your patient?"

"Yes."

"You're sure?"

"As nearly as I can tell from that photo, yes, that's the man. I remember him well. He frightened me. I blame myself for not realizing how very dangerous he really was."

Byrne opened the folder and took out the two pictures Feeny had given him.

"Was it this man?" he asked.

Mrs. Riordan looked at the shots of the man in the doorway, staring at something out of camera range, like a beast of prey watching its victim. "The same man," she said. "Your Lieutenant . . ."

"Block," Byrne supplied. "Lieutenant Block."

"That's the man I treated," said Mrs. Riordan. "He was the multiple personality."

Byrne fought down a sense of panic.

"Mrs. . . ."

"Riordan."

"Mrs. Riordan, you're going to have to substantiate this."

"Of course. I have some tapes of our conversations. It's a bit irregular to let anyone else hear them, but when there's such a clear danger to others, it's not unethical."

"We'll get to the tapes," said Byrne. "But right now let's start at the beginning. Who came to see you?"

"He said his name was Thomas Cater. He was troubled because of his 'family.' That's what he called them, his family, but what he meant was the different aspects of himself. At times he became a little girl named Kathy. He spoke of a man named Watts, whom he told me Tom-Tom had gotten rid of."

"He said Tom-Tom?"

"Not exactly. The girl mentioned Tom-Tom once, but I thought at first she was just using the name as an example of someone who was bad. If I'd known what she really meant, I would have come to you at once. I want you to believe that."

"I do, of course."

"In a slightly different context she referred to Tom-Tom again, but this time sympathetically. She said her father was mean to Tom-Tom. My guess would be that Tom-Tom was someone she knew as a child. Her brother—I mean his brother. When listening to the tapes it is very easy to forget I'm listening to a man. Or possibly Tom-Tom was himself as a little boy. It is a child's name, after all."

"Did the girl—or this Cater, or whoever we're talking about—did he ever mention Block?"

"Not exactly. I missed it the first time through, and nearly the second time, but there was another person mentioned. A 'good' person from whom all of these characters were being hidden. This may have been Lieutenant Block."

Byrne sighed and rubbed the sides of his nose.

"So who is he really?" he asked. "I can assume he's not really the little girl. Is he Cater?"

"I doubt it," said Mrs. Riordan. "I think the five personalities we've seen are all aspects of his character that he feels he must keep separate, and he has given them personalities of their own, copied from, or let's say molded around, someone in his life. Someone he loved, a sister maybe, or someone close to him, or maybe just someone who caught his attention once. I don't think any of them are the real person. We may never find the real person."

"Mrs. Riordan," Byrne said, rising, "We're going to try like hell."

Florio hesitated. When he stepped toward the house, he knew there would be no turning back. He might well have to kill Block, and he didn't want to do it. Block was his partner, his friend, a man he respected and admired. But of course it wouldn't be Block he shot. It would be whoever Block happened to be at that moment.

Florio had pieced it all together secondhand, taking what he could read of Kanter's assessment of himself and applying it to Block, reading past the straightforward grilling of Byrne and the detectives to ascertain the pattern they were establishing. The truth had been wasted on them all, which was not surprising. They had Block's word, Block's skein of circumstantial evidence, a name in an address book, misspelled, Florio's fingerprints at the scene of the first murder—had he slept with Alicia Caro on one of his many lost nights? Florio couldn't say no—Florio's picture in Keiner's camera, Florio's inability to account for his whereabouts on so many lonely evenings.

Florio had protested at first. He had told them, told Kanter again and again, that it was Block who had been curled up on the floor outside Sheila's door, whimpering like a child. Block who had turned at the sound of Florio's footsteps, risen up, snarling, like a demon. Block who had spoken in the indecipherable language as they struggled. Block who was going to murder his own pregnant wife, his own beloved Sheila.

Or not Block, exactly. Tom-Tom. Florio was vague on the theory of multiple personality, but Kanter had been leading enough in his questions for Florio to get the general idea. Kanter had been probing to find out what had set Florio off, what had triggered the change. Florio thought it was simple enough. The Tom-Tom murders had started when Block got married. What could be more disruptive, more threatening to the personality than love? Falling in love with Sheila had nearly destroyed Florio, and Florio wasn't crazy. What must it have done to Block, who was?

Block was not crazy, of course. Block was as sane as ever. When he jogged by and caught a glimpse of a man with a gun getting out of his car, Block doubled back and crept up behind him. He lay there now, atop a dune, fifty yards away. Florio had come to kill. The riot gun left no doubt about his intention. Block's first thought was for Sheila. He had to protect, had to stop Florio and save the woman he loved so much. Only after that did he think of his own safety.

Tom-Tom rose up from the dune where he'd crouched, watching the man with the gun. Block was useless to him now. Block wanted to save the woman. Tom-Tom wanted to save himself. And then take the woman. Alone in the house on a deserted beach with the woman. As he ran back along the beach to the house he began to giggle to himself.

Sheila waited on the screen porch at the rear of the house, looking terrified. She started to call out, but Tom-Tom put his finger to his lips, signaling silence. He opened the trunk of the tan Citation and lifted out a shopping bag with the name "Gristede's" on it. Sheila came to him at the car.

"Florio has escaped!" she said. Tom-Tom put his finger to his lips and hushed her. He grinned broadly and led the way into the house by the back door.

"McKeon said he might be coming here!" Sheila said in a hoarse whisper. "Sandy, what are we going to do?"

As they reached the kitchen she noticed something odd about him for the first time. His face was contorted with a grin, the left side of his mouth jutting upward, the right immobile. His eyes seemed to sparkle strangely, intensely. The look on his face frightened her.

He lifted the shopping bag, holding it toward her, but at arm's length from his body. His jogging suit was unzipped and his body was bathed in sweat. His voice was dancing in sudden spurts, breathlessly, excitedly.

"Something for you," he said.

Sheila glanced at the shopping bag which hung tautly from her husband's hand. She reached for it. He slowly pulled it away from her, moving it carefully as if it were fragile.

"No, no," he said, starting to chuckle. "Mustn't be impatient. You'll get it soon enough."

Sheila smiled uncertainly at the sound of his laughter. Like the smile on his face, it seemed forced, unnatural.

"What about Florio?"

"He's here. We have to get ready for him. This will help."

"What is it?"

He giggled harder and harder, the sound coming out in bursts through his clenched teeth, as if he were trying to keep it in. His shoulders shook with the effort, but she could detect no real humor in his laughter. She began to be afraid.

"I'll show you," he said finally. He indicated with a motion of his head that she should go to the bedroom.

"It's always better in the bedroom, isn't it?" he asked.

"Sandy, what's the matter with you?"

"Everything's going to be just fine," he said, his eyes gleaming. He held the shopping bag rigidly in front of them like a lantern to light the way.

"Why are you acting so strangely? Shouldn't we leave the house?"

"Oh, no," he said. When she hung back he grabbed her arm and propelled her in front of him into the bedroom.

"Sandy, you're hurting me!" She tried to face him, walking backward. When the edge of the bed touched her legs, he gave her a push and she sat. He leaned toward her, grinning, and she squirmed backward on the bed.

"What is it? Tell me."

"I'll show you," he said. He upended the shopping bag and a

snake fell onto the bed beside Sheila. With remarkable speed Tom-Tom shot out a hand and caught the snake behind the head.

Sheila sucked in her breath.

"Don't scream," he said sharply. He held the snake toward her as if she might want to examine it.

"Put your legs on the bed," he said.

Obediently she swung both legs onto the bed, where they stretched out uncomfortably straight.

"If you make a sound, I'll let it go," he said. Tom-Tom touched the snake's tail to her lap, slowly lowering it down as it curled itself into its natural coil. He held the head only inches from her body. The rattles announced the snake's annoyance. Sheila gasped, arching her body away, but there was nowhere to go.

"Sandy," she whispered through a constricted throat.

"Now, you just sit here quiet," he said, "and it won't hurt you. You don't want it to hurt you, and I don't want it to hurt you. I'm saving you for better things."

"Take it away," she said, almost soundlessly.

The snake spasmed in his hand, lunging desperately to get away. Its fangs jutted forward, missing her stomach by less than a finger's length. Sheila turned her head to the side, straining to get farther away.

"We're going to have a visitor," he said calmly. The dreadful grin had faded and he was speaking seriously as if he wanted to be sure she understood. "I don't know when, but sometime he's coming in. When he does, you're not to make a sound. You're not to move an inch. If you do . . ."

There was no need to finish the thought. The snake burst into sudden activity, wrapping itself around his wrist. Sheila closed her eyes. She was afraid she would be sick if she watched.

"If you hold still and don't make a sound, it won't bother you. You're nice and warm, it'll like that. You are nice and warm, aren't you?" Tom-Tom pressed his free hand into her lap. "Sure you are," he said. The grin had returned. Sheila could not imagine what had happened. This could not possibly be her husband.

He lowered the head of the snake onto her lap until it was

almost resting on the coils. With his thumb he stroked it gently behind the head, again and again. Slowly the snake became mesmerized, ceasing its struggles.

"I'm going to take my hand away," Tom-Tom said at last. "Don't move."

He stroked the snake's head once more, then slowly removed his hand. The snake was motionless for a moment, then gradually it seemed to come to its senses; the head came up on the long stalk of the neck, inch by inch, tongue flicking, testing the air.

"Don't move," said Tom-Tom softly, moving back another step, safe now from the rattler's strike.

Sheila squeezed her eyes shut, concentrating on keeping her thighs from trembling. The snake, contented, lowered its head once more, snuggling into the heat of Sheila's body. She could hear Sandy's footsteps receding from the room. In her mind she screamed for him not to leave her like this, but she was too afraid to speak. She heard the bedroom door close, and she opened her eyes. The nightmare had not gone away. The snake lay on her lap. The phone rang. It rang again and again and again, screaming its urgency. Eventually it stopped.

Florio shifted his elbows on the sand, trying to find a position that would ease the pain in his back. It was no use, the pain was continuous now and getting worse. Florio realized he couldn't wait much longer, or he might not be able to move at all. He had been watching the house for a long time, lying flat on his stomach just below the top of a dune. He had seen one brief movement within the house several minutes ago, a flash of a shape going past a window. He hadn't been able to tell who it was, and there had been nothing since. He did not know if Block was in the house. Tom-Tom. He had to think of him as Tom-Tom. If it were Block in the house, Florio would not be lying here cradling a riot gun. He hoped he wouldn't have to use the gun. If Block was Block, he could hold him at bay with it, call the police, and take his chances at explaining everything once Sheila was safe. That, after all, was the whole point, to make Sheila safe. But if Block was not Block, if he was Tom-Tom or any of the other personalities he could assume, Florio would use the gun.

He came slowly to his knees. He could be seen from the house now. If anyone was watching from behind the curtains, he would make an easy target. For the distance between the road and the house there was nothing but sand. Florio felt totally exposed and vulnerable.

As he came to his feet he was twisted with a spasm of pain that nearly drove him to his knees again. He stood motionless for a minute, trying to control the pain. He concentrated on the shotgun, making sure it was loaded with five shells of the double-ought buck. In the time it took to press the trigger five times he could blow out the entire wall of the house. If he was close enough. If he was too far away he would do little more than scratch the paint.

The pain subsided enough for him to walk. He would have to brace himself somehow if he fired the gun. With his back the way it was, there was no telling what the recoil would do.

As he neared the porch, a tremor of fear shook him. He had done this before, many times, approaching a door behind which a killer might be waiting, gun in hand. He had done it and at times he had nearly enjoyed it. At any rate the jolt of adrenaline which it evoked always propelled him forward, not back. But then he had never been alone. He had never been wounded. He had never been hunting his partner.

The creak of the floorboards on the porch sounded in his ears like a clap of thunder. There was no hope of his taking Block unawares, if he was listening. But then he had no reason to be listening, no reason to be wary.

Florio threw open the door and came in doubled over, immediately swerving out of the doorway where a waiting gunman's sights would be aimed. He had made the move many times before, but this time his back reacted as if he had been stabbed anew. The pain made him stagger; he couldn't straighten his legs. He fell forward awkwardly, coming to rest on one knee.

If he'd been waiting, I'd be dead, Florio thought. And if he's here, he knows I'm here, too. His eyes flicked over the room. There was no one there and nowhere to hide among the sparse summer furniture.

I'm not going to make it through this, he thought. I shouldn't have tried it. For a moment he felt very weak, as if his bones had melted, and he longed to be back in the hospital bed, tended by the nurse, safe, drugged from the pain.

Florio listened and heard nothing but the wind that blew continually off the ocean and his own heavy breathing. It took him a very long time to stand up and when he did he could feel blood flowing down his back and under the belt and into Kanter's tapered slacks.

At first Sheila was in panic. It took every last ounce of her self-control to keep from leaping from the bed. It might be worth it, she reasoned. Better to die from the snakebite than from fear. But she wouldn't be the only one to die. Her baby would die, too. The snake's head was practically resting above her womb. She could imagine the poison racing into the innocent life within her. It was only the fear for her baby's life that overcame her own and held her still on the bed.

She heard the noise on the porch, then the sound of someone falling in the living room. Involuntarily she shifted her weight slightly. The snake's head came up immediately, tongue flicking out, the eyes staring relentlessly at Sheila. She froze completely, holding her breath, forcing her eyes wide so they would not blink, until the snake lowered its head again. There was no longer any sound from the other room. The house had become completely silent. Concentrating on every second that passed, Sheila waited on the bed, her body tense but still.

The cramp started in her lower back, coming first as only a

twinge, a muscular warning of things to come. Sheila tried to relax, to ease the aching muscle, bunched in tension for far too long, without moving. She closed her eyes and tried to imagine that someone was massaging her back. She concentrated on her breathing, hoping to develop a complete relaxation.

The muscles tugged again, a slow gathering and tightening. If it came in full force, she knew she would not be able to help herself. She would scissor her body forward, right onto the snake's fangs, as all the other muscles in her body reacted instinctively to counteract the one gone berserk.

McKeon willed the phone to ring. Byrne was standing over him, hovering like a sharpened sword, and McKeon felt as if he were allotted only so many unanswered rings before the sword fell.

"Still no answer," McKeon said.

"Let it ring," Byrne said ominously.

"Maybe she's out on the beach," McKeon offered hopefully.

Maybe, thought Byrne. There were any number of perfectly acceptable reasons why Sheila didn't answer the telephone, and only one frightening one. Why did he assume the worst had happened? Because that was the only possibility that mattered, he admitted.

"Are the local cops on their way over there?" Byrne asked. He had already been told the answer, but asking made him feel as if he were doing something positive.

"They are, but they were quite a ways away. It will take them a while yet. The roads are kind of slow out there, I guess."

McKeon was beginning to feel stupid holding the ringing phone to his ear, but he wasn't going to be the one to quit. Finally Byrne took the receiver from him and held it to his own ear, as if to verify that no one had answered. Byrne could hear the distant ringing. It sounded hollow, as if echoing through an empty house.

Run, he said in his head. For God's sake, lady, run. Finally he hung up.

Movement then, footsteps, very cautious, very soft, moving through the living room, toward the bedroom. She could hear when they left the rug and touched upon the wooden floor. She could hear when they stopped just outside her door. She wanted to scream, to cry for help, but she was afraid the snake would react and strike. She clenched her jaws shut, her eyes strained to see someone come around the corner into the room. Let it be Sandy, she prayed. Not that leering, giggling monster. Let it be Sandy, oh, God, please.

Florio stepped around the corner of the doorway, pointing a gun at her. She gasped and instantly the snake was up, alert, tense. She froze. Florio hesitated, then began to move toward her slowly, the gun still pointed at her. The world had gone insane today and Sheila knew that in a moment she would either be dead or insane herself.

Florio tiptoed slowly toward her, his eyes on the snake now, the gun out in front of him, the barrel ever closer. He didn't dare shoot, not with a riot gun. Sheila would be hit, too. Her eyes were so frightened, he wanted to speak to her, to reassure her that he had come to save her, but first he must deal with the snake, which had risen fully erect. Nervously seeking refuge, the serpent moved higher, toward Sheila's cleavage, flicking its tongue in and out as it sought access to the dress. Sheila bit her lip to keep from screaming and she could feel the blood dripping down her chin.

Tom-Tom stepped silently into the doorway behind Florio. Sheila saw the demonic grin on his face, the leer of evil. She saw the rolling pin raised over his head.

Florio noticed Sheila's head jerk up and look at something behind him. He whirled just as Tom-Tom brought the rolling pin smashing down on the bloodstain on Florio's back. Florio

TS - R

grunted and stumbled against the bed, still turning. His back collided with the bed frame and he dropped the riot gun, groaning. The gun went off with a roar, missing Tom-Tom completely but tearing into the door where he had stood seconds before. Portions of the doorframe were torn off; plaster and lath fell in shreds from the wall. The door looked as if someone had attacked it with a wrecking ball.

Tom-Tom nonchalantly stooped and picked up the riot gun as Florio's limp fingers groped for it. He turned to look at Sheila, leering broadly. The astringent stench of cordite filled the room.

The serpent was insinuating itself into her bosom. Sheila's eyes were wide with terror as she looked into the face of the man who had once been her husband.

"Please," she mouthed, her lips and throat too dry to make the sound. "Oh, please!"

With an air of easy indifference Tom-Tom plucked the snake behind the head and lifted it, holding it in her face.

"Are you afraid of snakes?" he asked, laughing.

She squeezed her eyes shut but felt as if she could see the serpent's unrelenting eye through her closed lids.

"Oh, there are much worse things," he said. He sounded pleased.

With a negligent flip of his wrist, Tom-Tom tossed the snake away from him. It landed within inches of Florio's head and slithered with amazing speed out of the room.

When Sheila opened her eyes again, Tom-Tom was standing over her, his body wracked with spasms. Insanely, he seemed to be bursting with laughter he could barely contain. His eyes were wild and excited and little gusts of mirth escaped him through clenched teeth.

"Much worse things," he said when he had regained control of himself.

"Sandy." She started to rise from the bed. Tom-Tom pressed the barrel of the riot gun to her forehead and forced her down.

"You stay there, or I'll have to bring your little snakie back," he said. "You behaved when he was baby-sitting. Do you want him again?"

Sheila shook her head.

"No? You sure? Then you sit tight."

He nudged Florio in the ribs with his foot. Florio groaned.

"Get up, hero," said Tom-Tom.

Florio pushed himself partway up with his left hand. His right arm hung uselessly at his side.

"Give me your handgun," said Tom-Tom.

Florio slowly shook his head. "I don't have one," he said. Sheila could hear the pain in his voice.

"That was careless of you," said Tom-Tom. "You should have come better prepared, if you were after me. That's not showing the proper respect."

As he spoke, Tom-Tom skillfully frisked Florio, the barrel of the riot gun pressed behind his ear. When finished, he jabbed the barrel into the blood on Florio's back. Florio cried out and collapsed again.

"Not much of a hero," said Tom-Tom. He turned to Sheila. "He's not much good at saving you, is he? Even with practice."

"He came to kill us," said Sheila.

"Just me, I think," said Tom-Tom, grinning. "Isn't that right, hero?"

"He's Tom-Tom," said Florio. "I saw him that night, he was curled up in front of your apartment door, crying like a child. He was trying to get you out."

"It's not true," said Sheila.

"I *saw* him," said Florio.

The phrase resonated in Sheila's memory. "I saw him," Florio had said, reaching back, trying to pull the knife from his back. "I saw him."

"You're Tom-Tom," she said to Florio, but even as she said it she doubted it. Florio was not standing over her with a gun, her husband was.

"Why was he never at home at night, Sheila? The Caro woman was killed the night before you got married. Was he with you that night?"

"He wanted to be alone . . . his last night as a bachelor."

Tom-Tom laughed, a short, cruel bark.

"Was he with you the night the nurse was killed?" Florio asked. He knew Sheila had to understand her situation if they were to have any hope of getting out of it.

Sheila remembered the phone call that had summoned Block to the yacht in the boat basin. It came early in the morning, just as Block was coming home.

"Did you ever know where he was? Why wasn't he ever with you? I would have been."

Tom-Tom laughed again, a sneering sound. "Sweet, isn't it?" he said.

"What happened?" Sheila said, imploringly. "How did this happen to us?"

"Do you mean your husband?" Tom-Tom had removed the pillowcases and was ripping them into long strips. The gun rested negligently across his lap. Hopelessly far away, Florio realized. Assuming he could stand at all, he'd never be able to reach the gun before Tom-Tom blew him to fragments. Or, more likely, clubbed him to the floor so he could taunt him some more.

"Your husband was afraid of you," said Tom-Tom. He began to knot the strips of pillowcase together, testing each knot carefully, making a long rope of patterned percale. "Your husband was afraid of a lot of things."

"He wasn't," said Sheila. She was still not certain what was happening, but she sensed that to keep him talking was to keep some sort of avenue open.

"Oh, he was. He was afraid of loving. Very dangerous business, loving women. He was afraid any woman he loved would have to be killed, just like the other one."

"What other one?"

"Rachel, a long time ago," said Tom-Tom. "He was going to marry her and it made him so nervous I had to kill her. She shouldn't have told him she was pregnant. Of course I had to go away after that."

"Did he know?" asked Florio.

Tom-Tom tested a length of his pillowcase rope, jerking at it with both hands. "Oh, he didn't *know*, but that was just because he was afraid to look. He didn't want to look. He was too pure for that. But he was afraid of me anyway."

"Why do you say 'was'?" Sheila asked, bewildered.

"Block's gone. What good is he to me now? Once you're dead he'd be under suspicion. He wouldn't be any good for hiding."

"I don't believe you!" cried Sheila.

"Sandy's stronger than you are," said Florio. "He can come back."

"Sandy, please!"

Tom-Tom laughed, and for once sounded genuinely amused.

"Well, that was a nice idea, good try. Did you really think it's that easy? *I* decide when I come and go, not him. I'm the strongest, no one can keep me down. He was getting much too weak. Well, he married you, didn't he? Then you got pregnant. You shouldn't have gotten pregnant. But don't worry, I can fix that."

"What do you mean?"

"That would spoil the surprise," he said, approaching the bed with his rope. Prodding her with the gun until she rolled onto her stomach, Tom-Tom tied her hands together, and then her feet. Florio moved toward him slightly and Tom-Tom put a foot atop his wound, forcing him to the floor. He jerked Sheila roughly into a sitting position, then lifted her over his shoulder.

"Let's go to the kitchen," said Tom-Tom. "There are so many things to play with in the kitchen." A burst of excited laughter escaped him.

Florio could see Sheila's terrified face looking down at him, imploring him to save her. He groaned as he tried to get to his knees.

Tom-Tom turned in the shattered doorway, looking back at Florio.

"Do join us in the kitchen. You can crawl that far, can't you, hero? You'll enjoy watching. We'll have such a long time and for once we won't have to worry about being interrupted."

Florio heard Sheila begin to weep as Tom-Tom carried her

out of sight. He was on his hands and knees, his head hanging down like a wounded dog's, trying to think, to fight the pain and think. He knew why Tom-Tom wanted him to come into the kitchen. He couldn't kill Florio in the bedroom and drag him into the kitchen without leaving traces. He would probably wait until Florio was in the right spot, then kill him with the riot gun. He would press Sheila's fingers onto the trigger for fingerprints. And then he would do whatever he had in mind for Sheila. Florio remembered the Caro woman, the long agony of the woman Tom-Tom had crucified. With Sheila, he had promised, he would take even longer. Afterward, when she was finally dead, he would arrange things to make it look as if she had freed herself just before death and killed her torturer, Florio.

And Block? What would he do with Block? Another murdered pile of clothing? No, not if he went to the trouble of making Florio appear to be the killer. He would have to "dispose" of Block's body in some convincing manner. The ocean perhaps. He was clever enough to pull it off. And then Tom-Tom would simply disappear, emerging again years later, hidden by another personality, another character as innocent and unsuspecting as Block had been.

He needed a weapon. Something—anything—to give him an edge, if only for a second. Florio removed Kanter's belt. The buckle was a thin one, too light to swing properly. Using his left hand, fumbling at the knots, he unlaced one of his shoes and retied the laces through the belt buckle. Swung at arm's length the shoe would have considerable velocity, enough to stun a man, if it hit him in the face. If it hit him in the face. If it hit him at all. If Florio could bring it off with his left arm. If Tom-Tom didn't cut him in half with the riot gun the minute he stepped through the door.

"Come join us, hero," Tom-Tom called tauntingly from the kitchen. "I know you'll want to watch." Florio was glad to hear the contempt in Tom-Tom's voice. That might make him a little too confident. A little too careless. It was a reckless, desperate gamble at best. If Tom-Tom were wary, it had no chance at all.

Florio realized if he failed he would end up splattered on the walls. But then he was going to wind up that way, anyway. He might as well go down swinging.

"Come in here, hero."

Come and get me, thought Florio. You step through that doorway first and let me take the first swing. Time was on his side, Florio reasoned. Tom-Tom would not come in and shoot him in the bedroom. If that was his plan, he would already have done it. And he wouldn't try to manhandle Florio into the other room, that would be too dangerous.

Florio struggled to his feet. The pain was so intense he thought for a second that he would pass out. When his head cleared, he stretched his left arm out behind him, the belt taut with the shoe at the end.

"I can't move," he called. Come and get me now. Give me one swing before I go. I can wait you out.

Sheila screamed.

"You'll miss the fun," Tom-Tom called. "I'm really good with a coat hanger." He was so excited he could barely speak clearly. Florio could picture him standing before Sheila, shaking with excitement, the coat hanger . . . Christ, the baby. He was after the fetus.

Florio lurched forward. The pain pulled him over and he limped like a hunchback through the blasted doorway. Sheila was strung up like a side of beef, hanging by her arms from the overhead light fixture. Her feet were off the ground and she was swinging slightly. Tom-Tom stood in front of her, watching Florio. On the table beside him he had arranged the kitchen utensils like so many surgical instruments. Paring knife, coring knife, butcher knife, boning knife, cleaver, corkscrew, vegetable peeler, mallets. Florio remembered the horror of the food processor in Caro's kitchen. Tom-Tom held a straightened coat hanger in his hand. The riot gun lay on the table, pointing toward Florio, only inches from Tom-Tom.

Too far, Florio thought. Too far. He could never reach Tom-Tom before the riot gun cut him in two. He needed to take at least two more steps closer.

"Come on in, hero. Come a little closer so you can see the details."

Florio limped forward with his right foot. His left side stayed behind, the belt still hidden by the doorway. As he moved he shoved bits of lath and plaster aside. The results of the shotgun blast were clearer on this side of the wall. Jagged shards of the doorframe, bits of lath with nails sticking out, shattered wire mesh used to strengthen the plaster, flakes of plaster, and shreds of wallpaper were scattered all over the kitchen floor.

"Come on," said Tom-Tom.

Florio shook his head. "I'm in pain. I need some help."

Tom-Tom laughed. He lifted the coat hanger and with his other hand he reached between Sheila's thighs. It was what Florio needed. For a second, at least, both of Tom-Tom's hands were away from the gun. Florio took two gliding sidesteps into the room, keeping his right side in front of him. As Tom-Tom reached for the gun Florio pivoted his body and swung the weighted belt with all his strength.

The shoe caught Tom-Tom in the face just as he fired, causing him to jerk upward. Florio had fallen immediately, floored by the pain which felt as if a sword had sliced into his back. The blast ripped into the wall, creating, as the salesman had promised, a hole the size of a basketball. As Tom-Tom swung the gun toward Florio on the floor, Sheila lifted her legs and kicked. It was a feeble kick, but enough to knock Tom-Tom off balance. He lurched to one side and stepped on a nail protruding from a piece of shattered lath. Jerking his foot up, he collided with the table and fell to the floor, his head hitting the linoleum beside the refrigerator.

Stunned as he was, it took Tom-Tom a fraction of a second to recognize the sound of the rattle. It was a fraction of a second too long. The serpent had fled from the bedroom, seeking the safety, and warmth, behind the refrigerator. Now it was threatened again and it struck for the man's head. The fangs struck Tom-Tom in the neck. The pain was less than the shock. Confused, Tom-Tom jerked up, but as he did his hand dropped to the floor within inches of the snake. The serpent struck again, this time shooting its venom into Tom-Tom's arm. His hand was lodged in the crack behind the refrigerator. The third strike hit him in the finger before he could free his hand and roll away.

Florio began to crawl across the floor, dragging himself with his good arm. The riot gun was within easy reach of Tom-Tom, but the man didn't seem to care. He had curled himself into the fetal position, his fists pressed against his mouth.

"Please, not the snakes, Mama!" he cried, his voice that of a young boy. "Not the snakes again. I'll be good, I promise. Not the snakes, oh, please, no!"

Florio was within three feet of the gun when the crying stopped. Tom-Tom came to his knees and stared blankly at Florio crawling toward him. It's all over, thought Florio. He reached for the gun but he was far too short. Tom-Tom had but to lift it and pull the trigger. But he continued to stare blankly ahead. Florio noticed tears falling from the man's eyes.

Kathy moved under the table and curled herself into a ball, hugging her pain. It reminded her of the corncrib at home where she and her brother had gone to play with each other. She had loved Thomas, he had always been good to her. That was before Tom-Tom had come. That was before Thomas and Tom-Tom had started sharing, and a long time before Mr. Watts and Sandy Block had come. She never got to see Thomas anymore, she didn't know where he had gone, the others had driven him off. And then Tom-Tom had gotten rid of Mr. Watts. And now Tom-Tom had been hurt, she had witnessed that. She was sure he deserved it. But she didn't want Tom-Tom to die. She didn't want to die. But breathing was so hard, and her body felt so heavy, as if she could barely move it. It was so hard to make her chest go up and down.

Kathy heard the voices of the man and woman and wondered why they didn't help her. Couldn't they tell she was hurt? She tried to call to them but nothing seemed to come out. Why didn't they help her? Were they afraid of Tom-Tom? She wanted to tell them that they didn't need to be. She realized suddenly that Tom-Tom was dead. The snake had killed him. She felt sad about that, but at the same time much freer. He was gone at last. He wouldn't frighten her anymore. He wouldn't hurt the ladies anymore. If only she could breathe, Kathy would tell them not to be afraid.

The man tried feebly to rise, fell on his side and rolled very slowly to his back. From where Florio and Sheila stood, they could see he was barely breathing.

Sheila moved toward him, shaking off Florio's restraining arm.

"No!" he said.

"He's not Tom-Tom now," she said. "You can see that." He was not her husband, either; she did not know who he was. But he was dying.

Sheila knelt beside him. His chest didn't seem to be moving at all.

"Sandy!" she cried.

The man opened his eyes. Thomas Cater looked out on the face of the beautiful woman who knelt over him. He was alone now. All of the others who had protected him from life were gone. He had watched them all, all those years, from the tiny, infinitely remote place in his brain where he kept himself. He saw what they did, knew what they thought, but he never interfered, he let them do things the way they had to. They kept him safe. And now they were all gone.

"Sandy, I love you," Sheila cried.

Thomas Cater blinked his eyes once.

"I'll be good," he said.

Sheila heard a grunt and a thud behind her. She turned and saw that Florio had just cut the head off the rattlesnake with a cleaver. When she turned back to the man on the floor, he was dead.

The phone was ringing again, and beyond that, in the distance, was the sound of a police siren.

CONTENTS

ILLUSTRATIONS

FAMOUS CRIMINAL CASES

By the same Author

THE FIRST WAR CORRESPONDENT
THE OTHER SIDE OF THE STORY
FACT, FAKE OR FABLE ?
THE MAN BEHIND THE MASK

By courtesy of "The News of the World"

JOHN REGINALD HALIDAY CHRISTIE

FAMOUS CRIMINAL CASES I

by

Rupert Furneaux

LONDON

ALLAN WINGATE

First published in September 1954
by
ALLAN WINGATE (PUBLISHERS) LIMITED
12 BEAUCHAMP PLACE
LONDON, S.W.3

Made and Printed in Great Britain
by
THE WHITEFRIARS PRESS LTD.
LONDON AND TONBRIDGE

Foreword

THE period we shall long remember as that of Coronation year and the H-Bomb, from the close of 1952 to the start of 1954, produced a bumper crop of criminals. For months the names of these unfortunate people have been household words and some of them will no doubt pass into legend. Day by day we have followed the often grisly stories of their crimes; now their cases can be read from beginning to end.

Reg. Christie the mild-looking little man who thought his mission in life was to kill ten women (his score – 7), Christie the ex-criminal, ex-policeman, who framed poor stupid Evans (or did the not so stupid Evans try to frame his neighbour Christie?); Mrs. Merrifield who couldn't wait for her good fortune; Christopher Craig who shot a policeman and gloried in it; Bentley, who hanged because he called to him " Let him have it, Chris "; the Clapham Common boys who thought themselves little " Capones " and " Dillingers "; Whiteway the attacker of girls who accused a policeman of inventing his confession; Chesney the matricide who escaped to murder again; Kathleen Davies who, in squeezing £80,000 from foolish old men, added the threat of blackmail to the promise of bed; Maurice Williams, the " Ringer ", who tried to make a fortune by switching racehorses; Lord Montagu and his friends who fell victims to human prejudice; George Roberts, the deaf-mute with whom no communication was possible, who, though entirely sane and perfectly innocent of the murder of which he was charged, stood in jeopardy through a legal technicality, of being detained for life as a criminal lunatic.

These are the best or " the worst " of a wide selection; they are the ones who were found out. The really clever ones are those who stood in no dock and who did not fall into Mr. Pierpoint's trap.

These crimes gave rise to a number of controversies. The long debated question of capital punishment came to the fore in both the Bentley case and in reference to the execution of

Timothy Evans in 1950. The Report of the Royal Commission on Capital Punishment was published soon after the disclosure of these doubts. The issues involved in the two cases were quite different. The argument about the hanging of Bentley raised the question of the use of the prerogative of mercy. The doubts about Evans created misgivings about the absolute finality of the death penalty.

Many people think that Bentley should not have hanged. Others consider that full use must be made of the law as it stands to stamp out crime. Undoubtedly the execution of one of the two men who murdered P.C. Miles had a salutary effect on the criminal community; that Bentley hanged may well save the lives of policemen in the future. Bentley may have been unfortunate, but so was P.C. Miles.

Whether or not the doubts about Evans were justified, they bring into question the advisability of executing murderers who are convicted on circumstantial evidence. Obviously, if evidence comes to light to suggest that a mistake has been made, it is too late to right wrong if wrong has been done. Of necessity, most murderers are convicted on circumstantial evidence; their crimes are seldom seen; there can be no absolute certainty, only a high degree of probability that they are guilty.

A lesser controversy developed on the question of police methods in interviewing suspects and in obtaining confessions from murderers. Many murderers convict themselves by their own words; in other cases the confession which the police cannot obtain might have been the last link in the chain of evidence.

It is absolutely necessary that the police should do their best to obtain true statements from suspects but, however sure they may be, they must proceed along certain fixed lines. Vehement attacks were made on the police in both the Towpath case and in the murder of Patricia Curran. At the trial of the deaf-mute the judge criticized the methods adopted by the police. The Lord Justice General of Scotland has said that the dice are loaded against the man taken to a police station; that may be true but, in ninety-nine cases out of a hundred, he is the wanted man.

The public have the impression that when a body is discovered, and murder is suspected, the police commence a scientific investigation which leads to a suspect. This impression is the result of detective story reading; it is usually the other way round. The police at once start to interview as many people as possible and having found someone who cannot give a satisfactory account of himself and who appears to have some motive, they then fit the actual evidence to him. This is the only way that the police can catch a murderer. If they adopted Sherlock Holmes methods, they would never get anywhere.

When the police have found someone whom they think is the wanted person they apply polite shock methods and set all sorts of ingenious traps to get the truth out of him. It is essential that they should do this. It is nearly always the only way in which they can get evidence necessary to obtain a conviction. If they did not do so they might let a murderer out to kill other people. The outcry that would then arise would be far greater than any criticism of methods used on a particular occasion.

There is, however, a risk that once the police have decided that they have got their man they may, quite unconsciously, overlook evidence that points elsewhere. In the case of a suspect of feeble intellect shock methods may have the effect of reducing him to a condition in which he will say anything. The innocent are protected by the careful scrutiny given to " confessions ", and the conditions under which they are obtained, by judges.

Doubts about the death penalty and criticisms of police methods can only be properly considered against the background of crime. To-day we live in a period of vast increase of crime, especially in juvenile crime, the reasons for which are obscure. Six of the murderers dealt with in this book were under twenty-five years of age, eight had had criminal careers. Crime is on the increase, yet the chances of discovery and of retribution are greater than ever. In many cases murder is a continuation of a criminal career. Becoming over-confident by easy success, or by too lenient treatment, the criminal comes to think that he can get away with murder. The cases here demonstrated should go far to show that, in the long run, he can't.

Crimes may be lessened by publicizing the stories of its failures; the people here dealt with were failures. Most of them became criminals because they were lazy; lazy people are potential criminals. Others, of course, were " insane "—at least in the popular conception of the term. They acted irrationally because the circumstances that induced them to murder were more powerful than the fear of discovery and retribution. They may have known that what they were doing was wrong, which made them responsible for their action, but they could not control themselves.

Potential criminals who read these cases may take warning; happy will be the year in which there are no " Famous Crimnal Cases " to report.

Author's Note

The piecing together of the stories of these famous crimes has been made from a number of sources as well as from personal observation. Particular recourse has been made to regional newspapers such as the *Western Morning News*, the *Western Mail*, the *Northern Whig* and the London Suburban Group. The attention of those readers who wish to follow these cases further is drawn to :—

Dr. F. E. Camps   *Medical and Scientific Investigations into the Christie Case.*

William Roughead   *The Trial of Donald Merrett (Chesney).*

Paget & Silverman   *Should the Innocent Hang ?*

I

THE MONSTER OF RILLINGTON PLACE

WHEN the other tenants began to complain of bad smells in the house, Reg. Christie knew the game was up. The discovery of his murders was certain. He had been putting down disinfectant for weeks but, hearing that a complaint was being made to the local authorities, he fled on 20th March, 1953, from 10 Rillington Place, North Kensington, London, where he had occupied the ground floor flat since 1938. His wife, Ethel, had not been seen for months. He had told one neighbour that she had gone for a holiday to her relatives in Sheffield and another that she had gone to Birmingham for an operation.

On 24th March the new tenant of the flat, a coloured man named Beresford Brown, while searching in Christie's kitchen for a spot on which to fix a bracket to take his radio set, came across a hollow portion of wall covered by wallpaper. Tearing this paper back he found beneath it the door of a cupboard, one corner of which was missing. Peering in with the aid of an electric torch he saw the naked back of a woman. He ran from the house to the nearest telephone box and dialed " 999 ". His incoherent message, " body in my flat ", was flashed to all police cars in the area.

When the police officers arrived at the house they looked through the hole in the cupboard door, but they made no attempt to open it or learn the gruesome secret it contained for, in this same house three and a half years before, had been found the strangled bodies of Beryl Evans and her 14 months old daughter Geraldine. Tim Evans, their husband and father, had been convicted of their murder, and had been hanged, chiefly on the evidence of his neighbour John Reginald Haliday Christie. Now, there was a body, or perhaps even bodies, in Christie's flat!

Realizing the extraordinary nature, and possible significance, of the discovery, the Flying Squad men abstained from any investigation until the arrival of officers from the Criminal Investigation Department of Scotland Yard. They, in their turn, delayed taking action until the Home Office Pathologist, Dr. F. E. Camps, had been called to the house. When he arrived the door of the cupboard was pulled back. It disclosed a ghastly sight. Inside the recess, which was 5′ 6″ deep and 4′ high, with its back to the horrified observers, sat the body of a semi-naked woman. Behind it were other odd shapes wrapped in blankets. After the first body had been photographed in position, it was removed. Behind it lay two more bodies. Bodies 2 and 3 lay on their back with their legs in the air. Each of the first two " sat " on the head of the body immediately behind it. The position of the bodies indicated that the person who had placed them there must have climbed into the cupboard to secure the bodies to each other, as each was added.

A cursory examination of the bodies showed that they were all of young women, all of whom had been strangled. While they were sent to the mortuary for determination of identity, the police searched the rest of the flat. It was noticed that the floorboards in the front room were loose. The edges of two boards appeared to be cleaner than the rest; fresh nail holes, too, indicated that they had been recently relaid. The order " Take the whole floor up " was given. In the rubble beneath lay the body of a fourth woman, partly clothed and wrapped in a blanket.

In consequence of these grim discoveries the police became anxious to trace the late tenant of the flat, Reg. Christie, who, it was thought, might be able to help them with their enquiries.

At the mortuary a more detailed examination of the bodies showed that those from the kitchen cupboard had been gassed as well as strangled, and each bore signs of recent sexual experience at or about time of death. One had been dead for about four weeks, the other two for about eight weeks. The fourth body, that found under the floor of the front room, had been strangled only. She was middle-aged and had been dead from between twelve to fifteen weeks.

Identification of all four bodies was effected with remarkable speed and accuracy. A description of each of the bodies of the young women, with finger prints, was matched against lists of missing girls. Relatives or friends were then asked to confirm the identification. In the case of the fourth body, that of the middle-aged woman, the knowledge that Mrs. Christie had been missing for weeks led to its early recognition.

Within twenty-four hours of their discovery the causes of death and the identities of the four bodies had been established as :

> *Body I.* A young woman; dead about four weeks. Cause of death, asphyxia due to ligature. Carbon monoxide in blood, 36% saturation. Identified as Hectorina Mac-Lennan, aged 26 years. Last seen alive on 2nd March. Known to have stayed in Christie's flat on 3rd March. She came from a little village in the Scottish Highlands.
>
> *Body II.* A young woman; dead about eight weeks. Cause of death, asphyxia due to ligature. Carbon monoxide in blood, 40% saturation. Identified as Kathleen Maloney, aged 25 years. Last seen on 12th January. Born at Plymouth—and brought up by an aunt to whom she had written eight months previously from Holloway gaol, "I know I've been a bad girl, but I have learned my lesson since I have been here."
>
> *Body III.* A young woman; dead about eight weeks. Cause of death asphyxia due to strangulation. Carbon monoxide in blood, 34% saturation. Six months pregnant. Identified as Rita Nelson. Last seen alive 12th January. She came from Northern Ireland and in London had worked as a ward maid in a hospital and as a waitress in a café.
>
> *Body IV.* An older woman; dead twelve to fifteen weeks. Cause of death asphyxia. Identified by neighbour and by her sister-in-law, as Ethel Christie, aged 54 years, wife

10 RILLINGTON PLACE—CHRISTIE'S GROUND FLOOR FLAT

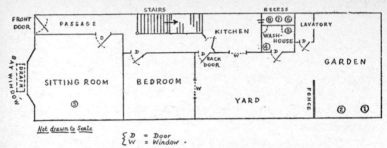

Not drawn to Scale

{ D = Door
{ W = Window .

1. Margarete Fuerst, 1943.
2. Muriel Eady, 1944.
3. Beryl Evans, 1949.
4. Geraldine Evans, 1949.

5. Mrs. Christie, 1952.
6. Rita Nelson, 1953.
7. Kathleen Maloney, 1953.
8. Hectorina MacLennan, 1953

of the missing tenant of the flat. The last known record of her was a letter dated 15th December (to which date the letter had been changed from 10th December) to her sister in Sheffield.

It was realized that the strangler of the three young women was a sex-killer who might strike again. Police throughout the country were alerted to keep a look-out for the wanted man, Christie; the " man with the staring eyes." Photographs of him were published in all newspapers.

Meanwhile at the " murder house " the police, having taken up the floors and dismantled the walls, turned their attention to the small garden of which Christie, as ground-floor tenant, had had exclusive use. A neighbour told the police that he had seen a man digging in the little rockery. Just beneath the surface the police found bones, some of which were identified as human. The greatest care was taken to collect every fragment. The garden was divided into squares and each square was dug to a depth of two feet and the earth carefully sieved. Each bone was numbered and a coloured chart was drawn to show where each had been unearthed. Amongst some of the bones fragments of dress material and part of the *Evening News* of 19th July, 1943, were discovered. A half-burnt skull was found in a buried dustbin.

When these bones were assembled they made up two skeletons, but the skull of one was missing. It was recalled that on 6th December, 1949, the skull of a female, aged about 34 years, had been picked up by some children playing on a bombed site in St. Mark's Road, a few hundred yards from Rillington Place. This, when matched with the skeleton, appeared to be the missing skull. How it came to be on the bombed site was explained later by Christie.

The examination of the two skeletons provided the following information :

I.   Female, aged about 21 years. Height 5′ 7″ to 5′ 8″. It contained a metal dental crown made of palladium silver alloy, which was chiefly used in Germany and Austria. Thus, the girl either came from one of these countries or she had had dental work done by a central European dentist.

II.   Female, aged 32/35 years. Height 5′ 1″ to 5′ 2″. (The one of which the skull had been missing.)

The skeletons conformed to the descriptions of two missing women. The first was identified as that of an Austrian refugee named Margarete Fuerst, who had disappeared in August, 1943, and the second as that of a woman named Muriel Eady, who had last been seen in October 1944. She had been employed at a factory at Park Royal where Christie had worked in that year.

Ruth Margarete Christine Fuerst was 21 years of age in 1943. She was 5′ 8″ in height. The foreign dental crown linked the skeleton with Austria. Muriel Eady was 34 years of age in 1944 and she was 5′ 1″ tall. Later, Christie admitted that the two skeletons were those of Fuerst and Eady.

Three other strange objects came to light. In the kitchen cupboard, after the bodies had been removed, a necktie, tied in a reef knot, was found. Under the floorboards of the hall passage a man's suit was discovered and in the garden a tobacco tin containing four sets of pubic hairs.

The search for Christie had been going on for seven days. On the morning of 31st March an unkempt man was seen peering into the window of a café at Putney. He asked a passerby for " 2d. for a cup of coffee." This man, a cycle shop-owner, named Bryars, thought that the beggar's face was familiar. He felt so sure that it was Christie that he telephoned the police. A few minutes later P.C. Thomas Henry Ledger saw the man leaning over the railings by the river. He spoke to him and recognized him as Christie. Just then the police van called by Bryars drew up. The police conferred: asked his name the man gave it as " Waddington." He agreed to accompany the police. In the van he threw his wallet to P.C. Ledger. In it was the identity card of John Reginald Haliday Christie, and a photograph of Christie as a War Reserve Policeman.

At the police station Christie made a long statement, the first of the three he was to make between his arrest and his trial in June. He confessed altogether to the murder of seven women at 10 Rillington Place by strangulation between 1943 and 1953.

In his first statement he said : " On 14th December I was awakened at about 8.15 a.m., I think it was, by my wife moving about in bed. I sat up and saw that she appeared to be convulsive, her face was blue and she was choking. I did what I could to try and restore breathing but it was hopeless. It appeared too late to call for assistance. That's when I couldn't bear to see her, so I got a stocking and tied it round her neck to put her to sleep."

On the bedside table, says Christie, was a bottle containing two phenobarbitone tablets, which had had twenty-five in it. " I then knew that she must have taken the remainder," he continued. Thus Christie claimed that his wife had been trying to commit suicide and that he had assisted her. He then described how he had buried her body under the floor of the front room. After Christmas, he sold his furniture and his wife's wedding ring for 37s.

The rest of his statement dealt with the deaths of the other three girls.

In Ladbroke Grove, he was accosted by a drunken woman who demanded money to take her round the corner. Christie said he was not interested but the woman followed him home and forced her way in. Then, " I went into the kitchen and she was still on about this thirty shillings. I tried to get her out and she picked up a frying pan to hit me. I closed with her and there was a struggle and she fell back on the chair. It was a deck chair. There was a piece of rope hanging from the chair. I don't remember what happened but I must have gone haywire. The next thing I remember she was lying still in the chair with the rope round her neck. I don't remember taking it off. It couldn't have been tied. I left her there and went into the front room. After that I believe I had a cup of tea and went to bed."

The next morning he put her body in the kitchen cupboard. Sometime after this, in February, he was having a cup of tea in a café in Notting Hill Gate. Two girls at the table were talking about rooms. One of them asked him for a cigarette. He told them that his flat would be vacant soon. One of them came to see it that night. She offered to stay for a few days if Christie would use his influence with the landlord to let her have the flat. Christie was " rather annoyed " and told her that it didn't interest him. Then, " I think she started saying I was making accusations against her when she saw there was nothing doing. She said that she would bring someone down on me. I believe it was then that she mentioned something about Irish blood. She was in a violent temper. I remember that she started fighting. I am very quiet and avoid fighting. I know there was something, it's in the back of my mind. She was on the floor. I must have put her in the alcove straight away."

Soon after this Christie met a man and a woman who were looking for accommodation. They came to stay with him for a few days. They left but the girl returned alone. Christie tried to get her to leave. " She started struggling like anything and some of her clothing got torn. She then sort of fell limp as I had hold of her. She sank to the ground and I think some of her clothing must have got caught round her neck in the struggle." He felt her pulse but it wasn't beating, so " I pulled the cupboard away again and I must have put her in there."

Three weeks later Christie left the flat. " I went out," he said, " and must have wandered about because my mind was blank, but I know I intended to go back."

He was not told at this stage of the discovery of the two skeletons in his garden. When he was charged with the murder of the four women whose bodies had been found in the house, it was indicated that his defence would be one of insanity. The autopsy on the body of Mrs. Christie disclosed no trace of her having taken, as Christie said, phenobarbitone tablets.

In the proceedings at the Magistrates' Court it was shown that Christie had altered the date on a letter from his wife to her sister-in-law from 10th December to 15th December. " It was of some significance," the prosecution pointed out, " that Christie purported to send a letter on the 15th, when his wife had died on the 14th." Shortly before Christmas his wife's sister had received a letter from him in which he wrote, " Ethel has got me to write as her rheumatism in her fingers is bad just now. We are in good health and as soon as Ethel can write she is going to send a letter." Christie had also forged his wife's signature to draw money from her bank account.

When Christie was told of the discovery of the two skeletons in his garden he described, on 5th June, how their deaths had come about. He related how, when he was a War Reserve policeman in 1943, he had met an Austrian girl. She went home with him several times when his wife was away. He remembered that her name was Fuerst. He said, " one day, she undressed and wanted me to have intercourse with her. I got a telegram while she was there, saying that my wife was on her way home. The girl wanted us to team up together. I would not do that. I got on to the bed and had intercourse with her. While I was having intercourse with her, I strangled her with a piece of rope. She was completely naked. I tried to put some of her clothes back on her. I took her from the bedroom into the front room and put her under the floorboards. I had to do that because my wife was coming back."

When his wife was out next day, Christie took the body and put it in the wash-house in the yard. He then dug a hole in the garden and that night he buried the body and the clothing. His wife never knew. Later on he burnt the clothing and half-burned the skull in the dustbin.

After his release from the police in 1943, Christie went to

work at a factory at Park Royal. There he met a woman named
Eady. He offered to help her with her catarrh. She came to
his flat and he gave her an inhalation, into which he had inserted a rubber tube from the gas jet. " She became unconscious and I have a vague recollection of getting a stocking and
tying it round her neck. I am not too clear about this. I have
got them confused. I believe I had intercourse with her at
the time I strangled her. I think I put her in the wash-house.
That night I buried her in the garden."

In April Christie had informed his solicitor that he had
strangled Mrs. Beryl Evans in 1949. She, her husband Tim
and her child Geraldine lived in the top floor flat at 10 Rillington Place. Her body, with that of her child, had been found
in the wash-house on his premises on the 2nd December. At
the request of Christie's defence her body was exhumed on
18th May, 1953. This was done to check his statement that
he had gassed and strangled her and that one set of pubic hairs
found in the tobacco tin came from her body.

In his statement to the police on the 8th June, 1953, Christie
described how he had killed Mrs. Evans on 8th November,
1949. She had, he said, been having a row with her husband
and Christie found her trying to commit suicide by gas poisoning. He stopped her but next day at lunch-time she asked him
to help her. He understood that if he agreed to help her she
would let him be intimate with her.

Mrs. Evans, according to Christie, lay down in front of the
fireplace in the back room of her flat. He got down beside her.
But he was not capable of having intercourse with her owing
to his fibrositis. He turned the gas tap on and held it near to
her face. She became unconscious. " I think that's when I
strangled her. I think it was with a stocking I found in the
room. The gas wasn't on very long, not much over a minute,
I think. Perhaps one or two minutes. I then left her where
she was and went downstairs. My wife didn't know anything
about it."

When Tim Evans came home that night Christie showed
him his wife's body, and told him that she had committed

suicide by gassing. " I told Evans that no doubt he would be suspected of having done it because of the rows and fights he had had with his wife. He seemed to think the same." Evans, according to Christie, said he would take the body away in his van and leave it somewhere. Some days later Evans sold his furniture and left.

Early in December the police called and found a bundle in the wash-house. They asked Mrs. Christie if she knew what it was, but she said that she had never seen it before. Christie was afterwards told that they had found a body. He said that he had asked Evans, in November, to put in the wash-house some shoring timber and old floorboards that had been taken from his front room by the workmen who had been repairing the house. He had seen the wood in the wash-house where it was stacked in front of the sink.

Christie said that he did not know what happened to the Evans' baby (which was also found strangled in the wash-house). He related how, at the time when the police were on the premises making enquiries about the deaths of Beryl and Geraldine Evans, his dog had scratched up Eady's skull. He managed to cover it up and to get it out of the house at night under his raincoat. He dropped it on a bombed site. He said also that the pubic hairs had come from the three women in the kitchen cupboard and from his wife.

The examination of the body of Beryl Evans after exhumation disclosed that she had not been gassed, as Christie said, and that, although one set of pubic hairs matched hers, they could not have come from her body within six months before death. If Christie had gassed her, as he said, he too would have been rendered unconscious and there would have been an explosion in a small room with a fire.

Christie, whose age was given as 55 years, was tried for the murder of his wife at the Old Bailey on 22nd, 23rd, 24th and 25th June, 1953, before Mr. Justice Finnemore. The Attorney General, Sir Lionel Heald, Q.C., prosecuted and Mr. Derek Curtis Bennett, Q.C., appeared for the defence. Christie pleaded insanity. While he was on trial only for the murder of his wife, Ethel, evidence relating to the deaths of the other

women was heard. The Attorney General told the jury that
" there is every possible proof that he knew he had done wrong
and was making every effort to conceal it."

Christie's past life was recalled (this had already been made
public at the Evans trial in 1950). A number of convictions
had been recorded against him. He had been born in Halifax,
Yorkshire, in 1899. In 1921 he was given three months for
stealing postal orders. In 1923 he was placed on probation for
false pretences. In 1924, at Uxbridge, Middlesex, he was sentenced to nine months imprisonment for stealing. In 1929 he
was sentenced to nine months for a malicious attack on a
woman with whom he had been living. In 1933 he was sent
to prison for three months for stealing a car. His wife, who
had left him in 1924, returned to him in 1933. In 1934 he was
knocked down by a car in London and was in hospital for some
weeks. On the outbreak of war in 1939 he became a War Reserve policeman, earning two commendations for efficient de-
tection of crime.

In the witness box, Christie admitted to causing the deaths
of his wife and of the five girls and to having strangled Beryl
Evans in 1949, but he denied having harmed Geraldine Evans.

Asked if Fuerst was the first person he had killed, Christie
replied " I think so." He was asked " You don't even know? "
to which he replied " No." Questioned as to whether he had
killed anyone between 1944 and 1949, Christie shook his
head. " Do you mean you might have done? " he was asked.
Nodding he replied, " I might have done. I do not know
whether I did or not." Referring to his wife's death he said
with the tears running down his cheeks, " I put her to sleep."
Asked if he thought he was doing wrong when he killed these
people, he replied, " No, I did not, definitely."

A number of doctors were called to give evidence about
Christie's mental state. As the jury had no apparent hesitation
in finding Christie sane, and guilty of murder, the evidence of
these doctors will not be given here. Christie's sexual mania
was, it was said, traceable to his incapacity. As a youth in
Halifax he went with a girl but she was " disappointed."
She told his friends and he was given a name that implied that

he was not quite a man. As a result he had a feeling all his life that he was not so mature and capable as he should have been. One doctor found that Christie's alleged loss of memory about his murders was too inconsistent to bear examination, and too selective and patchy to have been genuine. " He always remembers things in his favour and forgets them when they are not," this doctor stated.

In his final speech the Attorney-General dealt with Christie's motive for murdering his wife. If Christie's wife knew about his associations with other women, or if he thought she was getting to know too much about it, or might get to know too much, " then that is ample reason why you might think that some murderous intention might arise in his mind."

In his summing up the judge said, " It is no misuse of words to describe this case as a horrible one and a horrifying one." He continued, " I do not know whether any jury before in this country, or perhaps in the world, has seen and heard a man charged with murder go into the witness box and say to the jury, ' Yes, I did kill this victim. I killed six others as well over a period of ten years.' "

Mr. Justice Finnemore told the jury that they were not concerned about what happened in the Evans case and whether the result was right or wrong but, he said, " I don't suppose a jury has had to hear a man say in the witness box, ' I killed one of them in respect of which another man was charged with murder, and when that other man, who was the victim's husband, was tried for the murder of his child, in a similar manner to the wife, I gave evidence in that box in this very court and it was put to me that I had murdered that woman and I denied it and denounced it as a lie.' And now you have heard him say, ' I am telling you, members of the jury, I did in fact kill that woman.' "

On the question of Christie's sanity, the judge told the jury, " The mere fact that a man acts like a monster, cruelly and wickedly, is not of itself and by itself evidence that he is insane."

The jury of nine men and three women took eighty-four minutes to find Christie guilty of the murder of his wife. He was executed on 15th July.

Inevitably the discovery of the Christie murders at 10 Rillington Place gave rise to grave doubts about the conviction and execution of Timothy John Evans in 1950 for the murder of his child in that house in the previous November. Evans was also charged with the murder of his wife, Beryl. At his trial Christie had been the principal witness for the Crown. In his defence Evans had accused Christie of strangling his wife and daughter. Now Christie had been shown to be a strangler of women. As he gave evidence against Evans the bodies of Christie's first two victims were lying in the garden at 10 Rillington Place. At his own trial he had admitted to using the wash-house, in which the Evans' bodies had been found in 1949, as a temporary depository for two of his own victims. In 1953 he had confessed to the murder of Mrs. Evans. Was it possible to believe, it was asked, that two similar stranglers had lived in the same small house and had killed and hidden their victims in the same tiny wash-house unknown to each other? Was Christie the murderer of Beryl and Geraldine Evans and had the conviction and execution of Timothy Evans been an appalling miscarriage of justice?

Obviously, had it been known at Evans' trial in January 1950 that Christie was then a strangler of women and that he would one day confess to the murder of Mrs. Evans, Timothy Evans must have been acquitted on " reasonable doubt " alone.

To allay public misgivings, the Home Secretary appointed a Special Enquiry, under Mr. John Scott Henderson, Q.C., to investigate these doubts. The execution of Christie had been fixed for 15th July and this could not be delayed. He agreed to be interviewed by the Enquiry.

The Report of the Enquiry was completed on the 13th July. Section 49 states :

1. The case for the prosecution against Evans as presented to the Jury at his trial was an overwhelming one.

2. Having considered all the material now available relating to the deaths of Mrs. Evans and Geraldine Evans, I am satisfied that there can be no doubt that Evans was responsible for both.

3. Christie's statements that he was responsible for the

death of Mrs. Evans were not only unreliable but were untrue.

Consequently, Mr. Scott Henderson found, " I have there-fore to report that in my opinion there is no ground for think-ing that there may have been a miscarriage of justice in the conviction of Evans for the murder of Geraldine Evans."

(The author wishes to state that the question of Evans' innocence or guilt has been fully discussed by him in another book, *The Big Frame,* written in collaboration with Mr. Michael Eddowes, and to be published by Cassell & Co.)

Mr. Scott Henderson's findings have been violently attacked in Parliament (29th July, 1953). The chief criticism of the Report is perhaps that it has singularly failed to allay public disquiet about the conviction of Evans.

According to Mr. Scott Henderson, 10 Rillington Place was inhabited in 1949 by two stranglers, each of whom accused the other of being the murderer of Beryl and Geraldine Evans.

The " events " of the Evans case are as follows. On 30th November, 1949, Timothy Evans went to the police in Wales and said that he had found his wife dead and that he had put her body down a drain at 10 Rillington Place, London. When no body was found there he amended his statement to say that he had said this to protect a man named Christie and that she had died as the result of an abortion attempt by Christie, and that he had last seen her body in an empty flat in the house where he had helped Christie put it. Christie had told him that he would dispose of it down a drain. He had told Evans that he would find foster parents for the baby and he had advised Evans to sell his furniture and to leave London. After making his statement Evans requested the police to take a message to his mother in London to ask Christie the address of the people to whom he had given the baby and to fetch her.

When on the 1st December the police searched Evans' flat they found no bodies, but police officers were sent to Wales to bring Evans to London. That night Christie made a statement. On the following morning the police again visited 10 Rilling-ton Place, where they found the bodies of Beryl and Geraldine Evans in the wash-house. That evening when Evans arrived from Wales, he was shown the clothes taken from the bodies and the tie that had been tied round the baby's neck, and he was told that they had been found strangled and concealed by timber in the wash-house. He then confessed to their murder. He was informed of all material facts before he confessed. He did not therefore show, as has been claimed, knowledge that could have been known only to the murderer. Subsequently he withdrew his confession and accused Christie. At his trial, however, he could give no reason either why he had confessed to their murder or why Christie might have strangled his wife and daughter. He was executed on 9th March, 1950.

Christie denied that he had had anything to do with these deaths, and he related how Evans had been quarrelling with his wife. Christie was shown up as an ex-criminal, with a long list of convictions.

The Report of the Enquiry appears to publish only evidence which supported its findings, ignoring as the *Observer* has pointed out " all the arguments and facts which seem to point in the opposite direction."

Mr. Scott Henderson says that he rejected Christie's confession because he was satisfied that Christie gradually came to the conclusion that it would be helpful in his defence if he confessed to the murder of Mrs. Evans. It was uncorroborated and there was nothing to suggest that Evans' confession was false other than the belated and inconsistent statement by Christie that he had killed Mrs. Evans but not Geraldine Evans.

It has always been the contention of the Crown in the Evans case that whoever murdered the one also killed the other, but while Christie *may* have confessed to strangling Mrs. Evans to strengthen his defence of insanity (on the basis of " the more the merrier ") he would not obviously have confessed to the murder of the baby, as her death was not a " sex-murder."

While the question of which man, Evans or Christie, murdered Beryl and Geraldine Evans in November, 1949, and hid their bodies in the wash-house sometime prior to 2nd December, will probably never be completely cleared up, there seems to be far more evidence now to indicate that Evans was innocent than there was in 1950 to prove that he was guilty.

Apart from the extraordinary coincidence that must be accepted if Evans was a murderer, a great number of facts have now come to light which point to his innocence. These may be briefly enumerated :

1. Prior to being told of the finding of the bodies of his wife *and daughter,* Evans acted and spoke as if the child was alive with the foster parents chosen by Christie. Although Evans sold all his furniture and all his wife's possessions, the baby's things were found in Christie's flat who, according to Evans, had said that he would send them to the people to whom he had given Geraldine.

2. Evans, when he gave himself up, said that he had disposed of the body of his wife only, yet *two* bodies were bound to be found.

3. If Evans was a murderer, he had run away leaving two bodies which must one day be discovered. He had gone, too, to relatives in Wales where he could easily be traced.

4. No rope was found round the neck of Mrs. Evans, as, according to Evans, it should have been.

5. Why, if the body of his wife was not in the drain, did Evans say it was, unless Christie had told him so?

6. Christie lied at Evans' trial on a matter on which he need not have lied unless he, not Evans, was the murderer. He denied telling Evans that he had medical knowledge and that he had been training before the war to become a doctor until stopped by an accident, and he denied having had an accident, although we now know that he lured women to his flat by pretending to have medical knowledge and that he did have an accident in 1934. He also stated that on 8th November, he had fibrositis which would have prevented him from carrying a body. We now know that, although he saw his doctor that night, he did not complain of fibrositis until four days later.

7. Christie's confession to having murdered Mrs. Evans *is* corroborated. He said that he killed her at lunchtime on 8th November. He may have chosen the lunch

hour because the workmen who were in the house were then out. A girl friend of Beryl's has said that at lunchtime on that day she went up to the Evans' flat but couldn't get any reply, although she heard strange noises within. That afternoon Beryl failed to keep a tea date with her grandmother.

8.   Christie did not gas Mrs. Evans because, unlike the other women who were murdered when the house was full of tenants, he murdered her when the house was empty. He gassed his other victims to ensure silence.

9.   Evans left 10 Rillington Place on 14th November. *If* he placed the bodies in the wash-house they must have lain there for at least eighteen days, yet neither Mr. or Mrs. Christie noticed anything strange in the tiny wash-house, which they used as a firewood store.

10.   Why, unless she suspected something or had learned something about the Evans murders, was Mrs. Christie murdered in 1952? Her murder was Christie's one mistake; unlike his other victims her disappearance was certain to lead to an enquiry. We know from a girl who talked with her in 1952 that she did " suspect."

It is held that the chief strength of the accusation against Evans is that he " confessed " to the murder of his wife and baby, and that he lied in his other statement and at his trial, but his confession may have been induced by shock at learning of the death of his child. Upon hearing of it, just before his confession, he said he had no wish to live. *All* his lies, too, were told to protect Christie, and to hide the fact that, as far as Evans then knew, his wife had died as a result of an illegal operation performed by Christie. Evans was quite illiterate. He had been in and out of hospital from the age of seven to twenty-one and he had had no schooling. He said that he had acted on the advice of Christie (who as an ex-policeman was a person from whom to accept advice) and Christie has admitted advising him in 1949.

Christie had opportunity and motive (sexual assault) for killing Beryl Evans. The young husband had conveniently quarrelled with his young wife, which supplied a " motive " for Christie to pin on him for her murder. That Beryl Evans *had been* sexually assaulted is shown by an internal bruise found on her vagina after death. This bruise is suggestive of the type of sexual assault that Christie performed on his dying victims. There is no reason to think that Evans was a sex maniac. The suit found under the hall passage can only have been hidden by Christie. It could not have been put there before 12th November, 1949, when the floorboards were re-laid. He may have thought that it was marked in some compromising way.

One of the unexplained facts of the Evans case is that thirty-two statements, taken by the police from twenty-three persons, and passed to the prosecution, were not made available according to the usual custom to the defence at his trial. These statements might have thrown doubt on to the question of Evans' guilt.

Despite Evans' confession, it seems almost certain that Christie, not Evans, was the murderer of Beryl Evans. He had then to get rid of the baby. He easily persuaded the stupid Evans that his wife had died as a result of an abortion (she was sixteen weeks pregnant) and that he would be suspected. Christie admitted to re-arranging her clothes to conceal the fact that her death had been caused by strangulation.

Christie was a cool, calculating murderer and an ex-criminal. The insignificant sentences he had received for his petty crimes led him to conclude that he could get away with the greatest crime of all. He very nearly succeeded. The murder of his wife was his undoing. He knew that her disappearance would eventually lead to enquiry. He then became careless. He might have gone on for years strangling stray women and burying them in the garden. Their disappearances would not have been noticed. He certainly murdered six, perhaps eight females. He admitted to many other murders, saying that he had disposed of the bodies on bombed sites. In his life story, published in the *Sunday Pictorial* (5th, 12th, and 19th July, 1953), he related that " in my strange dreams it has always been ten women I must kill." His next victim had been planned, but fortunately for her the "date" fell through. Various girls have said that they went with Christie to model for photographs at a " Studio " in Maida Vale, but the Studio has never been located.

The " Monster of Rillington Place " was a mild-looking little man, the type nobody notices. Though standoffish, he was always polite to his neighbours, doffing his hat to women and anxious to take photographs of their children. He liked to be well-thought of and he frequently told his wife's relatives about his " big, fine house in London." The big, fine house, or the murder house as it is known locally, is now relet to Jamaican tenants in each flat. There are no " spooks " at 10 Rillington Place.

II

MILES GIFFARD

MILES GIFFARD claimed to have been insane when he battered his father and mother to death in Cornwall on the 7th November, 1952, and then threw their bodies over the cliff. The murder of his elderly parents by a twenty-six year old son is peculiarly horrible, so much so that it is difficult to believe that such a callous act could have been perpetrated by a sane person.

Many murderers claim to have been insane. It is almost impossible to imagine that more than a few are really " sane " within the popular conception of the term. The human animal is created with the ability to " reason." Few people, if they stopped to " reason," would commit a murder. Hardly anyone can be foolish enough to imagine that they have any real chance of getting away with murder. The scientific investigation of crime has reached such proficiency that the dice are heavily loaded against the murderer. Test tube, microscope and human experience have made success unlikely and failure almost certain. Usually, the penalty is death. Yet, every year many murders are committed. Why? The answer is, of course, that murderers seldom " calculate " their chances. The circumstances that lead people to murder are more powerful than is the fear of discovery and retribution.

If a person who kills another " knows " that he is doing wrong, then he is " sane." He, or she, is only " insane " if at the time he can be shown to have suffered from a defect of reason with the result that he was incapable of knowing the nature and quality of his act. Many murderers claim to have had a " blackout " or sudden brainstorm, but loss of self-control is not " insanity." Others claim to have been insane because that defence is the only possible one. There are, however, borderline cases in which the claim of insanity may be real. But it may be real only in a medical sense. An insane person can still know that what he was doing was wrong.

The case of Miles Giffard is of peculiar interest because it underlines the difference between the medical and the legal interpretation of insanity. The defence that he was insane put forward on his behalf had a real basis. It was not a case in which insanity was employed as the only possible line of defence; it was shown that he had a long history of mental ill-health.

The facts are as follows :

On the morning of Saturday, 8th November, 1952, the battered body of Mr. Charles Henry Giffard, a prominent West Country solicitor who acted as clerk to the St. Austell Magistrates, and that of his wife, were found on the beach just above high water mark at the foot of the 100 ft. high tide washed cliffs of Carlyon Bay at Porthpean, six hundred yards from their eleven room house, " Carrickowl." Bloodstains were discovered within the house and along the path leading to the cliffs. Near the body of Mr. Giffard was found the shattered remains of a wheelbarrow. Mr. Giffard's Triumph car, and his eldest son Miles, who lived with his parents, were missing. Warning that something was wrong had been given by the Giffard's young maid, who had returned to the house late in the evening after her day out. That evening, shortly before midnight, Miles Giffard was arrested in Chelsea, London.

All this sounds easy. Bodies are found; within a few hours a man is arrested nearly two hundred and fifty miles away. It *is* easy, because a system operates. Details of the stolen car were circulated by the police. By midday on Saturday it had been found, parked in Tite Street, Chelsea. A trap was organized. Flying Squad cars were positioned along Chelsea Embankment and at points covering Tite Street. A plain van, less identifiable than the squad cars, stood by the kerb. In it fifteen policemen sat for hours. In another police car nearby a woman sat in the back to disguise its true nature. The watch was a long one; soon after 9.45 p.m., a young couple who passed by were challenged by the police, but the woman watcher in the police car shook her head and they were allowed to proceed on their lawful occasions. As time went by, the police tightened their grip on the street. Shadowy detectives emerged from their hiding places to warn pedestrians not to loiter. Then a taxi turned into the street and drew up at a block of flats. A girl alighted and went down some steps in the basement. The taxi started to drive away. At once, lights flashed and a warning was sounded. Police cars converged from all directions. The taxi was surrounded by policemen. The solitary occupant, Miles Giffard, thinking apparently that he was being attacked, shouted, " police! police! " He was taken to a police station.

Giffard was held at first on the charge of stealing the car, but on Sunday he was seen by Supt. K. Julian, Chief of the Cornish C.I.D., who told him that he had seen the body of his father and that he would be taking him back to Cornwall on a charge of murder. Giffard then made a statement, in which he admitted the murder of his parents. Two hitch-hikers told the police how they had been driven from Exeter to London during the night of Friday in a car answering the description of the one missing from Cornwall. Their statement discloses something of the mental state of a man on the run from the scene of the crime. The first man related :

" The driver told us he was going to London and agreed to take us all the way. He seemed preoccupied and chain-smoked from a box of hundred cigarettes. He had a good suit on and seemed to be a decent sort. We spoke about girls, and he said he was going to London to see a girl who lived somewhere in Chelsea. We stopped at Andover and went into a café. He joined us later and said he had bought some gin. When we left he looked tired and in need of sleep."

The other man said, " He did not seem to know much about the car and kept grating the gears. He dropped us at Chelsea Bridge, and turned back along the Embankment towards Putney. As he left he said, ' I might see you on Sunday night

MILES GIFFARD

By courtesy of P. A.-Reuter

on the road, I'm going back then.' During the drive up he told us he lived in a nice house at St. Austell. Our general impression was that he was a very good chap."

Driven back to Cornwall, Miles Giffard was formally charged with murder in the little court at St. Austell, in which his father had acted as clerk for twenty-three years. He pleaded not guilty and it was indicated that his defence would be one of insanity.

At Miles Giffard's four day trial at Bodmin in February, 1953, for the murder of his father, the defence fought to establish that he was insane when he battered his father to death and when he had tipped the bodies of his parents over the cliff, but the prosecution contended that the murder of his parents had been premeditated and that Miles had killed his father to take his car in order to drive to London to see his girl friend. Mr. John Scott Henderson, Q.C., led for the prosecution and Mr. John Maude, Q.C., appeared for the defence. The case was heard by Mr. Justice Oliver.

In stating the case for the prosecution, Mr. Scott Henderson told the jury, " I will leave you in no doubt that this was a premeditated murder . . . a murder planned and planned over some days." He said that Mr. Giffard " lived at Porthpean, near the sea in a house practically on the cliff edge called Carrickowl. Living with him was his wife, mother of the accused. On 7th November the only other people living in the house were the accused and the maid, whose evening out it was.

" The case of the prosecution is that on that day the accused had made up his mind to go to London. He wanted to go to London to see his girl friend. He had no money and no means of getting to London, and the suggestion of the prosecution is that he decided to kill his father in order to be able to take his father's car and fulfil his wish of going to London that night. He knew that his father would not have permitted him to go to London, and would not have given him any money. 7th November was a Friday. As early as Wednesday he had been telephoning his girl saying that he would be up at the end of the week. On the Friday both Mr. and Mrs. Giffard were away from home. There were two cars which were used by the family, one car which Mr. Giffard used, which he took every day to St. Austell.

" He spent the day presumably at his office, but was home for lunch at the middle of the day. After lunch the father went away again and did not come back until about sometime after seven o'clock. The mother that day had gone to Plymouth with the other car and was away the whole day. She was back roughly at the same time as her husband came back."

Mr. Henderson continued : " At 6.30 that afternoon the accused phoned his girl friend, a Miss Vallance, in London, to say that he was coming up to London that night, but that he would phone at 8.15 to confirm it.

" At about 7.30 he went out to the garage. Both cars were there—one a Standard car and the other a Triumph. Mr. and Mrs. Giffard had only just returned. He saw his father doing something to the Standard car, and he took a piece of iron pipe from the garden and hit his father over the head, rendering him unconscious, as his father was facing him, presumably getting out of his car. He then went into the house to the kitchen and from behind he struck his mother with the same piece of iron pipe over the head, rendering her unconscious.

" At 8.15 that night, as he had promised, he phoned Miss Vallance again, saying that he was definitely coming up with his father's car, and he made arrangements to see her early the next morning.

" He then went out with a view to taking the car, and he found that his father was coming round. He struck him again with the iron pipe, several times, and from the medical evidence which will be put before you, you will probably come to the conclusion that at that stage the father died as a result of the injuries which had been inflicted on him by means of that iron pipe. He went into the house and found his mother coming round. He struck her again and the medical evidence will probably satisfy you that the injuries she received did not kill her.

" He then decided to get rid of the bodies, and he took the garden wheelbarrow, and he put first his mother in the wheelbarrow and wheeled her through the garden out by a back gate and through a copse and over a field to the cliff's edge— a distance of about one hundred and ninety-five yards—and tipped her over the cliff down on to the rocks below. The pathologist will say that it was the injuries she received by striking the rocks that caused her death.

" He then came back and put his father into the wheelbarrow, took a shorter journey on this occasion to the cliff— some one hundred and twenty-four yards, and put his father, who was already dead, over with the wheelbarrow. Shortly after ten o'clock that night, after he had done some cleaning up, he set off in the Triumph car to London, and was arrested in London at twenty minutes past eleven on Saturday night."

Mr. Scott Henderson told the jury, " You aren't trying him in respect of any alleged murder of his mother, but in this case the story of the death of these two people—the father and mother—is so linked up that in considering whether or not he murdered his father, you will have to hear a lot of the facts relating to the death of his mother."

He continued : " Having told you the short story of the events which the prosecution will prove, may I give you a little more detail about the background of this offence. I have told you he had no money and no means of getting to London and that he would not get any money from his father. I need not give you a full account of this tragic family history. Let me read to you—because it is a connected account intelligently given of what he himself says about it."

The statement made by Giffard after his arrest, as read in court, related :

" Up to about twelve months ago I was studying firstly for the law as a solicitor, and latterly as an estate agent at Ringwood. My father made me an allowance of £15 a month. I could not settle down to my studies and this led to some difference between me and my father. I gave up working last November and then I got a legacy of £750.

" I went to live in Bournemouth and I spent the money by about March. I scrounged around a bit, and I did some work, about eight weeks. I was selling ice-cream for Walls. I then left them, and some time in June I went home to Porthpean. I stayed home until the middle of August, then I came to London and took a furnished room.

" I began to visit the White Hart public house in King's Road, Chelsea. I met a Chelsea pensioner who frequented that public house called George Bowden. About a month, no, six weeks ago, he introduced me to a young lady and her mother, with whom I became friends. Gabriel Vallance was the young lady, and her mother is Mrs. Allison. I became a frequent visitor to their house, at 40 Tite Street, Chelsea, where I was made very welcome.

" I had been living from hand to mouth. I had odd bits of money from various people, and there are some cheques which were R.D. I have been drinking very heavy, and about a month ago Gabriel began charging me about my untidy appearance. I told her my parents had arranged to send my clothing up, but this was just a lie to stall her off. I was tight for money at this time and had no means of tidying myself up, so about a fortnight ago I said I would go home and get my clothing myself. That is what I told Gabriel, but in fact I wanted to go home to try and get some money from my father. On Friday, 31st October, I decided to hitch-hike to Cornwall and I told Gabriel so. She was rather upset at me going. I went to Cornwall, arriving on 2nd November. I actually did hitch-hike. I phoned Gabriel practically every day. I had a row with my father over my spending habits and told her so, and he said I was to stop in Cornwall and continue with my studies.

" Gabriel suggested that I should come up to London, get a job and make myself independent of my parents. I decided to come back to London the following week-end, that is this week-end. About mid-week I made up my mind to come back to London. I telephoned Gabriel twice on the Friday, 7th November, the first time at half-past five, I told her I was coming up to do some business for my father. This was not true. I promised to phone her again at half-past eight, to confirm whether in fact I was coming and I told her if I did come my father had promised to let me use his car. It is a Triumph, the number is ERL 1. At the time of my first phone call my father and mother were both out. They came back almost together in separate cars at about 7.30 p.m."

Mr. Scott Henderson stopped to point out to the jury that what Giffard had said showed that he had made up his mind to go to London that week-end, and that he had made up his mind to do so in the middle of the week. He gave proof of this by quoting from a letter written by Miles to Miss Vallance, in which he said :

"What I was afraid of has happened. I have had the hell of a row with the old man, made far worse by the fact that as usual he is right. The upshot of the whole thing is that he has forbidden me to return to London at any rate for the time being. He says he will cut me off without even the proverbial shilling, so there does not seem to be any alternative until I get a job."

Later in the letter Giffard said, " I shall not be able to take you to Twickenham. Who will? I hope no one, I am dreadfully fed up as I was looking forward to seeing you to-morrow and now God and the old man know when I shall. Short of doing him in, I see no future in the world at all." As Mr. Scott Henderson pointed out : " That throws a wealth of light on the way his mind was beginning to work. That was on the Monday."

Continuing to read from the statement, Counsel stated that independent witnesses would be called to confirm it.

" My father was doing something to mother's car. Both cars were in the garage. God knows for what reason I hit them over the head with a piece of iron pipe. I hit him once then. He slumped to the ground unconscious. Mother had gone into the house. I went into the house after her. I found her in the kitchen. I hit her from behind.

" Everything went peculiar. I got into a panic. Shortly after this I made a second phone call to Gabriel in London about 8.15 p.m., and told her I was definitely coming to London with my father's car. I asked if I could come round to her house in the morning for a wash and shave.

" I went out with the intention of getting the car and found my father coming around. I hit him again several times, then I got the car out and went in to get some clothes and my mother was coming around then. So I hit her again. She was bleeding very heavily. They both were by this time. I did not know what to do. There was blood everywhere. I got out the wheelbarrow, put my mother in it, took her out to the point and pushed her over. I then went back and did the same with my father's body. I pushed the wheelbarrow over that time.

" I went back to the house and washed the place out. I went to my mother's room and took some pieces of jewellery. The two brooches and the ring shown to me are some of the jewellery. I took some money from father's coat pocket. I packed a change of clothing. My own clothes were very blood-stained. I then drove the car out and drove to London. I changed my clothing before I got to Oke-hampton. I threw the pair of flannel trousers and tweed sports coat, which were very blood-stained, into the river at Fenny Bridges, just past Exeter. I also threw the piece of steel tubing I had hit my father and mother with into the river at the same time.

" I then drove on to London. I picked up two hitch-hikers somewhere near Ilchester. I dropped them at Chelsea Bridge. I then went on to Tite Street and got there about 5 a.m., and parked the car in the side of the road about fifty or sixty yards from the house. I had a sleep in the car until about eight o'clock. I left the car and went to No. 40 Tite Street, where I saw Gabriel and her mother. When I left the car I left the ignition key in it, and also left some blood-stained clothing in it and shoes. This blood came on my clothes when I moved my mother and father. I told Gabriel I was up to do some business for my father and that I had put the car in the Blue Star garage. I said that I had an appointment at ten o'clock and that I would come back to lunch.

" I went off to Dawsons, Piccadilly Circus, where I sold

three pieces of my mother's jewellery, which I have mentioned, for £50. Later I telephoned Gabriel and told her I could not keep the luncheon appointment and that I would meet her at 2 p.m. at Leicester Square. I met Gabriel and her mother at two o'clock. We went to the Odeon Cinema, Leicester Square, and saw ' Limelight.'

" We left there at five o'clock and I went off on my own with Gabriel. We went to a public house and had a meal, then we made a round of various public houses. Eventually we arrived at the Star public house, Chesham Mews, where, upon leaving, I told Gabriel what I had done; that I had murdered my father and mother. It upset her very much, and we just moved on to further public houses drinking. I told her that she would not be seeing me again. I had previously booked a room at the Regent Palace Hotel in the name of Gregory.

" I think I told Gabriel that I was staying with relatives at St. John's Wood. Later I took a taxi after closing time and took Gabriel back to Tite Street. I was very drunk and after Gabriel had left the cab, and I was being driven away in the cab, I remember it being stopped. I cannot remember too clearly what happened. I had some sleeping pills which I had taken from my mother's bedroom. They were in my coat pocket. I intended to take them and kill myself." (A box of pills was found on him.)

" That is the whole truthful story. I can only say I have had a brain storm. I cannot account for my actions. I had drunk about half a bottle of whisky on the Friday afternoon before all this happened. It just seemed to me that nothing mattered as long as I got back to London. Gabriel just fascinated me. This statement has been read over to me and I have had the opportunity to make corrections I desire to do. It is a true statement."

Mr. Scott Henderson said that Det.-Supt. Julian had seen Giffard in London and had told him about the blood-stained articles which had been found in the Triumph car. Giffard had been asked to account for his movements since midday on the Friday, and in reply he had said : " I know what you are referring to. I wish to tell you everything about it with as little trouble as possible. Will Gabriel be brought into this?" He was cautioned, and it was then that he made his written statement, which he opened with the words: "I want to be frank. I did it. I don't want Gabriel brought into it. I want to tell you the whole story. Many of the things I have said to Gabriel are not true. I haven't been working for about twelve months. I have only said the things to make a bold front to her."

Having outlined the evidence that would be given to corroborate this statement, the prosecution, Mr. Scott Henderson said, would then submit to the jury that it was a case of deliberate murder; "not only a case of deliberate murder, but one which was well premeditated. However horrific you may think the story is, the prosecution will ask you to say that there can be no doubt it is murder, and that the one verdict you ought to bring in is one of guilty."

Not all the witnesses, or their full evidence, can be reported here, but what many of them said is important in view of Giffard's defence of insanity.

The maid, Barbara Orchard, said that when she returned to the house on the night of 7th November, she had seen a light in the garage and she heard a car being driven away. In the kitchen of the empty house she found bloodstains. She telephoned the police. She said that Miles Giffard had been on perfectly friendly terms with his father and mother. Mr. Rowe, the gardener, identified a length of iron pipe as one of several pieces that had been in the garden. Police witnesses described the finding of the bodies. A brother of Mr. Henry Giffard gave evidence of identification.

In the witness box, Miss Gabriel Leslie Vallance said that she was nineteen years old and lived with her mother at 40 Tite Street, Chelsea, London. She said that she first saw the accused about two months before the first week in November. She met him at a public house in Chelsea, the "White Hart." After that she became friendly with him, and he was in London for the two months after she met him. He left London on the Friday, a week before he was arrested, and said he was going home to get some new clothes.

She said that he had told her he had an allowance from his father, but she knew that at that time he was rather broke. He told her he was going to hitch-hike to Cornwall. She next heard from him on Sunday, 2nd November, when he phoned her. He told her that his father would not allow him to go back to London. " We were expecting to see each other again on the Monday. He was just going for the week-end," she said. The next she heard from him was a letter on the following Tuesday.

She agreed that she had received a letter from Miles in which he said that his father had stopped his allowance and gave him a pint of beer and twenty cigarettes a day, forbidding him to go into pubs, concluding with the words: " I love you terribly and it is really breaking my heart to leave you in that den of wolves there."

Miss Vallance said that she replied the same day, and in her letter wrote: " Your father is right about not letting you come back because you were very extravagant—partly my fault."

She said Giffard had telephoned her about 5.15 on the Friday and said he would probably be coming up to London the following morning, and was going to borrow his father's car. He said he would confirm it by ringing again at 8.15. He added that she could expect him at about eight o'clock the next morning, and asked if he could go to her house for a wash and shave. She refused, but later spoke to her mother, who agreed that he could come to the house and she telephoned to Miles at six o'clock and told him so. He telephoned her again at 8.15 and said he would be coming.

The Judge asked her: " Did he say how he would be coming? " Miss Vallance replied: " Yes, in his father's car." Giffard had arrived at her home at about eight o'clock the next morning.

He had gone off later to do some business for his father and she and her mother had met him later and they had been to a film.

When they came out at 5.30 her mother went home, and she and Miles went to a public house. They then had a meal and some more to drink in another public house, after which they went to the " Star " in Chelsea.

Miss Vallance continued : " While we were in there he said he had done something awful. I said : ' What, pinched your father's car ? ' And he said : ' No. Something worse than that.' I said : ' Let's go ' and outside the public house he said he had murdered his mother and father."

The Judge asked : " Did he use the word murder ? "— " Yes." Mr. Scott Henderson : " How did you take that information ? "—" I did not believe him." " What was his state at that time ? "—" He was very upset." " Before he told you what he had done, did he say anything about you, make any proposal or anything of that sort ? "—" Yes. He asked me to marry him, and I said, No, not until he had a proper job." " Was there anything else said then."—" Yes. He said : ' I cannot see you any more '." " That led up to him saying : ' I have done something dreadful.' ? "—" Yes."

Cross-examining Miss Vallance for the defence, Mr. Maude asked her : " From roughly about eight o'clock, all through the hours you were with him, did he seem delighted to see you and perfectly normal until you got into the Star public house ? " " Yes " she replied. Mr. Maude : " He is all right in the ' Star ' until he tells you he has murdered his father and mother and then he becomes upset ? "—" Yes." " He is perfectly all right, delighted to see you, no signs of anxiety or worry at all ? "— " He seemed very quiet." " And that is all ? "—" Yes." The Judge : " Does that mean unusually quiet for him ? "—" Yes."

Next police officers described the finding of a length of steel piping about two feet six inches in length and about one inch in diameter in the river at Fenny Bridges, and the discovery of bloodstained articles in the Triumph car. An additional part of Giffard's statement was also read in court.

" In June I went home to Porthpean and broke into my father's house. Then I came to London and spent the money. I was only in London for a week, staying in odd hotels. Then I went home to Porthpean again. Then I returned to London again to dispose of some stuff I had taken, a ciné-camera and a bracelet of my mother's. I sold the camera at a place in Paddington. I sold the bracelet with a jeweller in Piccadilly Circus. Then I went home. I was only up here for a day. I straightened it out with my father."

Dr. Frederick Dennis Maurice Hocking, Cornwall County pathologist, said that Mr. Giffard's injuries could be put into two classes : Those suffered before death and the very severe injuries suffered after death caused by falling on to the rocks head first. Dr. Hocking said that Mr. Giffard was dead when he was put over the cliff. The blows had killed him. " I should describe them as heavy blows, but not blows delivered with the maximum amount of force of which a young man might be capable. They were not blows of maniacal strength " he said.

Opening for the defence, Mr. John Maude announced that Giffard admitted that he had killed his parents, but relied for his defence on evidence of a history of mental disease which went back for twelve years.

" There is no doubt," he said, " that this man of twenty-six killed his father and mother. There is no doubt about that whatsoever, and you will notice that throughout this case I have asked hardly any questions at all. There will be no evidence showing you that something other than what he said in his statement was the real truth. There is nothing to contradict that. There is no question but that the father was struck in the garage, that the mother was struck in the kitchen, and so on, and there is no point in my going through all those facts.

" It is not the question of simply saying : ' Why on earth did this young man murder his father and mother? ' That is one question, which of course we are asking. But that is not the ultimate question. The ultimate question will be : At the time that he killed his father—because owing to the peculiarities of the law you are only trying him for the killing of the father, although you will no doubt be deciding in your minds that he killed both—was he labouring under what is called a defect of reason to such an extent that he did not know what he was doing, that is to say, that killing his own father was against the law.

" This is a case where over many years this young man, as a child and on through the years, has without doubt whatsoever been gravely ill mentally. This is not a case of somebody who suddenly faces the danger of being hanged, and then doctors suddenly appear, the man never having shown any signs of insanity before. There are such cases where that is perfectly genuine, where a man may suddenly develop a mental disease. But that is not this case in any shape or form.

" You realize now that Giffard killed his father and mother to keep an appointment with Miss Vallance. Do you think that is sane? The prosecution were relying upon the statement in Giffard's letter that life meant nothing to him at all, to show that his crime was premeditated."

Mr. Maude asked if a sane man would be writing to any living creature saying he was intending to murder somebody. There was no question that he was planning a murder at that time.

A nurse, who had looked after Miles, between the ages of four and nine, said in the witness box that he was a very nervous little boy who suffered from dreadful nightmares. In addition, if she went into a room without him knowing, he would throw himself on the floor, shrieking, " No, No, don't do it." She said that Miles had been very devoted to his mother and had been fond of his father.

His housemaster at Rugby, where Miles had been from September 1939 to December 1940, described his as " a very abnormal boy." The report of his form master in 1940 stated, " He ought still to be in the nursery." Asked how Miles had compared with an ordinary difficult child, the housemaster said " I should say that in my experience he was the most difficult I ever met." Rugby could not cope with him, and he had left.

Another witness, who had slept in the same dormitory with Giffard at Blundell's school from 1940 to 1944, said he had always found him a rather odd person, apt to be scruffy about his person, his manner and his speech, apparently backward and unable to keep up with school life generally.

As there was a very real case to prove that Miles Giffard was insane the evidence of expert medical witnesses must be given fairly full. Dr. Roy Neville Craig, who came specially from Ireland to give evidence, stated that until his retirement he had been in practice as a psychiatrist in the West of England for twenty-five years.

He said that Miles Giffard had been sent to him by Dr. Hood, of Truro, in 1940. The whole of his school career had broken down, Rugby was unable to cope with him any longer, and his parents had sought his advice as to what to do with him next. He had found Giffard, who was then only fourteen, dull, apathetic and very inaccessible to talk to. The most striking thing about him was his complete lack of insight. He failed to realize that there was anything wrong with him. He was completely blunted emotionally. His face was expressionless, and it was impossible to distress him or make him laugh. He showed no emotion of any sort.

Dr. Craig continued: " I subsequently found when I interviewed his parents that this had gone on, accompanied by night terrors of a very violent character, that in addition he was attacked by paroxysms of fear, that he became frightened for no apparent reason. He lied much more frequently than he told the truth and his lying was purposeless and aimless. His condition was diagnosed then that he was apparently suffering from a form of schizophrenia, which is rare and which attacks young people, and from which there is no recovery. This treatment was stopped because it was found that deep down in the mind was a condition too grave to go on with it any longer. It was not safe to try and ease the underlying difficulties any longer. It is possible that if you did you could precipitate an acute outburst which could do an enormous amount of damage.

" There was another reason. The one and only asset that he had which sustained him in his school life at all was his games. That was the only thing in which he appeared to succeed, and the treatment interfered with that; so as we had got him superficially better, I decided to leave well alone."

Asked by the defence, " Was it your opinion that he was normal mentally? " Dr. Craig replied: " I do not consider that he has ever been normal mentally. It was found that the origin of his terrors came from some sadistic nurse, who had

not only beaten him as a very tiny child, but had locked him
in a dark cupboard. That was checked and found to be true
and the nurse was dismissed."

Asked if there had been any signs whatever of Giffard as a
boy having been aggressive, the doctor said his make-up was
" rather of the timid, cringing type which avoids a struggle or
violence. At no time during the period he had known him had
Giffard shown any aggressive tendency whatever." Dr. Craig
said that at the end of the two years he had warned Dr. Hood,
the general practitioner, and his mother, of the possibility of a
recurrence of the schizophrenia.

He said he had seen Giffard's father occasionally in Cornwall in the last two years, and when he heard what was happening and how Giffard was behaving, he had warned Mr.
Giffard senior that something ought to be done about his son
before it was too late, as it appeared that he was deteriorating.
Mr. Maude questioned Dr. Craig about the statement which
Giffard had made to the police admitting the murder of his
parents and Dr. Craig said that in a schizophrenic case, a man
would be able to give a quite clear account of what had
happened.

Asked if he had formed any opinion of Giffard's condition at
the time of the killing of his parents Dr. Craig said : " Yes, I
think at the time he did this thing he was in a schizophrenic
episode. He would know what he was doing, but in schizophrenia there is a split in the mind—a split between the unconscious or primitive part of the mind and the more superficial, conventional part. When the split takes place the primitive mind takes charge, uncontrolled any longer by the conventional part. People in this condition know what they are doing
and know the consequences of what they are doing."

Asked if the whisky which Miles Giffard had drunk before
the murder intensified the chance of an outbreak, Dr. Craig
explained while it might have intensified the symptoms it
would not necessarily have precipitated the actual outbreak.
" It simply pours petrol on the fire," he said. Asked if there
was any other factor which seemed significant to the doctor,
Dr. Craig replied : " Yes, I think it is very important that he

apparently writes indicating what he was going to do, and it happened some days afterwards."

Mr. Maude : " Why is that significant ? " Dr. Craig : " Because I think it is so important to understand that that could happen as a result of this man's disease by involving a completely different mental mechanism from somebody cold-bloodedly and deliberately going to commit murder—a completely different mechanism altogether. Schizophrenic patients will develop a kind of fixed idea which dominates the whole of their thinking processes for the time being. It just takes charge over everything. In this case I think the fixed idea was to go and see this girl in London."

Asked his opinion as to whether or not Miles Giffard at the time of killing his father and mother, knew what he was doing was contrary to law, Dr. Craig said : " In my view he did not know at the time of killing that what he was doing was wrong in law or morally, owing to his disease of mind."

Prosecution counsel asked Dr. Craig if he did not consider that Miles Giffard's history since he had first treated him in 1941 was not that of a waster. Dr. Craig said he did not agree with the word " waster." Mr. Scott Henderson : " Isn't that a fair description of a young man scrounging money ? "—" As a doctor I cannot subscribe to that." " Was he not completely idle when he went to London ? "—" Yes." " Wasting his time and substance on drink and girls ? "—" Yes." " Do you know that he had to come back to London, admitting that he could not take the examination because he had not worked for it ? "—" Yes."

" That, by itself, is not evidence of a schizophrenic tendency is it ? "—" There are features in that which are quite characteristic of it." " There are many people who are quite sane and behave in that way ? "—" Yes, many people."

Dr. Craig said that Mr. Giffard, senior, had also consulted him. He was suffering from alcoholic neuritis.

Dealing with the fact that during a schizophrenic episode Miles Giffard would have acted irrationally, Dr. Craig said that putting his mother in a wheelbarrow and tipping over the cliff was very irrational. " Has it occurred to you that by throwing them over the cliff he may have thought to hide the wounds he himself inflicted?" asked Mr. Justice Oliver, adding that that might lead one to suppose a degree of reasoning, that Giffard had wanted to cover up what he had done, and that therefore he knew what he had done was wrong.

"I don't agree with that," replied Dr. Craig. The judge: "You appreciate that is the whole point in this case?" "I do," replied Dr. Craig, adding that it was accepted that in every schizophrenic defective reasoning and judgment were both cardinal symptoms. Giffard would certainly not have been capable of evolving a plan to put his mother and father over the cliff with the intention of simulating a fall, or hiding their injuries. Mr. Henderson: "There must have been some reasoning, otherwise he would not have moved them at all?" —"Yes." Dr. Craig added that the whole episode was irrational and alien to Giffard's nature.

Dr. Craig said that, using the word "rational" in its medical and legal sense, Giffard knew the difference between right and wrong when he interviewed him in prison; and had begun to know the difference between right and wrong on the Saturday, immediately following the death of his father and mother. "I think he was more rational, most probably, in prison than on the Saturday," Dr. Craig added. Mr. Scott Henderson: "Would he know when he went to the jeweller's and pawned his mother's jewellery that he was doing wrong?" Dr. Craig: "I think his sense of right and wrong, both legal and moral, when he did that, would probably be dimmed."

Dr. A. P. Rossiter Lewis, a Harley Street psychiatrist, who had seen Giffard after his arrest said that he concurred that on the day of the murder Miles was suffering from a defect of reason; and though he knew what he was doing to some extent, he did not know it was wrong either in the moral sense or in the sense of being against the law. Called by the prosecution Mr. Giffard's family doctor, Dr. Hood, said he had been a close personal friend of the Giffards, and their family doctor since the time they came to Cornwall at Miles's birth. He knew of no abnormality in Miles until an incident at Rugby. After four terms at Rugby he was consulted by Giffard's mother and father, who showed him the school reports. " The thing that is now clear in my memory was the emphasis which was laid on the fact that he was an extreme liar. I think from memory that one of the masters in his report said that he didn't appear to appreciate the difference between truth and lies."

Referring to a letter from Dr. Craig to himself which had been found at " Carrickowl," Dr. Hood said that he had asked Dr. Craig to set out the picture of Giffard's illness plainly, because the late Mr. Giffard had found a little difficulty in always accepting the views of the psychologists.

Mr. Henderson: " Was he a great disappointment to his father? " Dr. Hood: " He was a great disappointment when he failed at Rugby. His father was very proud of his success at games, and was exceedingly proud when he was chosen to play cricket for the county. His father gave a rather large party to celebrate his coming-of-age. His father made a speech and the boy made a speech, and I think one couldn't visualize a more happy picture." Mr. Henderson: " Was his father keen to talk about him? " Dr. Hood: " Not of late. It was a subject one rather avoided with his parents latterly." Mr. Henderson: " Do you know about his friendships with the opposite sex? " Dr. Hood replied that there had been a variety of girls whom Giffard appeared to have been very attached to, but they had only lasted a short time.

In reference to Mr. Giffard senior, Dr. Hood said : " I never knew Mr. Giffard senior to have any mental disturbances whatsoever. He made an effort and cured himself without becoming a teetotaller. That showed he had no mental weakness." Asked why, as a friend of the family, he had not suggested to Miles Giffard's parents that a mental specialist should be called in to see him again at this stage, the doctor said: " The picture was more of just an idle little waster." Mr. Maude: " Is that what you feel about him? "—" As a nonexpert, I am afraid it is."

Dr. John Matheson, principal medical officer at Brixton Prison, where Giffard was held for a few hours after his arrest, said that the tests carried out there on him did not indicate any gross abnormality in the functioning of the brain.

Asked about tests into the sugar content of Giffard's blood, Dr. Matheson said that Giffard was deprived of food for twenty-one hours to see whether his sugar content would fall below the danger level. The judge: " But what is the use of getting him below the safety-line by starving him? He was not starving on November 7th, was he? "—" No, but this is what the authorities lay down as being the way to make this test. Dr. Matheson agreed that Giffard was starved for twenty-six hours in all, apart from having a half-pint of glucose and water. The results suggested that further clinical examination and further tests should be done. " From all I knew about the events on November 7th I failed to find any evidence that Giffard may have been suffering from spontaneous hypoglycæmia. I think it would be most unlikely for an attack of that kind to occur that evening in view of his big lunch on that day, and the fact that he consumed half a bottle of whisky."

Dr. Matheson described Miles as a " psychopath " " a person who is completely selfish, who seeks to satisfy his own desires immediately without regard to the rights of others and without regard to any future possible consequences to him, and who is liable to use violence to attain his ends if thwarted."

Dr. Matheson said that taking a general view of the whole of the events of 7th November, he was impressed by the fact that all Giffard's actions seemed purposive and motivated. He had done certain things for a certain reason to gain a certain end. " He appears to have been acting on a plan from beginning to end and he was able to modify that plan as circumstances required." Putting the bodies over the cliff, disposing of the blood-stained clothes, and cleaning up afterwards, suggested that Giffard knew he had done wrong and was trying to hide the evidence that would lead to his conviction and punishment.

Making his final speech for the defence, Mr. Maude reminded the jury that their function in the case was no question of revenge or disapproval of Miles Giffard's conduct and he knew that whenever anyone said anything about him being a waster, they would consider things with deadly calm. Mr. Maude described the incidents on the night of 7th November

at " Carrickowl " as quite extraordinary. " Here is a young
man who had turned into a bad lot, a scamp, or whatever you
like to call him, but who had never shown any signs whatever
of violence. Does that not strike you as very important? In
this quiet Cornish home this young man had a father and
mother. That he was not above stealing from them we know.
That is dishonesty. That he had an uncomfortable time hitch-
hiking down from London, sleeping in a barn with rats, we
know.

" But is it to be suggested that the dishonest young man who
has had an uncomfortable night, and who wants to go back
to London to see Miss Vallance, kills his father and mother
with a sane mind? It is not suggested that there were any illicit
amatory relations going on. But it is suggested that this young
man wanted so much to see Miss Vallance that he would not
stop at murdering his father and mother in order to do so. Who
on earth does not think that anyone who did that was absolutely crazy, and will always be thought to have been crazy?"
Mr. Maude pointed out to the jury the inconsistency of the
theory that he had tried to cover up what he had done, and
driven off to London in a normal state of mind. " He was
motoring himself straight to the gallows. There was no hope
in it whatsoever," he went on.

" If he was just drunk and not insane at the time, can you
imagine the man would be able with his mother and father
lying there, to go through with that telephone conversation
as he did. The man who has committed a double murder, and
who is not intoxicated, picks up two hitch-hikers, tells them
where he has come from, why he is going to London—to see
his girl. Is not Dr. Craig right, that it is this fixed idea which
is behind all this? The man who knows he has battered his
parents to death, and knows he has done the absolutely futile
thing of putting them over the cliff in a wheelbarrow—can you
think these are the acts of a sane man? What sane person would
believe that Mr. and Mrs. Giffard had gone out on the cliff
and that both had fallen over at different points.

" There was the most childish attempt to sweep out the blood
in the kitchen and the garage. In fact, there was blood inside

the car, down the garden path and all over the place. Can anyone imagine that a sane person thought it was in the least likely
that it might be assumed that Mr. and Mrs. Giffard had fallen
over the cliff? While in the car on the way to London he
threw away blood-stained articles of clothing, yet in the back
of the car were masses of the stuff still. And the car is left in
Tite Street. Is the theory to be that this is a normal person,
except that he is evil and has been stealing from his parents,
has drunk heavily, and had not been working? No, the whole
picture is mad, it is insane. It is unique. It is outside anybody's
comprehension."

In his address to the jury, Mr. Scott Henderson said that
this was not a case of a man, the son of a gentleman holding
responsible positions in the county, and living in a nice house,
suddenly going wrong and committing a heinous crime. It was
a case of a man who, since 1947, was living an idle and disso-
lute life, going from bad to worse. " This is the culmination of
his criminal conduct."

He said that the first question the jury had to ask themselves
was whether Giffard had a mental disease. There was a complete
conflict of evidence about that. If he had had an acute attack,
however long it lasted, would not the psychiatrists have been
able to detect the disease when they saw him very shortly afterwards?

In his summing-up Mr. Justice Oliver said the submission
was that at the time these acts were performed by the man they
were trying, he was, in the eyes of the law, insane, so as not to
be legally responsible for what he did. " Insanity in law does
not mean the same thing as it means when a doctor certifies
someone insane " the judge went on. " Insanity in law has a
perfectly definite meaning.

" Two questions have to be answered. One, at the time he
did the acts causing the death, did he know what he was
doing? The defence does not pretend that he did not. He has
himself given a most minute and meticulous and apparently
accurate account of what he did. Then comes the second question, which is in fact the only one you have to ask. At the time
he did these acts, did he know that he was breaking the law,

did he know that he was doing something that is forbidden by law? " The judge said it seemed to him that very much of the argument of the defence was: " Can you believe in such a thing as that a young man like this would go and murder not only his father but his mother? That, in my opinion, is not the proper way to approach this, although you will give all due weight to it." His lordship went on: " Approach it from the point of view of that question. There is no gauge of human wickedness. Things have been done, particularly recently, so wicked that you could not imagine a man who knew what he was doing doing it. But they are nevertheless done, and you have in my view to put aside matters of that kind.

" Why should a man who doesn't know he has done wrong want to wash up, throw away his weapon and change his clothes? " Mr. Justice Oliver added that the jury might think that all the things Giffard said during the time between the killing and his escape in his father's car pointed strongly in the direction that he had known what he had done, and was doing his best to turn his back on it, the dominating thing in his mind being: " I have got to get back to that girl somehow. I have got to have money to do it." On the Saturday morning there was the picture of Giffard waiting in the car outside his girl's house, until 8 a.m. before he disturbed her. " Then, instead of spending the morning with her he takes his mother's only just stolen jewels, and sells them for £50. Is that the act of a madman or is that the act of an utterly wicked man? You will answer that question soon."

Commenting on the fact that Miles Giffard had not gone into the witness-box to give evidence in his own defence, Mr. Justice Oliver said to the jury: " He could have gone into the box perfectly well and been asked to answer some of the questions that are unanswerable. He would say: 'I do not remember,' but at least let us have a look at him, and ask him why he threw his mother and father into the sea over that cliff. It might have been able to throw some light on it, but we have not been given the chance. His memory is perfect; he knows everything he did, and all the order in which he did it. Why should he not come and tell us? "

Referring to the actions of the accused after the murder the judge said: "What reason can you think of for even trying to wash the place, except to think, hopeless though it might be, to conceal what he had done? His motive must have been—or can you think of any other?—to conceal what he had done. What other motive could there be for taking clean clothes with him except to try and conceal what he had done? What about throwing the steel weapon into the river? Was there any motive in that except to conceal what had been done? Of course it was hopeless. The sole thing disputed is whether the evidence has made it more likely than not that in your view at the time he did it he suffered from a disease of the mind, whereby he was not able to know that what he was doing was contrary to law. If you come to that conclusion you will say he was guilty but insane. If you come to the conclusion that no such case has been made out, you will find him guilty of murder. In no case, of course, can there be an acquittal."

The jury of ten men and two women came to the conclusion that Miles Giffard was guilty, in thirty-two minutes. He was condemned to death.

Shortly after the close of the case the Home Secretary received a letter from one of the jurors stating that he had been convinced that Giffard was insane when he killed his father. The juror said that because of a misunderstanding this disagreement had not been made known to the judge. It was thought by Giffard's solicitors that this letter might justify a reprieve, but no reprieve was granted.

Although Miles Giffard had no previous convictions, he was the criminal type. He had escaped prison for theft because he stole from his own father. While in London, though he had an allowance and had inherited £750, which he spent in four months, he borrowed money from friends without any intention of paying it back and he passed dud cheques. His attitude to life is given in his own words: "I believe in living life to the full—twenty-four hours a day. I'm spending my money while I'm young enough to enjoy it."

Miles Giffard was a young man with an assured future but he preferred to become a playboy. At cricket he played for his

county and he was known as a forcing batsman. He could
never be steady, in anything. From the time he left the Navy
in 1947 he was a problem to his parents. They, apparently,
treated him with lack of understanding. In a case such as this
some of the blame must be attached to the parents and they
have paid for their errors. Miles couldn't settle down to the law,
as his father had planned and he found it equally difficult to
adapt himself to estate agency. He took to drink and women.
He was a waster, but a waster with a certain fascination.
Women fell for him. As long as he had money he was seen
everywhere, usually with an attractive girl. Then he fell in love
with the one person who might have changed him. Ironically,
his father kept him from her. But the urge to see her again was
too much for Miles. Sane or insane, he planned the murder of
his parents in order to steal their car to achieve what he must
have known could only be a few hours of liberty. If he had not
written the letters, which were read in court, and if he had not
told his girl friend over the telephone that he was proposing to
come to London on Friday night, his plea of insanity might
have been accepted. But, as so often happens in murder cases,
the circumstances were more powerful than fear of discovery
and retribution.

III

CRAIG AND BENTLEY

THE night of Sunday, 2nd November, 1952. A South
London surburban home: life to the Craig family had,
apparently, reached rock bottom. Three days before their
eldest son, twenty-six-year-old Niven had been sentenced to
twelve years' imprisonment for armed robbery. Since the trial
at the Old Bailey, the younger son, sixteen-year-old Christopher,
had been strangely silent; he was bitter at the sentence given to
the brother he so much admired. That afternoon he had been
to the cinema and had seen a film called *My Death is a Mockery*,
in which a man is hanged for the murder of a policeman. After
supper, he went out saying that he was going to see a friend.
Usually he was home by 10.30 p.m. The night before a distur-
bing thing had happened in the Craig home: there had been an
explosion in the attic. Mrs. Craig had rushed upstairs but
Chris had told her that a firework had gone off by accident.
He had been playing with one of his revolvers; in light of what
became known later it is clear that he had been practising with it.

When eleven o'clock came, and then midnight, and Chris had
not returned his mother and father became anxious; then steps
were heard on the path; there was a knock at the door; it was
the police.

Earlier in the evening Craig had met nineteen-year-old
Derek Bentley. As he was banned from the Bentley home as
an undesirable friend for Derek, he had sent another boy in to
fetch him. Craig and Bentley walked down the road and
jumped a bus to Croydon. On the way, Craig showed Bentley
a revolver and handed him a knuckleduster. Getting off the
bus at Tamworth Road they got over a fence and climbed on

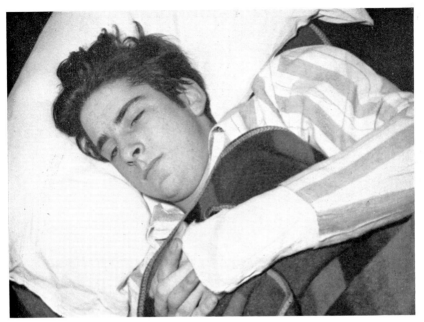

CHRISTOPHER CRAIG

DEREK BENTLEY

to the roof of a factory. They were seen by a woman who telephoned the police. Two police cars answered her call. Four policemen climbed the fence; Det.-Sgt. Fairfax, P.C. Harrison, P.C. Miles and P.C. McDonald.

Sgt. Fairfax climbed up a drainpipe and reached the flat roof of the building. By the fitful light of the moon he saw the two youths hiding behind a chimney stack. Approaching within six feet, he shone his torch and called, " I am a police officer, come out from behind that stack." One of the youths, Craig, answered, " If you want us, come and get us." The police officer charged in, seizing Bentley. While holding him he tried to grab Craig, who slipped away. Bentley twisted himself free and shouted, " Let him have it, Chris." This was heard by the other three policemen who had also gained the roof.

Bentley's words were followed by a loud report. Sgt. Fairfax was hit in the shoulder by a revolver bullet. Another shot missed him. Though wounded Fairfax knocked Bentley down and dragged him behind some roof lights. As the shooting went on he took from him a knife and a knuckleduster. Fairfax told Bentley that he would take him across the roof to the shelter of the doorway but Bentley said, " He will shoot you." When another officer joined them, Bentley said, " I told the silly bugger not to use it."

Fairfax shouted to Craig, " Drop your gun." This was answered by another burst of firing. P.C. Harrison tried to reach Craig but he was driven back. P.C. Miles, coming from the doorway, fell dead with a bullet through his eyes. From behind the chimney stack Craig raked the roof with bullets. P.C. Harrison, jumping over Miles' body, threw his truncheon, a bottle and a block of wood at Craig, who shouted, " Come on you brave coppers, think of your wives. I am Craig. You just got my brother twelve years. Come on, I am only sixteen."

Bentley, under arrest, told the police, " You want to look out—he will blow your heads off." As he was taken downstairs he shouted, " Look out, Chris, they are taking me down." There was a further burst of firing from Craig.

By this time the factory was surrounded by police and guns

had been issued. Fairfax, shouting, " Drop your gun—I also have a gun," ran towards Craig, who replied, " Yes, it is a Colt .45. Are you hiding behind a shield? Is it bullet-proof? Are we going to have a shooting match? It is just what I like." Then the police heard clicks from Craig's gun and his words, " There it's empty." Diving twenty-five feet to the ground Craig was seized by the police as he lay badly injured. He said, " I wish I was dead. I hope I have killed the bloody lot." In hospital that night Craig told the waiting policeman, " I had six in that gun. I fired at a policeman. I had six Tommy-gun bullets. Is the copper dead? How about the others? We ought to have shot them all."

Bentley, on being told that P.C. Miles was dead, said, " I did not kill him, guv'nor, Chris did it." He said that he did not know that Craig had a gun, but on the way to the police station he had said, " I knew he had a gun, but I did not think that the silly bugger would use it."

When Craig regained consciousness next morning, he asked if the copper was dead. He said, " I shot him in the head and he went down like a ton of bricks."

Christopher Craig and Derek Bentley were charged with the murder of Police Constable Miles. Craig's defence was that the death of the police officer had been accidental. He had fired only to frighten the police. Bentley's defence rested on the fact that at the time when the policeman was shot he was in police custody.

Craig and Bentley were tried at the Old Bailey on the 9th, 10th, 11th and 12th December, 1952, before the Lord Chief Justice, Lord Goddard. Craig was defended by Mr. E. J. Parris, and Bentley by Mr. F. H. Cassels, Mr. Christmas Humphreys prosecuted.

Setting out the case against Craig and Bentley, Mr. Humphreys said : " The case for the Crown is that Craig deliberately and wilfully murdered that police constable and thereafter gloried in the murder and he only regretted that he had not shot more. Bentley incited Craig to begin the shooting. Although he was technically under arrest at the time he was nevertheless still mentally supporting Craig in all that Craig continued to do. In English law—and you may think it common sense—he was in every sense a party to that murder."

Recalling the events of the fatal night, Mr. Humphreys drew particular attention to the remark made by Bentley to Craig, " Let him have it, Chris." The immediate reply to his words was the shot that wounded Fairfax. That statement, the prosecution submitted, was a deliberate incitement to Craig to murder Fairfax. It was spoken to a man Bentley knew had a gun. The shot that followed began the gunfight in which P.C. Miles was killed. That incitement, the prosecution submitted, covered the whole shooting thereafter, even though at the time the shot was fired that killed P.C. Miles, Bentley was in custody and under arrest. That Bentley was armed with a knuckleduster and a knife showed that he was prepared to use violence in the course of a common enterprise of housebreaking. Bentley's words to Fairfax, " I told the silly bugger not to use it," meant that Bentley knew that Craig had a gun and that he knew that he meant to use it.

Mr. Humphreys also pointed out that, at least nine shots had been fired and the revolver held only six, this meant that Craig re-loaded the gun during the gunfight. " The importance of that is merely as showing deliberate purpose in his mind as distinct from a foolish boy who happens to have a loaded gun and in fear, or in losing his head or whatever it may be, pulls the trigger."

The heroic story of the gunbattle was told by three surviving police officers, who swore to the words alleged to have been used by Craig and Bentley.

Craig's father, for the second time within a month, was called upon to give evidence about his sons at the Old Bailey. An ex-army Captain and now chief cashier of a bank, Mr. Craig said that Christopher had never been a violent boy; he was, in fact, a gentle boy. Although he had tried to teach him himself, Christopher had never learned to read or write. He suffered from what is known as " word blindness." Because of this he had been jeered at by other boys.

Christopher had, his father said, always been interested in firearms; he had wanted to become a gunsmith. He (Christo-

pher) had been fined at Hove for being in possession of a revolver. Mr. Craig was asked by prosecution counsel : " Did
you know he had sawn off the barrel of this revolver? "—" I
certainly did not." " Did you know it was sawn off in the attic
of your house? "—" No." " Did you know he had hidden in
your house a large quantity of ammunition."—" I did not."
" That included twenty-two rounds of .22, twenty-two rounds
of .23, forty-six rounds of .45, eight rounds of .303 and five
rounds of .303 blanks. You knew nothing about them? "—" I
did not." Mr. Craig had, he said, owned firearms for which
he had a certificate and he had been a keen marksman.

Both defendants gave evidence. In the case of Craig, it
mattered little what he said; the facts of the case against him
were evident, but Bentley, by what he said, seriously preju-
diced the court against him.

Craig said that in the previous year he had been fined for
having a firearm without a certificate. He was asked : " When
did you start taking an interest in firearms? "—" When I was
about four. I liked them when I was about seven." " Where
had you seen them when you were about seven? "—" My
father's." " What was the first weapon you yourself ever
had? "—" A cap and ball pistol when I was eleven. It was
about 150 years old." " Between the age of eleven and your
present age, how many weapons have you had? "—" Forty or
fifty." " Where did you get them from? "—" I swopped them
and bought them off boys at school." " Did you ever take any
of them to school with you? "—" I used to take all of them."
" Forty or fifty? " asked Lord Goddard. " Not all at the same
time " replied Craig.

Mr. Parris : " Whenever you had a weapon you took it with
you to school. Why? "—" To show it to the boys." " Why,"
asked Mr. Parris again and Craig in a low voice answered :
" To make myself look big." " Were you interested in firing
them? "—" I had fired a couple of them." Lord Goddard :
" Were you a good shot? "—" No, sir." " Did you know that
firearms could kill people? " Craig, after some hesitation,
answered " Yes." Craig said that it was his ambition to be a
gunsmith and that he took a gun to work nearly every day.

Mr. Parris: " The weapon in this case has the barrel sawn off. Why was that? "—" So that I could carry it and take it to work." " Why did you want to take a gun to work? "—" It made me feel big." " Did they ever say anything to you about not being able to read properly? "—" They used to take the mickey out of me." " What does that mean? " asked Mr. Parris: " Does it mean that they used to mock and taunt you? " Craig replied, " Yes, sir." Mr. Parris: " Because you could not read, did you go to the pictures? "—" Yes, three or four times a week." " What sort of films used you to see? "— " Gangster films." " Did you like that sort? "—" Yes, sir."

Next he was closely questioned about the events of the night of the 2nd November. Mr. Parris: " Sergeant Fairfax has said that at some time at that stage of the proceedings Bentley said, ' Let him have it, Chris.' Did you hear any words like that? " —" No, sir." " Where did you fire the first shot? "—" Down at the ground a few feet in front." " What happened to the officer? "—" He ducked to the ground." " Did you fire another shot? "—" Not then. He rushed at Bentley and I tried to frighten him and fired another shot." Mr. Parris: " Where were the other shots pointed? " Craig: " In the air. I think I fired one or two into this corner (indicating a point on the plan), on the east side." Lord Goddard: " How many times do you say you fired altogether? "—" Nine, sir." " So you reloaded the revolver? "—" Yes, sir." Mr. Parris: " Did you see the officer, Miles, come up to the roof? "—" No, I did not see him come on to the roof. The door opened. I thought someone was coming out to me and I fired another one to frighten them away. I fired it towards the house over the parapet." Lord Goddard: " How did it come to hit P.C. Miles coming out on to the roof? "—" It might have ricochetted off. I don't know." Mr. Parris: " Had you any intention at any time of killing that officer? "—" No, sir."

" You have heard the various things you are alleged to have said on the rooftop. Why did you say them? "—" It was all bluff so that they would not come up." Then Mr. Parris asked: " When you were standing there with the gun in your hands, what did you think you were like? " Almost inaudibly,

Craig replied, " Like the films." Mr. Parris : " Had you any intention of hurting any officer at all ? "—" No, sir." Lord Goddard : " Have you expressed any regret or sorrow that you have killed that officer? "—" Yes." " When? " asked the Lord Chief Justice. Craig replied : " When I was in prison." Mr. Parris : " Why did you dive off the roof ? "—" Because I knew I had hurt one of them." " What did you want to do to yourself ? " asked Mr. Parris. Craig's reply, " Kill myself " was scarcely audible. He declared that when he came to in hospital, " Someone hit me in the mouth and called me a murderous —— "

He was then asked about the statements he was alleged to have made after the gunfight. Craig replied," I don't think I said them." Earlier it had been stated that he had been given in hospital where he had been taken following the injuries he had received in diving from the roof at the end of the fight, a drug named pentothal. This was described in court as a drug " sometimes inaccurately called the truth drug." It is sometimes used to make people talk more freely than they would normally do.

Cross-examined by the prosecution, Craig made the following replies to Mr. Humphreys : " On this night you shot Police Constable Miles, is that right? " Craig : " Yes, sir." Mr. Humphreys : " You meant to shoot him, didn't you? "—" No, sir." " You meant to shoot any police officer who tried to prevent you escaping from the felony you were committing? "— " No, sir."

Craig said that he had known Bentley for about eighteen months. On the night of 2nd November he and Bentley were out to break into the wholesale confectioners and to steal what they could. Craig agreed that he had a loaded gun in his pocket but he stated that he was not a practised shot. He said that he had got the gun from a boy in Purley. Mr. Humphreys : " You had collected an amazing variety of ammunition and hidden it in your father's house. Where had you got all that from? "—" Caterham Barracks. I found it." Lord Goddard : " How did you get the ammunition from the Army barracks? " —" The ranges are out on some ground, and I found them,"

Craig was asked about the knuckleduster he had given to Bentley. " Where did you get that knuckleduster? "—" I made it." Lord Goddard asked for it to be handed to him. Putting his fingers through the holes he asked : " What is that spike for? " Craig's reply could not be heard and Lord Goddard repeated, " What is the knuckleduster for? " Craig : " You can put it on your hand." Lord Goddard : " To hit anybody. What is this dreadful spike for? You say you made it. What is the spike for? "—" I did not put it in. It was there. I just rounded it off with a file." " You have it on your knuckles and you have this spike on it," continued Lord Goddard, holding the knuckleduster on his hand for the jury to see. " It is a dreadful weapon."

Next he was questioned about the statements he had made in hospital; Mr. Humphreys : " Did you say in hospital : ' I was out to kill because I had so much hate inside me for what they had done to my brother ' ? "—" Did I say that? " " That is four days after you went into hospital. You do not suggest you could not have talked sensibly then? "—" I was injected every twelve hours." " I have heard all about the drugs. Are you saying that on 6th November you did not know what you were saying? "—" I say I did not say that. I do not remember saying that." Mr. Humphreys : " Did you say : ' Did you see the gun I had ? It was on the wobble, so I took it to work and sawed two inches off the barrel ' ? "—" That is ridiculous." " It may be ridiculous, but are you denying that you said it? "—" If I did, it shows the person who said it is not in his right mind."

Craig was next cross-examined about his words and actions on the fatal night. Mr. Humphreys : " Do you agree that you were out to commit crime this night. To break in and get what you could ? "—" Yes." " You agree you were well armed, both of you? "—" I did not know what Bentley had got." " And you intended to resist any person who tried to arrest you and prevent you committing that crime? "—" No, I wanted to frighten them." Lord Goddard : " You wanted to frighten them away so they would not arrest you? " Mr. Humphreys : " Do you think shooting a revolver in the air

will frighten policemen all round you from coming at you ?
You shot Fairfax at six feet range? ”—“ No.” “ How far
from you do you say he was? ”—“About twenty-seven feet.
No thirty-seven feet.”

A vital point in the cross-examination was reached when
Craig was asked about the words, “ Let him have it, Chris,”
alleged to have been spoken by Bentley. Craig replied that he
did not hear the words and that if the police did, they had
better ears than he had.

Mr. Humphreys: “ You say you shot nine times altogether? ”—“ Yes.” “ You shot all you could ? ”—“ I was trying to frighten them away.” Lord Goddard : “ And you knew
they were police officers because you heard him say when he
grabbed Bentley that he was a police officer? ” Lord Goddard :
“ Did you say, ‘ Come on you brave coppers. Think of your
wives’ ? ”—“ I am not sure, I might have done.” “ What did
you mean by that? ”—“ To frighten them. I was shouting
out.” “ You threatened to shoot them if they came on? ”—
“ No, I did not.”

Lord Goddard : “ Think of your wives—In other words :
Think your wives will be widows if you do come? ”—“ I was
trying to frighten them.” Mr. Humphreys : “ I am Craig;
you have just given my brother twelve years, come on you
coppers. Is that your way of frightening them or trying to get
them out from the cover behind the staircase? ”—“ No. I saw
the door fly open, I thought someone was coming out so I fired
again to frighten them again.” “ Is that your version of the
murder of P.C. Miles? ”—“ I did not know he was dead.”
Craig said that he knew Miles had been hit, but did not know
what had happened. Mr. Humphreys :“ He was shot by you? ”
—“Yes.” “And then an officer comes out and says ‘ Drop your
gun. I also have a gun ’ ? ”—“ He did not. Someone fired two
shots at me from somewhere I did not see.” “ ‘ Yes, it is a Colt
.45 : Are you hiding behind a shield ? Is it bullet-proof ? Are
we going to have a shooting match? It is just what I like?
Have they hurt you, Derek? ’ Do you remember that
speech? ”—“ I did not say it like that. A few times after I
fired the gun I said I had a Colt .45.”

"Is all the rest the imagination of the police?"—"No, it was just to frighten them. It was only madnesss to say that if you mean it." "Did you say it?"—"I do not remember." Mr. Humphreys: "Before you had any drug of any kind you said, 'I had six in the gun. I fired at a policeman.' Is that right?"—"I might have said I did not fire at a policeman." Craig denied saying: "Is the copper dead? How about the others? We ought to have shot them all" or "You are coppers, the other one is dead with a hole in his head. I am all right, all you buggers ought to be dead."

Mr. Humphreys: "All these officers when giving evidence of what you said are not speaking the truth, is that your story?"—"Yes." "From the moment you killed P.C. Miles to the moment you stepped into that witness-box to give evidence, have you ever shown the slightest remorse or regret for killing him—Not to anybody?"—"I might have done." Lord Goddard: "You were asked if you had ever shown any remorse or expressed any regret to anyone for having killed this policeman?"—"I have thought about that." "Have you ever expressed any regret?"—"Who was there to express it to?" "You saw plenty of policemen because they were watching you by your bedside?"—"I was hardly conscious." Lord Goddard: "Nonsense."

Bentley entering the witness-box was unable to read the oath. He said that he had been a dustman and a remover. He agreed that he had been told by his parents not to associate with Craig. He had met Craig on the evening of 2nd November, but he did not know why they went to Croydon. On the bus Craig had given him the knuckledusters. When they got off the bus he went to look into the window of a sweet shop. Without saying anything to him, Craig climbed over an iron fence. He followed him. They got on the roof. Bentley claimed that he did not know that Craig had a loaded revolver.

Describing the fight on the roof Bentley said: "Sergeant Fairfax came up and he took me and walked me across the roof. He said 'I am a police officer. I have the place surrounded.'" Mr. Cassels: "When he took hold of you did you make any effort to struggle?"—"No." "Or any attempt to strike him? "—" No." "Until the time the shot was fired did you know that Craig had a gun? "—" No, sir." Bentley stated that he was not being held all the time and that there was nothing to prevent him from joining Craig if he had wanted to do so.

With these words Bentley convicted himself. The police had stated in court that Bentley was in custody and under arrest from the moment that he had been seized by them. He had made no attempt to escape but here he was denying that he was in custody at the time of the shooting. But more of this later.

In cross-examination, Bentley told Mr. Humphreys that he had known Craig for years and had known him at school. Mr. Humphreys: "Then you knew of his love for firearms? "— " No." Bentley explained that he was leaving school just as Craig was coming to it. Mr. Humphreys: "You knew nothing about his mania for firearms? "—" I knew nothing." "You knew this night, before a shot was fired, that he had this gun on him? "—" No, sir." "Then what he has told the jury is a lie? "—" I would not say so." "But you have heard him in the box? Is it untrue? "—" Yes." "As between Craig and all these police officers on the one hand and you on the other hand, what you are saying is right and what the others are saying is not true? "—" Craig could have got muddled-up."

Mr. Humphreys held up a sheath-knife: "Just look at that knife of yours," he said, "Where did you get it?" Bentley replied that it was given to him by a friend a few months before. "Why were you carrying it that night? "—" It was in my coat and I was wearing it." "On the way to the warehouse you were given the knuckleduster? "—" I do not know." "What," cried Mr. Humphreys, "You don't know that he gave you the knuckleduster. Then why did you take it?" Bentley replied: "I don't know. It was something I put in my pocket." Mr. Humphreys: "Are you saying that you did not know that you were going to this warehouse to break in? " —" I did not know we were going to break in."

Questioning Bentley about the gunfight, Lord Goddard asked him: "Did you shout out, 'For God's sake don't fire' or, 'Shut up doing that' ? "—" No." Mr. Humphreys: "You were doing nothing to stop him doing what you did together to break in? "—" We came to break in and not to kill." " You were hoping that Craig would get away and you did nothing to stop him continuing to shoot? "—"There was nothing I could do." " You incited him to shoot further when you said : ' Look out, Chris, they are taking me away ' ? "—" He might have hit anybody. He might have shot me." Lord Goddard : " You mean that you were thinking only of your own skin? " Mr. Humphreys : " Did you think Craig was a thoroughly dangerous and irresponsible person when he had a gun in his hand ? "—" At that time, yes." " And well before you ever got on to the roof ? "—" No, sir."

Bentley explained that he met Craig at the end of the road. " We stayed on the corner for a little while, and then jumped on a bus going to Croydon." Lord Goddard : " What were you going to do in Croydon? "—" I did not know." " Did you and Craig make any arrangement to break into anywhere? " —" No." He agreed that on the bus Craig gave him a pair of knuckledusters which he had not seen before. He put them in his pocket. They got off the bus at Tamworth Road. " We looked in the window of a sweet shop. I was still looking in when Craig climbed over an iron fence . . . " Lord Goddard asked : " Without saying anything to you? " Bentley : " Yes." " What did you do? "—" I followed him over the fence." " Why was that? "—" I don't know." Lord Goddard : " You were going to break in? "—" I don't know why I went over the fence." Bentley said that up to the time when they got on the roof he did not know that Craig had a loaded revolver.

In his final speech to the jury Craig's counsel said : " Craig has become a symbol of wayward youth." Mr. Parris went on : " We say for the defence that he is not guilty of murder but of manslaughter, which, in all conscience, is a serious enough crime. Before he can be found guilty of murder you must be satisfied that an act of his killed Police Officer Miles. That is not disputed. The second thing is that there must be malice aforethought, constructural or actual—an intent to murder, an intent to do him grievous bodily harm or to use violence on the officer deliberately to resist arrest."

The defence claimed that if in the course of the struggle injury was caused accidentally, then it would be manslaughter.

Mr. Parris continued : " What the defence say is that in the course of the events of that night, this boy accidentally caused the injury to Police Officer Miles. The prosecution say that boy was a veritable walking armoury, and if it were a man you were dealing with in possession of his full senses and understanding, you would be quite right to infer he meant to use those terrible weapons. But you are not dealing with a man, you are dealing with a stupid boy. The very extravagance of his armoury shows it was there for bravado and not for use."

While Craig's defence was well-nigh hopeless, the case of Bentley turned on two points. These were stated by his counsel who told the jury that they could only convict him if they were satisfied that he knew that Craig had a gun and that he had incited Craig to use it.

In his final speech for the prosecution, Mr. Christmas Humphreys said that the crime of housebreaking represented the common purpose of the two young men. Both were armed; both intended to resist arrest and to use violence to resist arrest. Mr. Humphreys went on : " If you find, as against Craig, that he shot that police officer with a lethal weapon, knowing he was a police officer or that those around him on the roof were police officers in the course of the commission of a felony such as housebreaking is, and in the course of resisting his lawful arrest for the offence he was then committing, I ask you to say that that is murder. It may be suggested here that you should find a lesser verdict of murder—that of manslaughter, unlawful killing but without the intent to kill. That could only arise if there was, in the course of the facts I have just set out, the element of accident or excusable mistake in the shooting by the accused man of the officer in question."

Bentley, said Mr. Humphreys, agreed that he knew they were going to break into a warehouse and had agreed that he was on a common enterprise of crime with Craig. He said he did not know that Craig had a gun. " You have heard from Craig of his boasting and bragging about his great arsenal of guns and wanting to be a gunsmith. Is it not amazing that the friend he had known for years did not know it? Can you believe it?" Mr. Humphreys ended by saying: "What may be the result of your verdict is no concern of yours or anybody else in this court. I must ask you to return a verdict of wilful murder against each of these two young men."

The summing-up by the Lord Chief Justice, should be read in detail; Lord Goddard said: "In many respects this is a very terrible case and it is one which it is desirable that you and I should approach in as calm a frame of mind as we can. Here are two lads, one sixteen and one nineteen, admittedly out on a shopbreaking expedition at night, armed with a Service revolver, a dreadful weapon in the shape of a knuckle-duster, and two knives. The result is that a young policeman is shot dead while in the execution of his duty. You may think it was almost a miracle that others were not shot too. One of them, Sergeant Fairfax, was wounded, but fortunately only slightly. Let us put out of our minds in this case any question of films or comics or literature of that sort. These things are always prayed in aid nowadays when young persons are in the dock and they really have very little to do with the case.

"These two young men or boys, whatever you like to call them, are both of an age which makes them responsible to the law; they are over fourteen. It is surely idle to pretend these days that a boy of sixteen does not know the wickedness of taking out a revolver of that description and a pocket full of ammunition and firing it when he is on an unlawful expedition when the police are approaching him. You will remember that as far as Craig is concerned, by his own words he supplied a motive for what he was doing, for he said he hated the police because they had got his brother twelve years. It seems to show that his brother was convicted of a very serious offence to receive a sentence of that length."

Lord Goddard emphasized that the jury had to consider the case of each of these lads separately. "Let us take first of all the case of Craig. It is not disputed and should not be disputed that he fired the shot that killed the police constable. You are asked to say that the killing was accidental and that therefore the offence is reduced to manslaughter. Gentlemen of the jury, it is the prerogative of the jury in any case where the charge is of murder to find a verdict of manslaughter. But you can only do it if the evidence satisfies you that the case is properly reducible to one of manslaughter. The law of this country with regard to murder is this : If a person does an act towards another wilfully, that is to say, intentionally, which a reasonable person would know may cause death or grievous bodily harm, and death results, that is murder."

Lord Goddard continued : " If in an ordinary case in which no police officer was concerned, you thought a prisoner only meant to fire wildly and to simply shoot off a revolver in a grossly negligent way, but was so negligent he deserved punishment and death resulted, that would only be manslaughter. There is a further consideration in this case in which I want to direct your particular attention. Miles, the dead man, was a police officer, and the law has for centuries—even since there has been a law in this country—given special protection to police officers while in the execution of their duty. It is more accurate to say that in the case of killing a police officer the law does not give the accused the same defence as in the case of other persons. I am going to direct you that this is the law : if a police officer has arrested or is endeavouring to arrest, and that includes coming on the scene for the purpose of arrest, a person and the arrest, if effected, would be lawful, and that person for the purpose of escape or preventing or hindering the arrest does a wilful, that is to say an intentional act, which causes the death of the officer, he is guilty of murder whether or not he intended to kill or do grievous harm.

" There is no question here but that the attempted arrest by police officer or police officers was lawful. Therefore, if in the course of a lawful arrest the prisoner does an act which kills a police officer that is murder unless the act, that is the firing of the pistol, was accidental. Was it a wilful act which caused the injury? The question is not whether the result was accidental in the sense that more harm was caused than was intended. And now I have explained the law to you it may be you will have some difficulty, as I don't hesitate to say I have, in understanding what defence there can be for the prisoner Craig. There he was on this roof armed—and his revolver was loaded when he took it there and he had spare ammunition and he had some time to reload. The revolver contained six chambers and he fired altogether nine shots and two did not detonate, so he tried to fire eleven shots. If that is not a deliberate act of deliberate firing it is difficult to understand what would be.

" But you will remember and bear in mind we are only concerned with the death of Police Officer Miles on this indictment. Miles was killed by the third shot this youth fired. The first shot hit Detective-Sergeant Fairfax. That may help you to come to a conclusion whether this man was deliberately firing at the officers. The first shot hit the police officer, but fortunately did little harm. The second shot was fired, according to Fairfax, when Bentley was on the ground. Other police officers were heard to come up the stairs, and then the third shot was fired in the direction of the stairs and P.C. Miles fell dead. The aiming does not seem to have been bad does it— three shots and two police officers hit? One was fortunately hit only slightly and the other was hit between the eyes so that the blood gushed out and he fell dead instantaneously. That was not the only shooting. The next shooting was spoken of by another very gallant officer, Constable Harrison, who was working his way on his back along the sloping roof towards the prisoner.

" When Fairfax went back to the roof armed with an automatic he called out that he had a pistol and thereupon, according to Fairfax, the prisoner said : ' Come on then coppers. Let us have it out.' P.C. Jaggs said the prisoner shouted : ' Come on you brave coppers—think of your wives.' To Harrison he said : ' I am Craig. You have just given my brother twelve years. Come on you coppers—I am only sixteen.' " Lord Goddard turned to the jury and remarked : " You may wonder why he said : ' I am only sixteen.' Possibly you may know that the law does not allow a capital sentence to be passed on a boy of sixteen.

" Taking all those facts together is it possible—you will

always find a merciful verdict if you can—to find that that
shooting was accidental? You have got to find, before you can
reduce the case to manslaughter, that the shooting was accidental."

Turning to the case against Bentley, Lord Goddard said:
" These two youths are tied together for the murder of a policeman. It is quite unnecessary where two or more persons are
engaged together in any unlawful or criminal act to show that
the hand of both of them committed the crime." The simplest
illustration he could give the jury was that if two men went
out housebreaking and one broke in and the other was stationed
outside, both were taking part in the enterprise and both were
equally guilty. " Now let us see what the evidence is with
regard to Bentley. The first thing you have to consider is:
Did Bentley know Craig was armed? Can you suppose for a
moment especially when you have heard Craig say why he
carried a revolver, that it was for the purpose of boasting and
showing he was a bigger man, that he would not have told his
pal he had a revolver? Is it not inconceivable that Craig would
not have shown him the revolver he had? That is quite apart
from what Bentley said afterwards."

Looking at the table on which the exhibits were placed,
Lord Goddard said: " Let us see what Bentley had on him.
Where is that knuckleduster? " Holding the knuckleduster up,
he continued: " Bentley was armed with this knuckleduster.
Have you ever seen a more horrible sort of weapon? "

Ordering " Hand up those knives—that sheath knife—the
big one," he went on: " I do not know what parents can be
thinking about these days letting a boy of sixteen—although
they say they did not know—have a weapon like this to take
about. It is not new, you can see. That is what Craig is taking
about. Now, where is that other one? " Another knife was
handed to the judge. " This is a similar knife which Bentley
had. You can see it is sharp and pointed. What is he carrying
that for? Not even with a sheath on it. Although Bentley said
he did not know that Craig had a gun if the evidence of the
officers is overwhelming, you can say he must have known.

" The most serious piece of evidence against Bentley is that he called out, if you believe the evidence, to Craig, ' Let him have it, Chris,' before the firing began and the very first shot struck Fairfax. Gentlemen, those words are sworn to by three police officers, Fairfax, MacDonald and Harrison. Do you believe that these three officers have come into that witness box and sworn what is deliberately untrue? Those three officers who on that night showed a devotion to duty for which they are entitled to the thanks of the community."

Lord Goddard turned to the jury and said slowly : " You owe a duty to the prisoners. You will remember and realize I know that you owe a duty to the community. If these young, but not so young that they are not responsible in law, men commit crimes of this sort it is right quite independently of any question of punishment that they should be convicted; unless you find good ground for not convicting them it is your duty to do it. I have reminded you what the defence is; I think I have sufficiently reminded you what the prosecution is. With these words I ask you to go to the very serious and solemn duty of considering your verdict."

The jury of twelve men found both defendants guilty in seventy-seven minutes. In the case of Bentley, they made a recommendation for mercy.

With the black cap on his head, the judge told Bentley : " You are nineteen years of age. It is, therefore, my duty to pass on you the only sentence which the law can pass for the crime of wilful murder."

While Bentley was taken away, Lord Goddard addressed Craig. The black cap was removed; " Christopher Craig, you are not nineteen, but in my judgment, and evidently in the judgment of the jury, you are the more guilty of the two," said Lord Goddard. " Your heart was filled with hate and you murdered a policeman without thought of his wife or family or himself. Never once have you expressed a word of sorrow for what you have done. I can only sentence you to be detained until Her Majesty's pleasure is known. I shall tell the Secretary of State when forwarding the recommendation in Bentley's case that in my opinion you are one of the most dangerous young criminals that has ever stood in that dock. While the jury were out considering their verdict in this case I had to deal with another case in which you were concerned with another boy whom you led into it—holding up an elderly couple and stealing from them. It is quite obvious that the people of this country will not be safe if you are out of prison. I shall recommend the time I suggest to the Secretary of State that you shall be detained. The sentence is that you be kept in strict custody until the pleasure of Her Majesty be known."

When the two murderers of P.C. Miles had been taken away Lord Goddard ordered Det.-Sgt. Fairfax, P.C. MacDonald and P.C. Harrison, with Chief Inspector Smith, who had been in charge of the case, to stand before him. Lord Goddard said : " The conduct of the men of Z Division who on this night were concerned in the arrest of these two desperate young criminals is worthy of the highest commendation. They deserve the thanks of the community for their gallant conduct—all the police. They are deserving of commendation, but I have asked these three in particular to stand forward as they showed such commendable courage on that night. It is no light thing to face a burglar or housebreaker in the dark when he is armed with a revolver and firing in the way you faced them. I doubt not that all your comrades who were there that night would have shown exactly the same courage as you did. It so happened that you three officers were exposed to the worst of it, and therefore had more opportunity of showing the courage and resolution you did. The thanks of all law-abiding citizens ought to be tendered to you."

So ended the case of the two young gangsters who shot a policeman. They learnt, like many others, that in England you can't get away with murder. For Craig there could be no sympathy. To avenge his brother he fired the shot that killed P.C. Miles. It could only be regretted that he was too young to be hanged. At fifteen he had run away from home, armed with a gun, intending to steal a boat on the coast, and go to France. He was fined thirty shillings at Hove. While the jury was deliberating the murder charge, another boy was sentenced for armed robbery, " undoubtedly with Craig," as the prosecution stated.

But the case of Derek Bentley was rather different. Although in English law equally guilty of murder with Craig he had not fired the shot that killed the policeman, and, in fact, he had been in custody for fifteen minutes when the shot was fired. The jury had recommended him to mercy.

Like Craig, Bentley, too, had a criminal past. Like Craig he was illiterate. Both came from good homes. There the resemblance ended. Craig was the " leader," the stronger personality of the two. Bentley was mentally deficient (he had been rejected by the Army on that ground). As a child he had twice been bombed out of his home. At fourteen he was convicted of shopbreaking and he was sent to an approved school for twenty-one months. He was classified as an epileptic and reported as intellectually backward.

By finding Bentley guilty of murder, the jury decided that Bentley knew that Craig had a gun and he knew that he intended to use it to resist arrest. There can be no doubt that Bentley was aware that Craig had a gun but the full implication of that fact may not have sunk into his limited intelligence. There can be no dispute that Bentley spoke the words : " Let him have it, Chris," thus inciting Craig to murder but, at the time when P.C. Miles was killed, Bentley was under arrest, although he denied it in the witness box. It was questionable, too, whether his later remark, " They are taking me down, Chris," was intended to warn Craig not to shoot or whether it was spoken to inform him that he could now shoot without the risk of hitting his friend.

Bentley appealed against his conviction on two grounds; that his case had not been properly put by the judge to the jury and that the " joint enterprise " on which he had been engaged with Craig, had been brought to a close by his arrest, fifteen minutes before the policeman was shot.

The point was an unusual one and because Bentley's appeal was rejected, it is important to note the view taken by the Court of Appeal, stated by Mr. Justice Croom-Johnson :

" The argument advanced about that is that, whether there was a joint enterprise or not, a joint enterprise in which to the knowledge of both of them one of them was

to be armed, the appellant could not be held responsible
for the acts of the other because the joint enterprise was
at an end. That depends on what the jury thought was
the joint enterprise. If they thought it was an enterprise
to go and murder somebody and that was over and done
with so that the joint enterprise was finished, they might
very well have taken that view—I do not say that it would
have been the right view—but they might have taken the
view that the enterprise was finished as soon as one of
them was arrested, but they might equally have taken the
view, and there was ample material for them to take it
and no complaint is made of the summing-up with regard
to this, that the enterprise was not merely a burglarious
enterprise, but an enterprise in which they were to secure
themselves against those who came to apprehend them.

" In these circumstances, the jury might very well have
taken quite a different view as to whether the enterprise
had finished or not. It is a little difficult for Mr. Cassels
(Bentley's Counsel) because his own client was asked
specifically at the hearing whether he was under arrest at
the time Miles was killed. He would not have it. He
said he had not been arrested, that he was not under arrest,
that the police officer had not detained him, and all the rest
of it. In the face of that it seems to us that it is idle to suggest
that this point, if it be the point, about the arrest is one
which the jury could have taken into consideration and
about which the Chief Justice ought to have directed the
jury.

" The answers given in cross-examination by an individual on trial do sometimes have the result of destroying
the possibility of a good point of law being persisted in
which learned counsel has endeavoured to get on its feet
before the jury, and it seems to us that there is nothing in
this point on either of the two grounds.

" In our opinion there is nothing more than an ordinary appeal in a murder trial, an ordinary appeal which
is, in our judgment, without foundation and which is
accordingly dismissed."

The Court of Criminal Appeal considers only points of law. Bentley's conviction was confirmed but whether or not the sentence of death would be carried out rested on the decision of the Home Secretary.

By his words in the witness box Bentley had convicted himself of active participation in, and for incitement to, murder. He and Craig had gone together in a joint enterprise with the intention of resisting arrest. Bentley had incited Craig to shoot at Sgt. Fairfax and to kill P.C. Miles. It was a curious but an important point that, at the time when Miles was killed, Bentley was in custody. A person is under arrest from the moment he is touched by a police officer.

The rejection of the plea for a reprieve in the case of Bentley has led to a great deal of controversy. The matter was raised in the House of Commons. There was much to be said why he should not die; he had been recommended to mercy; the judge (The Lord Chief Justice) had said that he was the less guilty of the two; he was barely above the age limit; mentally Bentley was sub-normal, but, above all, he had been convicted only of participation in and for incitement to murder.

In the House of Commons Mr. Aneurin Bevan pointed out " a three-quarter-witted boy of nineteen is to be hung for a murder he did not commit and which was committed fifteen minutes after he was arrested. Can we be made to keep silent when a thing as horrible and shocking as that is happening? "

Bentley was hanged. Can his execution be condemned on moral or legal grounds? Can it be supported? The Home Secretary has an unenviable task. The prerogative of mercy is his and his alone. He is also responsible for public safety. Since the end of the war there has been a wave of crime, especially of juvenile crime; robbery has frequently been accompanied by violence and murder. In this case a police officer, in the execution of his duty, had been shot. Other police officers had risked their lives so that the law should be enforced.

As long as the death penalty is retained, it must be enforced unless there are reasonable grounds why it should be waived in a particular case. There is much to be said for the abolition of the death penalty in cases where the guilt of the accused person is established on grounds of a high degree of probability only. But, in this case there is no doubt that P.C. Miles was murdered. Under English law both youths were guilty of his murder. The only question that arises is whether Bentley, who did not pull the trigger of the gun, was guilty equally with Craig who did. The controversy about Bentley's sentence is emphasized by the fact that, because he was under eighteen years of age, the person who actually killed the policeman was not executed. But that Craig could not be hanged has no bearing on the question of Bentley's sentence.

Mr. R. T. Paget, Q.C., M.P., has advanced (Regina v. Derek Bentley; "*Should this Innocent Hang?*") legal grounds on which the execution of Bentley is questionable. Mr. Paget asks, "How long does this common responsibility endure?" He says that this is a question which the courts have never previously had to consider in a case of murder. Mr. Paget asks, supposing that Craig had escaped from the roof and had murdered P.C. Miles a day, a week, or a year afterwards, would Bentley still have been responsible? Mr. Paget believes that common responsibility endures only as long as the common enterprise was to resist arrest. This common purpose ceased when Bentley ceased to resist arrest and thereby withdrew his consent to that resistance. Bentley made no attempt to escape from custody, although he had the opportunity to do so. Unfortunately for himself, Bentley, in face of all the evidence that he was under arrest, denied it. Mr. Paget considers that he was entitled to be judged on the facts—not upon the idiotic answer he made under cross-examination.

Mr. Paget claims that "Bentley's case assembled in the highest degree every ground upon which the prerogative of mercy has formerly been exercised." That may well be but there was one special circumstance in this case which may have been the deciding factor. The man murdered was a policeman. Happily in this country the murder of a policeman is rare. The police go unarmed. As a result they must be specially protected. Capital punishment is not decreed, like other forms of punishment, both as a deterrent and as a reformative measure. Capital punishment is enforced as a deterrent and as a demonstration of the outraged sense of society. The execution of a man who kills, or who assists in killing a policeman, is justifiable on any grounds. What happens if he is not executed? We shall have the answer to this question when Craig is one day released, as eventually he will be.

IV

LOVE FROM A STRANGER

WHEN the business tycoon, peer of the realm, or what-have-you answered the telephone an alluring feminine voice told him, " A friend of yours—I've sworn not to mention his name, suggested I ring you. I'm in terrible trouble. I need money." In nine cases out of ten it worked. In fifteen years Kathleen Davies squeezed large sums out of foolish old men yet, in 1953 when she was sent to prison for blackmail, she was broke.

It all started in 1938. Kathleen was only fifteen when she learned that it was easy to wheedle large sums out of men, especially from old men. She knew the way to do it. She made them feel young again. She provided the romance they had never had and had always secretly desired. That a young and attractive girl needed their help flattered the male ego.

Her first " protector " sent her to the Royal Academy of Dramatic Art where she learned to act, off stage. During the war she toured with ENSA and afterwards she played a few minor stage and film parts under the name of Celia Lamb, but she found that a pout and a hard luck story raked in more cash. Repeated success made her over confident, when her men squeaked at the cost she threatened to tell their wives. That is illegal. It's worse; it's unethical !

Kathleen selected her prospective victims from the pages of Kelly's Street Directory, the Directory of Directors and Debrett. She studied the financial columns of the newspapers to see who was in the money. Then a telephone would ring in some palatial office. From one man she raked in £10,000 in cash alone. Two others paid her £1,500 a year, but she always

KATHLEEN DAVIES

asked for more. At last one of the mugs refused further contributions. " I'll tell your wife you seduced me," she said. " Do your worst," he replied. He informed the police he was being threatened. That was in July 1953.

When she was accused before the magistrate at Clerkenwell of demanding £300 with menaces and with intent to steal from " Mr. X " the prosecution described the case : " She is a thirty-year-old actress. He is a married businessman. The story in which they figure is the ' familiar case of a young woman who, having got on terms of intimacy with a respectable and well-to-do married man, uses that position to extort money from him under the age-old threat of exposure to his wife.' "

At her first trial at the Old Bailey, the jury failed to agree. Tried again in November she was found guilty and sent to prison for four years. She was defended by Mr. Derek Curtis-Bennett, Q.C.

The story of Kathleen's downfall can be reconstructed from the reports of the two trials. That one jury failed to agree was probably due to the reluctance of some men to apply a single standard to male and female behaviour. As Kathleen claimed her men were getting value for money. They were not averse to keeping her. Kathleen went wrong not in that she demanded money in return for her services, or favours, which is no crime, but that she extorted money by threats of exposure, which is blackmail.

After the publicity given to the proceedings in the Magistrates' Court, other men came forward to make complaint against her. One was a brother of Mr. " X " who had informed against her. These men sheltered themselves behind the anonymity of Mr. " C," " D," " E " and " Y."

Mr. " X " was allowed to write down his name, address and occupation, and also the address of his office. He said he was married and lived with his wife and two children. His pathetic story was as follows :

" On 13th July I received a telephone call at the office from a woman who said : ' I am Miss Lamb. I have been given your name by a very great friend of yours who assures me you would be able to help me.' I thought at first that she possibly wanted a job. I had never heard of her before and did not recognize her voice," Mr. " X " declared.

Celia Lamb came to see him at his office. She was, he said, a complete stranger to him. She explained that she had been sent by a very great friend of his. She told him : " I am in great financial trouble. I have had to pawn most of my jewellery. Can you help me? "

" I asked her," said Mr. " X," " several times who had sent her and who had given my name to her, but she kept on saying she could not give the name as she had promised this friend not to disclose it. She seemed in a very nervous and depressed state, and was obviously in need of help. Finally, after about half an hour, I agreed to lend her £10.

" I wrote a cheque and she wrote me an IOU. She seemed very grateful to receive that amount and said she would let me know the name of the person at the end of the week.

" On 16th July I rang her and asked her to let me know who this person was. I then saw her at her address at Pallister Road. I had a drink with her in a public house and she told me she could not let me know who the person was until next day.

" It was arranged that I should go to her flat the following day. I called there about six o'clock. We had several gin and tonics and I pressed her to tell me who it was who had sent her to me.

" She said the person was away until the following Tuesday and on that day would ring me up and tell me all about it."

Questioned, Mr. " X " admitted : " We got more intimate together. I went into her bedroom and intercourse took place." He left her flat at 7 p.m. " I gave her a present of £5. She did not ask for this money and I gave it of my own free will."

Ten days later " Miss Lamb " called him on the telephone and asked to see him. He was becoming suspicious because he could not find out who was the so-called friend who had given her his name. He arranged to meet Miss Lamb at the Café Royal and he took with him a lady whom he thought might know who she was. " Miss Lamb said : ' Why aren't

you alone as arranged?' I replied that I had brought somebody with me who might have recognized her. Miss Lamb
said : ' I have never been so insulted in my life,' and left us.
My friend was a lady connected with the theatre, and Miss
Lamb had told me she was hoping to get a part in a show."

In spite of this, Miss Lamb telephoned him later and tried
to arrange another meeting. When he told her he could not
meet her she replied : " Unless I see you I shall ring your
home." That evening she rang him at home, and said : " Unless I receive a cheque for £300 by to-morrow morning I will
inform your wife what happened at my flat." Mr. " X " did
not make any answer. He was angry but, " I was naturally
rather frightened." His wife was in the room when the call
came through. He decided to inform the police.

When on the following evening the telephone rang, Mrs.
" X " answered it. Miss Lamb asked if she could come to see
her. Mrs. " X " told the court : " I said I was not in the habit
of seeing people who did not disclose their business. The caller
said she could not disclose her business because she was speaking from a public place and would I believe it was very important. She then asked if she could come and see me that
evening. I told her I did not think that evening would be convenient to me and I would prefer to see her the next morning.

" She was so pressing about the urgency of her visit that I
agreed to see her at eight-thirty that night. I did not see her.
She rang again that night and I handed the receiver to my
husband.

" Later there was another phone call. It was Miss Lamb.
She said she had something very hurtful to tell me.

" I told her my husband was beside me and she said she
wanted him to hear what she had to say. She told me my
husband had behaved like an absolute cad; that she had a
gentleman's agreement with him and that he had gone back
on his word to give her £300."

Mrs. " X " said that Miss Lamb added : " If a man comes
to your flat and tries to seduce you and then arranges to meet
you at a café and arrives with a bespectacled woman, wouldn't
you think he was a cad ? "

She told Miss Lamb she would call on her the next day. She did not speak to her again. Mrs. " X " did not believe the woman's story. Her husband did not tell her the truth until the night before the case opened.

On the day following these telephone conversations Mr. " X," on instructions from the police, telephoned Miss Lamb. A detective listened in to the conversation about payment of the money. She was asked to call at his office. Mr. " X " then gave her a cheque for £300. " I asked her what guarantee, if I gave her the money, I would have of her not approaching me again," Mr. " X " told the court. " She said she wished to go to the South of France and I would not hear of her again.

" When she left I made a pre-arranged signal to Insp. Foster, who was outside. He stopped her, took her back to my office and told her he was a police officer." She said, " I was hard up. I did this in desperation."

Mr. " X " was questioned by Miss Davies' counsel; he replied that he liked the look of her from the start. He gave her £10 because he was interested in her and felt sorry for her. He had gone to her flat, he said, to find out the name of the mutual friend who had put her on to him, but he agreed that he had rung her up and asked her to buy a bottle of gin.

Mr. Curtis-Bennett : " Did you think the bottle of gin might loose her tongue? "—" No, I did not."

" You made advances to her? "—" Yes."

" Was that to find out the name of the man? "—" No."

Mr. Curtis-Bennett asked : " You are a very substantial man financially? " Mr. " X " replied " Yes." He had, he agreed, asked Miss Davies for her telephone number and he said that he was interested in her.

Mr. Curtis-Bennett : " You actually told her she was a very attractive girl ? "—" I may have done. Yes."

" Did she not say from the outset she wanted to know if you could lend her £300? "—" £300 was never mentioned."

It was suggested to Mr. " X " that, being " attracted and possibly overcome by the woman," he had told her he would let her have £300 and on that basis slept with her, but he denied it.

Mr. Curtis-Bennett : " You were attracted by her and quite clearly intended to see more of her after she first came to your office ? "—" To find out who sent her to me."

" At her flat did you tell her you had made arrangements to let her have the £300; that it was silly of you, but she was very attractive and charming and that you were prepared to help her ? "—" No."

Mr. " X " denied saying to Davies on the telephone : " I will let you have your cheque. I will drop it in on the way to the office."

Questioned about handing over the cheque for £300, he agreed that he wrote it and passed it to Davies on police instructions, and also that, having told his wife everything, he was not acting under menaces.

Then came some awkward questions.

" Have you had an experience like this before? "—" No, not really."

" Have you had pressure brought upon you before by a lady, anything approaching blackmail ? "—" Possibly."

" How long ago was that? "—" Three or four months."

" Was that the only similar occasion? "—" Yes."

" From then on I suppose you were very nervous of having affairs with other ladies. If you had some sort of experience of blackmail you were a bit wary? "—" It has nothing to do with this case."

Mr. " Y," brother of Mr. " X," had had, he said, a somewhat similar experience. Mr. " Y " said he had a telephone message at his office from someone who called herself Celia Lamb and said : " I have been told to get in touch with you by a mutual friend."

" It was arranged that she should call at my office, and she did so," Mr. " Y " told the court. " She said she was in great trouble financially, that she was an actress and that things were very bad. She said she had to sell jewellery to meet her debts, and must have financial assistance at once."

He had believed her and he gave her £10 as a loan for which she had given him a receipt. But she had not repaid the money. He did not send the woman to his brother. The first he knew of her going to his brother was when he read a newspaper report. Asked " Would you have given her £10 if she had been a man? "—" If she had been sent by a mutual friend, yes."

" Had she been in your flat? "—" Yes."

" Have you slept with her? "—" Yes."

Mr. " Y " had, he agreed, met her ten minutes after the phone call—at a teashop. Between January and May he had seen her about once a month. He had paid a grocery bill of £75 for her and he estimated that in all he had given her about £220.

Mr. " C " said he had been approached by Miss Davies but that he had not given her any money. She told him she was " broke " and could not pay the grocer's bill. He decided not to help her and told her he thought she had a bet that she could pick someone out of the telephone directory who was " mug enough " to pay her money.

Mr. " D," a titled man of about sixty, said that Miss Lamb had told him on the telephone that she understood he was an understanding and generous man and asked to meet him.

" I refused to see her under any circumstances," said Mr. " D." Then, looking at Davies, he added : " I have never seen her in my life before and I don't know how she got hold of my name."

He agreed that he appeared in " Who's Who," and was a prominent person.

Mr. " E," a company director, said " Celia Lamb " telephoned him early in 1952. She called at his flat and finally he gave her £8 to get rid of her. He received the money back later " after considerable trouble."

Mr. " F " and Mr. " G " told similar stories about being telephoned. But Mr. " F " said he told the caller to tell the " mutual friend " to contact him, and he heard nothing further from the woman. Mr. " G " said he told her he was not a fool and put down the receiver. He, too, heard nothing more.

Kathleen Davies told the court that a woman had given her a list of forty-five men who would help her, " as I was an attractive girl." Asked if the list was composed of elderly married men, she replied, " No, they were men of affluence." " Plump birds was the expression," suggested prosecuting counsel.

Mr. " Y " had given her, she said, between £350 and £400. She knew he was married, but never threatened him in any way. " I met him one day in Frascati's Restaurant and told him I was not, after all, pregnant," she said. " It was after that he gave me the £80. He said he could not see me any more because it was costing too much." It was towards the end of their affair that he told her about his brother, Mr. " X," she added.

She had refused to disclose to Mr. " X " who the mutual friend was, because she had promised not to. " I said I was hard up and wanted to borrow £300 to pay off certain debts and that I wanted to go to Paris where there was a job waiting for me. He was a little nonplussed but gave me £10 for my immediate needs. He told me I was an attractive girl and said he would like to take me out. I mentioned £300 at our first meeting."

A few days later he had telephoned and he had asked to come to her flat. " He told me to buy a bottle of gin and he would pay for it," she went on. " When he arrived we had a drink and he started making advances to me. I asked him about the loan and he said he had managed to scrape £300 together and would let me have the money the early part of the following week. It was after this that intimacy took place. He left £2 to pay for the gin and a further £3 as a present." Replying to Mr. Derek Curtis-Bennett, she said : " It is not true that I told him I would tell his wife what happened in the flat if he didn't let me have a cheque. I did say ' Let me have the cheque you promised.' "

Miss Davies told the court that Mr. " Y " was very sweet and charming, but Mr. " X " was just a funny little man, the exact opposite of his brother.

Asked what she was going to do with the list of men she had been given, she replied, " I thought I would try and get into business of some kind." " That's just what you did," pointed out the prosecuting counsel. When counsel suggested she got men to part with small sums of money until they slept with her, when it became more expensive, she replied, " I think not. I have only slept with two."

Counsel : " Mr. ' X ' paid £220 plus £6 plus £10, the £6 and £10 being for services rendered. That was what it cost him to meet you? "—" If that is the way you put it, yes."

Counsel : " You were intimate with Mr. ' X ' once. It cost him £5 and there would have been £300 but for the police? "—" That was my price £300. I would not have been intimate with him otherwise."

Asked, " How did you manage to live? " she replied, " I always had friends to help me. I had certain men who helped me. Some men help you without wanting to be intimate with you."

" When did you start being kept by rich men? "—" I had two rich men who have kept me."

Addressing the jury in the second trial, Mr. Curtis-Bennett said that Mr. " X " had admitted that within three days of meeting a complete stranger he was intimate with her. He had experienced blackmail before with a woman—not Miss Davies —and he had said in evidence that he was wary of women. " Being wary of women, he is in bed with one three days after meeting her. What he was like before he was wary of women we shudder to think," said Mr. Curtis-Bennett.

Kathleen Davies was found guilty of demanding £300 with menaces from Mr. " X," of obtaining £10 from his brother, and £6 from Mr. Nigel Fane, an insurance broker, with intent to defraud. In passing sentence the judge told her : " You are not a young and innocent girl but a woman of years with a knowledge of the world. I have no doubt you went into this with your eyes open."

It was shown that Kathleen Davies had been placed on probation in 1942 for two years for obtaining £3 1s. by false pretences and £3 19s. by fraud.

Of all the thousands she had received, nothing remained. It had been spent on gay parties and on expensive clothes. The complete realist to the last, Kathleen regretted that she had been caught. She was a little surprised only that the game had gone on for so long.

Men were her business for fifteen years, but she found them, she says, " a spineless bunch." A man could be a Napoleon of Commerce, but to Kathleen Davies he was often just another middle-aged mug.

V

THE MURDER OF THE BLACKPOOL
WIDOW

IT is difficult to imagine a murder more foredoomed to failure than that of the Blackpool widow, Mrs. Sarah Ricketts. Even old ladies of seventy-nine seldom die suddenly without apparent reason and Mrs. Ricketts was a particularly healthy old lady. In giving her rat poison Mrs. Louisa Merrifield took the off-chance that a doctor would issue a death certificate without a post-mortem examination. At first glance Mrs. Merrifield's action seems to have been hasty. After an acquaintance-ship of only twelve days the aged widow had made a will in her favour, leaving her the bungalow in which she lived. Mrs. Merrifield, who was only forty-six, would not have to wait that long to enjoy it. Then, a few days later, Mrs. Ricketts made Mrs. Merrifield's husband, Alfred, a joint beneficiary. He and the widow seemed to be getting too friendly. Mrs. Merrifield may have suspected that he would be liked so much by Mrs. Ricketts that she would be cut out of the will altogether and left out in the cold. Mrs. Merrifield had been " out in the cold " most of her life. How could she see £4,000 slip through her fingers when security was at last in sight?

Mrs. Ricketts died on 14th April, 1953. Louisa May Merrifield and her seventy-year-old husband Alfred Edward Merrifield were tried at Manchester in July for the murder of the old lady to whom they had acted as housekeepers.

The events and conversations (made known at the trial) that led up to and followed the death of Mrs. Ricketts are as follows :

12*th March*

Mr. and Mrs. Merrifield, having answered an advertisement

MRS. MERRIFIELD

by Mrs. Ricketts offering free accommodation to anyone who would look after her, moved into her bungalow in Devonshire Road, Blackpool.

24th March

Mrs. Merrifield called on a solicitor in Blackpool and instructed him, on behalf of Mrs. Ricketts, to prepare a will leaving her property to Mrs. Merrifield.

26th March

Mrs. Merrifield met an old friend, Mr. David Brindley, telling him, " David, I have had a bit of good luck. Where I have been living an old lady *has died* and left me a bungalow worth about £3,000."

Some time in March

An elderly man and a woman bought rat poison from a chemist in Manchester. The man was wearing a deaf aid and complained of having ulcers on his leg.

31st March

Mrs. Norah Lowe, of Alexandra Road, Blackpool, who had employed Mrs. Merrifield for a time in February, received a letter from her which read :

" My Dear Mrs. Lowe,

" Just a line or two to say I hope you are O.K., as I am doing very well. I got a nice job nursing an old lady and she left me a lovely little bungalow, and thank God for it. So you see, love, all comes right in the end . . . "

31st March

Mrs. Ricketts' will was executed. The bungalow and other property was left to Mr. and Mrs. Merrifield. Mr. Merrifield now became a joint beneficiary with his wife.

9th April

Mrs. Merrifield asked Dr. Yule to examine Mrs. Ricketts to certify that when the will was made on 31st March Mrs. Ricketts was fit mentally and knew what she was doing. She said the reason was that the old lady might die at any moment from a stroke or some similar disease and she (Mrs. Merrifield) wanted to keep herself all right with the relatives.

Later when Mrs. Merrifield called to pay him half a guinea for the examination he told her he had no intention of signing a certificate to say Mrs. Ricketts was fit mentally and said he wanted nothing more to do with the case.

11th April

When Arthur Gardner—who came to pay the rent of his house to Mrs. Ricketts—called, the door was opened by Mrs. Merrifield. Mrs. Ricketts tried to attract his attention. " I think she was trying to tell me there was ' trouble in the camp ' by pointing at the Merrifields and shaking her head," he said.

11th April

Mrs. Merrifield said to a Mrs. Brewer who she met in the street, " We are landed. I went to live with an old lady and she died. She has left me a bungalow worth £4,000." She continued, " I am all right. It's all left to me until that old — got talking to her, and then it was left to us jointly."

12th April

Mrs. Merrifield visited the house of a Mrs. King. As she was leaving she said, " I'll have to be going now. I have to lay the old lady out." Mrs. King asked, " Why, is she dead ? " " No, she's ill, but she won't be long," replied Mrs. Merrifield.

13th April

George Forjan, a van driver, saw Mrs. Ricketts when he delivered supplies. Mrs. Ricketts couldn't find her money. She said, " I don't know what they are doing with my money." She complained of not getting proper food and said she was fed up with the Merrifields and " they would have to go out."

13th April

To an entire stranger in a bus queue, Elizabeth Barraclough, Mrs. Merrifield, who gave her name, was alleged to have said she had been to Wigan and when she came back her husband was in bed with the old lady. Mrs. Merrifield told her : " If it goes on again I shall poison the old — and him as well. She is leaving me a bungalow between me and my husband, but he is so greedy he wants it all on his own."

13th April

Mrs. Merrifield visited a Dr. Wood. She asked him to see Mrs. Ricketts as she was seriously ill. He asked how long she had been ill, and was told, " For some time." Mrs. Merrifield said that Mrs. Ricketts had not seen a doctor recently; she wanted Dr. Wood to call that evening. When he asked if it would do in the morning, Mrs. Merrifield replied, " What happens if she dies during the night? " Dr. Wood called after his evening surgery. He found Mrs. Ricketts looking the same as she had done when he visited her three years before. Mr. and Mrs. Merrifield were present when he asked Mrs. Ricketts when she had last seen a doctor. She said that she had been visited by a Dr. Yule, but he would not call again as she could not afford his fees.

Dr. Wood found that Mrs. Ricketts was suffering from mild bronchitis which she had had as long as he could remember. He found nothing else. He assured her that there was nothing to worry about but he prescribed some sedative capsules because she was " nervy." She asked him to call in the morning and he told her that he would ask his partner, Dr. Page, to call.

Dr. Wood remonstrated with Mrs. Merrifield for calling him out under what he thought were false pretences. She said she had been frightened in case something happened to Mrs. Ricketts during the night. Mr. Merrifield did not speak.

As Dr. Wood was leaving Mrs. Merrifield said something to him about a will, but being annoyed at having been called out, he said that he was not interested in her domestic affairs.

14*th April*

At midday Dr. Page, Dr. Wood's partner, was called by Mrs. Merrifield, and found Mrs. Ricketts dying. At 1.50 p.m. he visited the bungalow again and found Mrs. Ricketts dead. When he declined to issue a death certificate, Mrs. Merrifield said to him, " She is over eighty. She's been dying since she came to the place."

Dr. Yule was also called but he refused to issue a death certificate.

Mrs. Merrifield called at a friend's house and left a handbag saying that it could not remain at the bungalow as it looked as if there was going to be trouble. She said that it contained policies which she did not wish Mr. Merrifield to see.

Following upon a telephone call from Dr. Yule, two police

officers visited the bungalow. They examined the body but
did not find any marks of injury or violence.

15*th April*

Mrs. Merrifield called on the friend with whom she had left
the bag and asked her to keep it rather than, as she had previously asked, it should be given to a Mrs. Hands, as if the
police called at Mrs. Hands' they might want to search the
room. Later this bag was collected by a solicitor on instructions from Mr. Merrifield.

16*th April*

Mrs. Merrifield went to an undertaker and asked for
arrangements to be made for Mrs. Ricketts to be cremated at
once. When he asked if Mrs. Ricketts had any relatives, Mrs.
Merrifield replied, " No, Mrs. Ricketts didn't want the family
to know."

Meanwhile, a post-mortem revealed the cause of death as
phosphorus poisoning. In the opinion of the pathologist, it was
administered after 6.20 p.m. on 13th April in one large dose
or in successive doses through the night. With the phosphorus
was found bran, similar to that used in rat poison. The grounds
of the bungalow were searched with a mine detector for a tin
in which rat poison might have been contained, but no tin was
found.

17*th April*

Mrs. Merrifield made a statement to the police in which she
said that since going to Blackpool she had lived at about
twenty different addresses, doing domestic work and private
nursing. When she and her husband went to live at the bungalow in Devonshire Road, Mrs. Ricketts was ill and took to her
bed for a few days. There was no food in the house, only some
stout and bottles of spirits which Mrs. Ricketts said she took
as medicine for asthma.

" She used to have egg and brandy about three times a
day; she asked me to take over everything, including her
money to run the house," added Mrs. Merrifield.

After being given good nourishing food Mrs. Ricketts began
to look better, but about 9th April there was a change in her
condition. She kept coughing and complained of pains in her

stomach. The next day she was very indignant because Mrs. Merrifield sent for Dr. Yule.

When the doctor asked if Mrs. Ricketts had made her will she replied: " I am looking after them that look after me." The doctor told her she was quite *compos mentis* and knew what she was doing and Mrs. Ricketts replied: " Definitely."

On 11th April Mrs. Merrifield was up all night with Mrs. Ricketts. The old lady did not seem to improve and on 12th April she was seen by Dr. Wood. She continued: " I stayed up with her until midnight and then she dozed. I heard her moaning after I had gone to bed. I gave her an egg-cup full of rum. She asked for it, saying it did her good. She had it neat. She always did. As she seemed quiet again I went back to bed."

Mrs. Merrifield said she heard Mrs. Ricketts opening the sideboard drawers and then heard a box of tablets fall. At 1.45 a.m. and again at 3.15 a.m. she found Mrs. Ricketts out of bed. Each time she assisted the old lady back again. " She never spoke," added Mrs. Merrifield. " I kept giving her brandy. She had lost her speech but made me understand that she was thirsty. I stayed up with her until 8.30 a.m. on 14th April. Then I sent a message for Dr. Yule."

Mr. Merrifield also made a statement. After referring to Mrs. Ricketts's decision to change her will Mr. Merrifield is alleged to have said that on 10th April his wife told him: " Mrs. Ricketts is poorly and I think she ought to have a doctor. I don't want to get into any trouble if anything should happen to her suddenly, and I am going to get one."

When Mrs. Merrifield finished her statement the police officer, Det.-Supt. Colin MacDougal, said to her: " We have strong reason to believe that Mrs. Ricketts died as the result of something she had to eat or drink." To this Mrs. Merrifield replied: " That's funny, there has been nothing in the house since I have been here that would hurt her." The superintendent continued: " As you know, we have searched the house and have taken possession of certain articles, but have not found any substance or container which would appear to account for her death." She replied: " If my Maker sends for me now, my conscience is clear. There has never been anything in the house to hurt her."

18*th April*

To a reporter Mrs. Merrifield said: " I cannot understand what all the fuss is about, for days detectives have been coming and going and have searched the house, taking most of Mrs. Ricketts' clothing and her personal belongings away. Mrs. Ricketts prepared her own meals. She was a very difficult old lady. Before we came she had neglected herself and I had done my best to persuade her to go to a doctor, but she refused repeatedly. She has two married daughters but I have not seen either of them. Her death came as a big shock to me and my husband. I don't know what is going to happen now, but I believe Mrs. Ricketts made a will a few weeks ago, and she said we would always be able to live in comfort here. I understand she lost her second husband about ten years ago and that she lived mainly on income from investments." (*News of the World*, 19th April.)

When these odd facts became known, Mr. and Mrs. Merrifield were charged with the murder of Mrs. Ricketts by the administration of poison. They contended that the old lady had died from natural causes. Before their trial opened in July three things happened. Dr. Wood, who had been called in to see Mrs. Ricketts on the day before she died, died, but a deposition of his evidence was taken. The handbag which Mrs. Merrifield had left with friends was secured and it was discovered to contain, in addition to personal papers, a dessertspoon on which was found a small amount of dried substance. At an identification parade on 30th April the owner and the assistant from a chemist's shop in Manchester, at which a man and a woman had purchased rat poison in March, failed to recognize anyone.

The Merrifields stood trial before Mr. Justice Glyn-Jones. The Attorney-General, Sir Lionel Heald, Q.C., appeared for the prosecution and Mr. J. de V. Nahum, Q.C., for the defence. The trial lasted for eleven days, one of the longest in legal history.

The case for the prosecution was that Mrs. Ricketts had

died from a dose or doses of poisonous yellow phosphorus, which is used in the rat killer, Rodine, and that only Mr. and Mrs. Merrifield could have given it to her. Rodine could be bought without the purchaser signing anything. A one-ounce tin, costing one shilling, contains ten grains of yellow phosphorus, which is enough to kill five people.

The Attorney-General in stating these facts asked, " Who else was in the bungalow that night? We find that during the night Mr. and Mrs. Merrifield were alone in that bungalow with Mrs. Ricketts." They gave, he pointed out, Mrs. Ricketts her food and drink at the time when it was alleged that she swallowed the poison. But after Mrs. Ricketts' death no rat poison was found in the house, nor any spoon or glass with which it was administered. " Thus, if it was taken by accident or to commit suicide, *what happened to the rest of the tin?* " he asked.

The Attorney-General also asked the jury to consider, " What was in the mind of the person who put the spoon in the bag? " and he questioned whether it was consistent with someone's innocence that they should load all their belongings in a handbag when they know the police are coming. He said, too, that it was rather an extraordinary thing that Mrs. Merrifield should have told Mr. Brindley that the old lady had died about a fortnight ahead of the fact.

As usual there was considerable conflict of expert medical opinion about the cause of death. While one pathologist attributed the cause of death in the case of Mrs. Ricketts to phosphorus poisoning, another even more eminent pathologist gave the opinion that, although phosphorus had been taken (or given to) the dead woman, she had nevertheless died from natural causes. According to this view, provided of course that the phosphorus was shown to have been administered by the Merrifields, they were guilty only of attempted murder.

That Mrs. Ricketts had taken, or had been given, phosphorus there was no argument. The dispute raged round the questions whether it had killed her, and whether she had taken it herself or whether it had been given her by the Merrifields. Thus, if it was proved that the rat poison had been admini-

stered by the Merrifields, the jury could find them guilty either
of murder or of attempted murder, according to which pathologist they believed. Alternatively, if the jury found that there
was no evidence to prove that they had given it to Mrs.
Ricketts, then the Merrifields would be found not guilty.

The first pathologist, Dr. George Manning of the North-
Western Science Laboratory, who had carried out a post-
mortem examination on Mrs. Ricketts on 14th April, called
for the prosecution, said that in his opinion death was caused
by phosphorus poisoning and that the phosphorus was taken
in the evening or night of 13th April.

He then explained how he had carried out experiments to
disguise the garlic smell and taste of Rodine. By tasting it himself he discovered that both rum and blackcurrant jam masked
the taste. Brandy also masked the taste, but he could detect
the odour faintly.

The second pathologist, Professor J. M. Webster, director
of the Home Office Laboratory at Birmingham and professor
of forensic medicine and toxicology at Birmingham University
(a surprise witness for the defence), said that, though poisonous
phosphorus was found in Mrs. Ricketts, she may have died
from natural causes. In his view she had died from necrosis of
the liver. Mrs. Ricketts might have ingested the phosphorus
from fifteen minutes to five hours before she died.

When Professor Webster said, " I don't think I am in a
position to express an opinion " on the question of whether
Mrs. Ricketts could have taken the rat poison herself after
seven o'clock, the judge pointed out, " You haven't hesitated
to express vigorous and, I can almost say, even dogmatic
opinions on the strength of what you have seen and heard.
Do you feel unable to express an opinion on whether or not
it was possible for this woman to have administered rat poison
to herself after seven o'clock in the morning? "—" I must not
dodge the issue at all. I don't think it impossible."

Asked by defence counsel, " Do you rule out the possibility
of ingestion of Rodine rat poison by accident or suicide or
attempted suicide other than by murder between six-thirty in
the evening of 13th April, when she was examined by Dr.

Wood, and the time when she got in a coma about three-fifteen in the morning?" The judge intervened, saying, "If you are asking him to infer and express his opinion as to whether accident is more probable than suicide or more, you are asking him to assume the functions of a jury."

Professor Webster continued, "The sequence of colour and swelling of the liver as described by Dr. Manning is totally wrong. It is quite wrong to say that this lady died from phosphorus poisoning before the liver had time to swell." He was asked: "Do you attach any importance to the fact that no free phosphorus was found in any of the organs, except the intestines and stomach?"

Professor Webster: "I do. The importance I attach is this, that without the presence of free phosphorus in the other organs, one cannot state that death was due to phosphorus poisoning." Professor Webster also said that one objection he had to Dr. Manning's findings was that he had not heard that any phosphorus was found in the actual wall of the intestines.

The judge: "Does this mean that by coincidence this old lady died so quickly after swallowing phosphorus that it had no time to enter her body."

Professor Webster: "That is correct."

Asked: "Have you come to a conclusion as to the cause of death?" Professor Webster replied: "This lady, in my opinion, died from the effects of necrosis—fatty insufficiency."

The judge: "In forming that opinion you based yourself on the assumption that the evidence of Mr. and Mrs. Merrifield regarding her death were correct, or on the evidence of others who saw her, or was it immaterial?"

Professor Webster: "It was immaterial."

Mr. Nahum: "Can diet or lack of food have an effect?"

Professor Webster: "It can cause necrosis."

Replying to a suggestion from the Attorney-General that his conclusions were a "fantastic hypothesis," Professor Webster gave five reasons why Mrs. Ricketts may have died from natural causes:

There was hepatic necrosis;

There was no proof that phosphorus was absorbed;

There was no proof of phosphorus being recovered from the organs;

The period of death was equally consistent with either; and

If this was a Type One phosphorus poisoning there was no evidence of shock.

The Attorney-General: "Mr. Nahum has suggested that one cause of death might have been beer bottles from a brewery where rat poison was being used."

Professor Webster: "There are many rats in breweries."

The Attorney-General: "She might also have been struck by lightning."

Two further questions remained to be answered. With what had the rat poison been taken, or given? And what was the dried substance found on the spoon in Mrs. Merrifield's handbag?

Dr. Manning told of his experiments to mask the taste and smell of Rodine. Both rum and blackcurrant jam had done so. But while Mrs. Merrifield said in her evidence that she had given both rum and blackcurrant jam mixed with spirits to Mrs. Ricketts during the night she died, Mr. Cann, a chemist who gave evidence, said that he found no trace of jam in the body.

On the question of the spoon another chemist, Mr. Thompson, called for the prosecution, said that he found on it no phosphorus or bran, both of which are used in Rodine. But it would not be found if the spoon had been rinsed, he said.

Both these questions were left undecided but, unless the spoon was the one used to administer the Rodine, why did Mrs. Merrifield try to conceal it? Why, too, were no empty jars of blackcurrant jam found?

Next, an attempt was made to identify Mr. Merrifield as the elderly man who had purchased rat poison at a shop in Manchester in March. This did not succeed but it is interesting to see why it failed.

Miss Mavis Atkinson was asked to look round the court and see if anybody there had entered her shop, Cottons Chemists Ltd., Victoria Bridge, Manchester, as a customer. She nodded towards Alfred Merrifield and said: "The gentleman sitting next to the policeman—the gentleman wearing a hearing aid."

Merrifield smiled broadly—and Miss Atkinson said that he bought Rodine rat poison in March. With him was a woman, but Miss Atkinson could remember nothing about her.

She said that at Blackpool police station on 30th April she walked up and down a line of twelve men and stood for a few minutes looking at a man she recognized.

The judge: " Who was he? "—" The person who came into the shop to buy Rodine."

Sir Lionel: " Did you point him out? "—" No."

" Why not? "—" I was too nervous."

Cross-examined by Mr. Nahum, Miss Atkinson said she eventually picked out Mr. Merrifield in the magistrates' court at Blackpool on 28th May.

Mr. Nahum: " You knew perfectly well before going to the police court hearing that the man you failed to pick out at the parade was Mr. Merrifield, the man in court? " Miss Atkinson: " Yes."

" Between 30th April and 28th May I suppose you'd been reading the papers? "—" No."

" You don't read a paper? "—" No."

" Do you take the *Sunday Dispatch*? "—" I believe we used to. I don't buy the papers."

Mr. Nahum handed to Miss Atkinson a copy of the *Sunday Dispatch* for 3rd May, three days after the identification parade. He asked her: " Do you see a photograph there, as large as life, of Mr. Merrifield? "—" Yes."

" Before the magistrates, did you say ' On Sunday we had the *Sunday Dispatch*? ' "—" Yes."

" Weren't you vitally interested? "—" The police said something to me about avoiding looking at the papers."

" Haven't you the natural curiosity to look at the newspapers when they are plastered with photographs of the man you failed to pick out? "—" No."

Mr. Nahum handed her a copy of the *Daily Mail* for 16th May, and said: " Miss Atkinson, that's a very good photograph of Mr. Merrifield, isn't it? "—" Yes."

" Did you see that? "—" No."

Miss Atkinson said she saw a photograph of Mr. Merrifield in an evening newspaper on 30th April, about an hour after the identification parade.

Mr. Nahum : " I suggest to you that between 30th April and 28th May you must have seen photographs of Mr. Merrifield."

Miss Atkinson : " No."

The owner of the chemist shop, Harold Hague, pointed to Mr. Merrifield in the dock and said he had sold him a tin of Rodine in March. Mr. Hague said he failed to pick out anybody at the identification parade. He saw Mr. Merrifield's photograph in a Manchester evening paper on 15th May.

Mr. Nahum : " You said in the magistrates' court, ' I think I have seen photographs of Mr. Merrifield in the *Daily Mail* '." Here Mr. Nahum handed to Mr. Hague copies of the *Daily Mail* for 16th May and 28th May, and Mr. Hague said : " I have certainly seen that one "—pointing to the *Daily Mail* of 16th May. He added : " It is possible I saw the photographs in other newspapers."

Re-examined by the Attorney-General, Mr. Hague said he told a police inspector that he was not sure that Mr. Merrifield was in the parade.

The failure of the shop owner and his assistant to identify Mr. Merrifield was, as we shall see later, of considerable significance.

In the witness box, Mrs. Merrifield denied that she had been to Manchester to buy rat poison, that she had told anyone that Mrs. Ricketts was dead before she died, that she had aimed to get the bungalow or that she had called doctors in only to get a death certificate. The questions put to her and her answers are as follows :

Mr. Nahum : " Have you, in the course of your life, ever learned, been told, or read anything about phosphorus poison ? "

Mrs. Merrifield : " Never."

" Did you at any time, forcibly administer Rodine rat poison to Mrs. Ricketts ? "—" No, sir."

" So far as you were concerned with the actions of your

husband during those days, did he administer anything of a poisonous nature to Mrs. Ricketts? "—" No, sir."

Mr. Nahum : " Was there ever a day when she didn't have rum? "

Mrs. Merrifield : " No, never."

Mrs. Merrifield said she was up five or six times the night before Mrs. Ricketts died. " She cried bitterly. She said, ' You don't know how ill I am.' I said, ' You'll have to have your daughter down to see you.' She said, ' My daughters will not come here because they know more about my two husbands' deaths than anybody is aware of '."

Mrs. Merrifield was asked if she tried to get a doctor to certify that Mrs. Ricketts was fit to make a will.

Mr. Nahum : " When you said Mrs. Ricketts might die of a stroke or some such thing, you wanted to be quite sure there would be no trouble with relations? "

Mrs. Merrifield said she told a doctor that her second husband died suddenly and that she did not want to have any " nonsense about it."

As to getting a certificate certifying that Mrs. Ricketts was fit to make a will—" I didn't need it," said Mrs. Merrifield. " She had made a will."

Asked about the statements made by the people to whom she was supposed to have made certain remarks before the death of Mrs. Ricketts, Mrs. Merrifield replied, " I think it's just jealousy. They are all up to their necks in mortgage. I never said Mrs. Ricketts was dead before she died to anyone."

Asked how the spoon got into her handbag she said that as she and her husband moved from one address to another during various seaside jobs she sometimes carried her own cutlery in her handbag. " I thought I took them all out," she added. " But it is possible one had been left in."

Mrs. Merrifield was next asked by the Attorney-General about the drinks taken by Mrs. Ricketts the night she died. " Do you still say you did not give her anything to drink before three o'clock in the morning? "

Mrs. Merrifield : " I did not give Mrs. Ricketts Rodine to drink."

" As woman to woman you would naturally give her a drink if you thought she was ill and wanted a drink? "—" It's true that I gave her drinks."

" It's quite untrue to say from beginning to end that you never gave her anything to drink? "—" I never gave her a Rodine drink."

He asked Mrs. Merrifield if she gave Mrs. Ricketts quite a lot of brandy during the night. Mrs. Merrifield stated that she gave Mrs. Ricketts a teaspoonful.

Sir Lionel : " What did you do with the spoon and the egg-cup? "

Mrs. Merrifield : " I washed them up after breakfast as I always do."

" Was that the spoon you put in your handbag? "—" I did not put a spoon in my handbag."

She was then questioned about the will made by Mrs. Ricketts. Mrs. Merrifield said that after being with Mrs. Ricketts for about three weeks the old lady said : " I'll have the house turned over to you." " I said, ' Don't turn it over to us. I don't want to take the roof from over your head.' "

Sir Lionel : " At no time have we heard any suggestion that she wanted to turn the house over to you like that."

Mrs. Merrifield : " I've never been asked."

" Have you ever mentioned it to anyone until to-day? "— " No, never."

Mrs. Merrifield agreed that at first the bungalow was left to her and then her husband was brought in to the will, but she denied saying, " It was all left to me until that old b— got talking to her."

The Attorney-General asked : " It was true that you thought Mr. Merrifield was getting too friendly with the old lady? "— " Well, everybody has their suspicions. I found Mrs. Ricketts a very immoral woman." Asked to explain what she meant, Mrs. Merrifield indicated members of the Press, and said : " Is it all right to explain in front of these young men? " She continued : " I checked Mr. Merrifield because he was making a fuss of her. It's his nature."

Asked : " Were you not afraid that Mrs. Ricketts would

change her will and leave it all to Mr. Merrifield? "—" No, I was afraid of nothing."

Sir Lionel then referred to her remark that " I'll poison them both " and asked : " If you did, you'd be sure of having the bungalow all to yourself ? "

Mrs. Merrifield : " I never had any intentions to poison anyone."

" Wasn't Mr. Merrifield afraid of what you might do to one or both of them? "—" No, he had no need."

She also stated that she loved the old lady.

Next, she was questioned about the poisonous yellow phosphorus.

" You know that yellow phosphorus was found in Mrs. Ricketts' body? "

Mrs. Merrifield : " I don't know what colour it was."

" You know poison was found ? "—" I heard so. I read so."

" Do you know the doctors say it must have been taken during the last hours of her life ? "—" Yes."

" You know also that according to Dr. Manning the most striking sign of phosphorus poison for a bystander is great thirst? "—" I heard him say about the thirst."

" You have said Mrs. Ricketts suffered from great thirst in the early hours of the 14th? "—" She suffered from great thirst from the time of us going there. She was always on the thirst for her brandy and the drink."

" It is true, is it not, to say she was suffering from intense thirst in the early hours of 14th April ? "—" Yes."

" You have also told the jury that she complained of a nasty taste in her mouth? "—" Yes."

" But you know now, don't you, that a nasty taste in the mouth is a sign of phosphorus poisoning? "—" I don't know. There are plenty of nasty tastes."

To her own counsel, Mrs. Merrifield replied that she had no idea at that time of the proportion of phosphorus in Rodine. Nor did she have any idea what constituted a fatal dose of Rodine.

Mr. Merrifield, who was wearing a deaf-aid, took his examination in the witness-box very light-heartedly. He was rebuked by the judge for joking. " Tell Mr. Merrifield he would do well to remember his position and not to make little jokes," said the judge. In reply to questions he stated, " When my wife and I took this position I found the old lady a small lady and very feeble. She had had a stroke in the right arm and leg. She had both arms wrapped up in cotton wool and bandages —just like elephant's legs. I thought she was a very, very heavy drinker for an old lady. In fact, I helped to drink some of it myself when she gave it to me."

Mr. Nahum : " What do you drink ? "

Mr. Merrifield : " If somebody asked me to have one, I would have a mild beer."

He told how his wife usually left on Mrs. Ricketts' bedside table a small bottle of rum, a small bottle of brandy, a pint glass of water, a packet of aspirin and a carton of stomach powders every night.

Mr. Nahum : " It is suggested by the prosecution that during the night before Mrs. Ricketts died you and your wife together gave this old lady Rodine rat poison to kill her."

Mr. Merrifield slammed his fist down on the ledge before him and said : " An outrageous false statement, sir."

" Have you any knowledge of Rodine ? "—" No, definitely not."

Asked about Mrs. Ricketts' will, he related how she called him to her bedside and said :

" My word, Mr. Merrifield, you are being good and kind to me. I want you to keep on as you are doing, you and your wife, and I'll make it so you'll have a home here for the longest day you'll live."

To the question : " Do you remember anything being said about a solicitor and a change of her will ? " he replied " The old lady said something to me about altering her will. In what form I couldn't tell you."

" What change did you think she had in mind ? "—" I think she was referring to making me the sole legatee, because she gave me so much praise for the way I looked after her." He said he did not tell his wife at the time about the talk of changing the will.

Next, he was questioned about his wife's handbag : he was asked why he thought it might be dangerous. Mr. Merrifield replied : " My own safety."

" Were you afraid it might contain something like this? " asked counsel, producing a packet of Rodine in its crimson paper cover from behind him. Mr. Merrifield quickly turned his head away, saying : " Don't show me that. I have heard so much about it this last four months I see it in my sleep."

" You have seen something like that before? "—" No, unless it has been in some shop or chemist's when I have not had occasion to enter."

" You have seen something like this before? "—" I have not, and don't ask me again."

" You said in a chemist's shop? "—" Quite possible, but I have never handled it."

" You have a recollection of having seen something like this before? "—" I have told you ' Yes,' and that is as far as my knowledge goes in rat poison."

Mr. Merrifield was questioned about allegations that he bought a tin of Rodine in a Manchester chemist's shop in March. He replied : " Definitely not, I've never been in Manchester for five solid years. I've never left the boundary of Blackpool for twelve months." He stated that he had ulcers on his legs. He was told, " A Mr. Hague has said you came into his chemist's shop and bought Rodine."

Merrifield banged his fist on the witness-box and said : " Perjured evidence, all cooked up by Scotland Yard men."

The judge : " That will do."

But Mr. Merrifield objected : " This is a British court of justice, gentlemen. I'm giving my evidence in the fight for my life and my wife's."

Asked if he had seen the chemist's assistant, Miss Atkinson, who identified him as the man who bought rat poison, before, he answered : " No, definitely not, sir, I've no idea where their premises are."

" It is suggested that together with your wife you murdered Mrs. Ricketts by giving her rat poison. Had you ever had

any knowledge about rat poison at all ? "—" No, definitely
not."

" It is suggested that on the Monday night, after Dr. Wood
left, and during the whole of that night or part of it, you and
your wife together, or with knowledge, gave this old lady rat
poison to kill her."—" Outrageous. False statement. Outrageous."

When Mr. Nahum said it had been suggested that he was
guilty of some impropriety with Mrs. Ricketts, Merrifield replied : " A more infamous statement has never been made in
a court of justice. Definitely not true.

" Fancy; an old woman of eighty years of age, paralysed
down one side. It's definitely not true, sir. Outrageous. Look
at my wife. A young woman. Fancy me getting into bed with
an old woman of eighty. It's an outrageous statement."

As Mr. Nahum commenced his final address to the jury,
Mr. Merrifield started to cry. Mrs. Merrifield and the warders
tried to console him but he continued to cry. Then he said in
a loud voice : " I cannot stick this. It is not fair. Let me go
down until they have finished this. I cannot stick it." The
court was adjourned to give him time to recover.

Mr. Nahum continued, and pointed out that there was not
a scintilla of evidence to show how Rodine got down Mrs.
Ricketts' throat, if indeed it did. It was only guesswork.

One thing was abundantly clear and that was that the old
lady " liked her drop of rum." What she would say if she was
given rum with Rodine in it he did not know, but would she
drink it voluntarily? " It is the most filthy looking liquid
imaginable," he added.

Next, he dealt with the conversations Mrs. Merrifield was
reported as having had with various people before and after
the death of Mrs. Ricketts. He asked : " Is anyone in their
right senses, who is going to murder someone else, going to go
to a friend or a stranger and say the person they are going to
murder is dead already? "

Setting out the case he said : " That this case is hedged in
with suspicion no one who has heard the trial would gainsay.
Let us not lose sight of what is the very crux and kernel of

this case—the two things which the prosecution must prove. In my submission the first is that a dose of yellow phosphorus was introduced into the body of Mrs. Ricketts and that dose actually caused her death. The second thing is that it was by the hands of the accused that that vital dose was introduced into her body. That had not been proved."

Coming to the will, he asked : " Is there any merit at all in the suggestion that they murdered her rather than wait for her natural death—this old lady of eighty? "

Mrs. Ricketts was estranged from her two daughters. They never went to see her, except very rarely. She had no friends.

" Is there anything strange or sinister or wrong in her leaving it to the couple who she had described as looking after her well? " asked Mr. Nahum.

The prosecution suggested there was something sinister that made Mrs. Merrifield get a solicitor and then a doctor to certify Mrs. Ricketts as fit to make a will.

" Is that a proper thing to do or is it a sinister and improper thing to do?

" Let us visualize that these two people made up their minds to poison Mrs. Ricketts. They buy a will form. They don't call in a doctor. They get her to make a will in their favour, administer the poison to her, she dies ; a strange doctor is brought in; she is a lady of eighty; they tell the doctor she fell ill in the night and they came down next morning and found her. May not that have been a pretty good way—the way the murderers would work if they really were murderers? "

Mr. Nahum continued : " The prosecution say that if you bring a solicitor and bring a doctor that is evidence of guilt. If you don't bring both that is also evidence of guilt. There is a saying, ' Heads I win, tails you lose.' That is the way this case is being run in two or three aspects; the same sort of system is being pursued by the prosecution."

Mr. Nahum then dealt with the evidence of the deceased Dr. Wood, who had pronounced Mrs. Ricketts fit on the night of 13th April. Dr. Wood said that Dr. Page or someone was coming the next morning. " What for? " asked Mr. Nahum. " To view the corpse?

" Mrs. Merrifield went out at eight-thirty the next morning to try to get a doctor. That was held against her. It was the same thing again—' Heads I win, tails you lose.' "

Mr. Nahum continued, " You cannot take away from the defence the visit of Dr. Wood. The very next morning Dr. Page was due to arrive.

" The prosecution alleged that between these two visits Mr. and Mrs. Merrifield gave Mrs. Ricketts a deadly dose."

As for the alleged threat that Mrs. Ricketts was about to change her will, Mr. Merrifield's recollection was that it was to be altered in his favour. " If she was going to change the will in his favour he would have no motive to kill her before she changed it," said Mr. Nahum. " If it was going to be changed in his favour to the exclusion of his wife, he would have a very good motive for not killing Mrs. Ricketts."

Coming to what he described as the " absolutely vital " medical evidence, he referred to the clash of opinion between the two pathologists, Dr. Manning and Professor Webster. " If you accept Professor Webster's evidence (that Mrs. Ricketts died from natural causes) this cannot be murder. If you accept Dr. Manning's evidence (phosphorus poisoning) this case could be murder—subject to proper proof that the accused administered the poison to Mrs. Ricketts. Can you be certain that Dr. Manning is right? Or don't you think there must be a doubt as to Dr. Manning's conclusion? "

The judge, Mr. Nahum pointed out, had said, " Was it not a remarkable coincidence that the old lady had died from natural causes and that phosphorus had been found ? " Yet " wasn't it a fantastic coincidence that at 10 Rillington Place, W.10, there were two stranglers—Christie and Evans? " asked Mr. Nahum.

" If Mrs. Merrifield had been a murderess the two subjects she would have avoided most in conversation would have been death, and death in connection with Mrs. Ricketts.

" As for the prosecution's evidence about Mrs. Merrifield hiding her handbag, which contained a spoon, that was nothing more than a ' vast red herring.' There had been no Rodine rat poison found in the bag, and no trace of it on the spoon.

" The crux of the case as far as Mr. Merrifield was concerned was his alleged identification by Mr. Hague, a Manchester chemist, and his assistant, Miss Atkinson. At seventy-one, Mr. Merrifield did appreciate one thing—the mighty injustice of that identification. He turned to you and more eloquently than I or any advocate could have done, finished by saying, with tears in his voice : ' There was I sitting between two warders, and they said : " That's the man." ' "

Mr. Nahum described Mr. Merrifield as quite guileless, a tragic simpleton, incapable of doing what the prosecution suggested.

At the conclusion of his address to the jury, Defence Counsel was asked by the judge : " Supposing the jury find that one or other or both of these accused administered Rodine rat poison to Mrs. Ricketts, intending to kill her, and that she died not of the rat poison but of natural causes—what is the proper verdict ? "

Mr. Nahum : " My lord, it must be attempted murder."

The judge : " That is clear ? "

Mr. Nahum : " Quite clear."

The judge : " You agree, Mr. Attorney ? "

The Attorney-General : " Yes, my lord."

In his closing address the Attorney-General told the jury that if they had nothing else but the evidence of Professor Webster and Dr. Manning, they might have difficulty in satisfying themselves that the old lady's death was due to phosphorus poisoning.

But Professor Webster took no account of the fact that Mrs. Merrifield said Mrs. Ricketts suffered from a most intense thirst on the morning she died.

She also complained of a very nasty taste—both symptoms of phosphorus poisoning.

He went on : " I am bound to submit that there is a most terrible case against these two people. I told you in opening that there was only one thing missing and that was evidence of administration of the poison. However unpalatable it may be, you cannot avoid the conclusion that there is the strongest evidence of how and when this poison was administered."

Of suggestions that the old lady's death might be an accident he said: " There is, of course, the possibility that a dying rat came through the window and that phosphorus was deposited that way. How it got into Mrs. Rickett's throat would be a further matter for speculation." He described as " fantastic " the suggestion that the old lady took rat poison and then got up in the middle of the night and put the tin in the dustbin.

The Merrifields, Sir Lionel went on, showed a determination to get what they wanted at all costs—to get the bungalow and say it was time the old lady was on the way out.

He added: " It would be to the satisfaction of anyone to be able to say: ' Oh, well, he is a harmless old gentleman. We can let him out.' I cannot ask you to do that. I am submitting that not only is there evidence against Mrs. Merrifield of the clearest kind, but evidence that they acted together."

Mr. Justice Glyn-Jones, summing-up for the jury, said of Mrs. Merrifield: " You may have formed the opinion that she was a rather vulgar and stupid woman with a dirty mind. I do her no injustice in telling you that. But the fact that she is a vulgar and stupid woman is no ground to convict her of murder."

As for Mr. Alfred Merrifield, " He was at times somewhat foolish."

On the question whether Mr. Merrifield was the man who bought the rat-killer, Rodine, the judge advised the jury, " as strongly as I can," to reject any identification or recognition in the magistrates' court or here.

" It is perfectly clear that by the time Mr. Hague or Miss Atkinson gave evidence they had the opportunity of seeing photographs of the defendants in the newspapers."

The jury must ask themselves, said the judge, three questions:

1.   Did either of these two, or did both of them acting in concert, administer rat poison to Mrs. Ricketts?
2.   If they did, was it with intent to kill?
3.   Did the poison, so administered, kill Mrs. Ricketts?

The judge then dealt with the theories put forward about Mrs. Ricketts' death.

The prosecution said she died from poisoning. The defence said she died from natural causes.

The prosecution said Mrs. Ricketts was at seventy-nine a very fit woman for her age. The defence said she was frail and ailing.

The "extreme conflict" of medical evidence led the judge to ask the jury to examine five points:

1. On Thursday, 14th April, rat poison was found in Mrs. Ricketts' stomach;

2. The rat poison was administered during the previous night;

3. The only people in the house that night were Mrs. Ricketts and the Merrifields;

4. Was the rat poison taken by accident or intention?

5. Or did one of the accused administer it to her?

The judge then discussed the details of evidence of Mrs. Ricketts' will, in which she had left her bungalow and some small personal property to the Merrifields.

"It matters not," said the judge, "that Mrs. Ricketts made a will in her favour. The point is: Did the fact that the will had been made in her favour operate on Mrs. Merrifield's mind subsequently?"

The judge concluded: "Of all the forms of death by which human nature might be overcome, the most detestable is that of poison, because, of all others, it can least be prevented by courage or foresight. Such a murder is rarely if ever committed in the presence of eye-witnesses who can give direct evidence of administration of poison."

Leaving the court room at 3.53 p.m., the jury deliberated for five-and-three-quarter hours. They returned at 9.30 p.m. Asked by the clerk, "Are you agreed on your verdict?" the foreman replied, "We are partly." The Clerk: "In regard to Louisa Merrifield, do you find her guilty or not guilty of murder?" When the foreman replied "Guilty," Mrs. Merrifield sagged and her face went grey. She was supported by the wardress and a nurse. The foreman then said that the jury had disagreed over Alfred Merrifield. He was taken to the cells below. He was smiling.

To Mrs. Merrifield the judge said, "You have been convicted on plain evidence of as wicked and cruel murder as I ever heard tell of." She replied, "I am not guilty, sir." She gazed fixedly at the judge while he passed sentence of death upon her.

The jury's disagreement on the charge of murder against Mr. Merrifield raised some strange issues. If he was to be retried would the Home Secretary permit a condemned person, Mrs. Merrifield, to give evidence? Would her execution be delayed to allow her to do so? Or should her evidence be taken in prison? These difficulties were overcome by the decision not to put Alfred Merrifield again on trial.

Why did the jury find the wife guilty but fail to agree about the husband? The jury accepted the fact that Mrs. Ricketts had died of poison and that Mrs. Merrifield had administered it with intent to kill. Her actions before and after the death of Mrs. Ricketts were those of a guilty person. Why should she have taken so much trouble to hide the spoon unless it was the fatal spoon? Of course, Mrs. Ricketts *may* have actually died from natural causes, but if she died before the phosphorus had worked then Mrs. Merrifield was still a murderess by intention. Some members of the jury must have decided that Mr. Merrifield had nothing to do with it. In this they were quite right. There was no particular evidence against him, except that he had been in the house. His forthrightness in the witness-box probably made a favourable impression on a north country jury. But, above all, he made no attack on his wife, despite her innuendoes against him, and despite the very evident possibility that he would have been the "next on her list." Mrs. Merrifield would hardly have been content with Mrs. Ricketts bungalow only half in her name. Mr. Merrifield seems to have had "two" lucky escapes.

Mrs. Merrifield, the "poisoner," was, as is so often the case with murderers, an ex-criminal, though a petty one. In 1946 she served eighty-four days in prison (the same one as that in which she was hanged) for obtaining duplicate ration books for two of her children and for possessing five more which she had obtained illegally. In 1947 her three children, one a baby of a year old, were deemed in need of care and protion. They were taken from her and placed in a home.

Born at Wigan in 1906, Mrs. Merrifield was the daughter of a coal miner. When she grew up she worked in a mill and then became a cook. She married in 1931, Joe Ellison, an iron worker. They had four children. He died in hospital in 1949. The coroner sent certain organs for examination which showed that he had died from an infected liver. " Death from natural causes," was recorded. While calling to see Joe in hospital, his wife became friendly with another patient, Alfred Merrifield, a widower and the father of ten children.

Three months after Ellison's death in January 1950 his wife married again, to a Mr. Richard Weston, a retired mine manager of eighty years of age. " Such a nice man," as the new Mrs. Weston called him; " plenty of money, too," she would add. They were married for only three months before he died of " heart failure." Unfortunately his money or pension went with him, and his wife was out in the cold again. On 19th August, 1950, she married Alfred Merrifield. For two and a half years they did odd jobs, caretaking and domestic service, then Mrs. Merrifield spotted Mrs. Ricketts' advertisement.

Mrs. Merrifield suffered from a common failing. She thought that she was better than she was. She had, as her Lancashire friends observed, " fancy notions " about her own importance. She wanted money and position. She was disappointed when Richard Weston died; she had to go back to the old life, living in " digs " with no future. When she learned that Mrs. Ricketts proposed to leave her the bungalow, she became greedy; she couldn't wait and she feared that Mrs. Ricketts might change her mind again and leave it all to Alfred. Then she would be out in the cold again.

VI

MUTE BY VISITATION OF GOD

POSSIBLY the strangest case to come before the courts in the year 1953 was that of George Roberts, who was acquitted at Glamorgan Assizes in March of the murder of seventy-eight-year-old Elizabeth Thomas who had been found beaten and stabbed to death in her cottage in the little village of Laugharne, Carmarthenshire, on the evening of 10th January.

Deaf and dumb from birth, quite illiterate and understanding only the most elementary signs, forty-six-year-old George Roberts was found not guilty not only because it was impossible to convey to him, or for him to understand, the nature of the charge upon which he was being tried but inasmuch as, without any competent statement from him, there was no evidence to present to the jury. Roberts was suspected of the murder of the old lady because he had been observed near her cottage shortly before her death and he had been seen with a knife in his possession some months previously. His arrest arose from the belief that the signs he made during an interview with the police could be interpreted. They may have been correctly understood, but no one could be sure. Obviously, no " statement " obtained in this manner could be admitted in evidence.

This is what happened in the little village of Laugharne on the evening of the 10th January.

Shortly after 6 p.m. a man named Ronald Jones heard screams coming from the whitewashed cottage of Miss Elizabeth Thomas. The old lady appeared to be crying for help " as if she was being hurt," Mr. Jones related subsequently.

He heard her call a name and there was a scuffle of feet inside
the cottage when he tried the door. Mr. Jones informed
Police-Sergeant Morgan who was nearby. Hurrying to the
house the sergeant looked through the keyhole and saw, by
the faint reflected light of a lamp, some person leaning over
towards the door. This person wore a light-coloured cap but
Morgan could not tell whether it was a man or a woman.
While he was rattling the door the lamp went out. The sergeant
climbed in through a window and in the passageway he found
the old lady, still alive and moaning, lying on the floor with
her head towards the front door. On the floor was a substantial stick to which were adhering hairs from Miss Thomas's
head. She had a fractured skull and injuries and wounds on
her body. She died next day in hospital without regaining
consciousness. Her assailant had apparently got away at the
back of the house. The night was dark and foggy.

Miss Thomas, who was a native of Laugharne, had lived
alone since the death of her brother two years before. For
more than fifty years she had been in service at a local house.
Her savings amounting to £200, which she kept between two
mattresses under her bed, were found intact. If gain had been
the murderer's motive, he had been disturbed before he could
search the house, but whoever he was he had had the presence
of mind to extinguish the light when he *heard* someone at the
door. The crime was committed between 6 p.m. and 6.15
p.m. Miss Thomas had been seen standing in the road directly
opposite her home just before six o'clock.

Early the next morning Roberts accompanied the police to
Carmarthen where he remained until 14th January without
any charge being made against him. He was allowed to go
but on the 18th he was again seen by the police and in consequence of what he is supposed to have conveyed by signs he
was charged with the murder of the old lady.

When Roberts was first interviewed questions were put to
him through Mrs. Beddoe-Davis, a deaf and dumb expert.
Through her Detective-Sergeant Jones told him that he had
reason to believe that he was near the scene of the crime. Mrs.
Davis interpreted his reply as follows :

" I was walking along Clifton Street at four o'clock and
went as far as the church. I came back about four-thirty. I
saw Miss Thomas on the doorstep and saluted her. She is
my friend. I did not speak to her, only saluted her as I went
past. Then I walked home and had food. There was
another man with me when I went home. I was home
at about five o'clock and did not go out again."

When it was put to Roberts that he had been seen near
Miss Thomas's house at about 5.30 p.m. he replied : " No,
I was not there. I had my food and I sat in the chair reading."
By " reading " he meant looking at pictures.

According to the police Roberts had made signs indicating
that he had thrown a knife into the sea.

Mrs. Davis stated in court that Roberts understood crude
signs, a little lip-reading, some correct deaf and dumb signs
and mime, but his counsel asked, " How far have they been
guessing what they thought he was saying."

Detective-Inspector Spooner of Scotland Yard told the court
of his interview with Roberts on 18th January. " I noticed
Roberts looked worried, and he made signs that he wanted to
say something. I gestured an outline of a woman to him. He
nodded. I then produced to him two photographs which
showed Miss Thomas's cottage. He pointed to Miss Thomas's
house and nodded. He then made a sign that he wanted to
write something. He was given a pencil and a sheet of paper.
He then commenced to draw a house. When he had completed the house in the centre of five he put down the pencil,
gestured a woman, bowed his head sadly, and touched his
eyes with his handkerchief."

Detective-Inspector Spooner said that Roberts then drew
two houses on both the right and left of the first house. He next
drew a sketch of himself, pointed to the sketch, then to himself, and then to the middle house. Again he gestured a woman
and made thrusting motions with his arms. The Inspector
continued, " I then showed him a knife and he nodded. He
then made a movement from that particular house in the
middle, over its top, along the top of the two houses to the
right and down by the side of the end house to where he had

pictured himself. He then indicated walking down the road
to the left of the picture and then on and beyond."

A number of local people told the court what they knew of
Roberts, who had lived all his life in the village. Miss Vaughan
said that Roberts had worked for her for thirty-three years
doing odd jobs. She had found him very intelligent within his
limitations and she had noticed that he was very observant.
She said that his needs were very simple. He did not seem to
bother about money. "As far as I know all he used his money
for was to buy cigarettes and comic papers."

Thomas Langdon of Laugharne said that he had seen
Roberts earlier in the afternoon of the murder wearing a light-
brown cap. Langdon agreed that he had found "Booda," as
Roberts was known locally, to be a decent fellow during the
twenty-five years he had known him. He had never known
him to lose his temper. Asked, "He lives in a world of his
own, doesn't he?" Langdon replied, "Yes." He related that
Roberts could only understand the simplest of signs and not
the deaf and dumb language. As an illustration he explained
that "going to the pictures" would be conveyed to Roberts
by turning a cinematograph handle; "Sunday" by holding
the hands in prayer, and "the passing of a night" by placing
the hands together at the side of the head. While Langdon
demonstrated these signs Roberts nodded rapidly. Langdon
said that he had never known Roberts to possess a knife.

Miss Ethel Watkins said that five days after the crime
Roberts called to see her and he seemed very overcome. He
sat by the table, rested his head on it and "shed a tear." He
made her understand that he had never beaten up an elderly
lady.

When Mr. Jones, who had heard screams coming from Miss
Thomas's cottage as he was passing, gave evidence a sign
language expert, Mr. T. A. Crellin, tried to explain to Roberts
what Jones was saying. Roberts shook his head and shrugged
his shoulders. Mr. Crellin told the court : " It would be simply
useless to put all this to him. I can't do it. You would have
to take him to the place and show him." When Roberts was
asked to plead to the charge, the interpreter said, " He would

not understand sufficiently to make a plea of guilty or not guilty."

Submitting that there was no case to answer the defence pointed out that the case was a mass of contradiction. A large number of witnesses who had known Roberts for many years had said that he was of such a mentality that he could understand only the simplest of signs and only by similar means could he get over to people what he was trying to say. " On the other hand you have complete strangers who have come into this court to say that they knew better than all these people who had known Roberts for years."

The actual evidence against Roberts was inconclusive; the principal scientific officer at the Forensic Science Laboratory at Cardiff said that green distemper taken from Roberts's mackintosh resembled in colour and ingredients the distemper taken from the wall of the cottage passage, but white material found on the coat differed from the white material in the sample of plaster. No bloodstains were found on Roberts's clothes and no fingerprints of his were traced in Miss Thomas's cottage. It seems inconceivable that the murderer could have escaped without some trace of blood on his clothes and equally impossible that he could have avoided leaving a fingerprint inside the house. When the murderer " heard " the police knocking at the door, he, whoever he was, turned out the lamp and he must have " groped " his way out at the back.

When Roberts came up for trial at Carmarthen the first question to be decided was his fitness to plead. As a result of the arguments put forward his trial was transferred to Cardiff. Before he could be tried on the murder charge it had to be decided whether he was " mute of malice " or " mute by act of God." It had also to be decided whether the question of his fitness to plead could be tried separately to the charge of murder. The point was one of vital importance. If the jury found Roberts unfit to plead on the murder charge the judge had no alternative but to commit him to Broadmoor where he would be detained during " Her Majesty's pleasure." Thus, because of a legal technicality, a man who was perfectly sane and who might be entirely innocent could be kept in prison

GEORGE ROBERTS

for life. As the defence maintained that there was no evidence to prove that Roberts was the murderer of Miss Thomas the judge was reluctant to dispose of the case by accepting a plea of unfit to plead. A jury was empanelled and after hearing evidence from a man who said that during his acquaintance with Roberts for twenty-nine years he had not spoken and could not hear the jury found him mute by visitation of God.

At his trial at Cardiff a plea of " Not guilty " was entered on Roberts's behalf. At the end of the prosecution's opening address by Mr. Vincent Lloyd-Jones, Mr. Justice Devlin asked him : " Is it right that apart from the statements alleged to have been made by him the only evidence to connect Roberts with the crime is that about half an hour before the probable time of the crime he was seen observing the house." Counsel answered, " Yes."

Mr. Justice Devlin : " After that time he was seen walking away from the churchyard and some unidentified man was seen walking away from a waste piece of ground. You propose to strengthen it by producing statements from a man with whom there is no certain means of communication."

Mr. Lloyd-Jones said that he had seen the statements and had been instructed on the mode of communication and it was claimed by Mrs. Beddoe-Davis that she had been in communication with him and he understood her.

Mr. Justice Devlin : " If I should rule that these statements should not go to the jury is there any evidence on which a jury might convict? " Mr. Lloyd-Jones replied, " I think not, my lord." " I would have thought it impossible," commented the judge.

The judge then asked the prosecution to call their evidence relating to the alleged statements before any other evidence. When Superintendent David Jones gave evidence of calling at Roberts's home in the early hours of the morning after the murder he was about to give evidence of questions put to Roberts through his uncle when defending counsel, Mr. Edmund Davies, objected on the ground that it was hearsay. The judge ruled that any questions put through the uncle could not be given in evidence and the superintendent went on to speak of the occasion when he interviewed Roberts in the presence of Mr. and Mrs. Beddoe-Davis. The defence objected to this unless the interpreter was first called.

Mrs. Beddoe-Davis said that she had been conversant with the deaf and dumb alphabet since childhood and she was also experienced in making signs for illiterates. She had been an interpreter for the Llanelly and Swansea police courts for a number of years. She said that she had put questions to Roberts for the police and she had endeavoured to make him understand them. Asked if she was able to communicate with him, Mrs. Beddoe-Davis replied, " Perfectly." What was alleged to have been stated during the interview was heard in absence of the jury.

A long legal battle ensued over the attempt of the prosecution to establish that Roberts was unfit to plead. His counsel pointed out that for Roberts not to be tried on the merits of the case because of his affliction was horrifying. The defence was a complete denial of the charge. The judge ruled that, " To insist upon this issue of fitness being tried might result in the detention of a man as a criminal lunatic when he is in fact innocent. This would result in a public mischief and the person so detained would be assumed in the eyes of the police and authorities to be the person responsible for the crime. The investigations which might result in the apprehension of the true criminal would not then take place."

The judge found a procedure based on a case heard in 1876 which enabled the defence to have the general issue of the murder charge tried before the issue of their client's fitness to plead without abandoning their right to fall back on his unfitness to plead. He would swear the jury to try the general issue of murder.

When the prosecution opened the case against Roberts his counsel successfully opposed the admission of certain statements alleged to have been made by him and as a result the prosecution offered no further evidence. The judge directed the jury to return a verdict of " Not guilty."

For the Crown, Mr. Lloyd-Jones said, " Having investigated the matter it does seem that in all the circumstances the right course to pursue is not to proceed with the case and to offer no further evidence." The judge replied: "That is a very proper course. There is one matter that a little disturbs me." He drew attention to the circumstances in which Roberts had been taken to the police station. Mr. Lloyd-Jones said that Roberts was invited to go through the medium of his uncle, "subject always to whether the interpretation was properly carried out." "Having got there," counsel continued, "he apparently liked being there. He was not detained at all, and he left with reluctance having been there for some days for the purpose of the enquiries. He showed no dislike of being there, and after a certain time he was not kept there against his will. No pressure was brought upon him to elicit any confession. Anything he said then to Superintendent Spooner was volunteered by him so far as they were able to understand him." The judge pointed out that it was not often that one saw statements in the form of question and answer. Mr. Lloyd-Jones submitted that it was an interrogation conducted in circumstances of extraordinary difficulty.

The judge: "It is quite clear, is it not, that there is no power for any police officer to detain anybody in a police station for questioning? I should have thought that if a police officer wishes to take a man to a police station he must arrest him and to do that he must have reasonable grounds." Mr. Lloyd-Jones: "He was an unusual man. He was told to go several times, but he stayed." "An unwelcome guest, in fact," suggested the judge. Mr. Lloyd-Jones said that Roberts was not kept in a cell but in an upstairs room.

Addressing the jury the judge commented: "This man was taken to Carmarthen Police Station on the night of 10th-11th January after the crime and he was kept there until the 14th. No charge of any sort had been made against him and during that time he was questioned and questioned in a manner that was not designed merely to elicit facts, but was in the nature of cross-examination. Being released on the 14th, he made a further statement on the 18th, and it was only after that that he was charged with the offence. I am fully conscious of the fact that the police have a very difficult task to discharge. It is easy to criticize the way they discharge their duties. This case must no doubt have created at every stage difficult problems for them. But I should like to make it abundantly clear that a man cannot be detained unless he is arrested. It is of first importance that when any abuse of this practice, whether innocent or not, is brought to the notice of this court it should be very carefully scrutinized."

The judge pointed out that detaining a man in a police station without being charged is something that is open to misconstruction. "These are the safeguards on which the liberty of each one of us rests," he said.

Mr. Justice Devlin made it clear to the jury that Roberts was not being freed because of a technical reason. No jury, he said, could return a verdict of guilty on the evidence the prosecution had to offer against Roberts. He referred to the absence of the sort of clues normally found in such cases and commented that " the evidence comes down to the fact that Roberts was seen before and afterwards and the fact that he had previously had a knife in his possession. These things are coupled with certain statements said to have been obtained from a man with whom communication was almost impossible. You could never have been asked to convict on evidence of this sort."

Roberts was of course unaware that he had been acquitted of the charge of murder. He was equally unaware of the nature of the proceedings taking place around him and, presumably, of the significance of the word " murder." That he was free to go was conveyed to him by his solicitor by a " thumbs-up " sign. He left the court free to return to the little village on Carmarthen Bay, free to take up again the threads of his life as local odd-job man. Miss Vaughan, who had employed him for thirty-three years, said, " I am delighted that he has been cleared. I shall give him work again, for he is loyal and faithful." The Welsh poet, the late Dylan Thomas, who lived in the village, declared : " Booda was always quiet and harmless. Everyone in the village seemed to like him."

The murder of Miss Thomas remains one of the unsolved crimes of 1953.

VII

THE CLAPHAM STABBING CASE

THE evening of Thursday, 2nd July, 1953. The dancing on Clapham Common had finished. Round the bandstand lounged a group of youths affecting an Edwardian style of dress—tight stovepipe trousers and tightly buttoned jackets, slit down the back, or what are known as "zoot-suits." One of them tried to push his way past four young men who were sitting on benches; he was told there was plenty of room elsewhere. He returned to his companions. They conferred, casting hostile glances at the four young men who, foreseeing trouble, moved off to a drinking fountain. There they were attacked by six "Edwardian" youths. They heard someone say "get the knives out." Two of them, Carter and Ryan, made a getaway. The other two, Beckley and Chandler, ran off and boarded a bus at some traffic lights.

When the bus pulled up at a request stop, Beckley and Chandler were dragged off the platform by the gang of six youths. A fight ensued. Chandler got back on the bus but Beckley, after being hit a couple of times, ran off pursued by the gang. He was seen to collapse on the pavement and he was heard to shout, "Go on, stab me, stab me." He was left to die.

A lady on the bus saw one of the youths put what appeared to be a green-handled knife in his right breast pocket. The one who did so was wearing a gaudy tie which he removed and put into his pocket.

When John Ernest Beckley, who was seventeen years old, was taken to hospital he was found to have six stab wounds, four in the back, one in the chest and one in the abdomen. He

died that evening. Two of his companions, Chandler and
Ryan, also received stab wounds.

Two of Beckley's assailants, Ronald Coleman, fifteen-year-
old shop assistant, and Michael Davies, twenty-year-old
labourer, were tried at the Old Bailey in September for his
murder. The jury disagreed. The murder charge against
Coleman was dropped but Davies, at his second trial in October, was found guilty and he was condemned to death. After
his appeal had been dismissed he was reprieved. Coleman and
four other youths were sent to prison for assault.

Such are the bare facts of one of the most sensational crimes
of the year; a murder in anger; a murder of a youth by a
youth for no reason except spite and maliciousness. Davies and
his five companions were hooligans or, as the Americans say,
" hoodlums "; *they killed because they thought that they could
get away with murder.* They thought that, because they had
no respect for the law, or for its punishments.

As there are so many people involved, we can list them as :

The Attackers

> Michael John Davies, twenty-year-old labourer (con-
> victed at his second trial of the murder of Beckley).

> Ronald Coleman, fifteen-year-old shop assistant (jury
> failed to agree on murder charge; imprisoned nine
> months for assault).

> Terence Power, seventeen-year-old unemployed (im-
> prisoned nine months for assault).

> Allan Albert Lawson, eighteen-year-old carpenter (im-
> prisoned six months for assault).

> Terence David Woodman, sixteen-year-old street trader
> (imprisoned nine months for assault).

> John Frederick Allan, twenty-one-year-old labourer (im-
> prisoned nine months for assault).

The Attacked

> John Ernest Beckley, seventeen years of age (murdered).

> Frederick Chandler, eighteen-year-old bank clerk
> (wounded).

> John Francis Ryan, nineteen-year-old packer (wounded).

Brian William Carter, eighteen-year-old metal worker (unharmed).

The Girls (witnesses)

Sylvia Audrey Clubb (Coleman's companion).

Eileen Anne Brannon (with Coleman when he tried to pass the benches).

Sylvia Patricia Pilkington (Wood's companion).

Other Witnesses

James George Leaver	On common.
Bernard George Wood	On common.
Vivienne Chandler	On bus.
Leslie Herbert Mellows	On bus.
Mary Frayling	On bus.
Theresa Margaret McCarthy	On bus.
Brenda May Wood	After murder.

The six " Edwardians " were soon under arrest. Their attitude to the murder was made apparent by their remarks to the police. Told that Beckley had died from stab wounds, Coleman replied, " Not me. I was not on the common on Thursday night," but later he admitted, " I was in the fight on the common, but not at the bus stop. I didn't stab him." When he was charged with murder, he said, " No, sir. Nothing to say."

Davies, on the other hand, admitted being in the fight. " We all set about two of them on the pavement. I didn't have a knife. I only used my fists." When he was shown a tie taken from his home he admitted that it was the tie he had worn when " all this business happened." He asked, " What do you want it for? "

Power, when questioned, replied : " You have made a mistake this time. My name's Terry Clancey." Told he was known to the police as Power, he replied : " All right, have it your own way, but you won't pin anything on me. What a night to be picked up, Saturday night."

When Power was told he would be taken to the police station he said : " I wasn't on the common on Thursday, I went with my mate to the Crystal Palace." He added : " I want to tell you about it. Micky Davies told you I was there.

The —— won't live long after he comes out from this, because I'll do him. I only booted the fellow. I was not the one with the knife." Told he would be put up for identification he replied: "Don't do that. Someone is bound to pick me. I wanted to tell you I was there. I put the boot into him, but I never had a knife, and don't forget it."

Lawson said at first, "I didn't see any fight," but on second thoughts he stated: "I think I had better tell you the truth because you seem to know I was in the fight with Terry Woodman." He then made a statement: "They all rushed in, but I don't know why they started it. We jumped on to a bus and pulled them off. Woodman and I stood back. The others were punching and kicking."

Woodman, accused of being involved, replied: "Don't know what you are talking about," but later he said. "All right. I'll come clean, but I didn't use the knife. Two of the boys asked if we would like a fight—we took one each." Allan, on being questioned, replied, "Honest, I didn't use a knife. I was only in the fight at the fountain, I wasn't in the fight at the bus stop. If I knew who used a knife I'd tell you."

At their trial for the murder of Beckley, Coleman was defended by Mr. Derek Curtis-Bennett, Q.C., and Davies by Mr. David Weitzman, Q.C. Mr. Christmas Humphreys prosecuted and the judge was Mr. Justice Pearson. Originally six youths were charged with murder but no evidence was offered against the other four. Two of them gave evidence at the trial.

Opening the case for the Crown, Mr. Christmas Humphreys showed the jury a small knife with a bluish-green handle, a replica of the one with which it was alleged Beckley had been stabbed. He said in some sense it was a knife and in some sense a dagger. The blade could be moved up notch by notch until at the end it became a dagger. The blade was not long but it was long enough to kill Beckley. Evidence would be called, he told the jury, that Davies had such a knife and that he had threatened people who might inform against him.

Blood had been found, Mr. Humphreys told the jury, inside Davies's coat pocket, the pocket into which he had been seen to put something that looked like a knife after the stabbing.

Mr. Humphreys said it was alleged against Davies that he used the knife which killed Beckley and wounded two other youths. Against Coleman the case was more a matter of inference—that he knew Davies was going into a series of fights, which took place on Clapham Common and at a bus stop nearby, with a knife in his hands and was prepared to use it, and *with that knowledge* he joined Davies in that attack.

The cause of Beckley's death was established. A pathologist, Dr. Donald Teare, said Beckley had two incised wounds in the scalp about one-quarter of an inch deep. There were four wounds in the back one of which was three and one-eighth inches deep and had penetrated the main vein and reached the main artery, supplying the heart. That had caused a great deal of bleeding. There were two other wounds on the front of the body. The cause of death was haemorrhage from stab wounds. Dr. Teare explained to the jury how he had carried out a number of experiments on an unclothed body with a knife like the one exhibited in court, and he was of the opinion that the injuries could have been carried out with a knife similar to the one which was an exhibit in the case. A considerable degree of force had been necessary to cause the main wound. He estimated that after being stabbed Beckley would have been able to run about one hundred yards, perhaps a little further.

Dr. Lewis Nickolls, Director of the Metropolitan Police Laboratory, said that he had examined the clothing worn by the two defendants. There was no blood on Coleman's clothes but he had found a *reaction from blood inside the right breast pocket of Davies's coat,* on the lining of the right cuff and on the waistcoat and shirt. It was impossible to say if it was human blood, he added.

The chief question to be decided at the trial was the identity of the person who had stabbed Beckley. A number of witnesses were called to tell how the fight started and what had happened at the bus stop. An important witness was Frederick Chandler who had been with Beckley on the common and on the bus. He said that he, Beckley, Ryan and Carter were sitting on seats with their feet resting on the seats opposite. Coleman came up with a girl. " He asked to come through. Ryan asked him to walk round. No one else said anything. He asked to come through again, and Ryan again asked him to go round. He left us and walked towards a group of other chaps at the bandstand." No one had provoked him or said anything insulting.

Asked by prosecuting counsel: " What did you do? "—" We got up and started to move away towards a drinking fountain. At the fountain we were attacked from behind by eight or nine youths. Two people kicked me and punched me. I saw Ryan on the ground and Beckley was fighting with three others." Chandler ran off and boarded a bus at some traffic lights. Beckley was with him. Then at the stop a gang of youths, " about three," pulled them off the platform.

Chandler said three others joined in the attack. Two attacked him and the rest concentrated on Beckley. The fight went on for about ten seconds, then he got back on to the bus. The six chased after Beckley. Chandler continued: " I was feeling groggy when I got back on the bus. I felt something warm around my stomach and found myself bleeding."

Prosecuting counsel: " Did you see any knife used that night? "—" No."

Mr. Derek Curtis-Bennett, for Coleman, asked, " Did you see a lot of people about in tight trousers and strange looking coats, with a slit down the back—Edwardian dress? "— " I did not pay much attention."

Mr. Curtis-Bennett: " I suggest it is a habit there among habitués. Did you see anything of that sort? "—" I believe so."

" Did it rather look silly to you? "—" I suppose it did."

" Did you make any comment about it? "—" No."

Mr. Curtis-Bennett: ' So far as you know at the bus stop you received blows with a fist, or so you thought? "—" Yes, sir."

" It follows that the person who held the knife was probably concealing it and punching with a part of it through his fingers? "—" Yes, sir."

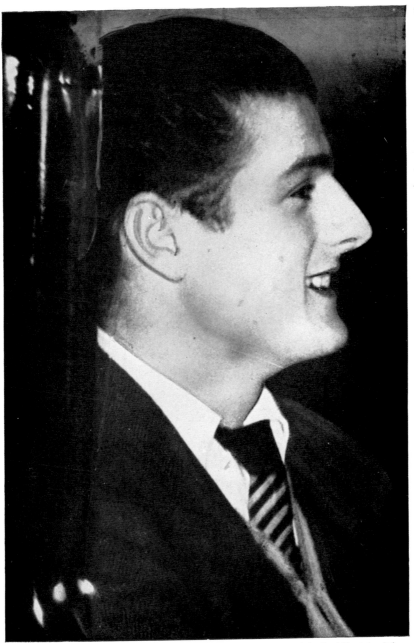

MICHAEL DAVIES

" You did not even see it ? "—" No, sir."

Replying to Mr. David Weitzman, for Davies, Chandler said that in the fight he did not recognize Davies. He discovered later that he had a stab wound. It was not inflicted at the fountain.

Ryan said he heard no terms of abuse used against Coleman. Describing the fight near the drinking fountain, he said : " One of the fellows attacking me shouted, ' Get out the knives.' I do not say who said that. When I saw there were so many I turned and ran for it."

When he was going home on the bus his shoulder felt stiff. " It was aching, and I put my hand up and felt the blood."

Eileen Anne Brannon said that she was with Coleman when he tried to push between the seats. One of the youths called him " a flash — ."

James George Leaver, a chauffeur, said that on the evening of 2nd July he went to Clapham Common with two girls, Sylvia Pilkington and Joan Condon. Coleman came up and told him of a remark made by some other youths. " Coleman said he was going to get a couple of boys," he continued. " Davies produced a knife and said, ' I will be all right with this,' or words to that effect."

Cross-examined by Mr. David Weitzman, for Davies, Leaver agreed that he was a particular friend of a youth named Bernard George Wood, whom he knew was likely to be in trouble over this matter. When counsel suggested that Leaver had invented his evidence about Davies having a knife and saying, " I will be all right with this," in order to protect his friend Wood, the witness replied, " No, sir."

Sylvia Patricia Pilkington, aged seventeen, who stated that she was Wood's companion, said that she had seen Davies on 2nd July with a knife in his hand. On the following day she had seen him in an amusement arcade and he gave her a message to take to Wood that no one knew who had done the stabbing. It would be bad for the ones who tell, he had threatened.

Sylvia Audrey Clubb, aged seventeen, who said she was Coleman's girl friend, said that Coleman had told her on the night of 2nd July that there had been some trouble on Clapham Common. The next night he told her Mike Davies and Johnny Allan had done the murder. Later, Davies said he would get someone to hurt her if she told anybody " who it was." Mr. David Weitzman, for Davies asked her : " You were ready to say anything to help Ronald Coleman, were you not ? "

" I wanted the truth known," she replied.

" I put it to you that it is not true that Michael Davies threatened you at all ? "

" Yes," she answered.

As she left the witness box the judge, looking intently at the gallery, warned the onlookers : " If there is any person in the gallery who is making signs to this person it is a very serious matter indeed. If it continues I shall have to ask that everybody in the gallery should be asked to leave. It is a most important thing that evidence should be given, and given freely."

Shortly afterwards a young girl who sat in the front row, wearing large loop ear-rings, left the gallery accompanied by two police officers.

Next, evidence was given by people who had seen the fight at the bus stop. Leslie Mellows, an ex-policeman, who was on the bus, said he saw Beckley and Chandler on the platform. As the bus pulled up a gang of youths pulled them off. Beckley and Chandler were struck and kicked and the lads were bending down to protect their faces. Coleman was one of the lads taking part; he was one of the foremost of them. As the bus moved off Beckley was leaning against the railings and there was blood running down his face. Mellows said he got off the bus and tried unsuccessfully to catch up with some of the youths.

Vivienne Chandler, aged fifteen, said that after the fight at the bus stop she saw one boy fall. There were five or six round him and she heard him say : " Stab me then. Go on." She went back to him after he had fallen and he tried to sit up.

Miss Mary Frayling, a secretary, said she was travelling on

the upper deck of the bus. As the vehicle approached the
" request " stop at Clapham Common North Side she saw a
group of boys running towards it. As the bus restarted she
noticed six or seven boys running on the pavement. They were
spread out and the one at the rear stopped, and another boy
went up to him and seemed to shake him. The boy who had
stopped then collapsed. The witness said she noticed the
youth who had shaken the other lad put something in his
right-hand breast pocket—it had a green handle. At the same
time he seemed to be shutting something.

Asked by Mr. Christmas Humphreys if she could recognize
that boy in court, Miss Frayling replied " Yes," and indicated
the defendant Davies.

Miss Frayling said that she did not know at the time that
what Davies put in his pocket was a knife. She thought it was
either a razor or a knife. She didn't actually see the blade.
She felt sure it was not a comb. Miss McCarthy, friend of Miss
Frayling, said they sat together on the bus. She noticed one
particular boy and thought he had a knife in his hand.

Next came two of the youths who had been in the fight.
Terence David Woodman, who had been originally charged
with murdering Beckley, said after the fight at the bus stop he
went with Lawson to the coffee stall where he heard Davies
say, " I only tried to run the knife up and down the fellow's
face," and he made a motion with his hands. Woodman agreed
that when he and Lawson were in prison they appreciated the
seriousness of their position and were exceedingly anxious to
do something to cover themselves. They were equally anxious
to show that someone else had a knife. Davies might have said,
" Someone had only tried to run the knife . . . , " but the witness added : " I cannot remember properly, but I thought he
said that he had."

Allan Albert Lawson, one of the four youths originally
charged with murdering Beckley, said he was at the bus stop
fight. Later he went with Woodman to a coffee stall where
they met Davies. There was some conversation about the
fight and Davies remarked, " I only tried to run the knife up
and down." Cross-examined by Mr. Weitzman, the witness

agreed that he had lied to the police in the first place when he said, " I did not see any fight." Mr. Weitzman : " I suggest Davies said, ' Someone must have run the knife up and down? "—" He could have done."

Bernard George Wood, aged twenty-one, admitted that he had been in the fight, but he had escaped arrest. He denied having carried a knife on that occasion but he agreed that he had once been fined £10 for carrying a gun without a licence. He told the court he saw Davies and Coleman on Clapham Common on the night of the fight. Coleman said that a fellow had called him a name. " I saw something in Davies's hand. . . . It was a knife and it was open. I did not see him open it," he explained.

Near the fountain on the common Wood said he saw three people fighting four others. " I and my friends joined in. Later the four ran away." Some time after that a girl came up and shouted that a fellow had been stabbed. Wood said he next heard Davies say, " ' There is no claret on it.' I knew what he meant."

Answering further questions Wood agreed he was very concerned about himself and anxious to cover himself up as far as he could.

Mr. Weitzman : " Did you decide Davies was the person who was going to be blamed for using the knife? "

Witness : " He was the only person with a knife."

Questioned about his reference to hearing Davies say, " There's no claret on it," Wood denied that was something he had put in in order to try and protect himself. Mr. Christmas Humphreys, in re-examination : " It has been put to you that you and others have put your heads together to lie to the jury to blame Davies to protect yourself? Is there any truth in that? "—" No."

Coleman was the first of the accused to give evidence. He told the court that his dress that night on the common was not completely Edwardian, as his coat did not have a split down the back of it, and his trousers were not as narrow as the usual style. He said that one of the youths on the benches, Ryan, had passed an offensive remark.

Counsel : " What were you going to do with Ryan who had insulted you? "—" Have it out with him. I might have started off with an argument. I would not have struck a blow to start with."

" Did you see anybody produce a knife? "—" No."

" Did you hear somebody say : ' Get the knives out.' ? "— " Definitely not."

The fight at the fountain had already started when he got there. " I ran up to Ryan and he struck me a blow. I went down and he started to kick me and then Davies and someone else rushed in and dragged him off."

Counsel : " What did you do then? "

Coleman : " I might have struck Ryan. I jumped up, everything broke up. Ryan started to run and we followed after him."

" Were you ever at the fight at the bus stop? "—" I never even saw that."

" Did you know anyone was going to use a knife? "—" No, sir."

" Did you see Davies? "—" I only saw him at the fountain."

Replying to further questions, Coleman said after the fighting was over he saw Davies. In his hand was a light-coloured object which Coleman said he took to be a knife. Davies asked him, " What shall I do with this? "

Questioned by Mr. Weitzman, for Davies, Coleman admitted he was very much afraid for himself at the time. " And very anxious, if at all possible, to put the blame on someone else? " Mr. Weitzman asked.

" No, sir. I would not put the blame on somebody else if it were not the truth."

" I am putting to you that you have invented this story about Davies and the knife? "

Coleman : " No, sir."

" And the words you suggest he has spoken? "—" No, sir."

" You were ready to lie in the first place to protect yourself? "—" Yes, sir, and I protected the others."

Mr. Weitzman, asking about what he had seen in Davies's hand : " You do not remember what really happened or what you really saw, do you? "—" Yes. I saw with my own eyes an object in Davies's hand."

" You do not know what that object was? "—" I did not see the blade, but I saw a light-coloured handle."

Answering Mr. Humphreys, for the prosecution, Coleman said he was not trying to pick a quarrel with the four youths who were sitting on the two seats, but he agreed he was prepared to quarrel with Ryan, because of his insulting remark.

Mr. Humphreys : " You went back to get reinforcements? "— " No, I spoke to ' Splinter ' (Wood)."

" And then, within a few minutes of your going back, there are eight or ten of you going towards these four boys? "— " They were all in a crowd."

" Are you saying you did not raise all the boys you could to go and attack these four? "—" Yes."

" And it is just after that Davies gets out a knife? "—" I did not see him get out a knife."

" Is Mr. Mellows wrong when he says you were the leader of the attack at the bus stop? He picked you out on the identification parade? "—" Yes, I was the only one wearing an Edwardian suit. I was not at the bus stop."

Coleman said he did not see Beckley fall because several youths were round him. When he saw them run he ran as well.

Mr. Humphreys : " Did you hear Davies say something about the knife? "—" Yes."

" Was that because you had seen that knife in Davies's hand before the fight started, and you knew quite well what he had been doing with it? "—" No, I thought he was in a panic when he asked me."

The second defendant, Davies, answering his counsel, Mr. Weitzman, in the witness-box, said when he was aged nine he was accused of stealing some cups and was discharged under the Probation of Offenders' Act. Later, he was convicted with three other lads of breaking and entering, and was placed on probation. He then joined the Merchant Navy for about fifteen months and his discharge certificate was marked " Very good." In 1951 he joined the R.A.F. and after twelve months was again discharged with a good character. Davies agreed that earlier this year he was again in trouble, being charged at London Sessions with shopbreaking. He was found guilty of receiving some of the property knowing it to have been stolen. There had never been any allegation of violence in these charges.

Asked about the evening of 2nd July, Davies declared he did not have a knife in his possession. He had never owned a knife similar to the one which had been exhibited in this case. He denied being one of the group to whom Coleman had complained that he had been insulted.

Mr. Weitzman : " Did you say on that occasion, ' I will be all right with this,' and produce a knife? "—" Definitely not."

He said, " I went for the big fellow because he was kicking Coleman. I just meant to keep him away from Coleman, but did not mean to do him any serious injury. There were three or four in the fight." He never heard anyone say, " Get out the knives."

Davies agreed that when Ryan ran away he chased him, and jumped on to the platform of a bus in order to catch him. As he boarded the bus someone shouted, " Here is one of them," but he did not help pull anyone off the vehicle. " I saw Woodman and Allan hit Chandler and I attacked Chandler as well," Davies went on. " I did not see anyone attacking Beckley, I was too busy with the other fellow."

Davies said he saw Beckley against the railings, but he did not go near him and ran off with the others.

Mr. Weitzman : " Is there any truth in the suggestion that you had a knife that night? "—" No, sir."

Cross-examined by Mr. Humphreys, Davies agreed that he must have been near Ryan when someone stabbed him, and the same remark applied to Chandler. He said after the fight at the bus stop he saw Beckley leaning against the railings. Blood was pouring down his face.

Mr. Humphreys : " You were seen to put a knife inside your right-hand breast pocket by Miss Frayling? "—" No."

" Then how did the blood get into your pocket? "—" I had struck Ryan and he had blood on his face and I keep a comb in that pocket. Miss Frayling is wrong."

In his final speech for Coleman, Mr. Derek Curtis-Bennett said: "You are not going to convict Coleman of murder because you may think he is guilty of assault or unlawful acts, or of behaving badly. You must cut all the prejudice out of the matter. Coleman had no thought of malice against Beckley. Were the jury satisfied that Coleman was there when Beckley received the fatal stab wounds?" he asked.

Mr. Weitzman, on behalf of Davies, reminded the jury that Beckley's three companions, Chandler, Ryan and Carter, had all given evidence. Not one of them had said anything to suggest that Davies was doing any more than the others. Not one of them uttered a word of evidence mentioning Davies by name or identifying him in any way.

Mr. Weitzman held up Beckley's blood-stained shirt and said: "If Davies held the knife, as the prosecution would have you believe, why was there so little blood on him? One would have thought there would have been much more. So far as his jacket is concerned we don't know if it was blood. Is it conceivable, if Davies was the man who did this, that there would not have been blood upon him which could be easily identified?

"A woman witness," he said, "had stated that from the top of a bus she saw Davies put something which she thought was a knife or a razor into his breast pocket. But there was a half light at the time and trees in the area were throwing further shadows. There was no evidence that anyone saw Davies touch Beckley or anyone with a knife or make any movement suggesting he was using a knife against anyone," he said.

In his final speech for the Crown, Mr. Humphreys said the case against Davies was that he was physically the actual murderer. The case against Coleman was that by reason of the part he played and the knowledge he had, he, too, was in English law guilty of murder. There was plenty of evidence, Mr. Humphreys said, "that Coleman knew Davies had a knife. I ask you to say that it is proved to the hilt that Davies is a murderer in every sense of the word and that Coleman, in law, is guilty of murder.

"During the fighting someone used a knife as a result of

which two boys were stabbed and one was murdered. It may be two persons had a knife, but there was no evidence that anyone, other than Davies, used a knife. A knife was seen in his hand before and after the fight, and there was blood on his clothes. Whether one or two persons used a knife was utterly irrelevant in law," counsel pointed out. " The case for the Crown is that this was a murderous attack, and these two are guilty in English law of murdering Beckley. Having received those wounds and bleeding seriously, Beckley was left to die.

" The case against Coleman was very different. No one saw a knife in his hand, but there was plenty of evidence that he knew Davies had a knife. Did the jury doubt that it was Coleman who led the assault at the bus stop? " he asked.

In his summing-up, Mr. Justice Pearson told the jury : " It was an essential part of the prosecution's case that Davies stabbed Beckley but not that Davies was the only one who stabbed him, or that it was necessarily his hand which struck the fatal blow. You may think the case against Coleman is by no means strong, but that is a matter for you. You cannot convict on mere suspicion. If you are left by the evidence in a state of uncertainty then the right verdict is not guilty."

But on the evidence presented the jury, after deliberating for three hours and forty minutes, were unable to arrive at a verdict. Davies had been shown to have owned just such a knife as with which the fatal wounds had been inflicted. He had been seen to put something that looked like a knife into his pocket, and in that pocket blood was found. Someone had stabbed Beckley, but which was the murderer? The charge against Coleman was dropped. Davies was sent again for trial on the murder charge.

The four remaining members of the gang, and Coleman, were sentenced to terms of imprisonment for assault. In presenting the case against them, Mr. Humphreys said : " That assault, violent and concerted, continued for the best part of half-an-hour over a wide range of Clapham Common, over the Queen's highway to the north of the common, and was so persistent and determined that some of the boys, as they had admitted, used a public conveyance, namely a bus, to enable them to cut off the escape of one of the boys whom they wanted further to ' beat up.'

" Coleman undoubtedly started the fighting. Thinking he had been insulted he collected a number of other youths who made this attack and they pursued the four boys across the common in various directions. The youths who had taken part in this assault then dispersed. Thereafter there was evidence that threats were used by some of them upon witnesses. The gravity of this offence was the persistence with which the assaults were carried out, the concerted action, and the fact that even a bus was not safe from this hooliganism. During the fighting three of the boys, Beckley, Ryan and Chandler, were knifed, but it was no longer alleged that a knife was used by any of these defendants."

Before they were sentenced (Lawson six months, the rest for nine months) evidence was given by the police of the previous careers of the defendants :

Coleman in the previous year, when he was fifteen years old, had been bound over, with other youths, for using insulting words and behaviour on Clapham Common. He was known to carry a sharpened paper knife in a homemade sheath. At school he was in a quarrel with another boy who was stabbed with a nail file. Coleman's explanation that it was an accident was accepted. In May 1953, Coleman had admitted to attacking a cinema attendant in a fit of temper because he had been told to behave in the cinema.

The police said Power had previous convictions for shop-breaking and larceny and he had been to an approved school. He was released on licence but when his licence was revoked he had escaped. Woodman also had one juvenile conviction. Lawson was a youth of hitherto excellent character. Allan had been in trouble with the police for shop-breaking and larceny. In 1950 he joined the R.A.F. for three years but deserted in January, 1952, and was absent until the date of his arrest. Davies admitted to having had convictions.

At his second trial in October the jury, after a retirement of two hours, found Michael Davies guilty of the murder of Beckley and he was sentenced to death. Mr. David Weitzman reminded the jury that there was no direct evidence that anyone saw Davies stab Beckley. Even if every word uttered by every witness called by the prosecution were true, counsel suggested to the jury that it did not prove that Davies inflicted the wounds on Beckley from which he died.

Summing up the judge told the jury: " Beckley had nine wounds; finally he sank to the ground stabbed to death . . . and that happened on Clapham Common North Side in this year of 1953 after our young people have been through public education. If someone deliberately and intentionally plunged some sharp instrument into that boy's body with intent to inflict grievous bodily harm and from those wounds the boy died, that is murder. A lot has been made of the fact that a number of other boys were concerned in the chase. A pretty state of affairs it reveals on Clapham Common in any view of the case."

Referring to a witness, Mary Frayling, the judge said she had a " balcony seat." From the top of a bus she saw a boy, whom she later identified as Davies, shake Beckley and then take out a green-handled object from his pocket, which she thought was a knife. " She was in no way concerned in this matter," continued the judge. " She is not the girl friend of any of the boys so that it cannot be said she was making up a story to shield anyone." Davies's defence was, the judge pointed out, " I never had a knife and I never used a knife." If the jury believed that and accepted that from him, there was an end of the matter. " The point is do you accept it, and ought you to accept it from him? " the judge asked. If the jury believed the witnesses called for the prosecution, it meant that before the fighting started Davies had a knife and had already drawn a knife.

Davies's appeal, on the ground that the judge had failed to apply to the testimony of one of the youths involved the rule relating to accomplices, having been dismissed, his solicitors took the case to the House of Lords. The Attorney-General contended that Lawson was not an accomplice and there was no obligation on the judge to warn the jury. The appeal was dismissed. In giving reasons for this judgment, the Lord Chancellor said :

"There was no reason why, if half a dozen boys fought another crowd and one of them produced a knife and stabbed one of the opponents to death, all the rest of the group should be treated as accomplices in the use of the knife and the infliction of the mortal injury by that means, unless there was evidence that the rest intended or conceived or at least contemplated an attack with a knife by one of their number, as opposed to a common assault. If all that was envisaged was a common assault (and there was no evidence that Lawson knew that any of his companions had a knife) then Lawson was not an accomplice in the crime consisting of its felonious use."

On 22nd January, 1954, it was announced that the Home Secretary had recommended a reprieve for Davies. For some months Davies's sister, twenty-six-year-old Joyce, had been seeking evidence in an effort to establish his innocence. After his second trial she put before the police information about a pair of blood-stained trousers. She claimed they had been exchanged between two people on the common soon after the crime.

All this happened in 1953. None of the youths concerned were over twenty-one. Five of them had previously been in trouble with the police. The significant fact is that the lenient treatment they had then received, instead of acting as a deterrent, made them think that they could get away with more serious crimes. By now, the five boys sent to prison for assault will be free. Davies may be in prison for many years, but eventually he will be released. What will these boys do with their second chance? The case of the Clapham Common hooligans will present an interesting example of the efficiency of modern " humanitarian " ideas on the prevention of crime.

By courtesy of Keystone

SIR DAVID MAXWELL FYFE, P.C., Q.C., HOME SECRETARY

VIII

THE BATH RACE-HORSE SWITCH

AFTER two lengthy trials four men were sent to prison in March 1954 for having conspired to cheat and defraud the Bath Racecourse Company Limited by falsely representing that a horse running in the Spa Selling Plate on 16th July, 1953, in the name of Francasal was in fact Francasal; and to conspiring to win money from bookmakers by similar false pretences. It was clearly proved, and it was accepted by the defendants, that a horse named Santa Amaro had run as Francasal. The defendants claimed that the switch of horses had been accidental, but the prosecution succeeded in convincing the second jury that the change of horses had been deliberate, and that if it had come off the four men would have stood to win £60,000.

The strangest aspect of the " Francasal " case is not that the greatest racecourse swindle of the century came unstuck but that it was expected to succeed. As a calculated risk the swindle seems to have had no more than an outsider's chance. Francasal's 10 to 1 win just after a break in the bookmaker's telephone line to the course was bound to cause suspicion.

Francasal was entered for the two o'clock race at Bath on 16th July. At the start of the betting odds of 20 to 1 were laid against Francasal by bookmakers on the course. At 1.30 p.m., the " blower," a private telephone line to the racecourse from an office in London used by bookmakers to pass bets to those on the course, went dead. Almost simultaneously, bookmakers throughout the country were inundated with large bets on Francasal. Quickly realizing that it was " live money " (i.e. bets from people in the know, not from " mugs ") the book-

makers tried to get through to the course to lay it off. If they
had been able to do this, the large amount of money invested
would have brought the starting price odds on Francasal down
to something near even money. Francasal would have been a
short-priced favourite. The odds offered by bookmakers are
based on the amount of money invested on a horse. As it was,
however, the horse started at 10 to 1. Sufficient money had
been put on at the course to bring the odds down from 20 to 1.
This suggests that there were others " in the know " apart from
the original conspirators. These others were probably the gang
who cut the telephone wire. In reaping their small reward they
spoilt the big coup.

The sudden disconnection of the " blower " service alone
would have been enough to create suspicion about Francasal's
10 to 1 win, but, apart from the fortuitous break in the wire,
the Stewards of the Jockey Club had apparently other suspicions of the *bona fides* of Francasal. From the time when
two unknown French horses had been landed in England it
was suspected that a switch might be attempted, especially
when only one of them was sent to a trainer and all trace of
the other was lost.

The arrangements by which the horses were switched are
discussed later. The defendants claimed that the change of
horses was accidental. No connection has been established between the horse switch and the break in the telephone wire.
Evidence relating to the cutting of the wire was not allowed
to be given at the trial of the four men who were found guilty
only of intentionally running one horse in the name of the
other.

Although Santa Amaro was a far better horse than Francasal, it is by no means certain that the gang gained anything
by the switch of horses. Two London bookmakers, giving
evidence at the trial, gave their opinion that as both horses
were unknown in England, it would have made no difference
to the odds which horse had run. The odds offered against
Santa Amaro at the start of the betting might have been even
longer than those on Francasal. If the money invested had
reached the course, the starting price on Santa Amaro would

have been no shorter than that of Francasal. It seems therefore that in switching horses the gang were trying to be too clever, but the suspicions roused by the sudden cut in the telephone service coupled with the success of an unknown horse were certain to lead to enquiry, and to the repudiation of the bets.

At the trials the prosecution set out to prove that (*a*) the horse switch was deliberate, and that (*b*) with the knowledge that a horse of far better form than Francasal was running large sums of money were invested. Five men were accused; one (William Rook) was acquitted. The other four were found guilty and sentenced. Harry George Kateley (three years), William Maurice Williams (two years), Gomer Charles (two years) and Victor Colquhoun Dill (nine months). The two trials lasted for forty days. One hundred and sixty witnesses were heard. Costs are estimated at £50,000. The jury at the second trial were shadowed by detectives each day from the time they left the court to the time they arrived back next morning. At the end of each day's proceedings they were warned by the judge not to allow anyone to discuss the case with them. When the case finished, one of the shadowing detectives invited the jurymen to join them in a social gathering. " We feel," he said, " that we know you so well, though we've never really met."

First, the horse switch.

Santa Amaro, having been purchased by Maurice Williams in France for £2,000, was brought to England on 12th May. It was collected at Folkestone by a transport contractor named Zigmund Webster, who delivered it to Layton's farm at Binfield. Six days later the horse was taken to Worcester to run in a private gallop against a horse of known form named Sun Suit which had been purchased for the purpose of the secret trial. Santa Amaro won easily. It was returned to France on 29th May and Sun Suit was sold.

Another horse named Francasal was bought in France for £820 for Maurice Williams. Francasal was entered for the Spa Selling Plate at Bath on 16th July and Santa Amaro was entered for the same race and for a race at Newmarket on the same day.

It has been clearly proved that the horse that won at Bath in the name of Francasal was in reality Santa Amaro. When the two horses were found by the police on 19th July, only Santa Amaro was wearing racing plates and the shoes contained traces of mud that came from Bath racecourse. Although the two horses looked alike they were in fact slightly different. Santa Amaro had two white tufts on its shoulders and there was a difference of one inch in height.

The two horses arrived from France on 12th July in the care of an English trainer resident in France named John Swaine. Webster collected both horses at Folkestone, taking one to Layton's farm at Binfield, Berkshire, and the other to his own farm at Sonning Common, where he put it in Box I. He did not know the names of the two horses. Both Kateley and Dill were present during these moves.

On the day following Webster was ordered to take the horse from Layton's farm to Bailey's training stables at Epsom. Collecting it before breakfast, he brought it to his own place where he put it in Box II. After breakfast he took a horse to Epsom. From there it went to Bath as Francasal. This was the horse that won, therefore it was Santa Amaro. Webster says that he made a mistake in which horse he took but he could only have made a mistake *if the horse he had brought from Layton's was Francasal*. If the horse he brought from Layton's was Santa Amaro, he took the *same* horse to Epsom.

According to Swaine the horse left at Layton's was Francasal. In his evidence he said he went with Santa Amaro and Francasal to the Layton's farm where he unloaded Francasal and put the horse into a stable. Santa Amaro was still in the horse box, which was then driven off. This was on Sunday, 12th July, and as he had been told earlier that it was planned to race Francasal at Bath on 16th July he advised Kateley, who was present at the farm, that Francasal should be immediately placed in the hands of a trainer. Santa Amaro had not had too good a crossing from France and he advised that the horse should be rested for a few days.

While Mr. Layton was unable to say which horse had been

THE TWO BATH RACEHORSES
On the left, SANTA AMARO; on the right, FRANCASAL

left at his farm, his wife and daughter did not think that the horse left there on 12th July was the same horse as had been left there on 12th May (which was Santa Amaro). According to them Mr. Layton had thought the same.

Thus, according to this evidence, Francasal having been left at Layton's was brought to Sonning where the mix-up occurred by accident. This was what the defendants claimed did take place, but it was not the view taken by the jury.

Having delivered, as he thought, Francasal to Epsom, Webster was told to send Santa Amaro to Newmarket on 16th July. The van driver was instructed to telephone a London number from Stevenage, about half-way, at 1 p.m. When he did so he was instructed to take the horse back to Sonning. Someone at Stevenage sent a telegram in the name of Maurice Williams to Newmarket stating that Santa Amaro would not run as the horse box had broken down and that it could not arrive in time. But no breakdown had occurred, and by then it would have been too late for the horse to have arrived at Newmarket for the two-thirty race in which it was entered. That afternoon the real Santa Amaro, running as Francasal, won at Bath.

After suspicions had been aroused, the police were instructed to trace the two horses. It was vital that they should be found before they could be disposed of. They were discovered on 19th July. The real Francasal was found at Webster's stable. It had not been shod with racing plates and so could not have been the horse which ran at Bath. It was then discovered that another horse had been stabled with Francasal for a few hours before being moved. This horse, later identified as Santa Amaro, was found on a farm at Padworth, eighteen miles away, wearing racing plates.

Mr. Williams, the registered owner of the two horses, was traced with some difficulty. The name " Williams " had been used by a number of people in connection with the horses. Dill had arranged for the horses to come to England and Kateley had taken part in the transaction. The police were certain that the horse originally left at Binfield was Santa Amaro. It had, according to their view, been sent to Bath as Francasal deliberately. Webster was wrong in thinking that he had made a mistake.

Second, the telephone cable.

Examination showed that the private telephone line to the course at Bath had been deliberately severed with a blowlamp. It was thought at first that it might have been cut by lightning. A roadsweeper, Bert Glass, told the police that he had seen the cable cut. While he was working in Weston Lane, Bath, he saw a lorry draw up. Two men carrying a ladder placed it against the hawser carrying the cable. A man in overalls climbed the ladder and applied the flame of an acetylene burner to the cable. Another man strolled over to Glass and told him, " We've been having a lot of trouble with this cable. It's the damp getting through a flaw in the lead covering. We'll have to weld it to keep the rain out." The men then drove away but Glass noticed the registration number of the van.

In September a thirty-one-year-old rag and scrap metal dealer of Rhondda, Leonard Phillips, was sent to prison for three months for being concerned in cutting the cable. He said: " If I had known it was going to turn out like this I would not have done the job. It was chicken-feed compared to what they got and I know what I am talking about. A fellow I know as Bill came to see me. He offered me thirty-five nicker to do a job—' an easy,' he said. It had to be done by one-thirty dead on that Thursday."

Thirdly, the betting.

It was proved to the satisfaction of the second jury that four of the five defendants had conspired to run one horse in the name of the other in order to make a substantial sum by betting. The four convicted were : George Kateley, a bookmaker, called by the judge the " head and brain of the conspiracy "; Maurice Williams, the registered owner of the two horses, described by the judge as " the life-long friend of Kateley and with him the originator of this conspiracy "; Gomer Charles, a Cardiff bookmaker, said by the judge to have provided the money to buy the second horse; and Victor Colquhoun Dill, Old Etonian and ex-colonel, who was " brought into the conspiracy by Kateley and Williams to give it an atmosphere of respectability." The other defendant, William Rook, was acquitted. He had acted in good faith in giving Williams an introduction to his trainer and in arranging for his own jockey to ride " Francasal."

On 7th March Kateley and Dill, calling themselves Williams and Colquhoun, took over the bookmaking business of J. Davidson & Co., at Hampstead. The business was in reality owned by Maurice Williams. Dill acted as manager. Credit arrangements were made with bookmakers all over the country on references supplied by Gomer Charles. On the day of the race Dill was instructed by Williams to place bets on Francasal to the extent of £3,500. He spread this amongst some thirty bookmakers. Some of these when they found that they could not get through to the course tried unsuccessfully to contact Davidsons by telephone. After the race bookmakers were instructed to withhold payment on bets on Francasal.

The defendants claimed that they had planned a betting coup and that Francasal had been entered at Bath for that purpose. The mistake in horses had happened accidentally. Williams and Kateley did not dispute that Santa Amaro had run as Francasal. The other three defendants went further and said that even if the switch had been deliberate they knew nothing about it. The jury had to decide whether the switch was deliberate, or whether it had happened accidentally, and if there had been a common design that one horse should run as another.

In finding that the switch of horses had been deliberate, the jury decided that the horse left at Layton's farm was Santa Amaro and that the change was not due to a mistake made by Webster. He had been ordered to take the horse from Layton's. This was the horse it was intended to run at Bath. It was supposed to be Francasal, but it must have been Santa Amaro. By finding Williams, Kateley, Charles and Dill guilty, the jury decided that they must have known that Santa Amaro was the horse left at Layton's, and that they had caused it to be taken to Epsom and to Bath as Francasal.

Two particular actions of the gang pointed to their guilt. Having taken a great deal of trouble to test Santa Amaro, whose form they knew, why did they run Francasal, whose form they did not know, at Bath? They invested some £6,000 on a horse for a betting coup whose form was not only unknown to them, but which was a far inferior horse to the one they owned but did not run. They then pretended that the other horse could not fulfil its engagement at Newmarket because of a breakdown in transport.

Then, assuming that the switch of horses was a mistake and that the defendants had set out to do no more than stage a legitimate betting coup with an unknown horse, the break on the blower service which occurred at the exact moment when their bets were being laid increased their potential return from £6,000 to £60,000.

While the most telling point in favour of the innocence of the accused lay in the apparent pointlessness of the switch of horses, it is clear that they would not have risked the same large sum of money on Francasal as they were willing to do on Santa Amaro. Why they did not run Santa Amaro in the first place is inexplicable. They would then have made a considerable sum without risk. The severance of the blower service (whoever did it) vastly increased their profits but it inevitably led to suspicion, to enquiry and to the withholding of winning bets, so much so that it is more than possible that it was the work of others who had heard a whisper of the betting coup.

The jury took four-and-a-half hours to arrive at their verdict, finding four of the defendants guilty. Of those convicted, it was shown that Kateley had been imprisoned for nine months in 1932 for receiving a stolen car. Williams had two minor convictions. Charles had been warned off all racecourses by the Jockey Club after a previous case in which he had given evidence in a horse switching case. These men were the principals. Dill had only been an employee. He had a distinguished military career and had also been on the stage.

The "Francasal" switch will go down in racing history as a carefully planned but rather stupid attempt to take the bookmakers' money. The plotters made elementary mistakes; their failure to have the real Francasal shod with English racing plates gave the game away. It failed because unnecessary complications were introduced into the plot. As an example of roguery it does not compare with the most audacious racing swindle of all—the race meeting that never took place. This was in 1909. While the gang who engineered this scheme robbed the bookmakers for a large sum, they missed making considerably more through one unfortunate oversight. Their identity has never been established.

Late in July a man calling himself Mr. Martin called to see the editor of *The Sportsman*. Mr. Martin represented the Trodmore Hunt Club of Cornwall. He asked the editor whether he would kindly publish the club's race card for August Bank Holiday. The editor was quite willing but, owing to the number of race meetings organized for that day, he could not send a reporter. That did not matter, said Mr. Martin. The club would telegraph winners and starting prices after each race.

On August Bank Holiday *The Sportsman* printed the Trodmore card and subsequently the results. During the afternoon a number of men placed bets with ready-money bookmakers. The coup was carefully planned. They picked only one winner, ignoring the other races. The horse, Reaper, conveniently "won" at 5 to 1, but when they came to collect their winnings a snag arose. While many bookmakers paid out on the results printed in *The Sportsman*, others relied on the *Sporting Life*, in which no mention of the Trodmore race meeting had been printed. The resourceful Mr. Martin found a way to overcome this; he arranged for the *Sporting Life* to print the results already published by *The Sportsman*. In doing so, however, by a printer's error the odds were given as 5 to 2.

When bookmakers started making enquiries, no such place as Trodmore was found to exist. By that time the organizers of the race meeting that never took place had vanished.

IX

THE TOWPATH MURDERS

AT 8.15 a.m. on 1st June, 1953, the body of a young girl was found floating face downwards in the river near Richmond, Surrey. After the police had been notified, detectives made a detailed examination of the towpath. About a mile away from where the body was found they discovered a splotch of blood. From it drag marks led to the river. Nearby were a pair of girl's shoes. Then they found another patch of blood-stained grass and another pair of shoes indicating that two girls had been attacked. When the body had been identified as that of sixteen-year-old Barbara Songhurst, it was learned that her friend, eighteen-year-old Christine Reed, was also missing. The second pair of shoes were identified as hers. Next day, her bicycle was dragged from the river. Her body was discovered on 6th June.

Both girls had been savagely attacked. Both had been sexually assaulted. Both had been virgins. Barbara had been assaulted before death, but it was not possible to say in Christine's case whether she had been assaulted before or after death.

The nature of their wounds had a direct bearing on the identification of their assailant. Barbara had a deep semi-circular wound on the left cheek, which was fractured. This was consistent with a blow from a sharp axe-blade. On her scalp were crushing lacerations and in the back of the chest were three stab wounds, which had been inflicted with a sharp instrument, possibly a double-edged stiletto type knife, approximately an inch wide at its widest part and at least four inches long. The blows had been dealt with such force that the killer had to wrench the knife free each time he struck. Abrasions on

ALFRED WHITEWAY WITH HIS WIFE AND CHILD

the body showed that the blows had been inflicted when the girl was lying on the grass.

Christine's body had four crushing lacerations of the scalp, made by a blunt instrument similar to the one used to attack Barbara. Christine had six stab wounds and through one of them four separate thrusts had been made. The knife must have been raised and lowered three times in the wound after it had originally been made. On her forearm were protective wounds indicating that she had attempted to push her assailant away.

The murderer had used an axe and a knife. Investigation showed that in 1951 and 1952, 1,000 daggers, similar to the murder weapon, were sold in Kingston and Richmond. Any one of these might have been the murder weapon.

The two girls had spent the Sunday at the river bank camp of three youths. They had left and returned, finally cycling away along the towpath about 11 p.m. This, coupled with information about the river tides, approximated the time of the murder at about 11.30 p.m. A man named Nixon, who was sitting with his girl friend a few feet from the river, heard the girls cycle past about 11.30 p.m. The police commenced looking for a powerful man, who owned an axe and a stiletto, and who could not account for his movements between 11 p.m. and midnight on the night of 31st May. His clothes would probably be blood-stained.

Twelve days after the murder of the two girls, on 12th June, a middle-aged lady, who was exercising her dogs in Windsor Great Park, was attacked by a man. Early in July this lady, Mrs. Birch, told the court how this man, Alfred Charles Whiteway, had dismounted from his bicycle and asked her the way to the " Holly Tree." As she turned to point the way she felt a hand on her mouth. His other hand caught her throat. She cried out but he put his forearm under her chin, pressing hard. He told her, " Keep quiet. Just come into the bushes. I won't hurt you, I promise." She managed to break away and call " Help." He again caught her round the throat, so that she could hardly breathe, warning her, " I told you to be quiet. It's too late now, lady."

Mrs. Birch managed to say, " I'm fifty-six and I've just got over a serious operation." Whiteway replied, " Give us a little kiss," and she told him, " I will give you my purse. I'll give you everything I have with me." Taking it, he ordered her not to tell anyone because he had a knife and knew how to throw it, and he rode away on his bicycle. When he was charged Whiteway said, " I am the person who attacked the old woman. I want to get it squared up."

Five days after this lady had been attacked, on 17th June, two police officers saw a man on Oxshott Common acting suspiciously. Three weeks previously, on 24th May, a fourteen-year-old girl had been assaulted there by a cyclist wearing a blue shirt. The policemen invited the man to accompany them to the station. He sat by himself at the back of the car. After being questioned at the police station he was allowed to go. On the following morning another police driver found an axe under the driver's seat. He, P.C. Cosh, took the axe home and used it to chop firewood. It was returned to the police station on 15th July as a result of something said by Whiteway who was by that time in custody on other charges. Asked about his axe he said, " Kingston police have got it. They found it in the police car." He explained that he had watched the policeman through the driving mirror and that he had taken the chopper from inside his leather jacket, put it on the floor and slid it under the driving seat with his foot. Poor Cosh was severely censured for his bit of scrounging but he could hardly have realized the significance of his " find."

On 28th June Whiteway was arrested for his attack on Mrs. Birch, who had picked him out in an identity parade. In July he was charged both with assaulting her and with the attack on the young girl on Oxshott Common on 24th May. The police suspected that they had also got the " Towpath Murderer " for, on 29th June, Whiteway was asked to account for his movements on the night of 31st May. He made a statement in which he said that owing to housing difficulties his wife and year-old daughter lived with her parents at Kingston, while he lived with his parents at Teddington. He went on : " I see my wife every night, sometimes for the whole evening. I generally go about seven-thirty and stay until about ten-thirty or eleven-thirty. We have discussed the Teddington murders and have worked it out that we were together that night. We did this because we read in the papers that everybody had to make sure where they were."

On Sunday, 31st May, he cycled to his wife's home and they had taken their child to Canbury Gardens nearby. After a quarrel he left his wife and cycled through Richmond Park. He returned to Canbury Gardens about 10.30 p.m.

" I saw my wife there with our child and we stayed together until eleven-thirty or just before that. We walked to her home and I had a cup of tea on the doorstep. I left her and went home by way of Kingston Bridge and Sandy Lane, Teddington; I did not stop anywhere, but went straight home. I got in at about five to twelve and saw my uncle who asked me to put the clock on. I put it on to twelve-fifteen. I did not go near the towpath on 31st May. The last time I had a knife was about six weeks ago. I used to take it to the park and throw it at the trees. I know the Songhurst family, as they used to live in our district. I knew Barbara when she was about six, but I have not seen her since. I did not know Christine Reed."

Thus, according to Whiteway, he had an alibi, but he admitted that he knew Barbara Songhurst. The police now knew, too, that he was an attacker of women, and that he had a criminal record.

At 12.10 p.m., on 1st July, Superintendent Hannam told Whiteway that he was making enquiries about the murder of the two girls. After he had been cautioned, Whiteway said: " I guessed this would come before long. It looks like me, I grant you, but when that job was done I was with my wife at her home." Asked if he knew where the girls were murdered, he was alleged to have replied: " I am going to keep my mouth shut, or you will pin it on me. I had nothing to do with the girls. . . . You are wasting your time. The bloke that did that job is mad." But his right shoe, taken from him, showed a strong reaction to blood!

Seven days later, on 8th July, he made another statement,

in which he said :

"I first met my wife about two years ago. I saw her in Bushy Park with another girl and took a fancy to her. I followed her to her home and spoke to her, and she agreed to meet me later. I wanted to get married to her, but she was a bit young and we knew her mother would not agree. I had once been friendly with a girl named June who is now married to Daniel Songhurst. I knew Barbara and all the family. My wife's mother has never been very friendly to me. We got married in 1952. I usually saw my wife every evening. I have always been very fond of knives. I have only one at the present time, a sheath knife."

He told how in May he had been practising knife throwing at a tree near the river, when he was joined by another man, Mr. Tarp. His big "gurkha" knife had fallen into the water. He went on :

"I can also throw a chopper at trees; in fact I throw it better than I do knives. Sometimes, I take my mother's chopper in my saddlebag when I go throwing. I remember quite clearly taking the chopper back in my saddlebag and putting it in a cupboard. So far as I know it is still in the house. I looked for it once in the cupboard and could not find it. I am quite certain I did not go up the towpath that night. I know nothing about the murders of Barbara Songhurst or Christine Reed. I did not know Christine Reed, and so far as I know I have never seen her."

On 1st July, Whiteway told the police how he had hidden the axe in the police car.

Meanwhile, he was charged at Chertsey with the attack on the young girl at Oxshott on 24th May. She had, she told the court, been walking with her dog on Oxshott Common. As she left the main road and went down a quiet lane towards Black Pond she heard a cyclist behind her. She turned round and saw it was Whiteway.

She called her dog so that he would not be run down and felt a blow on the back of her head. She was pushed into some bushes and she saw Whiteway holding an axe. As he dragged her along, he told her it would be all right. She tried to keep him talking in the hope that someone would come along. He told her to remove certain clothing, but she said, " No." He then tried to pull her blouse off. She tried to push him off and she felt his gloved hands round her throat. She could not breathe and he managed to remove some of her clothing and to commit an offence. Then he again put his hands round her throat. She did not scream out because it was a lonely spot and she thought he would strangle her.

She was able to get up and dress, although she felt dizzy when she raised her head. Whiteway went to the path to see if anyone was coming. He came back, picked up his cycle and rode away. She ran to the path where she met an elderly man who took her to hospital. The girl added that Whiteway asked her age before he assaulted her and she told him she was fourteen.

When Whiteway was told, on 1st July, that the police were making enquiries about the assault on this girl, he had replied :

" Do I have to tell you? " he said. " It has been worrying me. I did assault her. She told me she was fourteen. I don't know what made me do it. I was out on my bicycle, a blue one, just riding around. I noticed her walking along the road. She had a dog with her. She went up a footpath into the woods and I followed her in. I had a wood chopper in my saddlebag. I had made up my mind to seduce her and had got the chopper out of my saddlebag. I caught up with her on the footpath and I hit her on the head with the back end of the chopper. She was half stunned and I half carried her into the bushes. I seduced her. She did not struggle. I think she was frightened to death."

Whiteway said that he was sorry for what he had done and that he could not think why he had done it.

On 30th July Whiteway was again questioned about the towpath murders. He was interviewed in Brixton prison where he was on remand for the two cases of assault. He was shown the axe that had been found in the police car and the Kukri knife that had been recovered from the river. In respect to the axe, he said : " Blimey, that's it. It's been buggered about. It was bloody sharp when I had it. I sharpened it with the file." Shown the knife, he said, " That's it, you got it out of the water, didn't you ? " He asked : " Were you kidding about the blood on my shoe? " When he was told that heavy blood-stains had been found on one of his shoes he turned pale. Trembling, he said, " You know bloody well it was me. I did not mean to kill 'em. I never wanted to hurt anyone." He then said :

" It's all up. You know bloody well I done it, eh? That shoe buggered me. What a bloody mess. I'm mental. Me head must be wrong. I must have a bloody woman, I can't stop myself. I'm not a bloody murderer. Block 'em yes, every time, but not kill 'em. I only see one girl, she came round the tree where I was stood and I bashed her no harder than the other kid and she was down like a log. Then the other screamed out down by the lock. Never saw her till then I didn't. I nipped over and shut her up. Two of 'em, and then I tumbled the other knew me. If it hadn't been for that it wouldn't have happened. Put that bloody chopper away, it haunts yer. What more do they want to know? I blocked 'em both, that is what I can't stop. Why don't the doctors do something? It will be mental, won't it? It must be. I cannot stop it. Once yer tell you sods a bloody lie, buggered for ever. Give us it, I'll sign it."

Told that the murder dagger had not been found, he said, " So you have done it on me. I shall say it is all lies like the blood. You can tear the last one up—I did not give it." He asked the police if they were kidding about the blood on his shoe.

At his trial at the Old Bailey in October 1953 for the murder of Barbara Songhurst, Whiteway denied that he had made this confession. He accused the police officers of fabri-cating it. He stood on his alibi but it could not stand up under scrutiny and the prosecution showed that his axe was one of the murder weapons. Whiteway had also owned a knife similar to that used to kill the two girls, but this knife, the other " murder weapon," was never found. He was tried be-fore Mr. Justice Hilbery.   Mr. Christmas Humphreys prosecuted and Mr. Peter Rawlinson, Q.C., appeared for the defence.

Presenting the case to the jury, Mr. Christmas Humphreys pointed out that it was no part of the case for the Crown to prove motive. Barbara may have recognized her assailant and he had then killed her to silence her. " Such an axe as caused the injuries to these two girls was not only found in possession of the accused, but was found in circumstances in which it was obvious that he was concealing it," said Mr. Humphreys, and a long-bladed knife had been seen in Whiteway's possession a few days before.

The wretched P.C. Cosh told how he had found the axe and had taken it home. He was asked : " Why did you put it away in your locker and not report it? "—" The practice among drivers is that anything found in the car is claimed by the driver finding it." Judge : " You are not suggesting that if a man leaves a jemmy in a car the officer claims that? "— " No, sir."

Roy Tarp, a schoolmaster, said that one Sunday morning about a month before the murder he saw a man throwing a knife at a tree. He identified this man as Whiteway and he recognized the Gurkha knife exhibited at court. The man was also, he said, throwing an axe similar to the one produced in court. Whiteway had thrown a smaller knife as well. Mr. Tarp tried a throw with the large knife and it went into the water. Whiteway failed to find it but it was afterwards recovered by the police. Another man identified this knife as the one he had sold to Whiteway.

Whiteway's sister was handed the axe and she was asked : " Can you tell me whether you have ever had an axe like that at home? " She looked at the axe for about thirty seconds and amidst dead silence replied : " We did have one like this, sir." She said it was normally kept in a cupboard near the back-door and she used it to chop firewood. She missed it, five or six weeks before the police came to see her. Asked, " Have you ever seen your brother with a knife? " she replied, " Yes, sir. A sheath knife." " Can you remember when you last saw him with it? "—" No, sir."

The youths with whom Barbara and Christine had spent the Sunday had also possessed knives, but a pathologist, Dr.

Arthur Mann, said that their knives could not have caused the wounds. The defence did not suggest that these young men had murdered the girls.

The next exhibit was Whiteway's shoe. "On the right shoe," said Dr. Nickolls, head of the Forensic Laboratory at Scotland Yard, "I found there was a strong reaction for blood round the sewing near the lace tags, and also round the outside edge of the junction of the sole and the upper, and also on the inside edge. I took the shoe to pieces and in the dust which was round the stitching holding the upper to the sole, I identified the presence of human blood. The type of reaction obtained was similar to that found if the shoes had been extensively blood-stained and subsequently been washed or rubbed in very wet grass. I found no blood on the left shoe." A pathologist, Dr. David Haller, called for the defence, handed the shoe, said that the blood gave a positive reaction which was only possible with human blood. The judge: "Dr. Nickolls said it was human blood between the sole and the upper. You cannot differ from that?"—"No, my lord."

Mrs. Nelly Whiteway, eighteen-year-old wife of the accused, said that they were married in February, 1952. They had two children. After living for a short while in furnished rooms she had returned to the house of her mother who did not get on well with her husband. She used to meet him when he finished work. Asked by the defence: "On 31st May what time did you see your husband?" She replied, "About four-thirty in the afternoon." She explained that they had quarrelled and that she had gone home. Later, she went out again with the baby and met him in Canbury Gardens. This, she said, was about ten o'clock.

Questioned further, she made the following replies: "How long did you remain talking to him?"—"About one hour." "Then you left together, you pushing the pram and he wheeling his bicycle?"—"Yes." Mrs. Whiteway said that they went to her home and she made tea. Her husband did not go into the house but stood on the porch drinking tea. He probably had two cups of tea. Mr. Rawlinson: "Then what happened?"—"He asked me to look at the clock to see what the time was." Mr. Rawlinson: " It was getting late and he asked you to look at the clock? "—" Yes, sir." " Were you surprised that he asked you to look at the clock? "—" No, sir." " What time was it? "—" Eleven-thirty." " Did you tell him? "—" I did." Mrs. Whiteway said her husband kissed her good-night and left for his home. She did not see which way he went with his bicycle.

To the questions of prosecuting counsel, Mrs. Whiteway agreed that it was very difficult to remember the time of her husband's movements on 31st May. There were, it was pointed out, discrepancies between times given in her statement to the police and her evidence in court. She said: " I must have got mixed up. I made the statement to the police on what we used to do every Sunday." Mr. Humphreys: " Would it be true to say you don't remember and you did not remember then what you did on 31st May? "—" No."

Whiteway's alibi was obviously a shaky one. His uncle, Mr. Charles Langston, said he remembered his nephew coming home that night at about 11.30 p.m. by a clock which was ten to fifteen minutes slow.

Before Whiteway's confession was read, the judge overruled a submission by the defence that the statements taken from him were inadmissible. Superintendent Hannam denied that he had manufactured Whiteway's alleged statement. The superintendent also denied that at the interview he called Whiteway " Alf." Mr. Rawlinson: " Did you say to him, ' How is our stubborn Mr. Alf? '." Superintendent Hannam: " No, sir." " And did he reply: ' As stubborn as ever '? "— " No, sir." " I suggest that Exhibit 24 (the confession) is a statement manufactured by you? "—" That is absolutely un-true." " I suggest no such words were ever used by Whiteway on 30th July or at any other time? "—" If you are now re-ferring to Exhibit 24, my answer is that they are his own words from his own lips." " I repeat the suggestion that that state-ment was invented by you? "—" I repeat it is a shocking sug-gestion and I am pleased to deny it." The prosecution asked the police officer: " Was it obvious that this was the confession of a murderer? "—" It was." " And you took care when you

L 2

took it down? "—" I did."

In the witness-box, Whiteway said that on Sunday, 31st May, the day of the murders, he met his wife at Canbury Gardens. She had the baby in the pram. Later, he took them home, arriving about 11.30 p.m. "I stayed about ten minutes," said Whiteway, "I had a cup of tea made by my wife and drank it on the doorstep. I did not go in." When he left he cycled home over Kingston Bridge and along Sandy Lane. The time on the clock of a department store which he passed showed eleven-thirty-five. When he reached home his uncle, who slept in the same room, was awake and asked him to put on the clock to twelve-fifteen as it lost twenty minutes overnight. It was pointing to eleven-fifty. Whiteway agreed that he hid an axe in a police car when he was taken to Kingston police station on 17th June.

In answers to his own counsel he told how he had been throwing knives at a tree with Mr. Tarp. His Kukri knife was lost in a pool of water. He was asked: " Did you lose any more knives while Tarp was out of your sight? "—" Yes, the sheath knife. I missed the tree when I was throwing from about forty feet." Answering the judge, Whiteway said he saw the knife fall into some bushes. He searched for it but could not find it. Counsel: " Having lost two of the knives, what did you do? " —" I packed up." Whiteway also described how on 17th June he was taken to Kingston police station in a police car and was seen for two or three minutes. Counsel: " Did you leave your axe in that car? "—" Yes." " Did you hide it? " —" Yes, underneath the front seat." " Was that in connection with another offence? "—" It was."

Whiteway, answering Mr. Rawlinson in re-examination, said he used to see Barbara Songhurst when they lived in the same road up till 1945, but he could not remember what she looked like.

Mr. Rawlinson: " Have you ever said to Superintendent Hannam that you left your wife's house before eleven-thirty? " —" No." " Have you ever said you arrived home after twelve o'clock that night?"—" No."

Whiteway said he had not sent the clothes that he was wearing that night to be cleaned. Mr. Rawlinson: " In the final statement did you say, ' Put that bloody chopper away, it haunts yer ' ? "—" No, sir, I did not." " Does that chopper haunt you? "—" No, sir."

Whiteway denied that he had made the confession attributed to him. The statement was handed to him, defence counsel asking: " First of all, is it true? " Whiteway replied: " No." " Did you say anything like that to Superintendent Hannam? "—" No, sir. Nothing at all." " Was anything like that read over to you by Superintendent Hannam? "—" No, sir." " Was any statement read over to you at that interview at all ? "—" No, sir."

Mr. Christmas Humphreys, for the prosecution, asked Whiteway if he carried an axe about in his bicycle saddlebag. Whiteway replied: " Yes." " Had you the axe with you on 31st May?"—" No, sir." " It was sharp before 17th June?"—" Fairly sharp." " More than that, wasn't it very sharp?"—" No."

Mr. Humphreys: " Now we will come to your shoes. You have heard the evidence that your shoes had a considerable quantity of blood on them? "—" Yes." " And some of it was human blood? "—" Yes." " Where did it come from? "—" I do not know." Whiteway said that he had cut himself when he was employed at Decca's some three weeks before 31st May. The blood might have come from that. " Are you suggesting the blood on the shoes might have come from the cut? "—" No." " The news that blood had been found on your shoes was a great shock to you? "—" It was in a way, yes." " Such a shock that you began to say what you had not said before? "—" No." " You remember on 30th July, after you had made the statement, suddenly shaking when Superintendent Hannam mentioned about the blood on your shoes? "—" Yes." " And you turned very pale and were trembling? "—" No." " That is untrue? "—" Yes." " You said," continued Mr. Humphreys, " You know bloody well it was me who done it? "—" I didn't," replied Whiteway.

Coming to his alleged statement, he was asked : " You agree that if you made that statement it is a confession of murder, isn't it? "—" It is." " You are alleging that these two officers forged that statement and committed perjury in putting it before the jury? "—" I am saying I never said it." " Are you saying you were asked to sign a blank piece of paper? "—" No, there was writing on it." " Are you saying that you signed a piece of paper with a caution on it? "—" I only signed one caution." " What did you think you were signing in the middle and half-way down the page? "—" I did not know." " What did you think you were initialling at the bottom of the back page? "—" I don't know." The judge: " Did you initial a blank page? "—" No." " What did you initial? "—" A page with writing on it." Mr. Humphreys: " What did you think you were signing? "—" I did not read it."

Whiteway was questioned by Mr. Humphreys about other statements he is said to have made concerning his movements on Sunday, 31st May. He was handed one alleged statement and asked: " Do you say in that that you left home at 7.45 p.m. and went off to Richmond Park? " Whiteway: " No, sir, eight-forty-five." Mr. Humphreys asked him to look at another alleged statement in which he said he left home at 7.45 p.m. " In two written statements you signed that the time was seven-forty-five? "—" Yes, sir." " Do you remember Mr. Hannam saying that your wife and friends had made a statement that didn't in the least accord with what you said? "— " He only mentioned one statement." " Have you changed your story to accord with what they have said? "—" No, sir." " But to-day you are saying eight-forty-five? "—" Yes." " It makes a difference, doesn't it, when you are covering a period when these two girls were murdered? "—" It does, sir." Mr. Humphreys referred to the interview Whiteway had with Superintendent Hannam on 1st July. He asked him if he remembered saying: " When the job was done I was with my wife," and how he knew that the time was eleven o'clock. Whiteway said that he had read the time in the newspapers.

Mr. Humphreys: " You had a rather distinctive bicycle, easy to be picked out? "—" Yes." " So the following day you went by train to see your wife, a ten-minute bicycle ride away? "— " Yes."

The prosecution sought to call as a witness the young girl who had been raped by Whiteway on Oxshott Common. She was allowed to be sworn but, after arguments had been heard in the absence of the jury, her evidence was disallowed. The fact that a young girl had entered the witness-box may have given the jury an opportunity of guessing what her evidence might have been. The prosecution had hoped to establish a similarity between the attack on her with an axe and the attack on the two girls on the towpath who had also been violently raped after having been rendered unconscious with a blow from an axe.

In his final speech to the jury, defence counsel said : " Negative evidence can be just as important as positive evidence. Nobody knows exactly what happened to those two girls, and nobody knows exactly what happened near this tree. It may be those two girls stayed on with those campers a little longer and did not get to this tree until well after midnight. It may be those bodies did not become bodies until much later— possibly one o'clock—in which case Whiteway was back at home, as he had been since five to twelve. There is going to be the one issue, and you may think perhaps the most vital and important issue—was the confession ever made ? "

Mr. Rawlinson pointed out that if the case rested without " the confession " there most certainly would be an acquittal. " If Whiteway never made that statement as he says he never made it, the only explanation is that that statement was fabricated by somebody, and it is suggested his signature was put upon it by means of a trick."

" We have heard a lot about blood, but there is no evidence of blood on this man's clothes. There were nineteen wounds on Christine Reed and at least seven on Barbara Songhurst, yet there was no blood on this man."

In the final speech for the prosecution, Mr. Christmas Humphreys referred to the accusation that the police had invented Whiteway's confession as " the most tremendous attack ever made in that court." The prosecution, Mr. Humphreys said, were satisfied of Whiteway's guilt even without his confession. " Do you believe," he asked the jury, " that any officer would be so fantastically murderous as to forfeit the whole of his career by plain, wilful forgery and foul murderous perjury against an innocent man, as to write out this statement and fake and fool him into signing it ? " The alleged confession, he declared, was a reconstruction of the crime. It exactly fitted in with the scientific corroboration.

He went on : "Whiteway knew this area very well; he seemed to have been in the habit of carrying an axe in his bicycle saddle-bag; he seemed to have been very interested in other weapons. When Whiteway was made to believe that one of his shoes was blood-stained he had gone pale and had trembled. Could they have clearer evidence? As to his clothing, do not be misled by what might sound attractive. Are you satisfied that the clothing taken from him was what he wore on 31st May other than the shoe? It might have been that in the month he got rid of the clothing or cleaned it. There was no evidence that could amount to an alibi." He referred to the times given by defence witnesses, as " a clumsy attempt to fit their evidence in some coherent way to an alibi."

In his summing-up, the judge referred to the tragic thought of these girls riding along after they left the camp in good spirits, little knowing that this awful death was waiting for them along that towing path. There is no doubt that within a few minutes they were struck down, rendered unconscious and not very long afterwards stabbed to death. The weapon with which the girls had been struck down was just such an axe as Whiteway owned. " Now comes the great question. Who then was it? What sort of person do you think it must have been? He must have been, must he not, a man who had such a weapon as that axe, much sharper than it was when it was recovered after that extraordinary piece of conduct by the officer Cosh. Apparently that man who did this must have had a double-edged knife. You might expect him to be a man who knew that spot very well. Mr. Tarp had said Whiteway had an axe like that and he had also said Whiteway had a knife with a blade five or six inches long, and his recollection was that it was double-edged. It was not until much later that the axe was recovered, and when it was recovered the accused said :

' Blimey, that's it. It's been buggered about. It was sharp when I had it. I sharpened it with a file.' "

Dealing with the accusation made by the defence against the police officers concerning a confession alleged to have been made by Whiteway, the judge said it was impossible to over-state the gravity of this accusation. Of the alleged statement taken by Superintendent Hannam on 30th July, the judge pointed out that Whiteway had said in evidence : " I did not say the paper was blank when I signed it. There was writing on it." " That is a very important thing to remember. If that is so, and if it is a concoction from beginning to end by police officers, when did they concoct it and write it? Is the theory that this imaginative police officer had written this piece already before he went to the interview, taking it with him with a determination first of all to get another statement from the accused so he could fraudulently insert this statement somewhere, and induce the prisoner to sign it without obser-ving what he was signing? Whiteway denies there is a word of truth in the statement. If he did say it, it is a confession, and he is guilty. There is no escaping from that."

The jury of ten men and two women found Whiteway guilty of murder after fifty minutes deliberation. He was condemned to death. It was ordered that the indictment for the murder of Christine Reed and the two other indictments alleging rape and attempted rape against two different women should re-main on file.

In discussing Whiteway's appeal, Lord Goddard said : " This case is one of the most brutal and horrifying that has ever been before this court and any other court for years. It is just as well that the public should know," he went on, " that this man was arrested for attempted rape in Windsor Park on a lady walking out for the afternoon. She managed to pre-vent herself being raped and complained to the police. White-way was arrested and committed for trial. In the course of inquiries that were being made he admitted that he raped a girl of fourteen at Oxshott. This was the conduct of the man who was convicted of the ghastly murder on the towpath."

The great question raised by the Towpath Case is : Would

Whiteway have been convicted if he had not confessed ? Without it there was strong circumstantial evidence against him, evidence that hardly left his guilt in doubt. He was a rapist and an attacker of women, although that could not be shown to the jury; he owned an axe and he had tried to conceal it. He had possessed a long-bladed knife similar to the one used by the murderer. His shoe was blood-stained. He knew the area well and he had been in the vicinity at the time of the crime. His alibi was doubtful, but, above all, he had a motive for murder, for Barbara Songhurst knew him. Having attacked her, it was her life or his liberty. Fear of discovery led Whiteway to murder.

The police knew what sort of man he was; they knew that he was the murderer they were seeking. For the protection of the public it was their duty to persuade him to confess. They were accused of inventing the confession, but consider the public outcry that would have been raised if they had had to let him go and he had then murdered others. No one who reads Whiteway's confession could imagine that a police officer could have invented *such* a statement.

Seldom has the death penalty been more justified than in the case of Whiteway, the twenty-two-year-old labourer who bludgeoned, raped and stabbed Barbara Songhurst and Christine Reed and then flung their bodies in the Thames. Yet the fact that death was the penalty for murder did not deter Whiteway who had previously assaulted women without killing them. Seeing two young girls cycling along the towpath he attacked them. Then one recognized him. She had to die and her friend had to be silenced too.

Once again we find a murderer with a previous criminal career. Apart from his attacks on women, one of which dated back to fifteen months before the murder of the two girls, Whiteway had been at an approved school and in prison for theft. Thus in our selected year out of eight chosen murder cases, six of the murderers have previously been criminals. This suggests, does it not, that there is something wrong with our methods of dealing with criminals? Every criminal who gets away with a light sentence is a potential murderer.

X

A MOTIVELESS MURDER?

●

PATRICIA CURRAN, the nineteen-year-old daughter of a
Northern Ireland judge, was found murdered in a wood
close to her home, Whiteabbey, near Belfast, on 12th November, 1952. Of the thirty-seven stab wounds in her body eight
might have proved fatal. She had apparently been seized from
behind by an assailant who held her with his forearm pressed
tightly round her throat as he slashed savagely at her face with
a razor-sharp pointed instrument. As she sank to the ground
her killer knelt by her side stabbing maniacally at her body.

Her murder appeared to be motiveless. It had not been
committed for gain for her handbag was unopened, its contents intact. A torn undergarment suggested that an attempt
had been made on her virtue. If such an attempt had been
made her assailant had not succeeded in his criminal assault.
Nothing in Miss Curran's life suggested any reason for her
murder. It was at first thought that, as her father was a judge,
the motive might have been revenge, but after enquiry it was
ruled out.

There were few clues: the murder must have occurred between 5.30 p.m. and 5.45 p.m. Her satchel had been *placed*
on the ground which suggested that she may have stopped to
speak to someone she knew. An attempt had been made to
conceal the body. It was thought probable that her assailant's
clothes would have been stained with blood. The police commenced looking for a man who could not account for his movements between 5 p.m. and 6 p.m. They directed particular
attention to men of known sexual abnormality.

Two months elapsed before a man was arrested. The man

then charged with her murder, Iain Hay Gordon, a twenty-one-year-old aircraftman from the nearby R.A.F. camp at Edenmore, had been questioned a number of times after the murder. He admitted knowing Miss Curran slightly, but he claimed to have been in camp when the murder was committed. While the police were not satisfied with his explanation, it was some time before they could break his alibi. At his trial in March, Gordon was found guilty but insane. The jury were satisfied that he did not know at the time that what he was doing was wrong. No reason why he should have killed a chance acquaintance came to light; insanity was the only way in which his act could be accounted for. There was no evidence that Gordon had premeditated her death, but it is not without significance that he left the camp, just after he had returned there, carrying a murderous weapon. He certainly knew very shortly after the murder that his act had been wrong for he made an attempt to conceal the body and he went to considerable lengths to concoct an alibi.

After a number of interviews with the police in which he denied being the murderer, Gordon confessed to Miss Curran's murder. The police were violently criticized by the defence for the manner in which they were supposed to have obtained his confession but, as in the case of Whiteway, they were fully aware that they were dealing with a man who, unless he was apprehended, might murder again! In such cases it is absolutely necessary that the police should place the protection of the public first. The police are waging a " war " against crime. Several cases have occurred where they have had to let a man go free from want of evidence and that man has murdered again.

Patricia Curran, who worked as a secretary in Belfast, left the city by bus for home at 5 p.m. She alighted from the bus at 5.20 p.m. and she was seen to set off in the direction of her home. When she did not arrive it was assumed that she was visiting friends. Later in the evening, when her parents became anxious, the police were called. Her barrister brother, Desmond, who had gone to bed, was told at 1.30 a.m. that his sister had not returned home. He has described how he found the body. " We decided to search the grounds. I went into the shrubbery and searched in a zigzag fashion. I heard my father searching also. I found my sister's body lying beside some bushes on its back. The right arm was stretched out and the right hand and wrist were bent like the neck of a swan. The legs were straight out."

The time of the murder was established with some degree of accuracy. Miss Curran had been seen to leave the bus at 5.20 p.m. Her body was found half-way up the drive to her home, five minutes' walk away. A small boy as he was going up the drive to deliver newspapers heard a factory hooter blow : this went off at 5.45 p.m. As he came back down the drive, he heard a noise which frightened him. He took to his heels and ran.

In company with all the men at the R.A.F. station at Edenmore, Gordon was asked to account for his movements on 12th November between 5 p.m. and 6 p.m. He was interviewed a number of times, but although his story remained consistent it was finally shown to be false in every material particular. His attempts to manufacture an alibi fell to pieces when those with whom he was supposed to have been failed to support it. Two women also came forward to say that they had seen him outside the camp at 5.10 p.m. and 6.10 p.m.

When he was first interviewed on the day following the crime, Gordon volunteered the information that he had met the Curran family some months previously. He said that he had been down at Whiteabbey post office about 4.30 p.m. for the Air Force mail. He had returned to Edenmore and went for tea to the airmen's dining hall, and he was in the dining hall from five o'clock until five-ten and left, accompanied by Corporal Connor. He said that Corporal Connor and he walked towards the billet, that he remained in his billet reading or writing, and then for a time he went to the office in Edenmore in which he worked, and after the N.A.A.F.I. opened he went into it for a cup of tea. The N.A.A.F.I. opened at 6 p.m. He said much the same three days later, adding, " I was in the Central Registry from about 6.30 to 9 p.m. with one visit to the N.A.A.F.I. roughly between 7.30 and 8 p.m. I went to bed between 9.30 and 10 p.m." In reference to the murdered girl, he stated: "I knew very, very little about Patricia, and absolutely nothing about her private life. She struck me as being very intelligent and full of life—the last person anybody would wish to harm. Patricia never talked about what she had been doing during the short time I did see her."

Corporal Connor said that he had been with Gordon up to five o'clock and had had tea with him. Some twenty other men, when asked if they had seen Gordon between 5 p.m. and 6 p.m., made no response. On 29th November the police again interviewed Gordon and told him that they were not satisfied with the explanation he had previously given them. He then repeated his story, adding only that he had changed into civilian clothes on the evening in question. Nothing was then found on these clothes to cause suspicion. Spoken to by the police again on 10th December, he was asked how well he had known Patricia Curran. He replied: "I first met Desmond Curran at the Presbyterian Church and he invited me to his home in the Glen. He introduced me to the family. I was there on about four occasions. I just conversed with her when at her home in the presence of members of the family. I have never been out with her."

Between this interview and the middle of January Gordon was not again questioned by the police. He had, however, a conversation with Desmond Curran on 23rd December which is not without significance. Gordon, who was going on leave to Scotland, telephoned Desmond Curran and they arranged to meet. When they discussed the murder, Gordon said that he had been in camp between 5 p.m. and 6 p.m. Desmond Curran stated during the proceedings at the magistrates court: "I asked him how he thought the crime was committed and he said he thought it had been planned by someone who knew the place well. *He thought the motive was fear of Patricia because she had found out something about someone.* I asked Gordon what he thought about the weapon, and he said revolvers were used now. He wondered what was the advantage of an Italian stiletto. He said he supposed it would go in and out more easily, but thought an English or Irish knife might be used. He said he could not understand why, if Patricia was killed by the fourth blow, twenty other stabs were inflicted. When I asked him how he knew she had been killed by the fourth blow, he replied, ' Wasn't it in the paper? ' "

When they were questioned those with whom Gordon stated he had been with on the evening of 12th November contradicted his story. Corporal Connor reported that Gordon had asked him to say that they had been together after 5 p.m., but he had not seen him after that time. Another aircraftman, William Scott, said that Gordon had asked him, " Will you tell the police inspectors that you saw me on the night of the 12th? " Scott said that he had replied, " I cannot do that as I did not see you." He heard Gordon ask others the same question, and on their refusal, to say, " You lads, being friends of mine, might stick up for me." A counter assistant at the N.A.A.F.I. said that on the morning following the murder Gordon had asked her if she was sure he was in the night before. She told him that she wasn't daft and he went out. Later on he came in to borrow a scrubbing brush.

While Gordon had declared that he had not left the camp at the material time, two women had seen him outside it. The wife of the commanding officer had noticed him going down the road at ten minutes past five and the other had seen him at 6.10 p.m. coming out of the Glen where the body was found. On 23rd January she picked Gordon in an identification parade as the man she had seen on 12th November.

On his return from leave on 13th January Gordon was again questioned by the police. He said, " I started going to the Presbyterian Church in Whiteabbey. About October, I first met Desmond Curran. He spoke to me when I left the church. He told me his name and started discussing religious topics. After some conversation he invited me home for lunch. He introduced me to his father and mother and brother Michael. Patricia was not there. I believe Desmond and I discussed moral rearmament. I used to see him every Sunday and after this first visit I went to the house on three other occasions, each time at Desmond's invitation. It was during the second visit that I met Patricia. She was a nice, quiet girl, but I did not think much about her as I had no interest in her. Desmond was my friend. I had very little conversation with Patricia. I have never been at the Curran house in uniform, as I very seldom go out in uniform. Patricia never expressed any opinion about my friendship with Desmond. . . . I always made an appointment with Desmond when I saw him on Sundays at church. I have never walked up the Glen road without seeing the family. The two evening visits were made towards eight o'clock. I walked up the Glen alone. Patricia was there both evenings. I only saw the Currans' dog in the house. I got to know the dog fairly well. After the evening visits I walked down through the Glen on my own. Desmond did not escort me to the main road. I am not frightened of the dark. I have never walked up the Glen with Patricia."

He continued: "I did not see any of the friends of the family when I visited the Curran house with the exception of Michael's girl friend. There may have been one male friend. Desmond was the only one interested in moral rearmament as far as I know. I had previously asked a clergyman if there was any objection to my seeing Desmond. While I was with him I told him that a person made an immoral advance to me. I told Desmond I had rejected the advance. We spoke about homosexuality. I have no inclination that way, and, as far as I know, neither has Desmond. I continue to be friendly with Desmond still."

Asked about his movements on the evening in question, Gordon said: "I was not worried. Corporal Connor was sitting two or three seats away from me at the time. He came to me and said: 'You say you were with me.' He gave no reason for saying this. He never said why he wanted me to say this, but it might have been because he was on his own at the time. Everybody else was discussing between themselves who they were with. I said to Connor: 'I cannot very well say that.' Another airman, who was standing by, said: 'It won't matter.' I said to the corporal: 'What are you going to say?' He said: 'Say you had your tea with me and walked over with me to the billet.' I was not too happy about it, but I said to

him : ' Are you sure it's all right? ' He reassured me everything would be all right with something like : ' Don't be daft.'
I had serious misgivings about it, but did in fact agree to tell
the R.A.F. police a lying story. It was a lie because I was not
with Connor on the evening of 12th November. I do not remember seeing him at all that day. That is the truth. It was
not for my own ends, but I agreed to say I was with Connor,
though I realized it was a murder investigation. I have no idea
where Corporal Connor was on the afternoon of the murder.
I do not know why he approached me about the alibi. Though
I have discussed the matter with Desmond Curran I have
never told him about Corporal Connor approaching me about
an alibi. I know very little about the Corporal's movements.
I never carried a screwdriver or a penknife in my pocket or
any kind of weapon. I was not in the Glen on the afternoon
of 12th November. I did not murder Patricia Curran." Thus,
not only was Gordon's alibi a lie, but he tried to throw suspicion on an innocent person.

On the following day, Gordon changed his story. He
described how he had left the camp soon after 5 p.m. " I then
walked back alone to Whiteabbey and met Patricia Curran
between the Glen and Whiteabbey post office. She said to me :
' Hello, Iain,' or something like that. I said : ' Hello, Patricia.'
We had a short general discussion. I forget what we talked
about, but she asked me to escort her to her home up the Glen.
I agreed to do so, because it was fairly dark and there was
none of the family at the gate to the Glen.

" It was just about the Glen entrance where she first spoke
to me. We both walked up the Glen together and I think I was
on her left-hand side. After we walked a few yards I either held
her left hand or arm as we walked along. She did not object
and was quite cheerful. We carried on walking up the Glen
until we came to the spot where the street lamps' light does
not reach.

" It was quite dark there, and I said to Patricia : ' Do you
mind if I kiss you,' or words to that effect. We stopped walking and stood on the grass verge on the left-hand side of the
drive. She laid her things on the grass and I think she laid

her hat there as well. Before she did this she was not keen on me giving her a kiss, but consented in the end. I kissed her once or twice to begin with and she did not object. She then asked me to continue escorting her up the drive. I did not do so as I found I could not stop kissing her.

" As I was kissing her I let my hand slip down her body between her coat and her clothes. Her coat was open and my hand may have touched her breast, but I am not sure. She struggled and said : ' Don't you beast ! ' or something like that. I struggled with her and she said to me, ' Let me go or I will tell my father.' I then lost control of myself and Patricia fell down on the grass sobbing. She appeared to have fainted be-cause she went limp. I am a bit hazy about what happened next, but I probably pulled the body of Patricia through the bushes to hide it. I dragged her by her arms or hands, but I cannot remember.

" Even before this happened I do not think I was capable of knowing what I was doing. I was confused at the time and believe I stabbed her once or twice with my service knife. I had been carrying this in my trouser pocket. I am not quite sure what kind of a knife it was. I may have caught her by the throat to stop her from shouting. I may have pushed her scarves against her mouth to stop her shouting. It is all very hazy to me, but I think I was disturbed either by seeing a light or hearing footsteps in the drive. I must have remained hidden and later walked out of the Glen at the gate lodge on the main road. As far as I know I crossed the main road and threw the knife into the sea. I felt that something awful must have hap-pened and quickly walked back to the camp.

" I went to my billet and arrived there at roughly 6.30 p.m. There was no one in the billet at the time, and I saw I had some small patches of Patricia's blood on my flannels. I took a fairly large wooden nail-brush from my kit. I got some water and soap from the ablutions and scrubbed the blood off my flannels. I must have done this but I do not quite remember. As far as I know no person saw me doing it.

" I am very sorry for having killed Patricia Curran : I had no intention whatsoever of killing the girl. It was solely due to a black-out. God knows as well as anybody else that the furthest thing in my mind was to kill the girl, and I ask His forgiveness. I throw myself on the mercy of the law, and I ask you to do your best for me, so that I can make a complete re-start in life. I should like to say how sorry I am for all the dis-tress that I have caused the Curran family. I have felt run down for quite some time, and the black-out may have been the result of over-studying and worry generally. I am also sorry for the distress and worry I have caused my dear father and mother. I ask my parents' forgiveness, and if I am spared I shall redeem my past life."

How this statement was obtained was explained in court by Superintendent Capstick of Scotland Yard. Gordon was told that the police knew that he had been telling lies and he enquired: " Did anyone see me leaving the Glen? " Asked if he would be willing to be put up for identification, he refused, saying, " The Lord and my mother know I can speak the truth and I am going to do so. I am sorry I told you lies about the murder." He then said, " I did it in a black-out."

The police were questioned as to why they had spoken to Gordon about sexual matters. The county inspector replied : " From the very beginning of this investigation I was interested in people who had been convicted or suspected of sexual offences and I was even more interested in persons who had abnormal sexual habits. For that reason I thought it was im-portant to find out as much as possible about people who had these habits who were being interrogated. It was a line of enquiry followed throughout the case with many other people."

When Superintendent Capstick agreed that he had discussed sexual matters with Gordon, defence counsel suggested that these matters were introduced solely for the purpose of putting pressure on the accused man. Superintendent Capstick stated that Gordon had admitted gross indecency and sodomy with certain men.

When Gordon's civilian clothes were examined human blood-stains were found on the grey flannel trousers and in the pocket, where he may have placed the murder weapon. Other blood-stains were found on other articles of clothing.

There was no dispute that Gordon was the murderer of Patricia Curran, but why had he killed her? According to his confession it was in a moment of sexual frenzy.

Iain Hay Gordon was tried for the murder of Patricia Curran before Lord MacDermott, the Lord Chief Justice, between 2nd and 7th March, 1953. The twelve jurymen were not allowed to go home until the trial was concluded. The Attorney-General, Mr. Edmond Warnock, Q.C., appeared for the prosecution and Mr. H. A. McVeigh, Q.C., for the defence. Gordon pleaded guilty, but insane.

Referring to Gordon's early life, Mr. McVeigh described it as " a saga of misery." Evidence would be called, he said, to show that Gordon was not responsible for any crime. At the time he was insane in the legal sense. Gordon wept as counsel told of his early life in Burma, of the trip home by sea after the Japanese invasion, and of the illnesses he suffered. In the R.A.F. he was a lonely sort, continued Mr. McVeigh, the butt of jokes in the camp, always embarrassed and blushing on the slightest occasion. Occasionally he broke into tears. He could not be reprimanded and the ordinary discipline of the camp could not be applied to him. He was a very queer customer, willing and anxious to do his best, but never really doing anything properly.

Gordon's mother gave evidence. She spoke of the hardships Iain had undergone on the evacuation from Burma and on the voyage home to England. " When he grew into his teens," she said, " he became increasingly difficult." He was highly-strung and sensitive and resentful of correction. Questioned, she agreed that she had never seen him do anything cruel. Gordon's father read letters he had received from him after the murder, in one of which he stated :

" Patricia was one of the nicest girls that I ever had the good fortune to know. She was so nice and polite, quiet and helpful, so full of life that she was a perfect joy to know. Patricia Curran was the last person that you would have thought anybody would wish harm."

Gordon went on to say that when he was told of the murder, he just could not believe it. " There must be some mistake, I thought. That kind of thing just does not happen—not on your own doorstep, anyway." He said that Patricia Curran was the last person anyone would wish to kill. He continued:

"There is nothing that I, and many, many others, would not do to see that nice girl restored to life again. But that can never be : we just have a memory, but what a sweet and fragrant memory it is. I want to see the worker of this iniquitous deed brought to justice, not for vengeance's sake, but so that the murderer may be able to pay the penalty for this dastardly, foul crime."

Three days later Gordon wrote again telling his father how he had been interviewed by the police and questioned because he had known the murdered girl, " as far as I am concerned there is nothing to worry about, but I will be relieved when the killer is arrested."

R.A.F. witnesses spoke of Gordon's childish behaviour, his mistakes and his fear of reprimand. He had been called a " clot." Evidence was given of an accident he had had a year previously, in which he had sustained a fractured skull and possibly damage to the brain.

Dr. Arthur Lewis, a consultant psychiatrist of Harley Street, London, gave his opinion that Gordon was suffering from a disease of the mind known as schizophrenia, together with a condition named hypoglycaemia, and from a defect of reason. Dr. Lewis was certain that Gordon did not know what he was doing was wrong. His mind did not register what was taking place. Questioned by the Attorney-General : " Was he not trying to lie himself out of responsibility for this crime," Dr. Lewis replied : " He was, I am satisfied, telling lies, but I think that he did not know fully what had happened. There was a loss of memory and he made certain deductions about the whole matter and viewed the whole of the incidents as though he were a different person looking at something someone else had done."

" He consistently lied to five different policemen? "— " Yes." " And not only did he lie but he tried to get his comrades to lie in support of his alibi? "—" Yes. And I would like to add that in the first instance he lied to me." " He knew that

he was in a fix? "—" I think he did." "And was determined to lie his way out of it if he could ? "—" Yes." Dr.
Lewis also stated : " I am perfectly satisfied that there was
no sexual urge apparent and that he did not have a full sexual
inclination as we know it."

Dr. Mulligan, resident superintendent of St. Luke's Hospital, Northern Ireland, said that in his opinion Gordon, on the
evening of 12th November, had no intention of committing
any crime. Dr. Mulligan did not find anything to indicate that
Gordon was suffering from an attack of hypoglycaemia on the
day of the murder. In his opinion Gordon was not now suffering from the disease of schizophrenia, nor was he on 12th
November.

Lord MacDermott : " From what you have heard in court,
are you in a position to say if Gordon was suffering from disease
of the mind on 12th November? " Dr. Mulligan : " He was a
psychopath. That is a recognized defect of personality." Lord
MacDermott : " Is it recognized as a disease of the mind ? "
Dr. Mulligan : " It is well recognized." Lord MacDermott :
" Are you able to say whether when this man killed Miss
Curran, he then knew what he was doing? "—" He knew what
he was doing when he attempted to strangle her or stifle her
cries." Lord MacDermott : " If he struck her or attempted to
stifle her cries did he know that it was wrong to do that? "—
" He did."

Thus, we have much the same situation as occurred in the
case of Miles Giffard. The jury had to decide whether Gordon
was a schizophrenic or a psychopath. In deciding that he was
insane, they acted, apparently, on the assumption that a murder without a motive must have been the work of a maniac.
They found that Gordon had no intention, and no " malice
aforethought," to murder Miss Curran. That Gordon killed
Patricia Curran was described by his counsel as " inexplicable " and " inconceivable." Strangely enough the prosecution
seems to have thought the same, for we find Mr. Hanna, in
his final words to the jury, saying, " The Crown seeks no victim : the Crown is not moved in this case by any spirit of
vengeance."

The judge pointed out to the jury that they could bring in one of three possible verdicts—guilty, not guilty, or guilty but insane. His Lordship told them that one of the difficulties in cases of that kind was that the word " insane " had a number of different meanings. It may be, he said, that the prisoner is insane now. It may be that he was insane on 12th November, but it does not follow that he should be found guilty but insane. A man could be insane; he could even be in an asylum and yet be responsible for his actions and capable of being found guilty of murder. It had been laid down that the jury ought to be told in all cases that every man must be presumed to be sane until the contrary was proved to their satisfaction, and that to establish a defence on the ground of insanity it must be clearly proved that at the time of the offence the accused person must have suffered from a defect of the mind so as not to know clearly what he was doing, or if he did know, that he did not know it was wrong.

The jury found Gordon guilty but insane. No reason why Gordon should have attacked and killed a girl he hardly knew could be found. He may have acted in a momentary black-out, as he said, but the fact that he had left the camp just after he had returned from Whiteabbey carrying a service knife in his civilian clothes has not been accounted for. A possible explanation may lie behind his remark to Desmond Curran on 23rd December (reported during the proceedings in the magistrates court), where Gordon suggested that " the motive (of the murderer) was fear because she had found out something about someone." We know from the police evidence that Gordon was a homosexual. It may be that Miss Curran had learned of this and taxed him with it when she met him by chance at the entrance to the Glen. She may have said that she would inform her parents. Gordon then attacked her in fear of exposure; but this is, of course, pure supposition.

Although of no significance, it may be remarked that three days after Patricia Curran was murdered in Northern Ireland, a Joan Curran was murdered in Southern Ireland.

XI

CHESNEY

RONALD JOHN CHESNEY, having committed the "perfect" murder, took his own life five days later because his nerve failed. If he had bluffed it out it is unlikely that he would have been charged, far less convicted, of the murder of his wife and mother-in-law in Sunset House, Montpelier Road, Ealing, on the night of 9th-10th February, 1954. That he was their murderer is certain. It is as certain, but it is as "unproven" as it is that he was the murderer of his own mother in 1926.

Chesney was a murderer who escaped to murder again. Human life, even the lives of his own wife and mother, meant nothing to him, if they stood in the way of his ambitions. He cheated the gallows at the age of nineteen because the police bungled the investigation of his mother's death, because the jury, which included six women, boggled at sending a boy of that age to the scaffold, and, because the trial was held in Scotland, the defence were able to call England's leading pathologist.

Escaping a richly deserved fate, Chesney—or as he was then, John Donald Merrett—lived a life of crime, persuading those he met that he was a swashbuckling buccaneer born out of his time; a figure of glamour and romance. But it was all a fake; beneath the big black beard and golden ear-rings there ran a yellow streak, the yellow streak of a man who was too lazy to earn an honest living.

There was no need for young Merrett to become a criminal; he took to crime as a chosen way of life. He coldbloodedly shot his mother because she had discovered that he had been forging her name to cheques; twenty-seven years later he murdered his wife to secure a marriage settlement worth £8,400 and his freedom to marry another woman whom he would probably have deserted in a few months. He may have killed others; he was suspected by the German police of the murder of Heinrich Mosmann, whose body was taken from a river near Frankfurt only a few months before the Ealing murders. They believe that Mosmann was a member of an international gang of arms smugglers of which Chesney may have been " the Chief." There is much to confirm this : at the house in Ealing an arsenal of weapons was found; Chesney travelled about the Continent under a number of aliases; he had served a number of terms of imprisonment for smuggling; he was on the lookout for easy money.

The best way to deal with Chesney is to go back to the beginning : he was born John Donald Merrett, a name he changed to Chesney after it had acquired unpleasant notoriety.

Born in New Zealand on 17th August, 1908, Donald Merrett was brought to England by his mother in 1924. Sent to Malvern College, he left two years later with a brilliant scholastic record, but with a somewhat unsavoury reputation where money matters were concerned. As he had an obvious flair for languages his mother went to live at Edinburgh so that her son could study at the University for the Diplomatic Service. Each day Donald went off to his lectures but, unknown to his mother, he attended them only for six weeks. He went instead to the local dance halls where he soon acquired a particular girl friend. At night he retired to his room to study; once the door was locked he slipped out of the window and down a rope to the ground. To his mother he invented an ingenious reason for the presence of the rope on the window; it was put there, he said, to prevent him from falling out if he walked in his sleep. The ten shillings a week pocket money allowed him by his mother went nowhere; soon he was forging her signature to cheques. Some of the money he obtained went on the purchase of a .25 calibre automatic pistol, with fifty rounds of ammunition. He bought this on 13th February, 1926.

On 17th March his mother was shot with this pistol. The

housemaid had cleared the breakfast table and had gone downstairs to fetch coal. Mrs. Merrett was writing at her bureau;
Donald was at the other side of the room. The maid heard a
shot, a scream and a thud. A few seconds later Donald came
downstairs and told her, " My mother has shot herself." Going
upstairs the maid found Mrs. Merrett insensible on the floor,
bleeding from a wound in the right ear. In the bureau lay a
pistol and two letters from her bank saying that her account
was overdrawn.

Rushed to hospital, Mrs. Merrett was put in a room reserved
for suicide cases. Although she was at times fully conscious no
one would tell her what had happened and the police made no
attempt to question her. She did, however, make some significant remarks. She asked the doctor what was the cause of the
pain in her ear, telling him, " I was sitting down writing letters
and my son Donald *was standing beside* me, waiting to post
the letter. I said, ' Go away Donald, and don't annoy me,
and the next I heard was an explosion and I do not remember
any more.' " To a nurse she said : " Didn't Donald do it? He
is such a naughty boy." She died on 31st March, her death
being attributed to suicide.

Questioned about his mother's wound, Donald, said it must
have been suicide. Asked why she might have wished to take
her own life, he replied, " Money matters." He said that his
mother was sitting writing. He was in a corner. " I heard a
shot. I turned and saw mother falling to the floor with a revolver falling from her hand." He admitted that he and his
mother were not on the best of terms. While his mother lay
dying, he forged her name to further cheques and bought himself a new motor-cycle. He was not asked to make a statement
until the day before her death.

When the police examined the sitting-room they found three
letters on Mrs. Merrett's bureau. The two letters from the bank
might have provided a motive for suicide, but it was learned
that her account at another bank was well in credit. The third
letter was the one she had been writing. It was a rambling,
cheerful letter, hardly the type to have been written by a person
who had suddenly shot herself. The police left this letter on

the bureau; Donald destroyed it, saying that it was blood-stained.

For some time after Mrs. Merrett's death nothing happened. As Edinburgh University refused to allow Donald to continue his studies, his trustees arranged for him to be coached at Oxford. Eight months later he was charged with the murder of his mother. At his trial in February 1927 the prosecution alleged that he had killed her after monkeying about with her money.

Donald's fate turned on the medical evidence. For the Crown, Professor Littlejohn demonstrated that the direction of the wound in Mrs. Merrett's head, its position and the distance at which the discharge had taken place, " all point to the weapon having been fired by another party." For the defence, Sir Bernard Spilsbury, the Home Office pathologist, who if the trial had been in England would not have been available for the defence, stated the opposite. He saved the worthless life of Donald Merrett. He gave his opinion that the wound could have been self-inflicted. He showed how the short light automatic pistol could be held against the side of the head without undue strain on the hand or arm. He pointed out that a " considerable range of movement in the shoulder joint was found in women on account of the habit of pulling up their hair." The famous London gunsmith, Robert Churchill, explained how he had carried out tests with the gun : " I could reproduce that wound by holding the pistol with the thumb on the trigger guard and the fingers of the hand on the butt. There was nothing," he said, " to exclude the possibility of suicide."

Donald Merrett did not give evidence. This strange fact went unnoticed. After a retirement of fifty-five minutes the jury of fifteen brought in a verdict of " Not proven." Five men had voted for a verdict of guilty, but all six women voted for " Not proven." Donald was sent to prison for one year for forging his mother's signature to twenty-nine cheques worth £457.

Within a few weeks of his release from prison Donald again made the headlines, by eloping with a seventeen-year-old ward in Chancery named Vera Bonnar. She became the Mrs.

Chesney who was murdered in 1954. Almost at once he was in prison again for obtaining £200 from shopkeepers at New-castle-upon-Tyne by means of worthless cheques. He got nine months with hard labour. He was barely nineteen years old. When Donald came of age and was able to inherit his mother's money, he made a marriage settlement from which Vera was to enjoy the income for life. If there were no children of the marriage, the capital would revert to him on her death, should his wife predecease him.

Taking the name of Chesney, Donald and Vera lived a wild life on their yacht in the Mediterranean. They gambled at the casinos and attended all the best parties. Although of " inde-pendent means," it is believed that Chesney had already em-barked upon smuggling as a means of paying for his expensive tastes.

To such a man as Chesney the war came as a golden oppor-tunity to show himself as the dashing hero. Serving in torpedo launches he became a lieutenant-commander, but it was noticed that he was never in the thick of a fight. He was full of chase when shooting at a retreating enemy. He was taken prisoner, but he escaped from Italy. After the war he and Vera separated. He became a professional smuggler. She went to live at Ealing on the income from the Merrett marriage settle-ment. His activities soon got him into trouble.

Although he had left the Navy he was recalled to face court-martial charges of the theft of a car and he was sentenced at Hamburg to nine months' imprisonment, which he served at Chelmsford. On his release he was imprisoned and fined, in 1947 and 1948, in France for smuggling and for trafficking in currency. In the following year he was heavily fined for offences against aliens regulations. In Brussels he was fined for abetting the illegal entry of a German girl named Gerda, who had escaped from East Berlin, where she was wanted for the murder of a Russian, and with whom he had gone through a form of marriage in Germany. In London, in 1949, he was sentenced to three months' imprisonment for smuggling 222 pairs of nylon stockings into this country and in 1951 he was sent to prison for another three months for attempting to export

RONALD JOHN CHESNEY

Bank of England notes at Newhaven. They were found by Customs men in a secret compartment of his Packard.

Operating from Tangiers and from Dueren in Germany, Chesney built up, under the guise of an import-export firm, a smuggling network operating all over Europe. He adopted his mother's maiden name of Milner. While in Germany he met the girl Sonia Winnickes, to marry whom he besought his wife for a divorce. He found her in a night club in Cologne. In 1950 he brought her to London to meet his wife. She was with him when he was arrested at Newhaven. After spending Christmas, 1953, with Sonia at Dueren he left, ostensibly on a business trip to Holland, but he went elsewhere with another girl from Dueren. Sonia rejoined him on 8th February, on his return from a short visit to England, in a hotel at Amsterdam.

On the afternoon of 11th February the bodies of two women were found in an old people's home in Montpelier Road, Ealing. Concealed by cushions in the sitting-room lay the battered and strangled body of sixty-eight-year-old " Lady " Menzies. The room showed signs of a violent struggle. In the empty bath in the locked bathroom was found the body of her forty-two-year-old daughter, Mrs. Isobel Vera Chesney. She had died from drowning but the water had seeped away through the faulty plug. She was wearing a nightdress and a cardigan. She had recently taken a large quantity of alcohol and numerous empty bottles were discovered in her bedroom.

If it had not been for the strangled body of her mother, Mrs. Chesney's death would probably have been attributed to an accident while she was drunk. But, even so, there would have been some strange facts to be explained. Why should she have entered the bath half-clothed ? There were no soap deposits in the bath and, stranger still, no finger-prints in the bathroom. There were bruises, too, on her lower jaw and on each elbow. She had, apparently, been jerked under the water and held under when she was too intoxicated to resist.

While it was obvious that the two women had been murdered, it was noticed that there was no sign of forceful entry into the house and none of its inmates had heard the two dogs, who did not like strangers, barking. Various indications, such as Mrs. Chesney's watch which had stopped at 2.30 a.m. suggested that the murders had been committed between midnight and 4.30 a.m. Reconstructing the crime, the police came to the conclusion that the two women had been murdered by someone they knew well. The murderer had intended only to murder the daughter, and he had hoped that her death would have been attributed to an accident. Interrupted by the older women, who recognized him, he had to kill her as well.

After examining certain letters found in the house the police guardedly announced that a man of " buccaneer-like " appearance, who was known to visit the continent regularly, could help them with their enquiries. They wished to trace also the younger woman's husband, Ronald Chesney, who had left England seven days *before* the murders. The older lady, Mrs. Menzies, had for many years adopted the title " Lady " Menzies, to which she had no right.

While the police were convinced that Chesney was the man they wanted he, apparently, had a cast-iron alibi. He had not been in England at the time of the murders unless, of course, he had returned secretly or under a false name. The police learned that he had ardently wished for the removal of his wife and that he stood to benefit from her death.

Chesney had, it was learned, tried to bribe three men to kill her. Two of them had shared a cell with him in prison. He offered one of them £1,000 to run her down with a car, and Chesney took him to Ealing to meet his wife, " So that you won't mistake her for someone else." Chesney said afterwards with a grin, " I would hate an innocent person to be bumped off." To the other man Chesney gave a plan of the house in Montpelier Road with the promise of £2,000 when the job was done. To a third man he handed an undated cheque for £1,000, which could be cashed only when he had collected the marriage settlement funds. None of them took the offer seriously.

Then, six days after the discovery of the Ealing murders, there came startling news from Germany. Ronald Chesney had been found shot dead by his own hand in a wood near Dueren. British newspapers were at last permitted to tell the full story of Donald Merrett, alias Chesney. Within a few days the police were able to trace Chesney's movements and to break his alibi for the perfect crime. Other information, too, came to light to link him further with the murders.

On Chesney's face and arms were deep scratches indicating that the old lady had put up a stout resistance. Skin found under Lady Menzies' finger nails corresponded with that scratched from his face. It is believed that at the time of the murder of the old lady he was wearing only pyjama trousers, and blood-stained trousers were found in his luggage. In his finger nails were discovered wool fibres similar to those of the cardigans worn by Mrs. Chesney and her mother. There was also a human blood-stain at the bottom of his brief-case. At least two people in Ealing had seen a man resembling Chesney both before and after the murder. He had affected a limp to confuse them.

Chesney had an obvious motive to murder his wife. He wanted money and his freedom. Her death released not only the marriage settlement funds which amounted to £8,400, but freed him to marry again. After " hearing " of the death of his wife, Chesney instructed his solicitor in England to obtain the release of the money and he informed him that he had made Sonia Winnickes sole beneficiary under his will. In his fare-well letter, he promised her £11,000. Mrs. Chesney was fully aware that she was worth more to her husband dead than alive. She told her adopted daughter that she was in fear of her life because of the marriage settlement, warning her that something that looked like an accident, but which was not, might occur.

In order to fake his alibi Chesney had left England, after a short visit, on 4th February. He sailed from Harwich to Hook of Holland on a British passport in the name of Chesney. He made a point of being noticed by immigration and port officials. On the 6th he registered at a small hotel in Amster-dam under the name of Milner. He had no beard and next day he shaved off his moustache. Sonia joined him there on the 8th, leaving again next day. Officially Chesney remained at the hotel until the 12th, but a chambermaid saw him leave with a small suitcase at noon on Wednesday the 10th. She told the porter, who believing that Milner had left without paying his bill, went to his room where he found his luggage. On the bedside table was a British passport in the name of Milner. The chambermaid noticed that his bed was not slept in on the Wednesday night. Chesney returned at 4 p.m. on Thursday, 11th February, two hours after the bodies of his wife and mother-in-law had been found in Ealing. He telephoned Sonia in Germany and it was noticed in the hotel that he was " rather nervous." He left early on the morning of the 12th.

The twenty-eight hours unaccounted for in his movements between noon on the 10th and 4 p.m. on the 11th would have allowed him to have travelled to England and back, but under what name had he travelled ? In his luggage had been found the unused half of a return ticket to England between Hook of Holland and Harwich on 10th February. If he had travelled to England by sea, how had he returned ?

Enquiries proved that he had travelled to England on the 10th slightly disguised under a false name. A K.L.M. stewardess recognized Chesney from a photograph. It was found that he had used a passport which he had obtained by fraud. Knowing a Chelsea photographer named Leslie Bernard Treville Chown, he had secured his birth certificate for one and sixpence from Somerset House. With this certificate and two photographs of himself he had obtained on 23rd June, 1953, a new passport for one pound by supplying fictitious names as a reference. Matched with the real Mr. Chown's, the signature on the passport was obviously a forgery. Chesney's return trip had nearly misfired. Due to bad weather the plane had to be diverted from Amsterdam to Dusseldorf.

After leaving Amsterdam on 12th February, Chesney returned to Dueren. Early in the following week he bought a copy of the *News of the World* on Cologne railway station. It contained the story of the man with whom he had shared a cell at Wandsworth prison, who said he had been offered £1,000 to kill Mrs. Chesney. Chesney now knew that the police in England would suspect that he was the murderer, He knew, too, that his carefully prepared alibi had failed. He had hoped that his girl friend Sonia should stay at the hotel in Amsterdam for the whole week, and vouch for his presence at the time of the murders, but she had remained for one day only. Sonia had discovered about the girl with whom Chesney had stayed at an hotel near Dueren when he was supposed to be in Holland. His quarrel with Sonia may have precipitated the murder of his wife which up to then he had tried to get others to commit. He may have felt that his last chance was the ability to offer her marriage. He could only do this if Vera was dead. On 15th February, he shot himself by putting a .45 calibre revolver in his mouth and pulling the trigger. Just before he did so he had sent a note to Sonia. It said :

" My dear Sonia,
By the time you read this letter I will no longer be here.
. . . You know I am innocent but with what has happened in the past it would be difficult to prove. . . . I ask your forgiveness,"

but it was not delivered until after his death.

Chesney, having got away with the murder of his mother, believed it was possible to stage the perfect crime. He knew that his wife would be drunk; her death in the bath would be put down to an accident. He employed the " Brides in the Bath " technique made famous by Joseph Smith in 1915. Vera's death would probably have been accepted as an accident if it had not been for the murder of the old lady. Even so, Chesney hoped to prove that he was in Holland at the time. While Sonia's sudden departure from the hotel in Amsterdam may have precipitated the murder, it endangered his alibi. Yet Chesney obviously calculated his risk carefully; but he did not foresee meeting his mother-in-law as he came out of the bathroom. He had to kill her too. Then he lost his head; he left his wife's *semi-clothed* body in the bath and he was too careful to wipe the bathroom clean of *all* finger-prints. He then failed to take the most elementary precautions; he did not destroy the unused return ticket from England and his blood-stained pyjamas. Even so, although the coroner's jury returned a verdict of wilful murder against him, it is unlikely that, had he faced it out, he could have been convicted of murder; no single clue in the house pointed to him.

Fortunately for others in the future, Ronald Chesney's nerve failed him; the vision of the judge's black cap and the scaffold preyed upon his mind. He couldn't face it. The perfect crime was a flop because he wasn't the perfect criminal.

XII

AN UNSAVOURY CASE

THE trial in March 1954 of Lord Montagu, Michael Pitt-
Rivers and Peter Wildeblood for homosexual offences
with two R.A.F. men brings to light an unsatisfactory state of
affairs. The law as it now stands allows the State to infringe
the rights of individuals in a matter which is solely the concern
of each person. Society claims the right to dictate a particular
sexual choice. Obviously, society has a duty to protect young
people, but what consenting adults may do in private should
be their own affair. As a result of this case an enquiry is to be
held into the law relating to sexual offences and it is expected
that it will recommend that British law on the subject should
be brought into line with the more enlightened continental
practices.

We do not propose to go into the sordid details of this unsavoury case. The accusations of the two R.A.F. men are now
buried in the yellowing files of newspapers. Let them remain
there. The lives of three men have been sufficiently, and un-
necessarily, wrecked without reviving these details. What these
five men may or may not have done is no concern of ours,
but it is our concern that three men of hitherto unblemished
character should have been sent to prison because of a human
prejudice.

We may think that homosexual practices are disgusting
and horrible. We may mistakenly call them " unnatural," but
we must recognize the rights of those to whom such practices
are normal. Our present prejudice is at least three thousand
years old. It is based on ignorance of the nature of sex and
upon primitive superstition. It is unworthy of the twentieth-
century world.

The homosexual is an individual, of either sex, who prefers a person of the same sex to one of the opposite sex. There are many degrees of homosexuality. Some people are " bi-sexual "; they take what the opportunity offers, but others prefer a chosen sexual outlet. While women who prefer women are known as " Lesbians," there is no definite term for male homosexuals. While female homosexuality is illegal only in Austria, the social attitude to the male homosexual varies considerably in different human societies. It is illegal in Britain, Germany and in the United States, but in numerous European countries its practice in private by consenting adults is permitted.

It is incorrect to refer to homosexuality as being " unnatural " or to term it a " perversion." It is as old as humanity and it is found amongst most of the higher animals. Dr. Kinsey (*Sexual Behaviour of the Human Male*) has declared that its practice is widespread. From a great number of sample investigations he has stated that thirty-seven per cent. of men have during their lives some sexual experience with other men. Four in every hundred men are exclusively homosexual and thirteen out of every hundred are more homosexual than heterosexual. These figures relate only to those men who have actually had sexual experience with other men; many more may repress their homosexual desires. On this presumption there could be at least a million men in Britain who might be charged and sent to prison for homosexual offences at some time in their lives.

There is nothing new in this situation. It is not a modern phenomena. Male homosexuality may at times be more noticeable than at others but it is found amongst every race, colour and creed. There is little agreement about its cause and cure. It is an aspect of sex in which, due to biological or psychological reasons, gratification is sought amongst other members of the same sex. It is unnatural only in the sense that it cannot lead to procreation, but neither can normal sexual intercourse by control. While some homosexuals are born that way, others are so conditioned by early influences or by outside circumstances, such as the absence of women.

The social attitude to the homosexual has varied considerably. Arising from a primitive taboo on illicit sexual expression, which might involve the tribe in economic disaster, private sin became a public crime when primitive superstitions gave way to religious beliefs. Penalties against homosexuality became incorporated in legal codes only *after* priestly influence became effective. The Jews were one of the earliest peoples vainly to attempt to eliminate homosexuality by penal enactments. These Jewish ideas, through Christianity, are the basis of the present Anglo-Saxon attitude. To the Jews the practice of homosexuality was the sin of alien people : as such it was a sign of disbelief in the one God of the Israelites. The Hebrew word for a Sodomite implied a man dedicated to a deity, a religious prostitute. Amongst the Greeks, the other great civilization whose influence is felt to-day, homosexuality was tolerated and encouraged as a manly virtue. By the early Christians it was abhorred. By an Edict of A.D. 538, formulated by the Emperor Justinian, offenders were condemned to death, but the Christian attitude to sex, in which sexual enjoyment was discouraged, led to its increase rather than to its abatement.

Homosexuality did not become a felony in England until the reign of Henry VIII. Until then it was a religious offence for which penance was exacted. It was widespread in Saxon and Norman times. The body of William Rufus was refused burial in consecrated ground because of his homosexual tendencies. While the Church Canons during the Middle Ages point to its prevalence, religious monasticism and clerical celibacy led to its increase. With the dissolution of the religious houses in the Reformation the situation became so out of hand that by a Statute of 1533 the crime " not fit to be named " was made punishable by death. It remained theoretically a capital crime until 1828.

To-day in England two Acts of Parliament are in force. Men found guilty of homosexual offences are subject to punishment by sections 61 and 62 of the Offences against the Person Act of 1861. The Act lays down : " Whoever shall be convicted of the abominable crime of buggery, committed either with mankind or any animal, shall be liable to be kept in penal servitude for life or for any term not less than ten years."

Section 62 deals with attempts to commit the said abominable crime. Except in the case of assault the passive party, if over sixteen, is also guilty under the Act.

The Criminal Law Amendment Act of 1885, under section 11, makes acts of gross indecency between males in private a misdemeanour punishable with two years' imprisonment. If both parties are over sixteen they are equally guilty. Consent is no defence. Section 11 of this Act was inserted into the Bill, which otherwise dealt with female prostitution, by an amendment in Committee which was not debated in Parliament. It was under this law that Oscar Wilde was convicted and imprisoned in 1895.

No penalty will succeed in stamping out homosexuality; it might, however, be considerably lessened by a better understanding of human sexual needs.

Lord Montagu, Pitt-Rivers and Wildeblood were simultaneously arrested at their homes on 9th January, 1954. The charges on which they were subsequently tried and convicted arose from an investigation by R.A.F. security police. On the 16th December, a letter from Lord Montagu was discovered in the kit of Aircraftman Reynolds. On the following day in the kit of Corporal McNally a letter from Peter Wildeblood was found. Both R.A.F. men were suspected of homosexuality, a letter in endearing terms from Reynolds having been found in the possession of a man in Korea. Both airmen admitted friendships with Lord Montagu, Wildeblood and Pitt-Rivers. They stated that offences had taken place in 1952 in London and in Hampshire. This R.A.F. investigation took place while Lord Montagu was on trial at Winchester for an alleged offence against a boy scout.

When they were arrested Montagu and Pitt-Rivers were not allowed to communicate with their solicitors and, although the police did not have search warrants, their private papers were read and removed. In the case of Lord Montagu the police officer insisted on reading a batch of letters from the girl to whom he had been engaged. When told of the charges Pitt-Rivers said, " This is fantastic. What can I say? It is all part of this ridiculous witch hunt which is going on all over the country."

A number of interesting facts came to light during the preliminary proceedings.

Mr. Scott Henderson, Q.C., appearing for Pitt-Rivers, recalled that Mr. Roberts, prosecuting, had given an assurance in the case of McNally that there would be no proceedings against him.

Mr. Scott Henderson suggested that Reynolds should be warned, adding : " Mr. Roberts is not entitled to give an absolute assurance that there will be no proceedings."

Mr. Roberts said : " I am instructed by the Director of Public Prosecutions and the Air Ministry that in no circumstances will this individual be prosecuted. This court should be reasonably satisfied that the prospects of any proceedings are so remote as to be impossible."

Cross-examined by Mr. Fearnley-Whittingstall, for Lord Montagu, Reynolds admitted that when interrogated by R.A.F. police he made a statement giving the names of six civilians and R.A.F. other ranks. He said he had been a homosexual for about four years. He had been charged with an offence by the R.A.F. authorities but the case had been dismissed.

Reynolds said that he had made and signed three statements during interrogations.

Answering Mr. Myers, for Wildeblood, Superintendent Jones said that when he saw McNally in London on 28th December he knew that it was probable that the R.A.F. proceedings against McNally would go no further. He knew that proceedings were dismissed because it was intended to call McNally as a Crown witness.

Mr. Myers : " It was thought best that the proceedings against them should be discontinued ? "

Superintendent Jones : " That was the general opinion."

" Had it been arranged, and I use the word deliberately, that these proceedings should be dropped so that he could give evidence in this case ? "—" It had been suggested, yes."

" Was it suggested because it was thought the prosecution

would have a better chance if they called them as unconvicted people rather than as convicted? "—" Not necessarily."

Answering Mr. Scott Henderson, Superintendent Jones said that what he had said about McNally also applied to Reynolds.

At the trial, Inspector Stuchfield said that when he and a superintendent questioned the two airmen in the case they were not frightened or browbeaten.

On 31st March the following questions, as reported in Hansard, were asked in the House of Commons :

Sir Robert Boothby (Aberdeen East, C.) asked what undertaking was given to Aircraftman Reynolds and Corporal McNally with regard to their period of service in the R.A.F.; and whether they were to be retained in the service.

Mr. Ward, for the Air Ministry, in a written reply, stated : " No undertaking was given to these two airmen that they would be retained in the R.A.F. and steps have been taken to discharge them."

Sir Robert Boothby asked whether the undertaking given by the police to Aircraftman Reynolds and Corporal McNally, on behalf of the Director of Public Prosecutions, that no proceedings would be taken against them as the result of certain evidence given by them in a recent case was known to, or agreed to by, the Air Council.

Mr. Ward replied : " In the course of proceedings in the magistrates court at Lymington, on 23rd January, prosecuting counsel gave an assurance on behalf of the Director of Public Prosecutions and the Air Council that proceedings would not be taken against either McNally or Reynolds in respect of any matter upon which either of them was called to give evidence against Wildeblood, Lord Montagu or Pitt-Rivers. The assurance was given in the exercise of his discretion by the Director of Public Prosecutions in accordance with well-established procedure in order to ensure that they should not withhold evidence. The decision of the Director would have been nugatory had it not been supported by a similar assurance from the Air Council."

Mr. Ward also stated that in the course of investigations by the R.A.F. police, McNally and Reynolds alleged the commission by them of homosexual offences with twenty-four persons, three of whom were members of the R.A.F.

Thus, apparently, not only were the three defendants convicted on the testimony of two admitted homosexuals, but these men were accorded immunity from prosecution both for the offences in which they were accomplices and on other undisclosed offences of a similar nature, so that they could give evidence for the Crown.

At the trial at Winchester, before Mr. Justice Ormerod, Lord Montagu was defended by Mr. W. A. Fearnley-Whittingstall, Q.C., Pitt-Rivers (a farmer) by Mr. H. B. Hylton-Foster, Q.C., M.P., and Wildeblood (a journalist) by Mr. Peter Rawlinson. Mr. G. D. Roberts, Q.C., prosecuted. The jury was composed of twelve men. All three defendants pleaded " Not Guilty " to conspiring to incite the two airmen to commit serious offences and to individual offences involving the two men.

In stating the case for the prosecution, Mr. Roberts warned the jury to approach the evidence of the two R.A.F. men with " extreme caution." He went on : " They are put forward as men of the lowest moral character, who were corrupted, and apparently cheerfully accepted corruption, long before meeting the defendants. It is not to be laid to the door of the defendants that they were a party to the corruption at all."

Reynolds and McNally were, he said, accomplices and their evidence required confirmation and corroboration. " We hope to satisfy you from the very unusual association of these persons of such social disparity, and from letters and other documents, that there is copious confirmation to prove that Reynolds and McNally, if they tell the same story as before, are telling a story which, deplorably enough, is true."

The story told by McNally and Reynolds was as follows : Both were twenty-one years of age; both served at the R.A.F. hospital at Ely; both admitted to being homosexuals. McNally agreed that he had spent a night at the Regent Palace Hotel with a man named Jerry, in November 1953, but no offence took place : he had also referred to Jerry, in a letter to a man

named Chris, as " my husband dear." Reynolds said that he
had been a homosexual for four years. He knew " by instinct "
that McNally was a pervert. When his kitbag was searched
by the R.A.F. police, five letters were found from other
" friendly men." He had been charged in 1952 with an in-
decent offence. The charge was dismissed.

McNally met Wildeblood in March 1952. Later he brought
Reynolds along to meet Lord Montagu. The four men
attended a theatre in London and Wildeblood, McNally and
Reynolds went to stay at Lord Montagu's estate at Beaulieu,
Hampshire, in a beach hut where, according to the R.A.F.
men, offences took place. An all-male party was attended by
Pitt-Rivers who, because Lord Montagu was going abroad,
invited the other three to his home in Dorset where, again
according to McNally and Reynolds, offences took place.
Their accusations were unsupported save by letters written by
the accused men and by the implication that friendships between men of such social and intellectual inequality could
only have one meaning.

All three defendants denied the charges but Wildeblood admitted to being an " invert," a person who through no fault
of his own is subjected to desires to which a normal man is not
subject. Because he was lonely he had been in need of
an emotional friendship. Lord Montagu said that Reynolds'
evidence was entirely false. Pitt-Rivers said that Reynolds was
lying.

In his summing-up, the judge told the jury : " The prosecu-
tion depend very largely on the evidence of these two airmen,
McNally and Reynolds. On any view of the case, McNally and
Reynolds are accomplices."

Mr. Justice Ormerod went on : " If any crime has been
committed by any one of these men it has likewise been committed by McNally or Reynolds as the case may be. *I must
warn in the strongest terms that it is dangerous in the extreme
to convict a man upon the evidence of an accomplice, unless
that evidence is corroborated in some material particular by
some outside and independent evidence.* If you are satisfied,
having heard the whole of the evidence and bearing in mind the

warning I have given you about corroboration, that McNally and Reynolds are telling the truth, you may convict."

The judge defined corroboration as " Confirmation by independent evidence or some independent testimony which affects the prisoner by tending to connect him with the crime."

The jury might think that in some respects the evidence of McNally corroborated that of Reynolds, and vice versa.

" That is not corroboration in law : one accomplice cannot corroborate another accomplice."

The judge pointed out that the important question the jury had to consider was whether McNally and Reynolds were telling the truth. It had been admitted that there was a considerable degree of intimacy between the airmen and the three accused.

The jury had to consider whether this admitted intimacy was in itself corroboration of what McNally and Reynolds said.

The prosecution maintained that as there was such a disparity of background and lack of common interest between them, it would justify the jury in coming to the conclusion that the link between all of them was improper sexual practice.

According to the prosecution a letter written by Wildeblood to McNally could only have one meaning; it was a letter between two men who had been having the most intimate sexual relationship.

Dealing with the conspiracy charge the judge said : " If you are satisfied that these three men, knowing the circumstances, agreed to get these two airmen either to the beach hut at Beaulieu or to the house with Pitt-Rivers in Dorset for the purpose of having this illicit intercourse, the offence of conspiracy has been committed."

Of the individual charges against the three men, the judge said : " If you are not satisfied that those offences have been committed, any other charges probably fall by the way."

Referring to the two airmen the judge said, " It is said by the defence the whole of McNally's evidence in this matter is untrue, and that he has made it up to save his own skin or to shield someone else. The prosecution had submitted that whatever McNally had said about other people, the story he had told about Wildeblood was true. Reynolds has at some time made an allegation against Lord Montagu which he later withdrew. It is said that therefore he was making wild and irresponsible statements on which no reliance could be placed, and his evidence cannot be relied on."

Yet, despite the judge's warning about the evidence of accomplices and the admission of the prosecution that the witnesses upon whose evidence their case relied were men of the "lowest possible moral character," and despite the implication that McNally and Reynolds had been accorded immunity from similar charges if they became witnesses for the Crown, the jury, after a deliberation of four and a half hours, found the three defendants guilty. The only verbal evidence against Montagu, Pitt-Rivers and Wildeblood was that of two acknowledged homosexuals, yet the jury accepted their evidence as truth, and they rejected the evidence of a peer of the realm, a farmer and county councillor and a highly competent journalist, all of whom had excellent service records and were of the highest character.

The admission of Peter Wildeblood that he was an invert, and the association of men of the standing of Lord Montagu and Major Pitt-Rivers with two men so far their social inferiors as McNally and Reynolds *suggests* that the association was not an innocent one, but the only corroboration that the alleged acts did take place is the *suspicion* that they did. There is only the word of McNally and Reynolds that they did occur.

Thirty-six-year-old Michael Pitt-Rivers was sentenced to eighteen months' imprisonment, thirty-year-old Peter Wildeblood was also given eighteen months. Lord Montagu, who the judge said had been found guilty of less serious offences, received one year. In passing sentence the judge said : "I am dealing with you in the most lenient way."

McNally and Reynolds were "booed" when they left the court. Women jeered and hissed and shook umbrellas.

In the previous December Lord Montagu was found not guilty of an offence against a boy scout, the jury failing to agree on another charge. At the re-trial of the second charge, and at the trial of another man for a similar offence, the prosecution offered no evidence and both defendants were acquitted.

It is impossible to fail to notice the strange fact that the investigation which led to the charge concerning the airman against Lord Montagu appears to have been undertaken at the time when he was facing the charge relating to the boy scout. It gave opportunity for a second bite at the cherry—a cherry which someone seems to have been very anxious to eat.